CLAIMING MIA

Dot Com Wolves 1

ALISA WOODS

Text copyright © 2014 Alisa Woods

April 2019 Edition
Alisa Woods
Cover Design by Steven Novak

ISBN-13: 9781095554678

Claiming Mia (Dot Com Wolves 1)

LUCAS
I'm a mess. Broken. Lost my mate and almost myself. In no shape to help anyone.
Then the sexy girl serving me drinks stumbles into trouble with a bunch of wolves who are bad business—I should know. They're the competition. And they're as dirty at dot-com investing as they are predatory on young things like her. So I save her. Because I may be broken, but I'm not an ass.

Only she shows up the next day at my office. *As my intern.*
And now the Red pack is after her, putting us square in a pack war—one she doesn't even understand. I'm in no shape to claim a mate—*not* happening—but if I don't, the Red's jackass of an alpha *will*.

MIA

I'm just trying to earn my degree and dig my way out of poverty.

I was born a shifter—more of my bad luck—but I've kept that a secret, so it doesn't ruin my life. Shifters are monsters. *Criminals.* And I'm trying to *make* something of myself. This internship at the hottest internet business development firm in Seattle is my ticket out... *only the boss is a wolf.* And insanely hot. And he saved my life.

I'd break all the rules for this guy—except he wants nothing to do with me.

The wolves who *do* are the Big Bad Wolf kind. The kind I've always heard about.

I've got nowhere to turn... but to the one guy who doesn't want me at all.

***Claiming Mia* (Dot Com Wolves 1) is a super-hot complete story with HEA.**

(Formerly published as True Alpha).

Chapter One

LUCAS LEANED HIS ELBOWS BACK ON THE BAR AND pulled in a full draught of the human pheromones and perfumes swirling in the air. Musky fragrances mixed with sweet sweat, underscored by a tangy taste of arousal. And that was just the women. The males were overly scented as well, at least the human ones, as if they didn't understand the power of their own natural scent. The blue-neon sign outside the nightclub called it *The Deviation*. Inside, lithe human bodies pulsed to a techno rock beat coming from the live band on the stage. It was a ripe hunting ground for shifters and humans alike. *Prey*, his inner dark wolf panted, but Lucas back-handed that thought into the recesses of his mind. He may be hunting for a pleasurable companion for the evening, a temporary relief from the ghosts that haunted him, but he wasn't *that* kind of predator.

Not that there weren't plenty of those in the room.

This was neutral territory. He was rogue now, but even if he had a pack, he wouldn't make trouble in a closed environment filled with humans like *The Deviation*. The throng pushed right up to the bar where he stood, leaving little distinction between those dancing and those watching. Cutout panels behind the band let in beams of purplish light that stabbed through the tight crowd and washed everyone in a deep, otherworldly glow. The shifters were indistinguishable from the humans, everyone dressed in the same tailored silk shirts and curve-hugging black dresses that comprised the nighttime uniform of web entrepreneurs and their groupies.

Indistinguishable for most. But Lucas recognized a few.

Three shifters from the SocialHacks pack were in the thick of the dancing, hands running free over their female companions. His father's pack allied with the SocialHacks early on, their social media startup pairing well with his father's internet business development firm. Nearby was a trio from Red Wolf, another company that cultivated the dot-com businesses of Seattle and helped match them with investors. They were his father's bitter rivals—not only did they skate close to that invisible line shifters didn't cross, the one that kept the normal human citizenry of Seattle unaware of the wolves in their midst, but they were as ruthless in pack matters as they were in business. Lucas had seen more than one omega from the Red pack end up in a dingy alley missing a few vital organs. Tonight, the Red pack was hanging at the fringes of the crowd, watching. Like Lucas.

But that was all they had in common.

"How are you doing here, sir?" The soft voice behind him belonged to the female bartender. He could tell by her scent before he turned around: slightly musky with the dampness of the nightclub, but with a light woodsy taste. It wasn't perfume, which Lucas had an instant appreciation for.

He turned and gave her a smile. "I'd like another, please. Vodka, neat." She wasn't one of the celebrity bartenders who drew patrons to *The Deviation*, but he wasn't the type to drink the latest fad cocktail, either. In fact, he rarely was in a club long enough to finish a drink before a companion for the night found him. And having full command of his faculties, especially with a human, was key to leaving her satisfied, not sliced to ribbons.

The bartender gave him a fleeting smile, then dropped her brilliant blue-eyed gaze, brushed her long black hair out of her way, and reached under the bar for a bottle. He hadn't been to *The Deviation* in a while, but he guessed she was new—to the club, maybe to bartending as well. Her all-black uniform —slim dress pants and a collared shirt—had turned purple with the hazy light from the stage, but it fit her feminine curves in an understated way. He appreciated that, too, but bartenders weren't good prospects, not least because they might remember him the next time he came hunting.

She poured his drink, and he noticed her hand quiver. The liquid sloshed but not enough to escape the shot glass. He frowned and looked up, but she was already moving on, down the bar, to another customer. She gave that guy the same fleeting smile, but Lucas could see something wrong in it now. Something off. Her lips were slightly parted, her breaths shallow. She was panting, and not in a good way. The girl rushed through a bourbon-and-seven for her customer, then shuffled to the end of the bar, where her fellow bartender, a male, stood flirting with one of the female patrons. The girl had a quick, whispered exchange that Lucas couldn't hear over the pounding music, and then she slipped around the end of the counter and into the crowd.

Lucas straightened, looking for her over the sea of bobbing heads and waving hands. She was a tiny black-haired rabbit weaving through the weeds, tall enough to poke above them when she wasn't ducking under drinks held high or flailing arms. He wasn't sure why, but he couldn't stop tracking her.

He left his drink, untouched, and slid along the bar, keeping her in his sights. She broke free of the crowd near the back wall, where blue neon signs bulged with the letters of the club and the outlines of spilled electric drinks.

It was the same wall where the three Red pack members lounged.

The girl threw open a door which had been invisible a moment before, probably because it fit seamlessly into the black matte of the wall. Then she was gone, the door slowly easing closed behind her.

The Reds had watched her all the way out.

Lucas froze at the edge of the crowd, his unblinking stare trained on their bent heads and moving lips. *Not my territory,* he told his snarling inner wolf. *Not my pack.*

But he didn't look away.

Mia sucked in the cool night air of the alleyway outside *The Deviation* and nearly moaned with the relief. Jesus, the *smells* in that place. She'd been on since ten o'clock, and usually, she could make it through to the end of her shift at two: she just had to breathe through her mouth and take frequent bathroom breaks for fresh air. But tonight... it was as if all the college girls had decided to flash mob the club with a synchronized perfume attack. And the dot-com wannabe-billion-aire guys either came straight from the gym and overcompensated with Axe spray or somehow that was their *normal* smell. Add in the usual background *Eau de Deviation*, and the alcoholic whiffs from the drinks she was serving just weren't enough to ward it off. She had to get fresh air, or she was going to lose her dorm dinner of meatloaf and mashed potatoes—and it wasn't that good the first time around. Her sensitive sense of smell loathed closed spaces and aromatic people, and *The Deviation* had more than its share of both tonight.

Sometimes being a shifter well and truly sucked.

Who was she kidding? It sucked *all* the time. Mia had yet to find the hidden benefits of being able to transform into a wolf on a whim. Sure, she could smell the anxiety of her roommate while she studied for an econ test. Or the lecherous arousal of her English prof when he tried to "help" her during office hours. But she didn't count those as *benefits.* And an acrid stench of fear would constantly surround her if anyone found out her secret—not to mention no real company would ever hire a shifter.

She could tolerate a few more smelly shifts at *The Deviation* if that's what it took. Other than the stench, it was decent. Not too many slobbering drunks. Plus, she was twenty-one now, so she could serve, which meant better tips. She needed to keep this stinky job so eventually she could get a *real* one. One that paid well enough to get her mom out of that rat-hole apartment on Jackson Street and into something better. Somewhere Mia wouldn't have to worry about the crackheads shooting up the place and where the gangs hadn't ousted the police as the major power players in the neighborhood.

There were shifters in the crack gangs of Seattle, she knew that. Everyone did, though no one talked about it. And if anyone knew she was a shifter... well, that was all that would be left for her, too. Which was why she worked her tail off in community college and transferred to the University of Washington as a junior, as soon as she could wrangle a scholarship. But even the crappy dorm food cost money, so she had to keep her job at *The Deviation* if she wanted to graduate and get her mom out of the hellhole that was 12th and Jackson.

Breathe in. Breathe out.

Her stomach settled a little. Mia leaned back against the cool brick of the alley. The moon was nearly full, which didn't mean jack for her as a shifter. Werewolves that went all wolfy with a full moon were just fairy tales. She could shift whenever she wanted to—which was primarily *never*—and occasionally even when she didn't. But that hadn't happened for years, not since Bobby Johnson scared the shit out of her with one of his stupid Halloween pranks. It was a good thing she had been dressed as a ghost that year—she had only been ten, and the yellowed sheet had reached all the way to the ground. Covered her up pretty good, and Bobby never figured it out.

Didn't stop her from using some very wolfy-sharp claws to trash his mailbox the next night, though. Just on principle.

She closed her eyes and focused on calming the last heaves of her stomach. The music beat through the brick wall behind her, buzzing the back of her head. Just as she thought it might be safe to go back inside, the door next to her creaked open, letting out a throb of music that covered the footsteps of whoever was coming out. She popped open her eyes, blinking a couple of times to clear them, just in case it was patrons wanting to sneak a quick make-out session in the alley.

By the time she pushed away from the wall, she realized it wasn't a couple looking for privacy. It was three guys… and they were *big*.

The moonlight glinted off their black silk shirts. Mischief danced in their eyes. They stepped toward her, casually, as if they were about to ask her the time. One in the lead, two behind, probably mid-twenties. The lead one was pretty, the way boys sometimes are, without being the least bit feminine. In fact, there was entirely too much muscle beneath his tailored shirt. The other two were more conventionally handsome, but just as hulking, with beefy frames that spoke of hours in the gym or possibly some kind of professional sports. Their scent reminded her of cut steel, like they were fashioned from coldness and evil.

She could turn and run, but as soon as that thought blossomed in her head, two of the thugs fanned out, filling the alley with their smooth-moving presence. She wasn't quite surrounded, but she wouldn't escape either. Not without shifting, which she really, *really* didn't want to do. These guys were dot-commers. She could tell by the glint of their custom-made shoes and the close tailoring of their collared shirts. She was strong—being a shifter was good for that, at least—but even so, there were three of them. She would have to shift to have a chance. And if she did, they would talk. The police would listen. She'd be outed for sure.

The door slowly swung closed, muting the music to a dull thud.

Shit.

"It's pretty crowded in there." Mia hooked a thumb toward the door, pretty freaking impressed with herself at the steadiness of her voice. "I'm sure someone will be along any minute, looking for fresh air, just like you boys."

The lead one smirked then tipped his head to his evil partner in crime. He slunk back toward the door. Could he lock it from the outside?

Dammit.

"Come on, now," Mia said, her voice way

steadier than her ramping up heart would believe. "There are a *ton* of girls in there, *much* hotter than I am, who would love to go home with you three."

"Who said anything about taking you home?" The lead one leered like this was a game, and only he knew the rules. "Maybe you should run."

The hairs on the back of her neck bristled. Okay, that was not good. At all. These guys wanted to *hurt* her. She was *prey*... of the very worst sort.

Her inner wolf snarled. Some of it must have escaped her, but that only made him lick his lips like she'd just given him a delicious present. Mia curled her fists and took a step back to widen her stance. Maybe this was it. Maybe she'd finally lose her secret and everything else that went with it. But she wasn't letting them do whatever sick things they had planned without a fight. If they were lucky, she'd stop short of actually killing them.

Her wolf surged against her skin, battering her from the inside, wanting out. She wanted to claw their faces, sink her teeth into their necks. Mia held her wolf back, trying to think it through. She hadn't shifted in so long. She would get tangled in her clothes, probably fall on her face before even getting out a growl. And who knew what else the creeps might have... weapons... she swallowed, wondering if taking off her shirt might distract them long enough to get through the transformation…

The lead guy's nostrils flared. Even a human could probably smell the stink of fear on her. The guy by the door leaned a beefy hand against it, holding it closed, while the other one edged around her, cutting off her one route of escape down the alley.

The lead creep flexed his hands and stepped toward her—

With a scrape and a thud, the door flew open. The thug who had been holding it stumbled backward and tumbled to the moon-brightened pavement. Another figure stomped out and quickly scanned the alley. His gaze fell on Mia and raked across the length of her body. Even across the span of the twenty feet between them, she felt it, like a hot paintbrush across her flesh. His face was familiar, but her fear-addled brain couldn't quite place it. The man turned his glare to the creeps in the alley and used one hand to close the door behind him without looking.

Everyone had been frozen during all of this.

Then all hell broke loose.

The thug on the ground lunged up with frightening speed. He grabbed the man at the door, wrestling him away from it. The lead thug started taking off his clothes.

What?

He ripped off his shirt in one smooth motion, and before Mia could track its fall to the pavement, he had transformed into a snarling, bristle-haired red wolf the size of a bear. Mia jerked back, skittering to the side of the alley and flattening herself against the brick. The red wolf lunged at the man, while his sidekick tore off his own shirt and morphed into another wolf, this one so dark red, his fur was almost black. They led with their fangs, but somehow the man had slipped away, leaving them with nothing but a mouthful of shirt. The third thug, the one who hadn't transformed, was jerked backward, arms flailing out as he fell to the ground again. The two wolves snarled but held their place, pawing the ground. Their guttural sounds echoed off the hard walk. Her heart in her throat, Mia was frozen against the wall. She edged forward, enough to see what had stopped them.

A brown wolf, fur glistening white in the moonlight, had the door-holding man's neck in his jaws. The man-made gurgling noises like he was already drowning in his own blood. The brown wolf snarled and must have clamped harder because the man flailed against his hold even though that could only have made things worse. Mia flinched, holding the wall and her breath, the iron scent of blood assaulting her nose. The two red wolves pawed the ground, yipped, and returned the snarl, standing stiff-legged and tall. But after a moment, they both took a step back. Then slowly, slowly, they lowered their muzzles to the ground, arching their backs slightly to do so. Even slower, their red-bristled tails sunk to brush the pavement, then tucked between their legs.

Submission.

Her wolf recognized it right away, even though Mia had never seen another wolf in her life. But their actions flushed something through her—the shock of a cool shower on a hot day, both bracing and filled with relief. They had *submitted.* In their wolf form, the red wolves could no more attack the brown than they could fly—at least not now, not while their submission was still fresh, the authority of the alpha wolf still strong in their minds. Maybe later. Certainly once they were in human form again, and the alpha had less influence on their inner wolves. Mia knew what that felt like, an impulse that was stronger than her free human will, just from the few times she had let her wolf run free

—mostly in the Olympic Mountains, where no one would see or wonder. But even in those few times, her thoughts, her actions, her very being seemed ruled by the instincts of her wolf.

The brown wolf released the man. Dark red smeared his throat, but he must not have been seriously injured, because there wasn't blood spurting everywhere, and he managed to scramble away, still breathing. He ran past Mia, not even a glance back as he escaped down the moonlit alleyway, his imported shoes clacking on the pavement. The two red wolves still had their tails tucked, but now they were backing away, too. They snarled as they went, gaining volume as the distance between them and the brown wolf increased, until they yipped, tossed their heads, and turned to trot down the alley after their fellow thug.

The brown wolf stood straight, legs stiff, tail curled back... staring at her.

She stared back.

The only sounds were the thump of music from the club and the jerky breath heaving in and out of her, but the air was rich with the fight: the scent of blood, a tang of sweat, and the fading whiff of fear. There was a sweet under-scent, familiar but something she couldn't identify. The brown wolf was watching her with eyes deep as night and glittering with the moon. Then, as he held her gaze, he started to shift. Mia had never seen it in another person before. Only in herself, and when it happened, she wasn't exactly looking in the mirror.

His gaze stayed fixed on her as the skin and bones of his body morphed, rearranging in some magic Mia didn't understand even when it was her own body. He was a shadow lengthening, a form growing smoother and taller, trading fur for muscle, muzzle for square jaw, paws for long-fingered hands until finally, he stood tall and naked in all his... *glory.* There was really no other word for it. His shoulders were broad. Muscles rippled down his arms, catching the moonlight, kissing it, and sending it bouncing back to the night. The planes of his chest and stomach were silver-glazed marble, and farther down... Mia's face ran hot as she realized the under scent was arousal. *His* arousal. And his erection was as glorious as the rest of him, tall and firm, the moonlight bathing it with a shimmering glow.

She jerked her gaze back up to meet his.

He slowly stepped toward her, each footfall measured and cautious, like she was a skittish deer he might be frightening off. A fluttery panic rose up in her chest as he approached, making her want to run just like one—not because she feared him, but because he radiated such raw power. Even in his human form, he was stealing her breath, holding her paralyzed against the wall in awe. She couldn't imagine what he could compel her to do in his wolf form.

Anything.

Her inner wolf whimpered.

He bent to pick something off the pavement. Only after he stopped approaching her and fussed with the thing he picked up, did she realize it was his pants. She looked away while he dressed, although that seemed silly, so she looked back again. By then, he was almost upon her, and she startled, hugging the wall once more.

When he was far away and naked, he was something like a Greek god. Up close and shirtless, he was less divine and more humanly, heart-stoppingly gorgeous. His dark brown eyes peered at her, studying her again. He was maybe mid-twenties, with a chiseled face that had lost all boyishness. His chest was raked with four lines of red, where a claw must have found him in the fight, but his wounds were already starting to heal. As she watched, the lines slowly disappeared, just as she'd seen with her own skin many times. His chest was now bare of any marks except for his sprawling, black tattoo: a howling wolf in the middle with inky fur that bled into a thorny tribal design curling down his side. Her fingers ached to touch the silky black lines. He was close enough that his scent was nearly overpowering her—and not because it was strong. It reminded her of the fresh pines of the forest, mixed with a musky earth scent that was subtle and yet inescapable. It screamed *I am male* so loud that her knees went weak with it.

He lifted her chin with one finger. She held her breath while he inspected her. Then he released her from the finger touch, and her wolf wanted to nip after it.

"You're not afraid," he said softly.

"Should I be?" Her heart was pounding hard, and she was drenched in dampness, from the slick sweat of residual panic to the heat between her legs. He was *wolf*. He had to smell *that*. It made more heat rush to her face.

A smile lifted one side of his pinched-serious lips. "Most humans are after a wolf fight."

She let out a breath. He thought she was human. It almost bubbled up a laugh, but she held it in.

His smile drifted away, replaced by seriousness.

"I've seen wolves before," she said. Which, actually, was a lie. At least, she hadn't seen any *other* wolves before tonight.

He nodded, slowly. She couldn't decide if he believed her or not.

Then she realized… "But I won't tell. Anyone. I promise."

One eyebrow lifted. "Really? And why not?"

In that moment, she recognized him: he was her customer at the bar. One of the last ones before she shuffled out, ready to gag on the cocktail of pheromones in the club.

She gave him a tiny smile. "Because you tip well."

He smiled, and it was like the moon had brightened.

She stood in awe of it for a moment. Then she added, "And, you know, for saving my life."

He put a hand on the wall behind her and leaned in close. He drew in a breath, and his eyes half-lidded, then closed. Her pulse kicked up to *approaching heart attack* speed. Was he going to kiss her? Should she let him? Was there any possibility of her *not?*

Then she realized he was just… breathing her in. His eyes opened and peered into hers. He was close enough now that she could easily reach out and touch him. Kiss him. Her wolf whined a complaint, but she couldn't do either of those things. She was paralyzed by his nearness.

"Did they hurt you in any way?" he asked, his voice a whisper. "Tell me the truth."

She shook her head in tiny movements.

"You're sure you're all right?" His voice sounded strained.

She nodded with equally frantic small movements. Then, feeling like an idiot for not being able to form words, she forced out, "I'm okay. Really."

He drew in another breath—more of her scent, she was sure of it—and bit his lip. It ran a quiver through her. Then just when she thought she might not be able to stand it anymore, that she might have to bridge the gap between them and just *touch* him… he eased back from the wall and dropped his hand. Then he simply turned away, leaving her hunched up against the bricks. She relaxed and tried to regain some composure, but her wolf spun rings of frustration inside her. She watched as he picked through the discarded shirts, shoes, and pants littering the now-empty alley. He found his shirt, slipped it on, swiped up two shoes and socks, then returned to her.

"Tell me where you live." It was a command.

"McMahon Hall. At the University." It didn't occur to her until *after* the words were out of her mouth that telling a complete stranger in a moonlit alley where she lived probably wasn't the best choice. But she wasn't afraid of him in any way. He wasn't capable of hurting her, not intentionally, she was sure of it.

He nodded like he had expected her compliance without question, then glanced at the door to *The Deviation*. "It's not safe for you to come back here." He swung back to look at her with those intense, dark eyes. "They'll return. And they'll be looking for you."

That ran a shiver through her. What would she do now? She *needed* this job. But she didn't want to say anything. He'd just saved her life: she didn't want to argue. And he was right. Next time he wouldn't be there to save her. The pit of her stomach hollowed out.

Instead of saying any of that, she asked, "Do you have a name?"

"Yes." The corner of his mouth quirked.

That tiny not-smile did a thing to her insides. "I see. A funny guy as well as an action hero. You know, if you don't tell me, I'll just make something up."

His face lost its humor. "My name is Lucas." He gestured down the alley away from the club. "Come on. I'll take you home."

She looked back at the door. "I should tell them I'm leaving." At Lucas's dark look, she hastily added, "I'll say I'm sick. Not telling anyone anything, remember?"

He hesitated, stared hard at the door, then nodded his permission. She shuffled toward the club. A glance back showed Lucas waiting for her, still barefoot and shirtless in the moonlight-drenched alleyway. *Holy hell,* he was hot. Or maybe his hotness came from the fact that he just possibly saved her life. Definitely saved her secret. Either way, she would make quick work of telling her boss she was done for the day and get back to the alley.

She was afraid he might disappear into the night if she didn't.

Chapter Two

Lucas dropped Mia off at her residence hall with hardly a word. He had hailed a cab, so she didn't even get a chance to peek in his car. Her attempts at small talk on the way back were met with stony silence. It was as if he wanted to forget the night had happened as quickly as possible. She wasn't sure why he even bothered taking her back to her dorm. She could have taken the bus, just like she did to get to *The Deviation* in the first place. But there she stood, outside the door of her hall at one o'clock in the morning, still wearing her work clothes and watching Lucas slip away into the night via an anonymous yellow cab.

Her wolf clawed at Mia's stomach. "Well, what was I supposed to do?" Mia grumbled to her inner beast. "Hit on him after he saved me?" *Wow, thanks for saving me from the big nasty wolves, hot shifter guy. Wanna get some coffee?*

Mia shook her head. Seriously pathetic.

A thumping sound that was more reverberation than music came from the upper floors of McMahon Hall. Someone was up late, throwing a party, and suddenly her room on the 11th floor was the last place she wanted to be. The tree-lined street outside the dorm obscured her view of the Olympic National Park in the far distance, but the leafy arms of the branches overhead still gave her a sense of park's darkened forest. It was the only place she could run free, shifting at will under the cover of the wild. Only she *never* did that... or at least very rarely.

The events in the alley—the danger, the fight, Lucas's breathing her in—all of it had awoken her inner wolf in a way it never had been before. Every nerve ending seemed on fire, and yet there was some ill-defined hollowness inside her. It was an unfamiliar longing: to shift, to let her wolf free, to follow some instinct that was driving her. A long, low howl echoed around inside her head, making the hollowness ring even more empty. Like a whispered promise that could never be fulfilled. Only she didn't know what the promise was or what she wanted to fill the emptiness with.

Mia gritted her teeth and kept the howl locked inside. Letting it out in front of her University of Washington dorm wouldn't exactly be smart. And Mia *had* to be smart. She had to work hard, finish out her business degree at UDub, and land a job so she could take care of her mom. Her dad had never been in the picture, and Mia was an only child, so her mom was the sum total of her family. And if there was one thing her mom had taught her, it was that there wasn't anyone or anything more important than family.

If Mia couldn't go back to *The Deviation,* she would have to find another job to get her through school. She whirled away from the faux forest in front of her and marched into McMahon Hall, taking the elevator to the 11th floor and trying to ignore the stale dorm odors along the way. When the elevator doors opened, it was clear that her floor was once again party central for the building. Who knew the *Business and Arts* dorm would be rocking it so hard so often. Didn't these people ever study?

Unfortunately, her room was in the wing where the party action usually happened. Given the slightly bigger rooms, the open floor plan, the balcony, and not least the stairwell for students pairing off or sneaking down to lower floors, it made sense. It was just highly inconvenient. And periodically turned her home into an over-crowded, over-smelly nightmare.

People jammed the hall as she worked her way in. On a good day, the dorms were a hotbed of nasty—a decade of moldy feet, the residual crumbs of a thousand midnight snacks—but tonight, there was the added sickly stench of bootlegged party drinks. In the corner of the living room, between the silk plant and a five-century-old orange floral couch, sat a metal tub. Students crowded around it with their red plastic cups, waiting for their dip of whatever toxic brew they'd managed to cobble together. She was guessing Tom Collins was some-where in the mix by the overly-sweet lemon scent perfuming the room. How they got away with throwing these parties, she could never figure. They must be paying off the Resident Assistants in sexual favors.

Mia sighed when she found the door to her room was flung wide open with a dozen people she didn't know inside. She wasn't worried—she didn't have anything worth stealing—but she *was* hoping to get some kind of sleep tonight. Maybe forget about the harrowing events of the alley, and the fact that she was newly out of a job.

Her roommate, Jupiter, was flirting in the doorway to their room with some guy—probably her crush-of-the-week, a Southern guy named Jackson from her drama club. Jupiter was from Kansas with all that country-girl wide-eyed innocence on tap plus a heavy helping of roll-in-the-hay eagerness when it came to boys. When she saw Mia, she grinned and waved with far too much exuberance. Mia trudged over, debating whether she could throw everyone out without explanation. It was past one in the morning after all.

Her roommate had the world's coolest name and the world's most ridiculous wardrobe. Jupiter's outfit tonight was par for the course: purple leggings, an orange tulle skirt, and a bunched up UDub sweatshirt that was far too big. Probably belonged to Jackson.

"You know," Mia shouted to be heard over the low-thumping music, "being a drama major is really no excuse for that outfit."

"You're just jealous." Jupiter's smile was too wide, the kind Mia was used to seeing on her customers at *The Deviation*.

"Yeah." Mia smirked. "Jealous of the color blind."

Jupiter made a snort of disgust then frowned. "You've missed half the party!"

"Only half?" Mia threw a questioning look at Jackson, who was watching them with high amusement.

He just shrugged.

"Where have you *been?*" Jupiter asked with the outrage of the half-drunk for slights real and imagined.

"I had to work tonight, remember?"

"Oh yeah." Jupiter's freckled face scrunched up. "Wait, weren't you supposed to be at *The Deviation* until two?"

"Yeah, I, um… got off early."

Mia was saved from explaining by a guy barreling out of her room. All three of them made way for him as he headed for the bathroom and took a quick turn into the girls'. Their floor was coed—either he was confused, or he didn't think he would make it to the boys' bathroom.

Jupiter threw an unmistakable *ew* look after the bathroom perpetrator, then propped one hand on her hip. The other held a small blue-feathered purse that looked like a boa constrictor had thrown up a peacock. She took that thing everywhere, like a pet.

Then she focused on Mia again. "I thought you had gotten that awesome internship at… at…" She snapped her fingers, fast.

"SparkTech Partners," Mia supplied. "I'm starting on Monday."

Jupiter flailed her hand without the blue-feathered thing. "Which is why you need to celebrate!"

"It's been a long night." Mia gave a sad look to her bed inside their room. It currently held three senior boys each with a red cup balanced precariously on their knee. "What I really need is some sleep."

"But you just got here!" Jupiter exclaimed. Then something over Mia's shoulder caught her eye, and her roommate bit her lip, looking guilty. "I might have told a certain hot senior from drama club that you would be here by the end of the party."

"*Jeeter.*" Neither Mia's warning tone nor the nickname Jupiter hated, slowed her down one bit.

"Oh, come on!" Her roommate gave her a disgusted look but dropped her voice. "Cade is perfect for you. Tall, dark, and overly serious. He's just your type."

"I don't have a type." Which was a lie. She very much had a type. It was tall, muscular, and naked in the moonlight. *My name is Lucas.* Even the memory of him leaning close to her made the room feel warm. Mia closed her eyes and shook that thought from her head. There were so many ways that wasn't even close to happening again.

Jupiter bunched up the feathered purse and made begging hands and eyes. She mouthed, *Forgive me.* Then her roommate dropped the drama like a change in costume and beamed over Mia's shoulder. "Hi, Cade!"

Mia rolled her eyes before putting on a tight smile and turning to greet Jupiter's drama club friend. Cade arrived just as she turned, a red plastic cup in each hand. His white t-shirt hung on his broad shoulders like it enjoyed the ride, and his smooth, muscular grace made her think of a tiger: all restrained power and limber movement. Mia was tall, but she still had to look up into those crystalline blue eyes.

"Hey, Jeeter." He smirked at her roommate, then gave Mia a softer look. "Hey, Mia. Didn't expect you until later." His tone, plus a smile he was working to restrain, made it clear he was happy to see her.

Truth was, if she had a type before tonight, Cade would have been exactly it. A commanding presence, killer grin, and gorgeous blue eyes that didn't hurt to look at but sliced right into her heart... and that was exactly the problem. She couldn't afford the distraction of boys. And her previous attempts at boyfriends had been near disasters. Whenever they got too close, too *intimate*, her control slipped. That's when her wolf came out to play, and that had never ended well. Which pretty well explained why she had only slept with two guys before, both of whom had been so freaked by their first time that it was also their last.

Sex was problematic for her, to say the least.

Only with human boys, her wolf whined.

Don't even go there, she thought in return.

As much as any human could be, Cade was definitely her type.

He smiled and handed her a cup. "It's tremendously sweet," he warned. There was a small lift on one side of his smile.

"Thanks for the heads up." She inhaled a small whiff of the vapors coming off the cup. Vodka, one of the cheap brands, plus whiskey sour mix and a leftover dash from a cherry that must still be swimming in the tub. She held the cup close, warding off the stench of the room with her own personal alcohol vaporizer—which she appreciated much more than the drink.

She pretended to take a sip, just to be polite. "So are you guys ready for your show?" She didn't keep track of Jupiter's stage plays, but the spring quarter was coming to a close, so they must have something going.

His smile brightened. "Yeah. You should come. It's called *Silent Death*, and it's a period piece set around Paris in World War II. We'll be in the Penthouse Theatre tomorrow night."

"Sounds like a barrel of laughs."

He frowned. "It's really not that bad."

She bit her lip. Damn, she was tired. Losing her manners, as well as her patience. "I'm sure it is. I'm sorry, I'm just…" She waved her drink. "It's the vapors talking." She inhaled another whiff and shrunk away from some passing partiers swinging their cups as they talked. Another glance at her room must have given away her desire to be anywhere else.

Cade leaned forward, then he edged even closer, dipping his head to bring his lips near her ear. "You want to get out of here?" His hand touched her hair, brushing it back. He was so close that his

cologne and whiskey-sour breath suddenly over-
powered the rest of the dorm scents. "My roommate's gone for the weekend." His voice was low,
husky. He probably thought it was sexy, but Mia
thought he was mostly just drunk.

Her wolf growled. The last thing she needed
was to be propositioned by a half-drunk college boy.
Suddenly, it was all too much, too close, and she
needed out. In fact, she needed *everyone* out. Now.

She nudged Cade back, hand flat on his chest.
"Look, I'm done for the night."

Disappointment shadowed his face, but she had
no time for that.

She turned to her room, pushing past Jupiter
and Jackson. "Okay, everyone, the party's over.
Time to go! Find your own beds."

A round of grumbles, a pause as all eyes turned
to see if she was serious, then another set of
mumbling and complaints as they slowly rose from
the bed, the floor, even her desk. As the crowd filed
out, a couple spilled out of the closet, still tangled in
each other, and bringing half of Jupiter's crazy
wardrobe with them, including a long, green scarf
that wound around their feet and made them go
down.

Mia just shook her head. Jupiter waved goodbye

from the door and disappeared with the partiers, Jackson's arm around her waist. Mia was just as glad to see them go, too, and as soon as the last of them was gone, she locked the door.

First thing, she tore off the top cover of the twin bed that belonged to her, vowing to run it through the laundry before she used it again. Even with that bunched up and stuffed under her bed, only ten percent of her dorm room felt like it belonged to her. The other ninety percent was taken up by her frenetic roommate's endless leggings, half-used doodle pads, and extensive shoe collection. Mia had a picture of her mom on the shelf, about a back-pack's worth of clothes in the closet, a stack of books, and her laptop on the desk… and that was it.

It was almost like she had never really moved in. The room belonged to the partiers as much as her —they were all temporary occupants until they moved on to the next thing. Mia eased down into the bed, lying on top of the sheets, not bothering to remove her clothes. A complete and utter weariness sunk her into the mattress, and she looped her arm over her eyes, blocking out the overhead lights.

Her room was a cage—a tiny concrete and glass cage, with a bed too short for her long legs, and nothing of value to lose in a fire. She didn't belong here, not in any real way. It was a way station on the path to the things she actually needed, that was all. The emptiness made itself known again, a deep hollow in her chest, and her wolf whined, curling its tail down in defeat.

The lights still blared overhead, but Mia turned on her side and dropped off to sleep like she was falling off a cliff.

Chapter Three

IT HAD BEEN TWO DAYS, AND LUCAS COULDN'T GET her out of his mind.

His fingers drummed the edge of his tablet, and he tried again to pore over the numbers for the latest internet startup his brother, Lev, had found for SparkTech to consider for investment. After another five minutes of circling back over the same data again and again, he shoved the tablet away and rose from his desk. He just was too distracted. He flattened his palms against the floor-to-ceiling corner office window and hung his head between his arms. Back when he was a managing partner in his father's tech-focused investment firm, Lucas's status had commanded this office. Now he was just a principal, but his father had still allowed him to keep his luxurious view of the Olympic Mountains. The rain had swept through earlier, leaving a shine on the Emerald City in the early morning sun. He squinted against it and let his gaze roam over the high rises, flicking occasionally to the mountains beyond.

His wolf surged a bit each time he did.

He'd tried going for a hunt over the weekend, but it didn't help. He kept thinking about the girl, the one he'd stopped the Reds from playing with, like the other field mice they liked to torment. Lucas should have asked her name. He should have gone back to the club to make sure she quit on the spot. He should have moved her to a different dorm. *Something.* There were a hundred things he could have done, but instead, he rushed her home, thinking if he simply got her safely out of his arms reach that would solve everything, including the strange pull she had on him.

That part he understood least of all.

He paced the length of his office, but his gaze kept wandering back to the forest of glittering steel-and-glass high rises of downtown Seattle and to the distant trees beyond. A year ago, when he lost his mate, he lost a part of himself as well. He hadn't been fit to be alpha for anyone anymore, so he'd left his pack and gone rogue. He even left SparkTech and lived in the wild until he'd almost forgotten what it was to be human. He'd thought he *had* forgotten until Lev came looking for him and pulled him out of the dark hole of despair he'd fallen into. There was no fixing what had broken inside him, but Lev convinced him he could still contribute to the family business, even if he weren't part of any pack. It was just enough to keep him human, and after a while, he'd begun to believe he could keep the longings at bay with a shit-ton of work, his brothers nearby, and a steady supply of female companionship to ease the pain. Slowly, his wolf quieted. The mournful howling every night, crying his need for a pack of his own, eventually stopped. Lucas thought he'd finally found a way to carry on.

And then… *this girl.*

Human girls were a distraction, a temporary pleasure to sate his longings. They lasted a night, maybe two. Never more. And he'd found plenty who enjoyed what he had to give. They responded to his inner alpha even if they couldn't see how broken he really was. Which suited him just fine, until… this strange girl who needed his help. He didn't understand what pulled him to track her. Or why he went into that alleyway to stop the Reds.

She was nothing to his pack, just another human in the half million or so in the Bay area.

His wolf growled at that thought, and it came out as a throaty sound that echoed around his office. The door was closed, so he didn't even try to rein it in. He knew a lie when he heard one, even when he told it to himself. He might be broken, but no alpha could have stood by and let those sick bastards in the Red pack toy with someone the way they did. Much less a human girl, unprotected, unwary… although it turned out she knew more than he thought. She'd seen shifters before. And yet kept her silence about them.

That was intriguing, but it wasn't what haunted him. What kept him pacing through the weekend were two simple things: first, her scent had pulled him in, and he'd been tempted to claim her right there in the alley, something that didn't even make sense. Humans were for pleasure, not mating. But second, and more important, he had inflamed the tensions between his father's pack and the Reds… and he'd brought the girl deep into the heart of it. The Reds would go after her, track her, hunt her down, now that they knew she was important to him.

And after a weekend of pacing and hunting and

shredding the sheets in tumultuous dreams where he fulfilled that wish to claim her in the alleyway, he had finally admitted to himself and his wolf that she was, indeed, important to him.

The thing was, he had no idea why.

A knock at the door dredged his attention out of the depths.

Lev poked his head in the door. "Hey, man, just giving you a heads up."

Lucas sighed. "Let me guess. My extracurricular activities this weekend found their way to our father's attention."

He held his hands up. "Wasn't me, bro. Dad found out on his own. I just heard the howling." Lev was his youngest brother and part of his pack, back when he was a true alpha. But even when Lucas went rogue, Lev never really stopped being his beta. Officially, his brother had rejoined their father's pack. Unofficially, he still had Lucas's back, in family matters as well as business. There was a reason Lev had been the one to pull him out of the forest again. And why Lucas carried on, staying at SparkTech, making it work for Lev's sake, even if every day it shoved a hot poker into old wounds.

"I'll take care of it, Lev," he said, taking one last glance at the mountains. "Thanks for the warning."

Lev gave a short nod and disappeared back out the door.

Lucas took a breath, glanced at his neglected work on the tablet, and decided it was better to clear the air with his father than to wait for him to come Lucas's way. He locked the screen on his tablet, tucked it in his desk, and headed for his father's office.

SparkTech took up a good fraction of the 32nd floor of the Russell Investments Center in downtown Seattle. His father grew it from a pack-only business, just him and his brothers, to one of the most successful business development companies for technology startups in the Bay area. He liked to say Seattle was on its way to competing with Silicon Valley as a premier ecosystem for tech startups. And the investment opportunities *were* getting better, with startups these days being spearheaded by people from Google or Amazon as often as not. The industry was maturing, and his father had the vision to take it to the next level. He was the kind of alpha who could see the possibilities and seize them —the kind Lucas had wanted to be—but success breeds competition, and Red Wolf had been nipping at SparkTech's heels more and more in the last year. The competition was fierce to scoop up the next billion-dollar tech startup. For Lucas to have waded into that mess and possibly mucked it up even further with this business with the girl…

He took a deep breath and steeled himself as he pushed open the door to his father's office.

As befit the alpha of a company, his father had the finest office, a corner with a view of Mount Rainier, luxurious wood furniture, and glass-and-chrome bookshelves to hold the many trophies and accolades their investments had won. His father waited until Lucas had fully entered his expansive office, and the door had swung shut behind him. Even then, he fussed with something on his tablet.

He was making Lucas wait. Not a good sign.

When his father finally put down the tablet, his expression was cool. "Have you had a chance to look at the numbers for LoopSource?"

"I… um…" Lucas was thrown. He had expected to account for the girl, not the project Lev had tossed to him last week. "Still assessing. Their new platform is interesting, and it seems to be gaining traction, but I'm still checking out the CEO and their execution team. And I'm not sure the market is ready for them."

His father's dark eyes drilled into him. "Red Wolf seems to think they're ready."

Shit. "They're making a move to offer?"

His father let out a sigh, then came around his giant glass-and-chrome desk. Framed logos of their previous acquisitions, the ones that made his father millions and put him on Seattle's *50 Most Influential People* list, covered the surface like a small forest of Plexiglas-encased-money. And power. His father stopped in front of the desk, leaning back against it and folding his arms.

He stared at Lucas for a moment longer, then said, "Tell me about the girl." It was a command, and that tone would have made all of Lucas's fur stand on end if he was in wolf form. But he wasn't. And he wouldn't submit to his father ever again— not to be in his pack, or in any pack, for that matter. He had too much alpha left in him to allow it.

Still, Lucas dropped his head and winced, searching for an explanation that made any sense at all. When he looked up, his father was still waiting. "You know how the Reds are. They would have torn her apart."

His father's eyes narrowed. "You know her."

"No." Lucas swallowed. "Not really."

His father's face was stony, but Lucas could see the confusion flicker across it. His father had mated with his mother early on before they were even out of college. His mother was a strong wolf from an allied pack, but more than that—they were in love even before they mated for life. Lucas knew his casual sex habits completely baffled his father.

"You're not in my pack, Lucas." His father lifted an eyebrow. "That offer still stands, any time you change your mind, son." Then all tolerance fled his face. "If you *were* in my pack, we'd be having an entirely different conversation. As it stands, I really don't care what you do outside this office. Unless it affects the company, and then I care a tremendous amount."

Lucas flinched. He couldn't bring himself to say it was a mistake to interfere, but his father was right. He had to fix this. "What is Red Wolf saying?"

"I had a very interesting phone conversation this morning with Crittenden," he said, his voice rough with an unspoken growl.

Crittenden was the alpha of the Red pack and CEO of Red Wolf. Alpha to alpha. *Shit.* That had escalated fast. Lucas's gaze dropped to the floor, trying to get ahead of this.

His father continued, "He says he's willing to leave your girlfriend alone in exchange for us dropping pursuit of LoopSource."

"What?" Lucas's gaze snapped back up to his

father's. "That's absurd. They can't possibly expect—"

His father's steely look silenced the words as they came out of his mouth. "I told them I had no intention of dropping LoopSource. And if they hurt the girl, Crittenden would personally be held responsible by my pack."

Lucas's mouth dropped open. *Pack protection.* For a girl whose name he didn't even know. His father had gone way, *way* out on a limb for him, his wayward would-be alpha son. And if the Reds decided to push it, they could have a pack war on their hands.

Lucas shut his gaping mouth and stood straighter. "What can I do to help?"

His father cocked his head in approval of Lucas's understanding of the situation. "I would find a way to keep your girlfriend safe. I don't want her tempting some young pup in the Red pack into doing something stupid to make a name for himself."

"Understood." Lucas turned away, a calm filling him along with a peculiar shame. Protecting the girl is what he should have done from the start. It's what his father, a true alpha, would have done if fate had tossed him into the same circumstance. Before he reached the door of his father's office, Lucas turned back to face him. "Just so you know, she's not my girlfriend. She's just a girl who needed someone's help."

His father's face betrayed no surprise if he had any. "That doesn't matter now."

"I know." Lucas stared at the carpet by the door. "Just wanted to set the record straight."

As he headed toward his own office, the heat in his face grew stronger with each step. He'd put a lot in jeopardy to save a girl he didn't even know. However, he knew the failure wasn't in that act, but in the ones that followed. When he failed to find permanent protection for her. A way to keep her safe from the wolves hidden just under the skin of Seattle's most ruthless businessmen, now that she'd crossed onto their radar.

That was a mistake he was going to fix.

Chapter Four

Mia was dressed and ready to leave for the first day of her internship, but first, she had to pass the Supreme Gatekeeper of Fashion, otherwise known as her roommate, Jupiter.

"Absolutely not." Jupiter tsk-tsked her plain black slacks and white collared shirt. It was perfectly respectable business attire—Mia had looked it up online—plus it had the benefit of pulling double duty on the black pants she would no longer be wearing for *The Deviation.*

"Jupiter, please." Mia was already jittery enough, she didn't need this. "I'm going to miss the bus." The ride was only 23 minutes—she'd looked that up too—but if she didn't leave in the next five minutes, she would miss it and be late for sure.

"The first day requires a higher dress code," Jupiter admonished. "Then, if everyone else dresses like a bartender who just lost her job, then fine. Be that way."

Mia had told her roommate she couldn't go back to *The Deviation* because she would need help finding something new, but she'd been light on the details of why. She would keep her promise to Lucas, the hot shifter she spent half the weekend daydreaming about, but even without that promise, spilling to Jupiter about werewolves on the streets of Seattle was just a little too close to home for comfort. Mia had only had the weekend to look for a job, but so far no luck. If something didn't turn up soon, she could still go back to *The Deviation*. She hadn't technically quit, and her next shift wasn't until Wednesday.

Jupiter rummaged through the closet that housed both their clothes, but mostly hers. Articles of clothing started to sail across the room.

Mia watched as most missed the bed and landed on the floor. "Jeeter—"

"Hush!" Jupiter said, her voice muffled. "I'm finding you something decent." After a moment, she came out with a silky something in brilliant blue. She held it up to Mia. "Perfect! Matches your eyes exactly." She tossed that to Mia and returned to the closet.

Mia pulled in a breath. "Fine." She knew a losing fight when she saw it, and maybe if she hurried, she would still make the bus. She rushed through the buttons of her white collared shirt and threw on the blue silk one. It was sleeveless and made her arms feel naked. But it draped just right everywhere else and instantly made her feel more professional.

"Great! Jupiter, you're the best. I'll see you—"

Her roommate pulled back from the closet with a set of blue pumps in one hand and a black jacket in the other. "Oh, we are *so* not done."

"Jeeter, I've gotta *go.*"

Jupiter thrust the clothes at her. "Change while I get the pearls."

Five minutes later, Mia passed inspection and somehow ran the whole way to the bus stop in her roommate's heels. Thankfully, they wore the same size. Or perhaps not: if Jupiter hadn't been an exact fit, maybe Mia wouldn't have to endure quite so many mandatory makeovers.

But she couldn't argue with the effect the clothes had on her confidence. She was dressing the part of the business entrepreneur, and while she would probably spend the afternoon fetching coffee and making copies, she hoped there would be more to it than that. She'd taken quite a few classes in her major already, and she'd done her research on the company: at least as much as could be found on their website. She was there to learn, to make a great impression, and eventually, to score a real job. One that paid.

Her arrival at the Russell Investments Center downtown, as well as the long, slow ride up to the 32nd floor, were enough to bring her nerves raging back. SparkTech's name and logo were etched into the frosted glass doors, and when she pushed them open, her jitters took another jump up the nervous scale. She had never been in an office that was so… *luxurious.* The off-white carpet felt like she was walking on a thick, padded cloud. The walls were illuminated along the ceiling and floor, giving the effect that they floated on a glowing cushion of light. The dark burnished wood of the receptionist's desk shone with such a high state of polish that it reflected her unsteady approach in her blue heels. There was no one behind the desk, and the frosted doors off to the side weren't inviting. Neither were the glass tables and trim, off-white couches. A small fan whirred in the corner, an air purifier, then she realized the office had almost no scent—as if the small device had scrubbed all the normal human and office smells from the room. It was refreshing, comforting in a way she hadn't experienced since her last trip to the forest.

"Hello?" she called quietly. When no one answered, she teetered, uncertain. She almost turned around and headed back to the elevator, when the frosted doors swung open, and an impeccably-dressed mid-thirties woman strolled out, all smiles. She gave an approving glance over Mia's attire.

Mia kept her sigh of relief inside and silently thanked Jupiter for her wardrobe assist.

The woman shook her hand. "I'm Lena. Welcome to SparkTech. You must be our new intern, Mia Fiore."

"I hope I'm not late." Mia looked nervously for a clock, but there wasn't any.

"No, dear, you're right on time." Lena ushered her toward the door. She had a light citrusy smell that Mia was almost certain wasn't perfume… just her natural, clean-scrubbed scent. Oddly, it helped her relax even more.

Lena steered her down the hallway. The wide-open floor plan left plenty of space in the middle for groups to meet, while the offices ringed the perimeter.

"Most of the Managing Partners are out for the day," Lena said, "but the Principals are all in, including the one you'll be assisting for the term. You're just with us for the summer, right?"

"Both summer terms, actually," Mia said. "If that's still all right?"

"I'm sure that it is."

They stopped in front of an office at one corner with a name etched on the frosted glass. All the offices must have windows, or powerful internal lighting because the same frosted glass that comprised both walls and doors seem to glow with an effervescent light from within.

Lena knocked.

A gruff male voice called, "Come in."

Lena opened the door, and Mia put on what she hoped was a professional smile as she trailed behind Lena into the office. Mia kept the smile plastered to her face even as her eyes went wide at the incredible view out the windows. The city lay at her feet, with the Olympic Mountains in the distance. The noon-time sun filled the lushly appointed office with natural light.

Belatedly, she pulled her gaze back to the man sitting at the desk.

Then the smile on her face died.

Lucas.

She struggled for something to say, confused, shaken, but it was nothing compared to the fire in Lucas's eyes. He lurched to his feet but stalled out there, still standing behind his desk.

"Mr. Sparks," Lena said, her voice wavering a little. "I'm sorry to disturb you. This is Mia Fiore. You said you wanted our new intern brought right to you as soon as she arrived."

He knew? Mia's eyebrows hiked up, but the pure shock on Lucas's face said *no*, he was just as surprised as she was.

He was still frozen behind his desk. Finally, he said, "Right. Yes. Thank you, Lena. That will be all." His gaze was locked on Mia, looking her up and down, like he expected to find something else, anything else, besides *her* standing before him in a suit and heels.

Lena seemed to sense the live-wire tension as well, but confusion ruled her face. *Of course.* Why would Lucas tell his office assistant that he had saved a college girl from two snarling wolves over the weekend? In fact, the freaked look on Lucas's face had to be more than just shock at seeing her show up in his office. He had to be worried she was going to spill his secret—at his fancy investment job, no less. Mia forced a brighter smile and tried to send him reassuring looks, but the intensity on his face just burned them away.

"Well," Lena said, her voice strained. "I guess… just let me know if you need anything." Surprisingly, she was saying this to Mia, as if she was hesitant to leave her alone with Lucas. But that was exactly what needed to happen.

Mia gave her a broad smile. "Thanks so much for your help!" The cheery enthusiasm was probably a bit too much. But it worked in nudging Lena to the door and eventually through it.

As soon as the door closed, Lucas tore around the desk toward her.

Mia threw her hands up, not so much to stop him but to buy a second to get her apology out.

He still beat her to it. "What are you doing here?" His voice had growl in it, even more than she expected, and it sent a shiver through her. "How did you find me?"

That short-circuited her brain. "Find you? I wasn't stalking you! I've had this internship lined up for months." She snuck a look back to the door.

Through the frosted glass, she could see his name etched there, in reverse: *L. Sparks, Managing Partner.* Her research came rushing back: Lucas Sparks was one of the founder's sons in this family-owned business. Of course, she hadn't thought twice that he might be *her* Lucas. Which made her frown even more: he wasn't *hers* in any conceivable way. Except perhaps in her hot dreams about him over the weekend.

He was looming over her, emotions warring across his face, but he was holding something back. She jumped in with the apology, suddenly worried her internship might vanish in a puff of smoke, just like her job at *The Deviation.*

"I swear I didn't know you were here," she said in a rush. "I promise I won't say anything to anyone. Please, don't…" She swallowed as his frown just grew deeper. "Please don't fire me. I need this internship on my resume. I promise I won't be any trouble."

At that, the expression on his face broke. It wrenched something inside her, but she wasn't sure what, because he took a step closer and ran two fingers along her cheek, which completely stopped any thoughts in her head.

"Hey," he said softly. "No one's going to fire

you. Stop worrying about that right now."

His touch was a line of heat across her cheek, but his words worked through her, relaxing the tension that had hiked up her shoulders. That, and the nearness of him was like a balm that washed away her concerns. His scent finally reached her over the near scentlessness of his office: a freshly-cut wood smell with a musky hint of baked-in-the-afternoon-sun. Her body was likewise warming to the richly masculine quality of it, completely without her permission. When she peered up into his dark eyes, they were hooded, and she could tell he was breathing her in again, like before, when they almost kissed in the alleyway. It wasn't just her imagination. She was affecting him, too. Only now, he was her *boss*.

This couldn't end well.

Before she could think of what to say, he looked over her with a gaze that almost felt like a touch. "Mia." His voice was husky, and her name on his lips felt like a caress. "I'm really glad to see you're okay." He blinked, like he was coming out of a daze, then frowned. "I think perhaps we were destined to cross paths."

"Or just luck, I suppose." *Bad luck*, her mind was saying, but her wolf was whimpering again. Her inner beast didn't seem to think it was in any way bad.

Lucas frowned and pulled back. "It's better to have you working here, I guess, than at *The Deviation*. You *have* told them you quit, right?"

She bit her lip. "Well, no." When his eyes went wide with disbelief, she rushed the rest out. "I'm trying to find another job, but it's only been a couple days! I'm sure I'll find something soon."

He shook his head. "But you have *this* job now. Why do you need two?"

Why did she need two? Anger boiled up in her. Because she wasn't some freaking billionaire perched high in the sky, a son-of-the-boss hottie who made enough money to wear a tailored Italian suit like he was born into it. "Why? Because I don't have a corner office, Lucas! I'm a college student. And I need to eat on occasion, and maybe buy books, and *hello*, even the bus fare to come down here cost money! I can't afford to do an internship like this without *some* way to make enough money to live on." With the last of it, her anger boiled over. Sure he probably saved her life, but he obviously didn't know anything about her.

His face had settled into a scowl. "Whatever

we're paying you, I'll double it. Will that be enough to let you quit *The Deviation?*"

"Last I checked, double of nothing was still a big fat zero."

The scowl went two shades darker. "You're an unpaid intern."

"You're a genius." She pouted, regretting those words as soon as they were out of her mouth. She regretted it even more as he spun around and stalked back to his desk to pick up the phone. *Shit,* he was going to fire her. *Way to open up your big mouth, Mia, and—*

"Lena," he said into the phone, but he was staring straight at Mia with those intense, dark eyes. "I want to change Mia's pay class from unpaid to associate." There was a slight pause on the phone. "Yes, she's quite exceptional. Please get the paperwork started. Thank you."

He hung up the phone, and Mia's mouth hung open. Had he… did he just get her a *job?* A real, paid one? Lucas slowly came around the desk again, taking each step carefully, like he was walking a tightrope until he stood before her again.

Mia shut her mouth, which was still hanging open, and just stared up at him. *Why?* Why was he doing this for her?

"Do you have a cell phone?" he asked quietly.

"Um… yes." Her head was spinning, but she fumbled to fish it out of her jacket pocket.

"Call *The Deviation*. Right now. Tell them you're quitting."

He waited patiently while she texted her boss at the club. A kind of light-headed feeling took over as she pressed the *send* button. She really didn't have to go back to that stink-hole. She had a for-real job at a prestigious business development firm in downtown Seattle that smelled a little bit like heaven. With a boss who was the hottest guy she'd ever known.

And a shifter, whose secret she had sworn to keep.

She slid the phone back in her pocket and stared up into his eyes. His neatly tailored blue dress shirt tucked into his smoothly draped designer pants, which hung perfectly on him. All of it hid the muscles she knew lay underneath. The ones she had seen on grand display in the moonlight—an image she still couldn't get out of her mind.

"Why are you doing this?" she asked softly. Maybe he wanted sexual favors. Maybe this was some kind of *quid pro quo* that would land her in more trouble than she could handle. As he leaned closer, she had a hard time worrying about that. Everything about him radiated *safeness.* She knew he was a powerful wolf when he shifted. Even in her wolf form, she would be no match for him. Her wolf whimpered in agreement, but not in a bad way. In a way that made her mouth water a little with the idea of him *wanting* things from her.

Maybe this was just the kind of trouble she would like to handle.

"I want to make sure you're safe." His eyes blazed, raking over her and heating up her face again. His hand raised as if he was going to touch her, and her insides literally ached with anticipation. But at the last second, he held back. He leaned away, then took a half step back as if she had suddenly turned into something dangerous he needed distance from. "Your safety is the most important thing, Mia. You don't have any idea what those wolves would do to you if they found you. I want to make sure that doesn't happen."

The sudden coolness of his voice confused her. She didn't know what to say.

He dropped his gaze then turned and headed back to his desk. Without looking at her, he picked up his phone and dialed.

"I need your help on something," he said into it, then, "Thanks." He hung up.

When he looked up at her, his eyes were cool again, not blazing with the heat from before. "My brother, Lev, will show you around and get you settled."

"Thank you," she said, but awkwardness filled the air. She hadn't just imagined the attraction, had she? Was he just looking out for her, like a big brother might? She certainly didn't feel that way, but maybe for him…

A moment later, the door to his office swung open. A younger version of Lucas leaned in, his face boyish and open.

"Take care of her for me, will you, Lev?" Lucas's voice was all business again. "I've got some numbers I need to run for LoopSource."

Lev beamed, and he looked even younger. But friendly. "You got it, boss!"

Lucas frowned like somehow Lev's words irritated him, but then he picked up his tablet and focused on that.

Mia was still awkwardly standing in the middle of his office. Lev waved her out into the hallway with him.

Once they were alone, he grinned even wider. "So you're the girl, huh?"

"The… what?" she asked, suddenly nervous.

He faltered. "I mean… you're the *new* girl."

She gave him a quizzical look. "Was there an *old* girl?"

Lev winced, bit his lip, and did a whole facial gymnastics session that Mia could only watch in amazement. They were strolling down the hall, and he seemed to involuntarily glance at a darkened office, the only one that wasn't beaming light through the frosted glass. Having seen Lucas's office, the only way that could be was if the blinds were drawn tight, draped over, and all the lights were off. Etched on the doorway was the name *T. Sparks*.

Lev jerked his gaze away from the door and stared straight down the hall. "No, no, I was just saying…" He looked back to her. "I'm glad you've joined us. I'm Lev by the way." He held out a hand to shake. It was warm and friendly, just like the puppy-dog brown eyes and open smile. "What's your name, new girl?"

Her unease finally washed away. "Mia," she said. "Mia Fiore."

"Well, Mia Fiore, anything you need, just ask,

but for starters, how's this for an office?" He stopped at one of the brightly-lit offices halfway down the hall, only four doors down from Lucas's office, and swung open the door. It was a miniature version of Lucas's—not so richly appointed, but still the same luxurious furniture the rest of the company had. An air purifier hummed quietly in the corner.

"It's... amazing." She strode in and stared at the view out the window.

"Great!" Lev strode over to pick up a tablet off the desk—which, she guessed, was now *her* desk. "Let's get to work."

Chapter Five

LUCAS HAD MANAGED TO LARGELY AVOID THE GIRL —*Mia*—for most of the week. Even thinking her name rumbled his wolf into some kind of frenzy. And when she'd been in his office that first day… he'd damn near kissed her. It was as if her nearness was an intoxication for his inner beast. It had taken all his control to simply step back from her. Which really made no sense at all. His wolf had never had that kind of reaction to the other girls he'd bedded, or any female for that matter, not since… but if he couldn't think about Mia's name without rousing his wolf, he certainly wasn't going to conjure up Tila's…

He dropped his head into his hands, elbows propped on his desk, and closed his eyes.

Tila had been *everything* to him. Smart, funny, sexy, a natural in the business, as much as anyone in his father's pack. She *belonged* with him. But more than that... she fit into his soul. She was a piece of him, completed him. And when that was gone...

He huffed out his frustration and rose suddenly from his desk. He couldn't let that black void capture him again. He had responsibilities—to Lev, to the company, and now even to this girl, Mia. Keeping her safe was the only truly worthwhile thing he was doing now. Lucas strode to the window to look out over the city, only to be surprised to find the sun had set and the evening lights had begun to wink on. When had that happened?

He sighed. Avoiding Mia would only last so long. She was here for the duration, at the very least until he could be sure the Red pack had lost interest in her. Which could take longer than the summer term for her internship. Lev had set her up to analyze the LoopSource fundamentals, damn him. Lucas had a feeling Lev knew exactly how much he was tempted by her brilliant blue eyes and pale, silky skin. When he'd touched her face, he'd found it as soft as he had imagined all those times in his bed... his inner wolf whined its frustration.

It was tired of waiting.

Office romances weren't forbidden at Spark-Tech—his father's pack was filled with such pairings —but this was different. She was an intern, and a human one. Those other pairings had been long-term shifter employees and had his father's approval... he would *not* approve of this, not least because the girl was under pack protection until the Reds grew tired of her. Or moved on to some other distraction.

Lucas had a fleeting thought of simply bedding her. Once. Get this insanity out of his system. The other girls had only ever lasted that long, the initial attraction quickly wearing off once his physical needs were sated. Perhaps that was it—he was overdue for a physical release, and once he had it, he could put this whole business behind him.

His wolf snarled and pushed against him from the inside. His hands curled, nearly forming claws as he resisted the strength of the impulse to shift. He shook his head, forcing his hands to relax and his wolf to settle. He was fooling himself with that kind of talk. Mia was far from a one-night deal *already.* He needed a more permanent way to ensure she was safe, yet safely removed from him and not a constant, daily temptation. Even a trace of her scent lingering in the common area could bring out longings that needed to stay deeply buried.

That was it: he needed to wind up the Loop-Source deal. *Now.* Or as quickly as possible. He would bury himself in work, and that would get him through. Although it would also require that he worked with *her*, just on the off chance that she noticed something in the financials that he had missed. His wolf panted at that idea, and he knew he was lying to himself again. Yet as soon as the idea had been set loose, he couldn't rein it back in.

He glanced at the gray-black sky—it was void of stars due to the light pollution of downtown, and as dark as the night would get. The hour was late, but his father was likely still working. Lucas would update him on the progress on the LoopSource deal, leave a note on Mia's desk to see him in the morning, and then go home to hopefully sleep off this growing frustration. Maybe a few shots of vodka would ease his way into dreamland tonight.

He scooped up this tablet, gathered a few scattered printouts, and headed toward his father's office at the far end of the space owned by Spark-Tech. Sure enough, his father's office still glowed with the fluorescent lights within, but Lucas stumbled as he passed Mia's office. The lights were still on there as well. Was she really working this late? How was she planning on getting home? The bus sure as hell wasn't safe out of downtown at this time of night…

He kept walking but made a note to hurry back to check on her.

He knocked on his father's door and quickly entered on his command. His father looked up from a thick report he was wading through. Pages were spread across the desk, intermingled with several others.

Lucas eyed them. "Are you working LoopSource as well?" Sometimes his father would have multiple partners and principals studying all angles of a company.

"No, this is a separate matter." His father sighed and leaned back in his chair, threading his fingers together and examining Lucas. "Speaking of which, how is our new intern working out?"

"Fine." He tried hard not to look thrown by the sudden change in topic.

"She's quite capable, from what I've seen so far."

His father was studying his reaction, so he kept it cool. "Is that right?" Lucas could tell he wasn't fooled by the dodge when his father raised a single eyebrow.

But he seemed willing to let it go. "More to the point, I haven't heard from Crittenden recently."

Lucas frowned. "That's a good sign, right? Maybe they're losing interest."

His father gestured to the documents in Lucas's hands. "What are you seeing? Is LoopSource worth funding?

"It's looking good, but I still need more time. They're dropping some reports off in the morning. I'll need to wade through those. Or possibly get Mia to help with it." He cringed internally that he let that slip out, but pressed on. "Either way, I'll be working through the weekend to get some final numbers for you by Monday. But I'd be surprised if Red Wolf's already turned them down. The Reds will want to analyze those reports as well."

"Agreed," his father said with a sigh. "I'm afraid it's too early to hope they've given up—on Loop-Source or your young intern. And even if they lose interest in that startup, they'll likely reserve threats against Ms. Fiore for a future one. Have you moved her to a new residence yet?"

Lucas winced for real this time. "No, not yet."

He knew he needed to discuss that with Mia, but he'd been so busy avoiding contact with her all week that he'd never found the right time to bring it up.

His father shook his head. "Lucas, the University dorm system may be relatively safe, but once they find out where she lives…"

"I know," he said quickly. "I'll handle it."

"Please see that you do." His father gave him a nod that Lucas knew was a dismissal.

He stood straighter and retreated from his father's office.

Thankfully, the lights were still on in Mia's. He swung into her office, words on his lips to chastise her for working so late, but he stopped short. She had earbuds in and obviously didn't notice him barreling into her office. She had one hand worked up into her long, deep-black hair, mussing it substantially as she hunched over her tablet. He blinked, imagining his own hand in her hair like that and feeling the surge of his wolf heartily agreeing with that image. He slowly approached her, trying to catch her eye without startling her, but she didn't notice, just moved slightly in her chair, spilling open her jacket further to reveal more of her silky white blouse underneath. It was demure, but it still made his mouth water.

Finally, he was close enough for her to catch sight of him. She let out a shriek and jerked so hard, her chair slid on its wheels and went out from under her. In a flash, he dropped his stuff to the carpet and sped around the desk, where he hooked his arms under hers and scooped her off the floor. Her iPod was tossed to the floor, and the chair had slid away, but there she was, breathing hard and grasping onto his arms to stay upright, a wild look in her eyes along with that still-mussed hair...

Damn. He was in such trouble here.

"Oh my god!" she said, breathless. "You scared the shit out of me!"

Then she blushed, color rushing to her cheeks and making her pale skin blossom into something even more appealing. He was holding her far longer than necessary, but her scent was closing in on him —the normal light musk and crisp meadow flowers blended with a hint of sour panic that had him closing his arms tighter around her, his instinctual need to keep her safe pulling her closer when he should be letting her go.

"Are you all right?" It came out as a whisper. *Mine,* his inner wolf growled. Lucas's heart stuttered. He shouldn't feel this way about her. It made no sense...

"I'm… I'm okay." She wasn't pulling back, but she did move slightly in his arms. She was tall, but he was taller, and she had to look up into his eyes. Which she was doing right now. Her lips were slightly parted. Her chest was still heaving, pressing lightly against him with each labored breath.

He should turn away.

He should let her go.

Mine, his wolf insisted.

It wasn't true.

He didn't care.

He crashed his lips to hers, devouring them in a kiss so hungry it made his inner beast roar. He swept his tongue across her lips, tasting her, and she opened her mouth to him. He plunged in, claiming the sweet taste of her until she bent back with the force of it. Her taste was uniquely *her,* and he drank it in. His arms tightened around her body, molding it to his chest as his hands sought ways to bring her closer. His all-consuming kiss turned into many smaller ones, still hungry for her, but softer. Then he was nipping at her lips, taking them gently between his teeth and teasing them with promises of the sweet torments he wanted to lavish upon them.

The thud of a door closing jerked him out of the lust-filled haze that clouded his senses. He dashed a look to her door, but it had slowly swung shut, and they were only exposed to the nighttime skyline of Seattle, for any who wished to see the show they were putting on in the lighted office on the 32nd floor.

Lucas remained still, holding his breath, Mia safely caged in his arms as his father's shadow passed by the frosted glass of her office. He waited, silent as prey hidden in the brush until the outer door to SparkTech's reception area clicked shut. When he finally looked to her, Mia's face was flushed, her beautiful eyes wide, her lips swollen from his assault on them.

He drew in a breath, regret stabbing him, then released her and took a step back.

She teetered, and he almost came back to steady her, but he didn't trust himself to touch her again.

"I'll take you home," he said, his voice thick.

Her shoulders drooped. She was disappointed. Her kisses in return had been no less eager than his. Her arousal perfumed the air and felt like a physical force pulling him back. His wolf raged against his skin, wanting out. Wanting *her*.

She was far too dangerously addictive for him. There was no way he could just have a taste. No way he could touch her again and have any hope of holding himself back.

It took a moment, but she recovered. "I… I can take the bus."

"No!" His wolf surged, and he lurched forward with the force of it. He stopped himself just short of grabbing hold of her again. Slowly, with extreme gentleness, he placed a hand on her shoulder. Then he bore his stare into her eyes to impress upon her: this was not up for negotiation. "I will drive you home."

She quivered under his hand, so he released her. But her jerky nod was all the assent he needed. He scooped her iPod off the floor, righted her chair, and busied himself with gathering her things off the desk and his off the floor.

He would get her safely home as quickly as possible. Then he would figure out some way to forget what had just happened.

And never let it happen again.

Chapter Six

THE SCORCHING HOT KISS AND THE LONG, SILENT
ride home had Mia twisted in knots. She had apparently replayed some of it in her dreams that night if
her roommate Jupiter's knowing looks and Mia's
tangled sheets were any indications. She was just
relieved there were no rips in her bedding from any
accidental night-shifting. That hadn't happened in
ages, but then she'd never had a kiss be so powerful
that it possessed her: mind, body, and soul.

Lucas had insisted she no longer take the bus to
work. He said he would send a car and driver, and
sure enough, the next morning, a stretch limousine
showed up at her dorm room bright and early,
ready to pick her up. She was quickly exhausting

Jupiter's wardrobe, trying to find something appropriate to wear each day to SparkTech, but she took care to dress extra professionally that morning: a trim, black skirt, a muted-yellow light-weight sweater, and her long hair pulled back in a clip. Jupiter had laden her with a few gold bangles and pronounced her "perfect." Mia couldn't help hoping that would be Lucas's evaluation as well. She certainly caught a few stares from her fellow McMahon dorm students as she stepped out Friday morning in her yellow-gold pumps and business-smart outfit. The high-class limo with the door held open by a black-tie driver in a *Driving Miss Daisy* cap only added to the effect.

On the drive into downtown Seattle, the urban canyon streets were still gray, shadowed by the early morning sun. Mia couldn't decide what exactly had happened the night before. Lucas kissed her—had *thoroughly* kissed her—and his rock-hard erection against her body said he wanted to do much more than press his lips to hers. It wasn't just a kiss, either: more like a volcano of passion erupting. But then he had just… *stopped.* Was he afraid they would be caught by his father, the Senior Mr. Sparks, CEO of SparkTech? She had snooped a little online and found Lucas had graduated from the University of Washington four years ago, which made him at least twenty-six. Wasn't that a little old to be worried about what his parents thought? Or was it because she worked for Lucas? She decided that had to be it —he was afraid she might cry sexual harassment or some such thing.

As if anything sexual involving Lucas could be termed harassment of any kind.

And then there was the whole shifter aspect. To be honest, that was the part that excited her the most. He was *wolf.* And after what she had seen in the alleyway, he was an extremely powerful wolf, in both his human and shifted forms. She had always been drawn to powerful men—at least the kind who wore their power in their broad shoulders and in the muscles underneath their t-shirts. But Lucas was the kind of man she was truly meant to be with: strong, overwhelmingly sexy, and able to handle her in the event her inner wolf became unleashed. The thought of that alone made her squeeze her thighs together and hope the driver wasn't a shifter, wondering why his passenger was getting aroused by herself in the back of his limo.

The whole thing caught her completely off

guard. She was trying to get her degree, get a job, help her mom… she had never imagined she would meet another shifter along the way, much less one who would be so profoundly protective of her. So insistent in ensuring her safety. And who lit her on fire like no boy ever had. But Lucas was no *boy*… he was most definitively *all man*. And when he held her in his arms last night… it wasn't just the passion of his kiss that entranced her. It was the feeling of being utterly safe. Completely, passionately wanted. Of *belonging* in a way she had never felt with anyone else before.

Lucas seemed such a perfect match for her. It must have been fate—or something equally power-ful, perhaps destiny—that had drawn them together. Only he seemed to want to resist it. *Why?* And why was he so driven to care for her in the first place?

As her limo arrived at the Russell building, Mia realized the things she *didn't* know about Lucas Sparks far outnumbered the things she *did*.

She strolled into SparkTech, pleased she was one of the first to arrive, and immediately went to Lucas's office. If she could just get him alone for a little while, have a chance to talk, maybe she could reassure him that he had nothing to worry about—

he wasn't just her boss, he saved her life! She would never repay that by jeopardizing him or SparkTech in any way. And maybe, just maybe, he would see that he didn't have to hold back from her.

But as soon as she entered Lucas's office, he shoved a pile of reports into her arms and sent her away. She spent the day going over every line: they were already into Stage Two of their due diligence on LoopSource, and these reports were supposed to help SparkTech determine the market potential of LoopSource's new internet platform. It created apps that were super easy for casual internet users —basically it was a customization tool, but the tech part of this marketing report was thick with terms she didn't recognize and struggled to piece together. The report itself glowed with numbers that seemed to say LoopSource was the next big thing in mobile computing, but the *diligence* part of due diligence meant evaluating the report as much as the data within it. No matter what else happened with her and Lucas, she needed to prove she could be an asset to SparkTech—so Mia rolled up her sweater sleeves and dug in. Lunchtime flew by, and it was well into the afternoon before the grumbling in her stomach could no longer be ignored.

Just as she was ready to temporarily climb out

of her analysis hole, Lev popped his head in her door.

"Hey, new girl!" he said cheerily. "You know, we're not actually operating a sweatshop here. You're allowed to take breaks for lunch."

Mia let out a small laugh and leaned back from her desk. "Just trying to make an impression, I guess." She rubbed her weary eyes, unclipped her hair, and shoved her hands through it, stretching out the kinks.

"Oh, trust me, you're doing plenty of that." Lev opened the door the rest of the way, letting himself in. He held up a white paper bag he was carrying, then set it on her desk. "Sustenance for the eager young intern."

"You brought me lunch?" Mia blinked up at him, amazed. Was everyone at SparkTech determined to look out for her? It warmed something deep in her heart, something she hadn't felt with anyone other than her mom: a sense of family. Of *belonging*.

"Well, big brother Lucas told me to take care of you." He perched on one corner of her expansive desk. "I take those kinds of orders very seriously." But there was mirth in his eyes, and he gestured for her to look in the bag.

Inside was a chicken salad sandwich, fruit salad, and the most enormous, gorgeous-looking chocolate chip cookie she had ever seen in her life. It all looked gourmet. And very expensive.

"Wow, Lev, I…" She doubted she could repay him—she hadn't started getting checks from Spark-Tech yet—and she didn't want to insult him by offering. So she just peered up at him as sincerely as she could. "Thank you so much."

"Whoa! Hang on!" He chuckled and put up his hands as if to fend her off. "It's just a sandwich. But if you've been giving Lucas half that big-blue-eyed treatment, I can understand why he's smitten."

Her hand froze halfway in the bag. "Smitten?" Suddenly the jitters in her stomach went into overdrive. "What do you mean?"

He looked at her like she was crazy, then lowered his chin. "I thought you two were…" Then his eyebrows hiked up. "Oh boy." He laughed nervously. "You know, I really do have a big mouth. You need to just ignore whatever I say."

Mia frowned. "Does everyone think…? I mean, does the whole office believe…?"

Lev held up a hand to stop her. "Nobody thinks anything, Mia. We're all happy to have you here. Hey, if you and Lucas are just friends, all the better.

Whatever your magic is, new girl, you just keep doing it. He hasn't been this productive since…" His face morphed again into a stricken panic like he wanted to pull the words back in.

"Since what?" Mia's eyes went wide. There was something in Lucas's past. Something everyone was tiptoeing around.

Lev slipped off the desk. "And… that's my cue to go."

"Lev!" she chastised him, rising from her seat. How could she get him to spill what he knew?

"Eat your lunch, new girl!" he called over his shoulder on his way out the door. "You need to keep up your energy!"

And then he was gone.

Mia slowly sat down, then carefully laid out the lunch Lev had so thoughtfully brought to her. Something had happened to Lucas. Something that his family—including Lev and probably his father, who she had yet to meet—all wanted to help him get over. Or maybe recover from? She didn't know, but as she bit into her sandwich, she vowed to find out what it was and help Lucas in any way she could. If Lev was right—if she was having some positive effect on him—she wanted to do more of that. It was the least she could do for all he'd already done for her.

Her inner wolf yipped in agreement. Probably a little too enthusiastically. And she was likely just looking for a reason to spend more time with Lucas. But she had a hard time thinking there was anything wrong with that, either.

Chapter Seven

REFUELED BY LEV'S LUNCH, MIA DOVE BACK INTO the reports, and the rest of the day slipped past. Before she knew it, the cool white carpet of her office was turning a dusky orange from the setting sun. She had finished reading most of the reports and had some initial thoughts, but she hadn't really had time to process all of it yet. Just as she was wondering if she could take them home or if they were confidential to SparkTech, someone knocked on her door.

Lucas stepped inside without waiting for her answer and closed the door behind him.

Mia stared at him as he slowly approached her desk, cautious like she might spring out at him at any second. "Hi," she said trying to break the awkward silence that had already fallen.

"Hey." He gestured to the reports but remained on the other side of the desk from her. "How's it going?"

"Pretty good," she said. "I think the market might be ready for LoopSource, but I'm not really sure. I need more time to fully digest the reports. Is it possible to take them home?"

He smiled and seemed to relax a little. "Sorry, they have to stay in the office. I've been looking them over, too, and I think your intuition is right. But I'll be working the weekend to make sure before I take my recommendation in on Monday."

She smiled. "Maybe I could come in this weekend and help?"

His smile faded away. "That's not necessary." He dropped his gaze to the reports, drumming his fingers on the desk, looking uncomfortable again. "Look, Mia, about last night—"

She rose up from her seat, effectively cutting him off, and then quickly came around her desk. She did *not* want him apologizing for their kiss… especially if no one else in the office cared if they were together or not. He looked startled by her coming closer.

She stared up into his eyes. "I don't have a problem with last night."

He frowned. "Mia, it's not a good idea—"

"Why not?"

"You don't understand—"

"No, I don't understand." She took a breath and tried to rein in her frustration. "Lucas, tell me."

He stepped back, and she could tell she had pushed him too far. "Look, what's most important is your safety. And I came here to talk to you about that."

"Well, the driver thing is pretty cool. I think I can hang with that."

He didn't smile at her weak attempt to lighten things up. "You need to move out of your dorm."

"What?" Her eyes went round, and it was her turn to take a step back. "Move out of my... I can't just *move out*, Lucas!"

"Yes, you can." He had that resolute look that she was beginning to recognize as the *no negotiations* look. But this was totally ridiculous.

"I'm locked into the dorm payments for the summer!" she said, stating the obvious. "And where would I go? All the good summer leases are gone by now." The more she thought about it, the more she was convinced he had to be joking. She *hoped* he was joking.

"We'll take care of all that," he said, his voice uncompromising. "You don't have to worry about the money. We'll find a place for you. Starting this weekend. We can move you into a hotel tonight, then get you an apartment in the morning. You have to do this, Mia."

"I... what in the world, Lucas!" She couldn't believe he was serious, but her blood pressure was creeping up. He was *ordering* her to move out? And what if she didn't? Would he *fire* her? This was getting more and more... *crazy.* There was no other word for it.

"I'm just trying to keep you safe," he said, but his voice was more strained now.

She shook her head and crossed her arms. "You know what? You can work by yourself this weekend. I'm going home. *To my dorm.*"

She stomped around her desk, yanked open the drawer that held her purse, pulled it out, then brushed past him, headed for the door. "We can discuss this on Monday!" she called back over her shoulder. She only hoped she actually *had* a job on Monday. But she was *not* letting him order her around and move her out of her dorm and just...

gah! What was he thinking? The whole thing frustrated her beyond measure.

He was following right behind her. "Mia, stop."

"No," she said, without slowing down. "I am tired of this *keeping Mia safe* thing all the time." She wasn't really, but the idea that he wouldn't even discuss what happened between them but felt like he could order her around… even her inner wolf was growling about that.

He kept tailing her all the way out to the front of the office. "Mia, I'm just trying to…" He dropped his voice as they reached the elevator. A bunch of other people were already waiting for their chance to flee the office for the weekend. "Mia, stop," he said under his breath. "Listen to me."

Luck was on her side because the elevator dinged at just that moment. The other people filed in, and she followed right after. Mia glared at Lucas to keep him from following, and he stayed back, strung tight, watching as the elevator doors closed.

She left him behind on the 32nd floor.

The ride down was just a *little* awkward, but Mia ignored the stares.

At the parking garage level, she got off the elevator with everyone else, but as they dispersed to their cars, she remembered she hadn't called the driver. He had left her with a card for when she was ready, but she had left in such a hurry, she'd forgotten about it. She briefly debated taking public transportation just to make Lucas angry but decided that was childish. Instead, she fished out her phone and the card and started dialing. Before she could finish, a limo entered the far gate from the street level. It was the same one that had picked her up that morning—at least it had the same stretched length and tinted windows—and she wondered how they knew, but then a glance at the waning light outside reminded her it was already late. Most people were leaving for the weekend, and surely the limo company had other customers to pick up. They didn't just sit around all day waiting for her call.

Only she didn't see anyone else to be picked up —everyone had already disappeared into their cars. She put away her phone and flagged down the limo as it slowly rolled between the parked cars of the half-full parking garage. It came to a stop in front of her, but she couldn't see if the driver was stopping for her or not. She edged forward, looking around to double check if there was anyone else waiting. She was alone, so she crossed the rest of the space and reached the passenger side just as the driver's door swung open.

"You guys have great timing!" she said cheerily, returning the driver's smile. Then a chill swept through her. She recognized him—but he wasn't the driver she had this morning.

He was the red wolf from *The Deviation*.

She froze. He leered as he came around the front of the limo toward her, but just as she unlocked her legs, the passenger side door swung open, and a second man, another of the red wolves, scrambled out of the car after her. She didn't get two steps before he was on her. Her wolf roared as he grabbed her roughly from behind. Her arms and legs flailed, trying to wrench loose from him, but his arm was locked around her waist, and she couldn't get hold of anything. He was dragging her toward the car. In moments, they would have her. Her wolf raged underneath her skin, wanting loose so she could tear into him with her teeth and claws, but the first one grabbed her flailing arms and held her fast.

Two against one. Both wolves. Both bigger than her.

She took a fast breath and started to scream, but a beefy hand clamped over her mouth, and her shriek died in the echoing chamber of the parking garage. She prayed someone would hear her one muted attempt at a cry for help before she was stuffed in the open door of the car.

Suddenly Lucas was there, his own roar reaching them just before his fists. He hadn't shifted, but even in his human form, he was able to clock the guy holding her arms. He went down on the pavement in a heap, and she renewed her struggle against the man holding her, slamming her heels back, trying to catch a piece of him. He grunted so she must have hit something. As his hold on her loosened, Lucas yanked her free. When Lucas released her to go after him, she stumbled, falling over the body of the first wolf, who was still in his human form. Why weren't they shifting? She didn't understand, but she scurried away from the fallen wolf, putting distance between them and her before looking back.

Lucas was beating the shit out of her second abductor, the one who was still conscious. He had fallen to the ground, and still Lucas was pounding on him. She smelled blood in the air, and there was more on the car… she rushed forward.

"Lucas!" she shrieked. "Stop! You'll kill him!" She flailed for his arm as it pulled back for another strike, just barely catching hold of it. But her touch seemed to break through his rage. His chest heaved, and there was blood on his hand. She couldn't be sure if it was his or not, but he took a step back. The man was down, moaning, cowering on the parking garage floor.

Lucas blinked several times, still looking at her attacker, then he turned to her. For a moment, his face was blank, but then he slipped his hand around her waist and hauled her away from the limo.

"My purse!" she said, tugging against him to stop so she could retrieve it from the floor. She didn't want them having *anything* of hers. He bent quickly to scoop it up, then locked his hand around hers and towed her away. They ran down one ramp of the parking garage and then another, down to the next level. Her legs were unsteady with the adrenaline of the fight, and her heels clicked a jittery echo throughout the garage, but the sound was mostly drowned out by Lucas's heavy, pounding heels. They reached his car—it was some kind of Audi, red and black and sleek, but she would have preferred something less like a race car and more like a tank. Lucas practically yanked off the door getting it open for her, and she dropped into the low passenger seat as fast as she could. He raced around to the driver's side, and within moments, they were screeching out of the parking garage. She caught a final glimpse of the two kidnappers by their limo.

They were still human lumps on the ground. Only one was moving.

Chapter Eight

IT WASN'T UNTIL MIA AND LUCAS WERE WELL AWAY from the parking garage that he slowed to a speed that would keep them out of jail. Even then, neither of them spoke. Lucas's grip on the steering wheel was the same white-knuckled one she had on her purse. She clutched it to her chest as if that would somehow help. She didn't ask where they were going. She didn't care, as long as it was away from *them*. She could still feel their hands on her, grabbing her, hauling her away.

"Why didn't they shift?" was all she could manage to say. Her voice was strangely mechanical.

"They couldn't fight me in wolf form," he said, just as stiffly.

She supposed that made sense, given they had

submitted to him once before, although her brain still wasn't working well enough to put all the pieces together. They must have found out where she lived. They must have tracked the limo service that picked her up that morning. A chill seeped into her stomach, wondering what had happened to the original driver. Maybe they killed him. Maybe they stole the limo.

All so they could come after her.

She blinked and looked at Lucas. He had known she wouldn't be safe at the dorm. He knew more about this than he was telling her. But at that moment, all she could see was the blood that still covered his knuckles. The fury on his face.

He had saved her. Again.

They pulled into another parking garage, a high rise near the outskirts of downtown. She wasn't sure exactly where they were going until they were inside the building, and a gray-uniformed doorman greeted Lucas with, "Good evening, Mr. Sparks." By the time she and Lucas reached the 15th floor, she figured he must be taking her to his apartment. He still hadn't spoken a word, just held her hand in an iron grip the entire way, not letting go for a single moment since they left the car.

His electronic key opened the door. He closed and locked it behind them.

She barely had a glimpse of his glass-and-black-leather décor, before he grabbed hold of her face and consumed her with a kiss. They stumbled two steps back until she was flush up against the front door, his body pressing her into it, hard in every possible way: his fingers pushing insistently into her hair, his tongue invading her mouth, his erection pressing into her side. She dropped her purse and grabbed at his shoulders, trying to bring him closer, even though he had already welded her body to the door with his.

His hands left her hair and slid down her sides, feeling every curve until he reached the hem of her sweater. He leaned back and pulled her slightly away from the door, enough to quickly lift her sweater over her head.

Her breath caught, suddenly half naked in front of him. He paused for a moment, looking at her, and she had that sensation again like his gaze was a hot stroke over her exposed skin.

"I thought this wasn't a good idea," she said, breathless, hoping he wasn't suddenly changing his mind.

"I'm tired of trying to resist you."

His words were another sweep of heat across her, this one running straight down between her legs. He ripped off his jacket and lifted his shirt over his head in one fast swipe. Then he pinned her to the door again, this time his bare chest open to her hands. They roamed across it and ran up his shoulders. His mouth, hungry for her again, devoured her neck in small nips. His touch was electrifying her, every nerve sending hot races of pleasure to the parts that yearned for more contact with him.

He growled, tasting her more aggressively as he worked down to her chest. He gripped her bra with both hands, and she felt his claws come out and shred the fabric away from her body. The pieces of it dangled to her sides as her breasts fell free. Lucas dropped to one knee, and his face nuzzled in between them. One hand rolled her hardened nipple between his fingers, wringing shocks of pleasure from it, while the other cupped her breast to his mouth. He sucked and nipped all over her heated flesh, each small, circling bite causing more wetness to pool between her legs.

Her wolf whined with pleasure, and she dug her fingers into his hair while she watched him feast upon her. Then he slid his hands down her body again, feeling every inch as he went. When he reached the bottom of her skirt, he slipped his hands underneath and shoved up the fabric. Her underwear was torn from her body before she could suck in a gasp. With her skirt up to her waist and her underwear gone, she was bared to him. Another growl rumbled in his chest, and he dropped further, lifting her knee over his shoulder and burying his face between her legs.

Her head fell back against the door as his tongue slipped into her folds. She called out his name and some other unintelligible word, as a haze of pleasure washed over her. The tip of his tongue worked her, and she held on as he brought her wave upon wave of pleasure. It built a pressure deep inside that felt like it might make her burst. Just as she thought she might come, he pulled away. She panted and clung to the door, weak with pleasure, watching as he kicked off his shoes and unzipped his pants. When he freed his erection, it was even larger than she remembered, shining in the moonlight, the embodiment of everything masculine. It made her even more weak in the knees.

He cradled her against the door. She had never seen such pure desire in a man's eyes before—such animal lust combined with an eagerness that was pure wolf. He claimed her mouth again, plunging inside and sharing the taste of her own flesh. He slid his hands down to her legs, behind her hips, then quickly lifted her from the floor. She held on tight to his broad shoulders, his muscles flexing under her hands, and quickly wrapped her legs around his back. She could feel his cock hard and ready against her and could hardly catch her breath. Hardly believe this was happening.

His hands gripped the flesh of her bottom, and he thrust into her. He was so large and ground so deep that what breath she had escaped her. The hard muscles of his chest pressed into the deep soft-ness of hers and held there for a moment. Joined deeply, his face buried in her hair, he moaned, *Mine,* so softly, with so much growl, that she almost didn't hear it. Then he thrust again and again, each time rocking harder against her and sending waves of pleasure shooting through her. His grip on her tightened, and each thrust brought a noise of plea-sure from him that pushed her closer and closer. As he took her, owned her body against the door, she could feel his claws coming out, grasping onto her, holding her tight to him. Her wolf whimpered in response, whining for more, and her own claws raked across his back, holding on for the ride.

As her claws dug into him, his breath hitched,

and she was afraid for a split moment that she had hurt him. But his moans and thrusts just came harder and faster, finally pushing her to the edge. Her body pulsed, pleasure whiting out her vision, her sound, even her sense of smell, and there was nothing but him, filling her, joined with her, bringing her a pleasure she didn't even know was possible. It possessed every sense in her body. He growled with his final thrust, and his body shook, as his climax seized hold of him. Aftershocks of pleasure kept rippling through her. He moved more slowly now, his thrusts gentling, his hold relaxing. Finally, after a long moment of stillness, he pulled out and eased her to the floor. But he still held her, tenderly pulling her from the wall and planting a hundred soft kisses on her face and neck.

As they came down together, he kissed her once more on the lips, then pulled slightly away. He had a slight frown and reached behind his shoulder to swipe at the marks her claws had no doubt left behind. He came away with blood on his hand, looked puzzled for a moment, then peered harder over his shoulder. Her claws had scored a dozen red lines on his back and upper arms. His eyes went wide, and he whipped his head back to her, a storm gathering on his face.

Oh no.

"You're a *shifter*," he said, his voice filled with betrayal.

"I didn't think… are you okay?" She scrunched up her face and tried to peer at his back, but she knew it wasn't the marks that bothered him. It was the *lie*.

He stepped back from her, standing naked, but with clenched fists and stiff shoulders. "What's your pack?" he demanded.

"Pack? I don't… I don't have…" Her heart was wrenching in two. The air was still rich with their lovemaking, but it had chilled ten degrees with the angry stare he was giving her. He reached out, but his touch was no longer gentle. He held up her arms, searching them, grabbing hold of her shoulders to spin her, checking her back for something.

She twisted her head toward him. "What are you doing, Lucas?" The fear in her voice must have reached him, because he turned her back to face him, but more gently this time.

He continued to search her body with his eyes, his face still angry, but it had tempered a little. "You're not marked. Why aren't you marked?"

"I don't know what that means!" Tears were closing in on her.

He closed his eyes briefly and drew in a breath. When he opened them, he pointed to the tattoo on his chest. "Your pack mark. Where is it?"

"I don't have a pack," she said. "Or a mark. You're… you're the only one who knows."

Realization dawned on his face, and he took a step back. The anger settled further, but she could tell it still boiled under his skin. "You've been hiding it. All this time."

"Yes."

"From everyone. Your family?"

"I only have my mom," she said, a defensive bit rising in her. "But yes. From everyone."

"From me."

"Until now." She peered up into his eyes. Could he forgive her for that? He knew *now.* He was simply the only one she had ever felt safe telling. Couldn't he see that?

But his expression was still cool. "You don't have a mate or a pack," he said again as if triple confirming it wasn't enough.

"I swear, Lucas." She hesitated, then pressed on. "I want to be with *you,*" she said softly.

His dark brown eyes hardened to bitter coal. "You do *not* want to mate with me." Then he turned away from her and stooped to pick up his pants from the floor. The anger was back, judging by the vicious way he pulled them on.

"But… I thought you…"

He glared at her again. "I *thought* you were human."

It was a like a stab through her heart. "I'm sorry I didn't tell you," she said, fighting tears. Her wolf was crying, a mournful whine that echoed through her head. "I would have. Eventually. I just didn't know…" She gestured at the pile of clothes at their feet. "Things just moved so fast."

"Wolves do not just have sex, Mia. Wolves *mate,*" he said, the anger flaming back. "If you had a pack, you would have understood this. But since you don't, let me be very clear about it: you do *not* want to mate with me."

She crossed her arms over her bare breasts, suddenly feeling naked. But the anger in her voice rose to match his. "Maybe I do! You don't get to decide everything for me!"

He turned away from her, and his back stiffened. "My mate is dead."

She sucked in a breath. This was the thing—the pain that his family wanted to help him heal. The darkened office at SparkTech flashed before her eyes: *T. Sparks.* His mate. She had died, and he was struck down by it. Devastated. She could see it in his stance, and in the fierce protection he had for her. How much more would he have had for the woman he loved? Had *mated* with? She wasn't even sure what that meant, but it sounded... like family.

She edged closer to his turned back. "I'm sorry, Lucas." What could she say that would ease his pain? "I don't want to... take her place. I just want to be with you."

He sighed, long and deep. "You don't understand, Mia." He paused, then slowly turned to look back over his shoulder to her. "I killed her."

Chapter Nine

I KILLED HER.

Lucas's words froze Mia's body against the door where they just had sex, but her mind spun like a carnival tilt-a-whirl. He couldn't possibly mean what he said... not *literally.* He had said, *My mate is dead.* She assumed that meant his wife.

Did she just have sex with a wife killer?

A chill raced up Mia's body, from her bare toes on Lucas's impeccably polished wooden floor to her naked arms, where she clutched the tattered remnants of her bra defensively to her chest. The chill swept up her face to the top of her head, and the realization that Lucas might actually be a *killer* lifted her sex-mussed hair straight off her scalp. She tugged at her slim black skirt, still hiked up around her waist—a pretense at modesty that seemed more urgent the more the chill seeped into her body and chased away the remnants of heat-filled pleasure he had given her. A pleasure she had never experienced with anyone before. And yet all those passionate kisses, all those expert touches with his hands and mouth, the urgent way in which he said he couldn't resist her any longer and had taken her against the door… were those the acts of a killer?

She shook her head, not believing it. Not with the way he looked at her, cared for her… *protected her.* When all he had to do was walk away. Mia didn't know what dark thing in his past had taken his wife from him, but she knew this much: Lucas Sparks was no killer.

"You don't really mean that," Mia said to him.

He had turned his back on her. "I don't say things I don't mean, Mia."

"I don't believe you," she said, standing straighter. "You just blaming yourself for your wife's death or something—"

He whirled on her, instantly looming over her and menacing her with a dark look. The fear-chill raced through her again as he forced her back against the door with his powerful presence. "Do *not* presume you know anything about me. You don't belong to a pack. You hide your wolf from your family. You know *nothing.* "

Moments before, he had been pinning her to the door with his thrusts deep inside her. Now, he kept her there with the disdainful gaze he raked across her nearly-naked body. But even that look welled up heat across her skin. And holy hotness, the pleasure he'd wrung out of her in that short tryst against the door... in spite of the warring emotions in her head, her body still sang with the thrum of it. But now he wasn't just angry that she lied about being a shifter—there was something else fueling the darkness in his eyes. Besides, he was right: she *could* shift, she just *didn't.* At least not very often and usually at night when she was dreaming. Or when she was in the throes of passion, like she had been with Lucas.

"You're right. I know nothing," she said softly. Mia met his challenging look with one of her own. "Teach me."

He was close enough to kiss her. Her inner wolf whimpered for him to press her into the door again. But he only let out an exasperated huff and turned away, shaking his head.

She couldn't see why being a shifter would matter to him. *He* was a shifter, after all. The fact that her claws had come out and sliced into his back and shoulders hadn't bothered him a bit. He was *wolf*—she could see those scratches were already healed. But there was something about her being a shifter that made him want her *less…* when it just made her want him *more.* Only a shifter could pleasure her like that and not wear scars as a result. But it was much more than that: her inner wolf yearned for him in a way she'd never felt before.

She *belonged* with him.

Only he didn't seem to think so.

It had something to do with his dead mate— Mia's mind flashed back to the darkened office at SparkTech with *T. Sparks* on the door. Whatever had happened, however his wife had been killed, it took part of him with it… and that darkness still sat inside him, like the shrine of his wife's office, kept shrouded and silent. How could he work there every day, seeing that?

A new sympathy welled up inside her. Whatever had happened, Mia wanted to help him get past it. To understand that it wasn't his fault and that they could start something *new.*

If only he would let her.

He was attracted to her, she was sure of it. She just had to convince him to give in to that force pulling them together, to give them a chance. But to do that, she would need more than angry stares and turned backs from him. And she would need to understand more about shifters and packs and... *him.* There were dozens of questions buzzing her brain.

Lucas had picked up his shirt from the floor. He pulled it over his head.

She scooped up her sweater as well. "Those men who tried to kidnap me were the same ones from the alley. Why are they after me? Do they think I'm going to turn them in for being shifters?"

It wasn't like being a shifter was a crime in and of itself, but shifter DNA had some kind of magic—the DNA itself would shift, changing to wolf or human, depending on what form the shifter took. When Mia was wolf, she was truly *wolf*—her DNA matched her wolfy cousins in the wild. When she was human, her DNA was unique to her but just as human as any other person. Magic allowed them to shift, but science measured the result—which meant shifters in wolf form could commit crimes without leaving human DNA at the scene. And turning shifters in to the police so they could obtain samples of both sets of DNA for their databases was considered your citizenly duty.

"Those wolves are from the Red pack," Lucas said, not looking at her as he fixed the buttons on his shirt. "And the last thing they're worried about is you turning them in."

She fussed with her sweater and skirt to smooth them down. "Then why are they after me?" She reached down to pick up the tatters of her under-wear and bra, then realized... she popped back up and met his gaze. He had been watching her, once her back was turned. "Wait... you *know* them?"

The muscles in his jaw tightened momentarily. Then he said, "They're from Red Wolf Development."

Her mouth dropped open. "The *internet* devel-opment company?" *No. Way.* Red Wolf was a direct competitor for SparkTech.

His gaze dropped, then found her shredded undergarments. He winced and dragged his gaze back up to meet hers again. "The Red pack has been a bitter rival of my father's pack ever since they started up here in Seattle."

"Wait, wait, wait." Mia held up her hands. Her underwear dangled from one. Frustrated, she threw it back to the floor. The lump of material skidded across the polished wood to the thick stone tiling of Lucas's kitchen. She'd hardly had a chance to check out his apartment before, what with the rapid entry, fervent sex against the door, her secret revealed, and Lucas's sudden withdrawal and anger. And now *he* had been holding out on *her*.

Big time.

Steamy anger started to gather in her chest. She elbowed her way around him and stomped past the open doorway to his vast gourmet kitchen. Its multiple stainless steel ovens and sparkling black granite countertops looked hardly used. The lamps hanging over the bar to the living room glowed like small white ghosts, but the rest of the apartment was lit only by moonlight falling through the bank of windows along the far wall.

They hadn't even taken time to turn on the main lights.

She strode into the expansive center room. It was as richly appointed as the kitchen. A black leather couch and chair sat in the middle of the room and faced a large black-glass-paneled wall with a huge built-in flat-screen TV. Speakers were embedded in the wall, and a glass table spanned the distance between the couch and the entertainment center. A pair of strange Z-shaped chairs stood off to one side, next to a wooden table with white orb lights hanging over it. There were no pictures, just a few modern-art-looking adornments. The entire room was sleek and luxurious and probably cost double her entire year's tuition.

She paced along the back of the couch, running her hand on top of the glove-soft leather and trying to wrap her head around the situation. It suddenly seemed much worse than she thought.

Lucas stayed by the door, watching her.

She stopped and gripped the couch as she faced him. "Your pack is rivals with the Red pack." Her voice was surprisingly steady for the trembles running laps up and down her body.

"My father's pack is rivals with the Red pack," he said coolly. "I don't have a pack."

She narrowed her eyes. "You're not in your father's pack."

"Not since I formed my own." He met her stare. Cautious. Arms folded. *Still* holding back.

She pushed off the couch. "Dammit, Lucas, you have to tell me what's really going on here! Why does the Red pack want me? What am I to them? Is this part of some rivalry between your packs? Am I… am I…" Her throat was getting thick. "Am I just some kind of *prey* for them?" She could see it now: in that alleyway, those Red pack wolves wanted to play some kind of sick game with her. Lucas stopped them… but then he'd hovered over her ever since. Making her quit *The Deviation*. Getting her a driver so he could control her comings and goings. And today… today he wanted to move her out of her dorm!

"Is this all a game to you?" Her voice cracked then, and she braced herself against the couch because there was a sudden weakness in her legs. What had she gotten herself into?

Lucas's stance softened. He unfolded his arms and quickly crossed the room like he was going to hold her up or something. She stopped him with an upraised hand.

He scowled at her hand like it offended him. "This isn't a game, Mia. You've seen the Red wolves —they're brutal. They let their dark wolves come out to play, both in business and pleasure. I'm only trying to protect you from them."

"But they compete with you. With SparkTech. You have the same territory or something." She couldn't figure out the angle. Why her? Why was she in the middle of this?

He folded his arms again and leaned against the couch next to her. "They have a physical territory carved out in Seattle. And we respect that. But yes, they compete with us *in business*. You've seen the reports."

Her eyes went wide. "They want LoopSource." The mobile computing platform they were both diligently evaluating for SparkTech to acquire… until she stormed out, got attacked by Red wolves, then ended up in Lucas's apartment.

"And they'll do anything to get what they want." He edged closer to her, arms still folded. He wasn't touching her, but it was like he had cast a protective shadow over her. He was contained, but ready to spring out and hold her the moment she allowed it.

She shook her head, still not piecing it together. "But why me? I mean, I'm just a bartender. Or I was… wait! Did they *know* I was going to intern at SparkTech?"

Lucas's eyebrows lifted like he hadn't thought of that. "Maybe." Then they settled into a scowl again. "Or you could have just been a target of convenience. Either way, when I stepped in…" He struggled for words for a moment, then dropped his gaze. "Well, that's when they figured out they could use you as leverage. Against me."

"Because I was your intern." She frowned. That still didn't make sense.

"Because I saved you." His jaw worked. "They think I care about you."

She involuntarily glanced at the door, where they had just... what? Made love? Had sex? Gave in to their animalistic passions? That was probably closest. She dragged her gaze back to his deep, dark eyes. He seemed even closer, and the air between them was still perfumed by the lust of their bodies.

"Do you care about me?" she asked, almost a whisper.

"No."

The air went out of her.

He unlocked his arms and reached like he was going to hold her, then stopped when she flinched away.

"It's not that I don't..." He looked pained. "It's just... the Red pack thinks there's something more than there is, Mia."

Something more than there is. Namely, not much at all. It was just a casual screw of the intern for him. A burning sensation rose up in her cheeks, and then she realized... "Oh my god. We didn't even use protection!"

He looked surprised at that, but the heat in her face was turning up to volcano-level. How could she have been so *stupid?* She had unprotected sex with her boss, who was just out for a quick lay, then on to the next thing.

"Oh my god," she said under her breath, mostly to herself. She brushed past him, determined to grab her purse and get the hell out of there as quickly as possible, but his iron-strong hands grabbed hold of her shoulders, stopping her cold. "Let go of me!" It came out as a shriek, but she didn't care. It was too much: all the danger and heated sex and crashing betrayal... it all came to a head of fury at once. She growled at him, her claws coming out as she thrashed against his hold, but he wouldn't let her go.

"Mia!" he said, loud enough to be heard over her wolf's protest against the indignity, but his voice was strangely calm. "Mia, it's all right."

"What do you care?" Her words were half-growls, and she could feel her wolf growing more angry, taking more control. Her claws were shredding his shirt. "It's not *you* that might be carrying a wolf baby!"

At that, his grip became even stronger, more insistent, almost painful, except she could tell he was holding back, holding *her*, drawing her closer into his chest. His words quieted, and she had to strain to hear them, which had the strange effect of quieting her wolf as well.

"It's okay, Mia, listen to me."

"Lucas." This time it was more like a sob. She gave up fighting him and just tucked into the safe harbor of his arms.

He held her completely then, the tatters of his shirt brushing her face. "You're not pregnant. You're not going to *be* pregnant. You're not fertile right now. When I thought you were human, I assumed you were on some kind of medication that controlled fertility. Once I realized you were a shifter, I just assumed you knew."

"Know? How could I know?"

"Female wolves... know these things," he said softly. "You would have been taught how if you'd been raised in a pack."

The panic had subsided, and she didn't want to move away from his arms, but she needed to see his face. To tell if he was teasing or making some kind of awful joke.

She twisted up to look at him. "How do *you* know?" She could feel the slight chuckle rumbling in his chest.

"That's something young male wolves learn to

detect early on. The scent of a female in heat is… hard to miss. Also sometimes hard to resist."

She flushed at that—did she really go into *heat?* She had the normal hormone swings of any girl… at least she thought they were normal. At the same time, it was comforting that he understood all of this, even if she didn't.

Still, she wrinkled up her nose. "But what about disease? I mean… I assume I'm not your first conquest." This didn't seem like the right time to tell him he was *her* first. Or at least, the first that really mattered. The first time she had actually felt like she had been with a *lover,* not just a bumbling boy who was scared off by her wolf.

The humor fled from his face. "You're not a conquest, Mia."

"You know what I mean."

He held her slightly away from his body so he could look down into her eyes. "Have you ever been sick a day in your life?"

She frowned. She hadn't, of course, but she figured it was just a part of the quick-healing aspect of being a wolf.

"Wolves don't get the same diseases as humans, even in human form," he said patiently. A hint of the smile was back. "I couldn't have caught anything from you, or you from me. If you had been human, that is."

"And as a wolf?" She bit her lip. "Is that why you were so angry when you found out I was a shifter? Because I might have some wolf disease?"

His face darkened again. "Wolves don't have those kinds of diseases. Even in a pack, there's rarely any diseases that can be passed from wolf to wolf. We really don't get sick at all." He didn't move away, but his expression had cooled ten degrees. He dropped his arms from their hold around her.

She missed them immediately.

Her mind was still a haze from the panic and everything else, but she tried to line up the pieces. "So the Red pack wants LoopSource, and they're trying to use me as leverage against you to get it."

"Yes."

"Because they think you care for me." Then she hastily added, "Enough to stop them from kidnapping me."

"I couldn't let them hurt you in that alley, Mia." His eyes bored into hers. "And I didn't even know you then. I'm certainly not going to let them hurt you now."

A warm flush ran through her. She didn't know where that rated on the scale of *caring*, but she was pretty damn sure no one else besides her mother had cared that much about her. Ever. Certainly not her father, some loser shifter who knocked up her mom and left before she was born. Or any of her so-called boyfriends, who had likewise taken off as soon as her wolf became apparent. That feeling of *belonging* came rushing back: she *belonged* with Lucas, even if he couldn't see it. Some part of him must know it, too. She just had to find that part and bring it out.

"You're going to protect me, right?" she asked, looking up into his dark, serious eyes.

"Yes." There was no hesitation. In fact, he seemed to loom larger as he said it like this mattered to him. *A lot.* Like it wouldn't just be bad for SparkTech if the Red pack got hold of her… like protecting her was a point of personal pride *to him.*

"So, if I'm going to stay out of those creeps hands, then I need to know more about what I'm dealing with here, Lucas."

Thankfully, he nodded solemnly. "I take it your mother isn't a shifter. So that leaves your father."

"Who was a loser who booked out of town once my mother was pregnant."

Lucas wrinkled his nose in disgust. "So you're

half shifter by patronage. Can you fully shift?" He glanced at her hands and smirked. "Or is it just the claws?"

She shrugged. "I can fully shift, I've just been hiding it so long, I've never had much practice. And apparently, I really don't know jack about being a wolf." She frowned. "Tell me more about this Red pack. You said they didn't shift when they attacked me in the garage because they couldn't fight you in wolf form. What exactly does that mean?"

Lucas took a breath and seemed to relax, leaning against the couch. Then he shocked her by taking her hand. He turned it over to inspect it as if he thought he would find claws there instead of fingers. His touch was warm and gentle, and she couldn't help feeling that electric attraction she had whenever she was near him. At least during the times he wasn't yelling at her.

"Your wolf form is very different from your human form." He held up her hand like he wanted her to look at it. She did, but it was just her hand. "Do you feel her inside you? Wanting to come out?"

She nodded, entranced by the way he was looking at her. Like she was under his care, and that was just the way he liked it.

"Well, when you let her out, she'll control your every thought, feeling, or impulse."

"I've felt that," she said quickly. "I become much more… instinctual."

He smiled. "Exactly." He released her hand, and she had the same sensation of missing his touch. She reluctantly brought it back to cross her arms over her chest. "There are several instincts that are very strong with your wolf, but the strongest is probably submission."

Submit. She remembered the Red pack wolves with their arched backs and tucked tails.

"You made them submit to you," she said, her eyes widening slightly. Her heart rate ticked up a notch. Her wolf had understood it immediately, and it had both frightened and excited her. The idea of being under Lucas's command like that… she swallowed.

He was watching her carefully. "Yes, they submitted. Partly because I'm an alpha. Partly because I was going to rip out their friend's throat if they didn't."

"So, once they do that… does that mean you control them?" The idea was still running hot and cold shivers up her back.

"Not exactly." His jaw was tight. "If I

commanded them to do something, they would have a hard time resisting. It's like a compulsion. A desire to do the will of the alpha. But most of the time, submission isn't about giving orders—it's about being part of the pack. It's a swearing of fidelity to the alpha, who likewise is bound to protect those who have submitted to him. Or at the minimum, not to hurt them. Once the Reds submitted to me, they couldn't fight me… but I also couldn't fight them."

"Like a truce."

"In a way."

"So… does it last forever?" Something about that nagged at the edges of her mind—it seemed impossible that any bond, no matter how strong, could last so long.

"No, only until the next moon," he said. "Then you have to pledge again. It's a ceremony every pack does at full moon. But in the meantime, at least while they were in wolf form, they couldn't attack me. Or I them."

"Which is why you all stayed in human form."

"Because I wanted very much to beat the living crap out of them."

The laugh snuck up on Mia, and she flew her hand up to cover it. But Lucas had a half-smile, too, so she dropped her hand and bit the edge of her lip instead. There was a whole world of packs and ceremonies and... submission and commands... she very much wanted to learn more about.

With him.

The humor dropped off his face as the tension built between them again. It was always there, like static electricity charging the air, just waiting for the right moment to spark.

"What do we do now?" Mia asked softly.

He dropped his gaze, and the tension evaporated, leaving her cold again. "It's late. You'll have to stay here tonight. We'll find you another place in the morning." He lifted his gaze, challenging her. "You can't go back to your dorm tonight."

She nodded readily.

He seemed slightly relieved, but then a new tension bunched his shoulders as he straightened up from his lean against the couch. He gestured to a hallway poking between the kitchen and living room. It disappeared into blackness toward the back of his apartment. "You can stay in my room. I'll sleep on the couch. I need to call my father and brothers to let them know the situation anyway."

The disappointment was a barb stuck in her chest. But what did she really expect? That he would join her in the bedroom? He'd already made it clear that being a shifter made her someone he did *not* want to mate with… whatever that meant exactly. But she was in his apartment, at least for the night. And he had pledged to protect her, a promise she had no doubt he would keep. That gave her time to figure out the rest of Lucas's worries… and put them to rest.

"Okay," she said brightly. "But I have to warn you that my wolf might snore loud enough to wake the dead. Even on the couch."

He smirked and shook his head.

But she was pretty sure he watched her all the way to the bedroom.

Chapter Ten

Lucas bends over the girl, on her hands and knees in front of him. His cock is rock hard and ready for her, and he skims his hands forward over the smooth skin of her back. He takes his time, but he can feel her panting, smell her intense arousal. She wants him to finish the claiming, but this is special, and he won't be rushed. He threads his fingers through her long black hair, like a sheet of night cascading along her back, over her shoulders, and hanging down to caress her plump breasts. He can barely see them below her body, but his cock pulses at the sight. He makes contact with her entrance, but stops short of penetrating… not yet. She whimpers, and her hips buck against him, urging him on. He slides one hand back to her hip to hold her still, gripping hard enough to give warning, but he keeps his claws and his wolf at bay. He doesn't want to mark her creamy white flesh… his

other hand reaches into her hair, fists it, and pulls her head back, exposing her neck and turning her face toward him.

It's Mia.

A small shock runs through him, a tiny surprise, but he knew it would be her. She belongs to him. His wolf roars in agreement, and he whispers the word to her. Mine. His grip on her hair is so strong she can barely manage a small nod of agreement, but her full, rosy lips are parted, and she's panting. He can feel her urgency, her need, as strong as his own.

He thrusts inside her, and her sweet, tight wetness swallows him whole. She cries out in pleasure, and his wolf howls in triumph. Saliva pools in his mouth. Each thrust sloshes the growing liquid around his tongue a little more. He bends over her, still thrusting, still pleasuring her, but his canines are growing, and he won't be able to hold off much longer before he delivers the brief pain of the claiming. He runs the tip of his tongue along her shoulder, warning her, holding her ready, still pleasuring her as much as he can. But when he finally gives in to his inner wolf and claims her... she screams.

It's a horrific sound, a death screech. He jerks back, but there's suddenly blood everywhere: his hands, her shoulder, running down her sides. The girl falls to the ground, rolling on her back... and it's no longer Mia. It's Tila. His mate. His wife. The dark wet hole in her chest drips thin lines of blood down the perfect, white globes of her breasts—

Lucas awoke with a start, gasping for air and drowning in horror.

His claws were buried in the couch, holding him anchored there, or he might have bolted straight up to standing. The living room was sharp with shadows and the fall of moonlight through the windows, but everything was still. Quiet.

Mia is safe, he tells himself. *She's safe.*

Safely in his bedroom, a constant torment from behind the closed door. He was an idiot. He should have moved her someplace else, somewhere less tempting. He had already spent the first hour on the couch tossing and turning, trying not to think of her in his bed just on the other side of the wall. Trying to ignore his raging hard-on. He should have known his dreams would only be worse.

He sheathed his claws and shoved away the thin blanket tangled in his legs. He'd only worn flannel pants, no shirt, but he was drenched in the fear-sweat of the dream, and his chest was still heaving from it. He understood now, only too clearly, why he had been drawn to Mia before— somehow his wolf had known she was a shifter, even while Lucas was convinced she was human. As a female shifter, his wolf would have instinctively been drawn to protecting her. Once he had sensed her in danger, everything was primal after that.

Protect. Defend. Claim.

His wolf still wanted a mate, and he would pull out all the instinctual stops to drive Lucas into claiming one. But the man in him knew how dangerous that was... and how he couldn't ever allow himself to take a mate again.

He should have stashed Mia in a hotel far from him. He should have put her out of sight and out of mind. But instead, his wolf had him taking her hard against the door of his apartment and then keeping her in his bedroom. In his *bed*, for god's sake. And claiming her in his dreams.

Damn him.

Mia's female wolf presence was awakening things long buried. Bad things. Things that needed to *stay* buried, or he would have to go full-wolf again and retreat from the world entirely. Lucas swung his feet off the couch, placing them on the cool carpet, and ran both hands through his hair.

A quiet sound came from the kitchen.

Like a chair being moved across the floor.

Lucas was on his feet, flying silently across the soft strands of the flooring before he could even think. A dark figure lurked in the shadows of the kitchen hidden from the moonlight by the dangling pots, utensils, and the island in the middle. Lucas held in his growl in order to catch the intruder by surprise, but just as he reached the short figure, a glint of moonlight bounced off a sheath of long, black hair.

Mia.

His realization was too slow to stop his hands from grabbing her shoulders, but he managed to gentle his touch.

She still screamed.

His whole body shook with it, drenched with the echoes of the death-screams in his dream. But he didn't let go. "Mia!" he said hoarsely. "It's just me!"

She stopped her struggle against his hold and sank into him. He didn't know which was worse— his reflexive need to protect her, brought about by the look of terror on her face, or the fact that she was in his arms again, soft and close. Both brought his cock back to attention. He angled his body slightly away from her, hoping the shadows would cover it. The air was still rich with their lovemaking from before, so his erection shouldn't be too obvious by smell alone. Then again, having the smell of sex in the air didn't help with his constant state of arousal either.

"God, Lucas, stop scaring the crap out of me!" Her words were angry, but her body was still trembling.

"Stop sneaking around the kitchen." He loosened his grip, but instead of letting go like he should, he tugged her into the moonlight and rubbed her arms, up and down, trying to calm her.

"I was hungry," she said, voice smaller. The anger had dissipated. She was warming to his touch, he could tell.

And so was he. *Not good.* He dropped his hands and stepped back. The island behind him blocked his retreat, and he was suddenly trapped between her warmth and the coldness of the granite countertop. The moon bathed her in white, making her oversized t-shirt glow. His wolf growled possessively as he recognized his shirt draped on her thin frame. It barely covered her bottom, and he knew her underwear was still in shreds on the floor.

"I guess we forgot about dinner," he said, stalling, looking for a way out of the kitchen. He needed to get out of arm's reach of *her,* wearing nothing under his shirt. "Would you like something to eat?"

She stared up into his eyes and licked her lips. If his cock weren't already paying attention, that would have done it. And there was no mistaking her intention to do more with that far-too-tempting mouth when she leaned closer. He sidestepped her advance, much to his wolf's dismay, and shuffled across the kitchen to the refrigerator.

"I'm sure I've got something here you'll like," he said quickly. He yanked open the stainless steel door, blasting the room with a ghostly fluorescent light, and thankfully, sending a waft of cool air across the heated skin of his chest. Of course, the refrigerator's bulb also lit up his erection, tenting out his flannel pants like a beacon in the night.

He grabbed some milk and shut the door.

She watched him, not saying anything. In the shadows, he went to the right cabinet by memory, pulled down a glass, and poured it full of milk. It glowed slightly blue in the moonlight.

"Do you want me to warm it up?" he asked with his back turned to her, mostly to fill the tense silence.

"No, thank you." Her voice had a silky under-tone. Was she sounding like a sex kitten on purpose? Or had his mind gone completely demented?

What mind? he thought bitterly. *You're thinking with your wolf, Lucas.*

His wolf just panted, ignoring him completely. It was raptly attuned to the sumptuous bouquet of scents rolling off Mia: the arousal, either from before or now, he wasn't quite sure; a woodsy, clean scent, probably her fresh-washed skin before going to bed; and a lingering musky smell that had to be pure pheromones at work. That called to his inner beast the most.

Lucas turned toward her, trying to keep the lower half of his body in shadow. He handed her the milk, his arm outstretched, keeping as much distance as possible. "Here. This should help you sleep."

"Does warm milk had the same effect on wolves as it does on humans?"

Damn that sexy, sleepy voice again.

"Yeah." He should have beat a hasty retreat, left her to her milk, alone in the kitchen, but she held his gaze as she lifted the glass to her lips. She drank it down greedily, in several long gulps, then set the glass down on the counter with a resounding clink. She licked the milk that rimmed her lips, leaving them wet and glistening.

Dammit. "Mia," he said, warning in his voice. He would simply have to tell her straight out. He would protect her, but there would be no more—

His thoughts cut off as she reached down and lifted the t-shirt off in one swift motion.

If she glowed before, she was pure radiance now. He hadn't had a proper chance to just *look* at her before, too overcome by lust or anger or the fear of letting his wolf loose. But now, in the wan light spearing into the kitchen... she was a moon-borne goddess. Her breasts were the full mounds of his dream, only now her nipples were hard peaks begging for his touch. Her ink black hair fell in waves around her shoulders, lying softly on either side of her breasts. The moon turned her skin an ethereal silver-white, but her blue eyes glittered with a mystical light that oozed with ancient sexual power.

Her beauty spoke like an incantation to his inner beast.

He blinked. She took one careful step after another toward him, allowing him a long look, but closing the space between them in no time. His mouth was dry from hanging open, but just as he swallowed to speak, she reached him.

And went down on her knees.

Oh god. His wolf whined in anticipation.

Before he could think of words to stop her, she had freed his straining cock from his pants and taken it deep into her mouth. He gripped the counter behind him, his head tipping back with the intense pleasure of being inside her again.

"Mia." He meant it as a pleading to stop, but even he could hear the groan of pleasure in it. His wolf lolled in it, basking in each slide in and out of her mouth, his power over Lucas's mind growing with each bob. Her hand grasped his shaft, adding to the pressure and making him gasp.

He looked down at her. The sight of her lips sliding over his cock again and again entranced him. His hands found her hair, and he relished the silky softness of it, even as she moved under his touch. Tension coiled deep inside him, a climax coming that would obliterate him. It took everything he had to gently urge her to stop.

But as he lifted her to her feet, that made the situation no better. She was in his arms again, her breasts pressed to his chest, her arms around his neck, his throbbing cock heating the coolness of her bare skin.

She looked up into his eyes and whispered, "Take me."

And that was it.

He plunged his tongue into her mouth, devouring her more than kissing her. He tasted his own fluids inside her, salt and musk, and that ignited an even more powerful drive inside his wolf. His hands slid down to cup her bottom, and he lifted her feet from the floor. He carried her across the kitchen and made it as far as the table before he couldn't wait any longer. His wolf wanted to bend her over the tabletop, spread her legs, and plunge inside until she begged him to stop. But that was too close... too much like claiming... he couldn't risk it. Even now, his canines were pushing against his lips, craving her. Instead, he set her down on the table, palmed one gorgeous breast with his hand, and forced her to lie back on the cool wood. She arched her back away from the cold surface, but that just splayed her knees, a moon goddess spread open just for him.

He had told her that wolves didn't have *sex*... they *mated*. And it was true, at least in the two packs he'd ever belonged to. But no matter how much his wolf wanted to, Lucas couldn't allow himself to claim her. Yet, he was nearly powerless against the pull Mia had on him. That left him having sex with a girl who was all woman, but barely a wolf... and someone he could never call *mate*.

All he could do was pleasure her. And obtain some kind of relief for himself. He would plunge into her and make her come and do everything short of truly making her *his*. But then he had to find a way to keep her safely *away*. Otherwise, he might lose his mind in this madness.

He lifted her slender legs until her ankles rested on top of his shoulders, then pressed the tip of his aching cock against the dripping wetness of her folds. His wolf whimpered, disappointed, begging for more than just sex. *Mine*, his wolf whined. Lucas gripped Mia's hips and thrust deep inside her, driving back his wolf with a slamming wall of plea-sure. She cried out his name, which rallied his wolf even more, but Lucas buried him again in a haze of lust. Mia moaned, and he could hear her wolf whimpering as well, asking for release. He held her tight against his pounding cock with one hand, while he slid the other over the silky skin of her belly until he found the tight nub of her sex. He drew small circles, timed with the rocking of their bodies. It didn't take long for that to make her come. The waves of her pleasure made her tight, hot body grip him even harder. He gasped with the intensity of it but managed to hold his own pleasure back, while he continued taking her hard, driving his body into hers until her moans turned into shrieks again. Her claws came out, carving into the table, just as he brought her to a second climax. This time when she squeezed around him, he couldn't hold back. The pleasure shot through him, emptied him, buried him under an avalanche of sensation that quieted his wolf, finally and completely.

Their panting breaths rasped the air. The table joints squeaked from the abuse they were giving it. His pounding rhythm slowed, but he kept rocking against her, riding every last shockwave of pleasure, until she was ready for him to stop. They didn't speak. When they had both come fully down from their peaks, he gently untangled their limbs, lifted her from the table, and carried her back to his bedroom.

He would lay with her tonight. God help him, he would probably take her again. He would pleasure her as long as she allowed it, and as long as he couldn't resist.

But he couldn't bear to constantly *have* her, but never be able to really *claim* her.

In the morning, she would have to leave.

Chapter Eleven

THE SMELL OF EGGS AND BACON HAD NEVER BEEN AS heavenly as it was to Mia this bright and sunny morning in the apartment of an alpha wolf who happened to be her boss.

And now her lover.

Mia was sore in the very best way—a way she didn't even know she could be. She adjusted how she sat on the strange-shaped decorator chair at the kitchen table, thankful for the cushioned seat, even if the black leather stuck to her legs. Lucas was cooking breakfast, dressed only in those pajama pants that hung low on his hips. She knew for a fact that he had nothing on underneath the flannel because they had both just thrown on clothes when they climbed out of bed with the morning sun. His back muscles flexed as he stirred the eggs. His bare feet made no sound as he crossed the kitchen for plates. The ropy muscles of his arms worked to craft a breakfast for her after he had made love to her all night long. Or at least until they had both fallen asleep from sheer exhaustion.

The man was so damn sexy she could hardly stand it.

But he was strangely quiet now.

He hadn't been so quiet before, when he woke her this morning, asking for more of what they had done the night before. Her body still hummed from the pleasure he had lavished on her. And he had taught her more than one way to return the favor. It was like they had been locked in a secret time bubble where there was nothing but their bodies and the pleasure they would wring from them.

She supposed they had to come back to real life sometime.

She squirmed in her seat again, the memories bringing back a flush of pleasure with them. Lucas was plating their food and soon brought it over, returning to bring two glasses of juice as well. He took the seat opposite her, but the silence continued.

She was so ravenous, she didn't mind. They both consumed everything he had cooked in less than half the time it took to make it.

As they were finishing, he finally spoke. "We'll need to go by your dorm and clear out your things. Whatever is important to you, bring it. I don't know when it will be safe to go there again."

She nodded and glanced around at his immaculate apartment. "I don't have much. And it probably won't fit in with your gorgeous apartment, but I promise I won't take up too much space."

He scowled at his plate, hesitated, then finally lifted those dark eyes to meet her gaze. Her heart rate picked up even before he spoke. Something was wrong.

"You can't stay here, Mia." It was the same cool tone he had the night before, only minus the anger. Although that wasn't exactly right—he seemed angry at *something*, it just wasn't *her*.

Her heart sank. "Oh." She couldn't think of what else to say.

"Last night was… amazing," he said, the frown still deep on his face. "But it would be better if we just left it at that."

Her stomach twisted, the eggs suddenly feeling

like a rock inside her. "That's not what you said this morning." Anger was rising up in her like bile. He *did* just want to screw the intern, after all. It felt like he was throwing her away... but that wasn't right either. He was moving her out of her dorm because he wanted to protect her. He had *promised* to protect her.

He gritted his teeth, staring at his plate again. "I told you before," he said quietly. "I have a hard time resisting you." Then he looked up, and the heat was back—the same passion he had shown her all night long in his arms.

She held his gaze for a breathless moment. "Then don't resist."

He closed his eyes briefly and shook his head. "You don't understand."

"Tell me," she said, still holding her breath. If only he would open up to her about it... let out the darkness that was holding him back...

He dragged his gaze back to her. For a moment, she thought he might tell her. "Maybe someday, Mia." The painful honesty in his eyes ripped into her. "But for now... I'm sorry. I just... can't have you here." He rose up from the table, taking her dish as well as his into the kitchen.

She watched him go, a lump in her throat. "But

you're moving me out of my dorm." There was a tremble in her voice.

He set the dishes in the sink and turned back to her. "We'll find you a place to stay. Probably just a hotel for now."

She got up from her chair and stared across the chasm of cold the kitchen had become. They had made love in this room... or maybe they simply had sex. She wasn't sure anymore.

"You're not going to stay with me at the hotel." She didn't let it be a question, just a confirmation that she understood the conditions he was setting.

"I'll stay until I'm sure it's secure," he said. "Then I'll hire someone to watch over you."

She bit her lip. "But I'll still see you in the office?" That one actually was a question. Did she still have a job? Did she literally screw herself out of the best job she'd ever had?

"Of course." His stance softened, and he unlocked his arms. "You'll have a position at Spark-Tech as long as you need. Or want."

That made her heart skip a little. And it gave her time... time to convince him he was wrong to push her away. That there *was* room for her in his life.

"But no more sex?" she asked.

His arms locked up again. "No."

"How about kissing?" she asked lightly.

He cocked his head to one side. "This isn't a negotiation."

"No kissing, then," she said. "What about fondling? Over or under clothes? How about straight-up groping?"

He gritted his teeth. "Mia," he growled through them.

"I'm just saying…" She pushed in her chair. "If I accidentally brush up against you in the elevator, don't be surprised if some part of your body gets squeezed." She raked her gaze over his overly-hot, extremely-masculine body. She made it sound like a joke, but she wasn't so sure it was. Would she be able to keep from jumping him in the elevator? She wasn't entirely sure.

But it pulled a smirk out of him. "Duly warned."

She flashed him another flirty look, then turned away. "I call shower first," she threw over her shoulder as she headed back to the bedroom. His low chuckle followed after her.

In truth, her stomach was still twisting.

He had given into her for a night. But in the

bright sun of morning, he'd thought better of it and pulled back. She would just have to keep trying, not drive him away, and eventually, he wouldn't be able to resist the pull between them anymore. Her inner wolf was still basking in the glow of a night with her alpha, but she roused enough to yip in agreement.

Lucas and his wolf *belonged* with them. But they would have to be patient while he figured that out as well.

Lucas strolling through her dorm building, at her side in his casual-yet-upscale polo and slacks, felt like some kind of out-of-body experience: his powerful frame and confident walk were better placed in a boardroom, not next to a bunch of hungover college students stumbling in from whatever frat party they had crashed the night before. Lucas let her lead the way, but his presence was commanding: he swept the hallways with his gaze and narrowed his eyes at every person they encountered, probably assessing whether they were a threat or not. It was incredibly reassuring and made her feel safe, even if she didn't know from one minute to the next what kind of relationship they had. For her wolf, it seemed simple: he was her alpha, or at least *should* be. Even if Mia hadn't submitted to him in any real wolfish way… yet. Her inner beast paced and pawed the ground, eager to cement that thought into reality. But her human self wasn't at all sure about that—especially when Lucas was a volatile, crazy mix of employer, lover, protector, provider, breakfast-cooker, and mentor on all things wolfish.

If she were on Facebook, their relationship status would definitely be *it's complicated*.

Lucas let her step into the elevator before him, then followed and used his stare to keep a bleary-eyed boy from joining them. The door closed.

"Floor?" he asked.

"Eleven."

She looked at him, but he kept his gaze on the slowly climbing numbers. There was an invisible wall between them now, one she wanted to breach by taking his hand or touching his face—she wished she was bold enough to grope him in the elevator like she had threatened, but all her bold demands had been made in the shadows of his kitchen, alone, late at night. Not in a brightly lit elevator that could stop at any moment.

When they reached the 11th floor and stepped into the common room, Lucas's nose wrinkled. She couldn't blame him—the post-Friday-night-party stench was second only to Sunday morning's usual combination of spilled drink mixers, stale body sweat, and at least a couple hasty sexual encounters. Today there was an Eau du Cheetos added to the mix. Must have been movie night. At least there weren't any used condoms in the corner like she found the last time.

"Sorry about the Smells of Debauchery," she said.

"I'd kind of forgotten about the college stench." He threw her a small smile that felt like a lifesaver on her stormy sea of emotion. "Probably blocked it out."

She smiled in return. "The whole place could use one of those air purifiers you have a SparkTech."

His smile dimmed. "Well, at least you won't have to stay here much longer."

She grimaced, thinking that at least in the dorm she had someone to live with, whereas Lucas was about to stick her in a hotel by herself. Or with a bodyguard. Which would be fine if the bodyguard was Lucas, but that seemed to be off the table.

The hallway was empty, with the dead-quiet of too-early Saturday morning for most college students. The early risers were already gone, and the rest were probably sleeping it off. Mia dug her keycard out of her purse and slid it into the door. The blinds were closed, and the morning sun hadn't yet been introduced to her room. At first, she thought her roommate, Jupiter, wasn't home—probably spent the night with her crush from last week, Jackson—but then she saw Jupiter's telltale blue-feathered purse dangling from her wrist. Her roommate was buried under the blankets on her bed, face down, her wild red hair spilling out over the edge along with her floppy arm, but the covers were pulled up over most of her head.

Lucas tiptoed past her sleeping roommate like she was a guard dog, but they would need some light to clear out her stuff. Mia strode over to the blinds on their window and opened them with a loud *zip* sound. Light crashed into the room.

Jupiter groaned like she had been mortally wounded. "Et tu, Brutus Mia?" she croaked, still under the blanket.

"I'm not stabbing you, Jeeter," Mia said with a

smile. "Although I should for what you've done to the place." The open blinds had revealed the wrecked state of their room: overturned red cups, underwear she prayed was Jupiter's draped over the chair, and it looked like someone had crumpled every piece of paper from the printer and tried to score baskets with it. Only two made it in the trash can.

Lucas took in the disaster scene and just shook his head. She could only imagine what he was thinking.

Jupiter stirred but only to pull the blanket tighter over her head. Her voice was muffled, but Mia could still hear her moaned complaint. "Oh, cruel fate. Why do you mock me?"

"It's a little early for Shakespeare, don't you think?" Mia called. She emptied the remaining printer paper from its box and handed the empty to Lucas. They wouldn't need much more than that to pack up her stuff.

Jupiter's muffled voice sounded stronger. "That's not Shakespeare, Miss Business Major." She shoved the blanket off her head and struggled to sit up. "It's Homer Simpson."

Lucas had a small smirk on his face when Jupiter caught sight of him and shrieked. Then she covered her mouth, looking ridiculously embarrassed for that, rather than the bed head hair and Glenda the Good Witch getup: short, pink tutu, sparkles included, black and white striped tights that only went up to her thighs, and a stretchy, pink tank top that clearly revealed her bra had gone MIA during last night's partying. Or perhaps she took it off for bed. But judging by Jupiter's pool of goth mascara under her eyes, Mia guessed her roommate had simply fallen into bed last night in a drunken stupor.

Eyes wide, Jupiter dropped her hand, then belatedly pulled her blanket up to cover her chest.

Lucas's eyes were laughing through the whole shenanigan, but he didn't say anything.

"Jupiter, meet Lucas," Mia said with a sigh. How was she supposed to introduce him? There wasn't much she could tell her roommate, but by the way Jupiter's eyes were dancing all over Lucas and hopping back and forth between them, she was sure her roommate would figure a lot out on her own. And grill the rest out of her. "Lucas is my boss at SparkTech."

That should light a fire in Jupiter's brain.

Sure enough, her eyes went even wider.

"Lucas, meet Jupiter," Mia said before her

roommate could say anything embarrassing. "My roommate and clothing supplier."

"Nice to meet you, Jupiter," Lucas said. "That's a great name."

Man, he had a killer smile, and Mia could see it working its magic on her roommate. Her face was almost as red as her hair. Lucas extended his hand, and Jupiter stumbled out of bed to shake it. Then a horrified look overcame her. She dashed to the chair, snatched her underwear off, and stuffed it in a drawer.

"We're normally much neater than this, Mr., uh… Lucas." She yanked red cups off the desk and dropped them in the trash, then looked back to Mia. "I didn't know we'd have company." She clutched the blue-feathered purse awkwardly across her chest, hiding her bra-lessness.

Mia shook her head and picked up a picture of her mom off the shelf. There was a pathetic amount of stuff in her dorm that was actually important to her. She would need her books and her laptop, but beyond that… she tucked her mom's picture in the box.

"Mia?" Jupiter asked, frowning at the tiny amount of packing. "What's going on?"

"I'm moving out," Mia said tightly, really not

wanting to explain *any* of it. She checked with Lucas, but he just gave her a small nod. "At least temporarily."

Jupiter's eyes had narrowed to slits. "Why?" She was asking Mia, but her suspicious look trained on Lucas like a laser.

Mia took a breath and turned to him, but his lips were pressed tight. He would leave it to her to explain. Only Jupiter knew nothing about shifters and packs and venture capitalist competition. Mia could lie and say she was moving in with Lucas, but that would just make things worse.

"Turns out SparkTech's paying me really well," Mia said, which was true, as far as it went. "I just wanted to move out to a bigger place."

The stormy look on Jupiter's face jumped to Category Five Hurricane Level. She glared at the paltry amount of belongings Mia owned. Even the slim black skirt and yellow sweater she was wearing belonged to Jupiter. And her roommate knew it.

Suddenly Jupiter's demeanor shifted to Sunny Day With No Chance of Clouds. "You know what? I'm in desperate need of a shower!" She gave a quick nod to Lucas. "Nice to meet you, Mr. Spark-Tech Man." Then she turned and flounced in her tutu to the closet to dig through for some new clothes.

Mia sighed. She would have to explain later. If there was a *later*. She didn't know when she would be back to her dorm and her roommate again— from what Lucas said, that might be *never*. She put her books and laptop in the box, with a bunch of pens and pencils, careful to keep her mom's picture on top. Jupiter was still rummaging through the closet. Mia would wait until she was done to pick through and find the stuff that actually belonged to her.

Jupiter re-emerged with a whole rainbow of clothes clutched in her hands. She eyed Mia's outfit. "Hey, wait a minute, sister! You're not planning on walking out with my favorite sweater, are you?"

Mia's gaze dropped to the classy yellow top, much nicer than anything she owned. "No, of course not. I'll get it back to you, Jeeter, I promise —" She looked up to find Jupiter giving her a skeptical look.

"Yeah, sure you will. Come on." Jupiter held up a t-shirt and some jeans that belonged to Mia. "Come to the shower with me. You can change while Mr. SparkTech packs up your stuff."

Mia frowned. She had always returned Jupiter's

clothes before. And in good condition, too. She was careful that way. But by all rights, she should really dry clean the clothes she was wearing now, or at least wash them…

"Come on!" Jupiter said impatiently. "I've got stuff to do, too, you know!"

Mia checked with Lucas, but he just shrugged. So she strode over to her strange, temperamental little roommate, took the clothes from her outstretched hand, and led the way out of their room.

As soon as the door was closed behind them, and they were headed to the bathroom, Mia hoarse-whispered, "Geez, Jeeter! Impatient much?"

Jupiter whirled on her, grabbed her arm, and pulled her to a stop in the middle of the living area. *"Mia!* What in the actual hell is going on here?" The rage-storm look was back.

Mia should have known it was all an act from her drama-major roommate.

"I'm just… moving out…" God, how was she going to explain this?

"With tall, dark, and sexy?" Her voice hiked up. "Mia, you've only been working there for a week! Is he forcing you into this? Is he one of those weird controlling types? Because I know some guys who could help with that, Mia. *Big* guys. They could beat the crap out of Mr. Sexy if you need them to! You just say the word."

"No!" Mia backed up from her, agitation making her voice squeak. "It's nothing like that! He's just looking out for me."

"Looking out for you." The skepticism was back in full force. "By making you move out of your dorm."

"It's not like that." Although it kind of was... but not really. There were dangerous people out to use her against Lucas. She just couldn't explain it to her roommate.

"Is he making you quit school?" Her focus was intense.

"What?" Mia said, genuinely shocked. "No, of course not."

Her roommate's gaze did a quick check over Mia. If she didn't notice before, it was obvious now that Mia was also seriously bra-less under her sweater. If she was less endowed, it might not have been so apparent, but as it stood, it was hard to miss.

Jupiter leaned in. "You're sleeping with him, aren't you?"

Mia bit her lip. There wasn't much point in lying. "It's complicated."

"Ye-ah." Her roommate drew out the word like that was obvious. "Sleeping with your boss can be that way. I mean, damn, I get it, girl. The boy is hot sex on a stick, but *he's your boss.*"

"Okay, okay!" Mia threw up her hands. "Not necessarily my best choice."

Jupiter's look said, *you got that right.* "Is he at least good in bed?"

Mia huffed and gave her a *you've got to be kidding* look in return.

"Right. Stupid question." Jupiter pursed her lips. "The real question is: *is he worth it?*"

Finally, a question she could actually answer. "Yeah. I think so, Jeeter."

"So what's the deal with this moving out thing?" She still seemed concerned, but it had stepped down several hurricane levels to slow, tropical storm.

"I think... I think I might be in love with him." She hadn't thought of it that way *at all*, but it was something that might make sense to her over-the-top drama roommate.

"Damn, girl, I didn't think you had that in you." But her voice wasn't disapproving. "When you fall, you fall hard. And freaking fast."

"We're trying to keep it on the down-low in the office, though," Mia said, making it up as she went now. "I'm moving in with him, but the cover story is that I'm just getting another place. If they even ask. Which I'm hoping they won't." She wished it was the reverse, but at least it was a story that should hold up for now.

Jupiter blew out a sigh. "I don't know, Mia. It's strange."

"You're the Queen of Strange." Mia pointed a finger at her friend's streaked mascara and general bed head. "Not to mention Party Queen and Boy of the Week Champion."

"I'm not judging you," Jupiter said, looking offended herself. Then the frown returned. "I'm just worried, Mia. I don't want you to get hurt."

That made her eyes prick. She threw her arms around her roommate, crazy lump of clothes and all. "You're a good friend, Jeeter," she said into her flyaway red hair.

Jupiter squeezed her back. "All right, all right," she said releasing her. "I'm the emotional one, remember?"

Mia smiled.

"Let's get you out of those clothes." She dug

through the armful of clothes and peeled away a pair of black slacks and a brilliant blue shirt that looked like silk. "Here. At least you'll have one outfit to wear. Until you have time to shop."

Mia held the lightweight clothes in her hands, tears threatening her eyes again. "I can't take your clothes, Jeeter."

"Take them?" She looked horrified, but Mia knew it was fake. "You totally have to bring those back! Whenever you come down from your New Boyfriend High and remember to come visit me."

Mia couldn't help it—she hugged her room-mate again. When they broke apart, Jupiter rummaged in her pants and brought out her phone.

"I look like hell!" she proclaimed. "And you're not much better, Miss Hot For New Boyfriend." Her roommate held up the camera and hugged Mia to her. "What better time to take a selfie?"

Mia laughed, but before she could even protest, Jupiter had already taken the picture. Checking her phone, she nodded approvingly and tucked it away.

"That's going straight to Tumble, isn't it?" Mia asked.

"*Tumbler,* you dork." Jupiter grinned, then tugged her toward the bathroom. "A disastrous selfie is the perfect thing to remember you by."

More quietly, she added, "And those clothes will be a reminder for *you* that you can always come back."

Mia shook her head. "Jupiter, I'm not—"

She held up her hands. "I'm just saying, in case you change your mind. It's not like I'm getting a new roommate for the summer. Forget that noise. If you're not here, I'm keeping this place *all* to myself!"

Mia half-laughed and ducked into the bathroom right behind her roommate. She didn't know how temporary this move was going to be—her stay at the dorms at UDub was never going to be permanent anyway—but it was ever more clear that the only thing she would miss from McMahon Hall was Jupiter.

And it was sweet of her roommate to say Mia could come back, but she was a shifter living among humans. She never really felt like she belonged among the drunken, bed-hopping college kids anyway—not with her drive to finish school and find a way to get her mom out of the slums. But now that Lucas had awakened her inner wolf, living in the dorms just felt like a badly fitting dress that she constantly had to tug to sit right and not flash some part of her that she didn't want to reveal.

In fact, when it came to *belonging* somewhere, the

only person who had ever made her feel that way was back in her room, packing her things and moving her away.

And when she thought of it that way, it felt exactly right.

Chapter Twelve

THERE WERE EXACTLY ONE BOX AND ONE MEDIUM-sized duffle bag in the back of Lucas's car. That was the sum total of Mia's belongings. His wolf growled its disapproval, and Lucas had to agree: it wasn't so much that she packed light, but that she had nothing of permanence. One photo of her mother, but no personal effects. Nothing of her past. No hint of her dreams for the future, beyond an armful of business textbooks.

It was far too much like his apartment. And it made him angry.

She should have more of a life than that. Maybe *he* was a train wreck after Tila's death, but Mia still had everything ahead of her. Not with him, but with someone.

Until he dragged her into the mess that was his life.

After Lev had pulled him back out of not only the Olympic mountains but the deep, dark forest of his despair, Lucas had torn out everything in his apartment that reminded him of Tila—her clothes, the photos, every memento of their brief and beautiful time together. It wasn't that he didn't want her —he would have given his life for hers. There were nights he would gladly have laid down in a cold grave if it would have brought her back to life. He simply couldn't bear the torment of having her all around him all the time. He nearly left the apartment altogether, but in the end, Lev packed her things and took them away… and Lucas could breathe again.

He gripped the steering wheel harder, wheeling onto Interstate 5 to head downtown. Mia sat quietly in the passenger seat, her new clothes a perfect complement to her features. The ink black pants matched her long, dark hair, now pulled back and clipped behind her neck. The sapphire blue silk top brought out the power of those mystical eyes… only her gaze was turned away from him, studying the skyscrapers of Seattle in the distance.

He had to wonder what she was thinking. It was

the right thing to move her out of the dorm—she had to know that—but what of the rest of it? The sex... him pushing her away... his reluctance to tell her anything about *why*.

God, he was such an asshole.

He kept looking over at her periodically, but she didn't give any hints as to the thoughts swirling through her mind. They were halfway to downtown before she looked at him in return.

"Is the hotel near the office?" she asked.

There was a fatigue in her voice that he didn't like. At all. His wolf growled at him, and he agreed again: he had to do a better job of taking care of her. It was his fault she was in this situation. He needed to make it as easy as possible on her.

"Yes," he replied, "but I need to stop by the office for a minute first. We kind of left in a hurry on Friday."

She frowned, then seemed to figure it out. "The LoopSource reports."

"I was just going to pick them up and bring them with us to the hotel. While you take a rest, maybe get some lunch, I'll look over them. I need to have some kind of recommendation for my father on Monday."

She shook her head. "I'm not tired. Maybe I can help with the reports?"

His first instinct was to say *no*. The dark circles under her eyes belied her claim of not being tired. Dammit, *he* was tired. They'd spent half the night exploring each other's bodies. He couldn't bring himself to regret that, but she had to be lying when she said it hadn't drained her energy. Which meant she must really want to help with the reports. Or, more likely, find a way back into his arms. Which was definitely not something he could allow to happen again, no matter how much he wanted it. Or how much she did.

But that was on *him* to resist. Short of that, he would give her anything she wanted.

He looked forward again, studying the traffic and avoiding her gaze. "That would be great. I could really use someone to double check my analysis." That much was true—he'd be lucky to form half a coherent thought this weekend with her nearby. "But Mia…" He glanced back, and her blue eyes were still trained on him. "We're just working."

"Right. No sex. Not even kissing." The corner of her mouth lifted.

He looked back at the traffic. "I mean it, Mia."

"I know." This time her voice was soft, and when he glanced at her again, she was back to looking out the window.

Yeah, he was definitely an asshole.

Another ten tension-filled minutes later, they arrived at the parking garage for the Russell Building where SparkTech sat on the 32nd floor. There was no sign of last night's attack by the Red wolves—the limo was gone, there was no blood on the floor of the garage—but he parked as close as he could to the elevator door, just in case.

"You need to come inside with me," Lucas said as he turned off the car.

"Right behind you," she said.

He hopped out of the car and came quickly around to her side. He got there before she managed to climb out of the car in her tall, black heels. He took her by the elbow to help, but she pulled away—not strongly, yet he felt the rebuke nonetheless. And she was right: he would have to watch his tendency to put his hands on her without thinking. Still, he kept by her side, scanning the nearly empty concrete spaces for any bad actors. Or lurking wolves. There was nothing but the sound of her heels clicking on the tiled entryway to the elevator.

The ride up was just as tense. He wanted to get in and out of the office as quickly as possible. Then maybe they would have a chance to talk. Sort things out.

As they emerged on the 32nd floor, Lucas said, "I think we left the reports in your office."

"You don't think Lena would have locked them up after us?" Mia asked.

He was about to answer, but his attention was drawn to the light coming from his father's office. The other rooms were dark, the shades having been drawn for the night and not opened in the morning, but his father's was occupied. Or somehow Lena forgot to close up shop last night. She was meticulous, so he doubted that very much.

Mia's gaze was drawn to it as well. "Is your dad here?" she whispered.

He nodded. They paused at her office, halfway down the hall. "Go in and get the reports. I'll wait." He paused, then met her blue-eyed gaze. "I think it's time to introduce you to my father."

Her eyes went wide, but she scurried quickly into her office and returned with an armful of reports, both his copy and hers. He took them from her, then gently guided her toward his father's office with a hand at the small of her back. Just before they reached it, he remembered he wasn't supposed to be touching her. He dropped his hand and used it to open the door.

His father was bent over his own nest of papers spread on his desk. His head jerked up, and he was on his feet, claws out, before Lucas could say a word.

"It's just Mia and me," Lucas rushed out. He'd never seen his father so on edge, or so quick to shift. Things must be worse than he thought.

His father's body immediately relaxed, and the claws disappeared. "Lucas. Good. I'm glad you're here." He frowned and dipped his head to Mia. "Sorry, to startle you, Ms. Fiore. I'm sure shifters are the last thing you'd like to see at the moment."

A glance to Mia showed her rigid in the doorway, but he didn't think it was fear that held her there. At least, not fear of his father's claws. More like his father's position in the company. Her boss's boss, he supposed, although he hardly thought of the structure that way anymore, not since he left his father's pack.

"Father, there's something you should know about Mia." When Lucas called his father last night to report the attack, he left out the aftermath—including the hot sex against the door and the fact that Mia was a shifter. He had no idea if the Red pack had managed to bug their phones or what, but he didn't want to take any chances with that secret getting out. Yet now that they were in person… "Mia is a wolf."

His father's eyebrows flew up, and he did a double take of Mia before pinning Lucas with his gaze.

Lucas cut off the question he knew was on his father's lips. "She doesn't belong to any pack. She's really only half blood, on her father's side. And she's not pack-raised. She's been a recluse."

"Um… excuse me?" Mia said. "I am *not* a recluse."

He turned to her, an apologetic hand holding her off. "It's just a term we use. For shifters who are hidden from everyone, even their pack. Or their families."

"Kind of a pejorative term, don't you think?" She frowned at him.

He really didn't need this right now.

His father's chuckle brought his attention back. "She's right, you know." His smile for Mia was kinder now, softer than any Lucas ever had directed at him. It was the kind of smile he saved for his daughter, Lucas's sister, and the other females of his pack. Mia probably didn't realize it, but she had already won his father over, simply by being wolf and not taking any flak from Lucas.

This wasn't exactly a surprise. Lucas had long ago realized that all the alphas of his family—his father, his older brother Llyr, and not least, himself —liked their women strong. Alpha females in their own right. His inner beast growled its appreciation for something Lucas was just now figuring out: Mia was likely an alpha herself. Loner. Stubborn. Driven. She just didn't realize it.

And somehow he had been blind to it until that moment. Still stunned by that thought, his father's gruff voice brought him back out of his own head.

"After your call last night, Llyr and I and several members of our packs went to the parking garage right away." His father shook his head. "The Red wolves were already gone."

"I left one unconscious," Lucas objected, but he winced as well. He had waited too long to call, too wrapped up in getting Mia to safety—which was excusable—and giving into his wolf's craving for her—which was not.

"I don't doubt you, son," his father said. "Not least because I received a call shortly afterward from Crittenden. He claims it happened without authorization, and those wolves are being punished. But the offer, or I should say *threat,* still stands." He glanced at Mia, but his pointed, and definitely angry, look was all for Lucas.

"The offer that they'll leave Mia alone if we back down on Loop Source." At his father's raised eyebrows, he added, "She knows everything."

"Well... not really," Mia protested. "Who is Crittenden?"

His father's look for her was soft again. "He's the alpha of the Red pack. They have the same reports we do, Mia. They seem convinced Loop-Source is the next big thing in mobile computing, but they know we can outbid them. The only way they'll be able to score the deal is by getting us to back down." He glanced at the reports clutched in Lucas's hands. "I'm still waiting to hear whether LoopSource is worth our time..." He looked back to Mia. "But I promise you. Under no circumstances will we allow them to hurt you."

Mia seemed to relax a little under his father's warm assurance. The man in Lucas was glad to see it, but his wolf growled at the intrusion of his father's alpha. He pushed his wolf's jealous thoughts to the back of his mind. His father had already extended pack protection to Mia, and he was simply reassuring her of that. Lucas was lucky his father was willing to step in and help where Lucas couldn't without a pack of his own. He had little to offer Mia and no claim to make. His wolf had better get used to that fact.

"However," his father continued, "now that they've attacked, that puts me in a very bad position. Mia wasn't harmed, so technically, my prior threat to hold Crittenden personally responsible hasn't been triggered. But the fact remains that the Red pack violated our territory when they tried to take her. A pretty brazen act, even if it wasn't authorized by their alpha. And not something we can just let go."

"Are you planning to retaliate?" Lucas swallowed. This could escalate quickly. Which meant even more danger for Mia. Not to mention his brothers.

"I already have."

Mia's face had gone pale. "But I'm fine! I don't want anyone to get hurt over me."

"This isn't your fault, Mia," Lucas said. "This is pack business."

"Lucas is right," his father said, with an approval that unexpectedly warmed Lucas. "None of this is your responsibility. You're just a bartering chip to the Reds."

"Maybe you could convince them that I'm not… I don't know… anything special?" Mia's face had scrunched up, and the need to touch her became suddenly overwhelming.

Lucas edged closer and allowed himself to put a hand on her shoulder. "You're already special enough that I beat the crap out of them when they tried to take you." He gave a small smile. "Twice."

"Short of your death, Mia, we're not going to convince them otherwise. And there's no way we're going to let that happen." His father's gaze was hot on Lucas's back. He had to be wondering exactly what kind of relationship Lucas had with Mia, especially now that she had turned out to be a shifter. Lucas hardly knew what to call their relationship himself, much less how to explain it to his father. Besides, it was irrelevant to the discussion at hand.

Lucas's arm slid around Mia to hold her. She seemed to need it, and he couldn't help himself anyway. He turned back to his father. "What kind of retaliation did you decide upon?" Lucas knew his father would have given it a great deal of thought before putting any of his pack in danger.

His father sighed. "I didn't want to escalate the situation too badly, but we had to have a response. Last night, I sent Llyr and some of his pack to incur on the Red pack's territory—they didn't hurt anyone, just trashed one of Crittenden's offices. All in wolf form, no DNA traces. But it should show them we're serious. And that we can incur again if need be."

Lucas nodded. "Has Crittenden responded?"

"Not yet." The muscles in his father's jaw twitched as he clenched it. "The Reds have always been dangerous and running to the dark side of their wolves, but this new territory, even for them. Some of these younger wolves are overconfident and clearly willing to provoke a pack war. Maybe they're out to prove themselves. Maybe they've just gone a little too far into their dark side. Whatever it is, I want you to pull this LoopSource evaluation together *now*. Prove to me that making that deal is worth my time and money."

Lucas nodded. "You want to put it to rest."

"I want to rub their noses in it," he said with a hard look. This was the alpha he grew up with—the one who knew that sometimes you had to hit back hard to stop a bully.

Lucas let out a small huff of air. "Yes, sir."

He gave his father a short nod, then led a wide-eyed Mia from his office. Figuring out what to do with her—other than keeping her absolutely safe—would have to take back seat in his mind for a while. His father wasn't Lucas's alpha anymore, but he recognized marching orders when he heard them.

And putting the LoopSource deal to bed might just put all of this behind them.

Chapter Thirteen

Mia shouldn't have been surprised by the luxurious hotel suite Lucas found for her, not after working in the upscale offices of SparkTech for a week and having spent the night at Lucas's modern millionaire-bachelor apartment. But she was still amazed at the stunning views of the Bay, the private balcony, and the marbled entranceway to the enormous living area, easily ten times the size of her dorm room.

The only disappointing part was that the suite came with two separate bedrooms.

Of course, if Lucas carried through with his threat to hire a bodyguard, rather than staying with her himself, then separate bedrooms would be fine. But if Lucas was her bodyguard... her inner beast whined every time she glanced at the closed bedroom doors. It wasn't right to be separated like that. And Mia had to agree.

Lucas worked on the tan leather couch in the center of the living room, the paper LoopSource report spread on the low ebony table, and his laptop balanced on one leg as he compared notes. Mia had set up in a nearby chair that was shaped like a giant half-circle and had deep brown nubuck leather as soft as a baby's skin. All her notes and her laptop fit within the circular confines of the chair, and it was angled, so she had a view out the windows.

It was perfect for work, which was what she should have been doing. Instead, her gaze had drifted to the boats skimming the waters of the Bay. The waves sparkled with the afternoon sun, but from this distance, the boats didn't seem to move— as if the brightly colored sails were ornaments carefully placed to make the ocean more lovely. Lucas and Mia had been working for hours, but time felt likewise suspended for her. As if she was waiting for a gust of wind to come fill her sails and let her breathe again.

She turned away from the timeless marina and watched Lucas instead.

His brow was furrowed in concentration, and

she could tell his mind was lost in the numbers spread before him. He was attacking this due diligence analysis like their lives depended on it—in a way, she guessed that maybe hers did. Or possibly others in Lucas's family. The dedication he was throwing into his work warmed her heart, but she couldn't help wishing he would turn those intense, dark eyes to her every once in a while.

Her chair felt like it was a million miles away, even though, physically, Lucas was only a dozen feet from her. But he had made it abundantly clear that their first night together was supposed to be their last. Still, she hadn't given up hope of changing his mind. Thoughts of last night still sent shivers of pleasure racing down between her legs, but more than she needed mind-bending sex, she needed him to open up about his past. He'd only given her hints, but she knew that it was preventing them from being together the way they should. His past was keeping her from *belonging* to him in the present, the way her wolf wanted.

The way *she* wanted.

Strangely enough, she'd felt the pull of that *belonging* when she had met Lucas's father, the senior Mr. Sparks. The way he smiled at her was something she'd never experienced before—it was like a gentle love, not sexual, but powerful and caring nonetheless. Like she was something worth treasuring and protecting. She guessed this was how daughters felt when they actually had fathers.

It dredged up a nameless ache inside her: how different would her life have been if her father had stuck around? If he'd provided a pack for her to grow up in? She could have learned all the things a young female shifter needed to know. She could have embraced who she was instead of hiding it. She would have *belonged*. The ache grew into a stabbing pain like she had just discovered something broken inside her that she had never known existed.

She gasped in a breath involuntarily, then drew it deeper on purpose and let it out, breathing through the pain. No wonder that craving to *belong* had been working her so hard and so persistently.

"Are you all right?" Lucas's voice was gentle but pointed. Like he thought she was having a heart attack or something.

But it was only a heartbreak. From something that happened a long time ago.

She met his concerned gaze across the span of feet separating them. "Yeah, I…" She swallowed. "I just realized that…" Could she tell him? No… it felt too raw to share. "I was just thinking how nice it must have been to be raised in a pack. With other shifters who understood you. Loved you."

He frowned and glanced at the papers and computer in his lap as if he was wondering the relevance of that thought to what they were working on.

She let out a small laugh. "Not that I really know anything about being in a pack. Or being a shifter, for that matter." She waited for his gaze to meet hers again. "Or having a mate."

With that, his face sank into a scowl. But he folded up his laptop and set it aside. "What do you want to know?"

She tried to hold in her surprise, but she mirrored him by closing her laptop and setting it on top of her stack of papers. She wanted to leave her circular chair-island and sit by him on the couch, but she sensed that would be invading his carefully constructed territory of business surrounding and isolating him. Instead, she folded up her legs and tucked them underneath her.

He was watching her every move.

"What does it mean to have a mate?" she asked.

He sighed and looked away. Her heart lurched and then pounded erratically. She'd pushed too hard, jumping right to the heart of it. But she held her breath and waited, hoping. After a long moment, he pushed away the remaining papers surrounding him and turned to face her. He laced his hands, propped his elbows on his knees, and took a long moment before he looked her in the eyes.

"Being wolf means you have certain… desires, certain bonds, that humans do not." He paused like he wasn't quite sure he wanted to go any further. But then he took a breath and pressed on. "It's like the submission we talked about before. When you're part of a pack, you submit to its alpha. It's a ceremony, but there's also a real bond with real power behind it. You don't simply *promise* to obey the alpha; there is a deep compulsion to it. Not impossible to break, but nearly so."

"Like with the Red wolves—they couldn't break their submission to you. At least in wolf form."

"Right." Lucas took another breath, but this one seemed to be easier for him. "It's strongest in wolf form, but there is some carry over to human form as well. Just as you feel your wolf inside you, pushing and pulling you, encouraging one action or discouraging another… you'll feel the submission bond as well. For males, it is a compulsion to serve and protect. It's the bond that ties the pack together. For females… it's a little more complicated."

"Women usually are."

That drew a tiny smile out of him. "No doubt an ancient truth." But the humor quickly died on his face, and his gaze dropped to his hands.

Mia waited, watching the muscles in his arms move as he fisted and unfisted his hands.

Finally, he said quietly, "For females, the submission can be the same as males. Every female submits to the alpha just the same as the males of the pack. But submission can also be the first step to mating." He paused again.

Mia wasn't sure if he would continue this time. "What are the other steps?" She had to chase the words with a hastily sucked-in breath. Her wolf was at full attention.

He nodded, seemingly to himself, still staring at his hands. "First, submission. In wolf form, of course, because that's where the bond forms. Second, a coupling. This time in human form. Ritually from behind." He raised his gaze to hers. "And then the bite."

She had forgotten how to breathe. "Bite?" Her wolf whimpered: a needy, sexual sound that had heat pumping throughout her body.

"The male's canines will protrude and enable him to bite the female while coupling." His voice was dead. Leaden by words he wasn't saying or maybe by the weight of the emotion behind that technical description of what Mia could only imagine was a wildly passionate and, if the whimpering of her wolf was any indication, highly erotic act.

"That seems…" She was definitely laboring to breathe. "…painful."

He smiled a little. Bitter and sweet, and that tiny movement of his mouth nearly broke her heart.

"I've only mated once," he said, and there was a gentleness in his tone that tore at her. "Afterward, I ask Tila what she thought. I was… well, somewhat caught up in the moment at the time. But I'd been told that females don't experience the pain as you might expect… that it actually enhanced the…" He broke off, his smile fleeing. "She said it was the best experience of her life. That it made her feel like she belonged to me in a way that could never be broken." He stopped. His mouth worked but in wordless pain.

Mia was out of her chair before she thought about what she was doing. She flew across the space separating them. He *needed* her. She knew it. And she didn't care if he knew it or not.

He seemed surprised by her arms around his neck, but she held him tightly, cradling his head to her. Tears ran down her face, but she didn't brush them away, too intent on holding him until he held her back. He was breathing heavily, pulling in gasps, but eventually, his arms went around her.

But his hold on her was weak like he was simply keeping her in place. Like he couldn't bring himself to hug her back.

She held him that way until his breathing evened out again. Slowly, reluctantly, she released him and eased down to the couch to sit next to him. He wasn't crying or anything, but there was a tightness around his eyes that hadn't been there before.

"You must have loved her very much," Mia said softly, searching his face for some sign of what to say or do to ease his pain.

He laughed lightly, and it settled her heart to hear it. "Mating is something more powerful than love, Mia. It's almost as powerful as death." The smile faded. "The bite isn't just a symbolic claiming of the female, a ritual binding of the two more than just their physical lovemaking. There's an actual physical or perhaps chemical bond that occurs. I believe it's part magic as well."

Mia frowned, fascinated and slightly horrified. "Is there some kind of venom in the bite?"

He smiled again. "No, no. Although I suppose you could think of it that way. The male's saliva carries some kind of ancient magical substance in it. It's not unlike whatever triggers the shift from human DNA to wolf DNA in the first place. But when he claims her, his bite adds something to her blood that literally changes her DNA. She is then connected to him. Physically bound. She literally *belongs* with him: they are paired. Now, if she bears pups, they will be stronger, healthier, more fully wolf, than if they had been conceived without the claiming first."

Mia's heart rate picked up and raced faster with every word he was saying. This was it; this was the pull to *belong* to him that she had been feeling all along. Only he had already claimed a mate once before.

"Is this something you can only do once in your life?" she asked, breathless.

He dropped his gaze. "For the females, yes. They can only be claimed once, and the bond can only be broken by the death of the male. Then she's able to mate again, at least in theory. Most are devastated by the loss. It's not uncommon for females to die soon after their mates."

Mia's eyes were wide as he explained all of it. "And for the males?"

He shook his head. "The bond is really one way in a sense. *He* bites *her*, not the other way around. *She's* bound to *him*. The magic occurs inside her body. But it affects him as well. The submission becomes permanent, and it crosses over even stronger to your human form. And that works both ways. He must always protect her. She will always be his."

Mia frowned. "Wait... if she's bound to him, but he's not bound to her... does that mean he could mate with more than one female at a time?"

Lucas gave a disgusted look and shook his head. "No decent wolf would do that."

Mia swallowed. She already knew not all wolves were as decent as Lucas. Hell, she hadn't met any *humans* who were anywhere near as fiercely loyal and protective as he was. But regardless of that, she knew what she needed to know: that males could mate more than once. And the mating bond was severed by death. That had to mean... it was at least possible...

He could be her mate.

If he would have her.

She drew in a deep breath. Even if it were technically possible, that didn't say anything about the darkness she knew he still carried about his mate's death.

His mate. She understood now how much power those words held.

Mia laid a hand on Lucas's where it rested on his knee. "I'm so sorry, Lucas. I can imagine how hard it must have been to lose your mate."

He pulled his hand away and rubbed both hands over his face. "I told you, Mia. I didn't *lose* her. She's dead because of me."

"You can't really mean that," she said, pleading with him to let go of whatever ridiculous guilt he was carrying around. "You can't blame yourself for whatever happened. It's like you said. You were her *mate.* You were bound to protect her by this…" She waved her hand around, not really knowing what she was saying. "…this ancient magical bond. Whatever happened, it wasn't your fault."

Lucas stood so suddenly, it nearly rocked her off the couch. He took a stride away from her, then whirled back. Anger was lighting up his face, turning it a blotchy kind of red.

"Do you want to know how she died, Mia?" he demanded. "Is that what you want?"

His anger struck her mute.

But he wasn't waiting for a response. "I let her walk straight into a trap. Why? Because I was *busy.*" His eyes glittered dark and hard and cruel. "Too concerned with SparkTech and proving myself to my father and scoring the next big acquisition. I was too worried about *myself,* so I let her go, *by herself,* to meet up with people I didn't even *know.*" He was shouting by the end, then he turned to pace away from Mia, ending up by the windows overlooking the Bay.

She untangled her legs from the couch and rose up to follow after him. "But you couldn't have known—"

"It's my business to know, Mia." He turned around, fisted hands locked in crossed arms over his chest. "A true alpha would have known. Would have *made sure,* before he let his mate walk into a coven of witches out for blood."

Mia stopped in her tracks. "Wait... what? *Witches?*"

"There are a lot of things you don't know about our world. *Obviously,*" he said bitterly. "I'm sure you're already wishing you could go hide, go back to being a recluse again. Dragging you into our world is just one more example of how very much I am *not* any kind of real alpha anymore."

"I... I don't understand." Were there really witches in the world? She supposed it wasn't that ridiculous, given that shifters were certainly real, and the whole shifting thing was definitely some kind of magic... but she had never heard of it before. He was right—there was so much she didn't know.

"Well, let me lay it out for you." His voice was so cold it sent a shiver down her back. "So you'll know exactly who you're putting your trust in to keep you alive where other supernatural creatures are concerned."

"Lucas, I—"

"Oh no," he cut her off. "You need to hear this."

She held still, frozen by his words. Now that he had started, he wasn't going to stop.

"They were posing as a startup. One we might be interested in acquiring. This was our first meetup, but they had impeccable credentials. Then again, they *would*, given they were *witches*, and could conjure the illusion of just about anything that suits their purposes." His voice dripped an icy hatred. "Tell me, Mia, do you know how the police obtain both the human and wolf DNA of shifters they bring into custody?"

"I… what?" The sudden shift in topic and his angry, pointed words made her feel like the floor was tipping.

"The police bring in *witches*. They have a spell that forces the shift. And for that kindly assistance, the police look the other way on a lot of dark magic and witch mischief. Like wolf hunting."

Mia braced a hand against the window they were huddled next to. "You mean witches hunt wolves… but why?"

"The heart of a wolf is a powerful thing, both physically and magically. Especially the heart of a mated female wolf. Even more so for the mate of an alpha. She carries the strength of them both in her heart."

Mia could see his eyes glass over, but he was so tightly bound, arms locked over his chest, that she didn't dare touch him.

"The witches lay a trap, they catch a wolf, and then they…" He swallowed back a pain she couldn't even imagine. "They cut out her heart."

"Oh my god, Lucas." Mia's hand flew to her

mouth and trembled there, tears springing to her own eyes.

A growl rumbled inside his chest, and his words came out in angry bites. "They forced her to shift so they could have it in wolf form, where it was most powerful. By the time I found her, they were long gone. There was no way to even prove a murder had occurred."

Mia gasped, horrified. "Because she died in wolf form."

"They didn't just take her heart, Mia. They took mine as well." His dark eyes were filled with so much pain she could hardly look into them without sobbing herself.

He nodded at the horror on her face. "So now you understand how deeply I failed to protect her. And why I will never, ever fail someone like that again." He straightened and unlocked his arms. "I've arranged for a bodyguard to come watch over you. You'll be much safer in his hands. He'll arrive on Monday. Until then, I will do everything in my power to keep you safe."

Mia's heart was too drenched with pain for her to speak.

He peered into her eyes for a long moment,

then said, "I will guard you, Mia. But I will never claim you, or anyone, ever again."

With that, he brushed past her and marched to the couch. In silence, he gathered his papers and laptop and strode toward the bedrooms at the back of their suite.

The door slammed behind him.

Chapter Fourteen

Lucas didn't leave his bedroom in their hotel suite for the entire night, but Mia heard him howling in the wee hours of the morning. He must have shifted… no human throat could make that noise. Or sound so heart-breaking. If she thought he would have let her in, she would have banged on his door, but she knew he wouldn't.

If he was *wolf* in there… she wasn't even sure she *should* go in. His anger the night before had been a rake of white-hot claws across her heart, and she wasn't sure if he would be entirely in control of his beast. The one she heard was… *broken.*

So broken, she finally understood.

His mate had been brutally murdered by witches, all while he was magically bound to protect her. He didn't say it, but it wasn't just a broken magical bond that grieved him: his tender love for his wife was like a soft cloud around the words he used to describe her. Now that Mia understood this mating thing—this claiming process that wasn't just calling dibs on the last piece of pizza, but a profound emotional, chemical, and magical bond— she got why it had devastated him. And was still destroying him, even now.

She had felt that yearning for a mate herself, the wolf inside her own skin instinctively reaching out for it—and she was only half wolf with barely any grasp of how pack life worked. But she understood why her wolf was drawn to him now. He was an alpha. Her instincts would drive her to mate with the strongest male around—that bond would give her the healthiest children—and Lucas had literally dropped into her life, saved it, and looked damn fine naked. Not to mention what he could do to her in that state... the human part of her certainly approved. But maybe... just maybe... Lucas was right.

Maybe he wasn't the right mate for her.

There were other shifters in the world, and they weren't all criminals like she had thought before. There were even other alphas, like Lucas's father, who were good and kind. Who saved scared college girls from their own kind in darkened alleys, then moved heaven and earth to keep protecting her. It appeared there were plenty of packs in the city… some were awful, but maybe there were other friendly ones, too. Or perhaps there was a wolf inside the senior Mr. Sparks' pack who would be a more suitable mate for her. It was at least *possible*.

Her wolf snarled at that thought, but Mia pushed her back, deeper inside her mind. What did her wolf know? She was an *animal* for god's sake! Her wolfy instincts wanted to rut with the hot alpha that she knew—Mia got it, she even understood it, and her own human sexual cravings were far too happy to accommodate those instincts—but she was more than just an animal driven by lust and an innate desire to mate. She was *human*. And one thing she understood about humans was that when their hearts were broken, they really didn't need rebound sex or another hot body to jump in the sack with… what they needed was a friend.

If nothing else, she could be that for Lucas.

Outside their hotel window, the early morning sun inched its way across Seattle. Their suite faced the Bay, so the light was still gray-blue, reflected between the shadows of the skyscrapers on the water. Mia opened the blinds to let all of the natural light in, then she thumbed through an order guide for breakfast. She was no good at cooking, so it was fortunate the hotel had room service. In fact, given the five-star accommodations Lucas had set up for her, she was sure the food would be amazing. And feeding a hurting heart was a good place to start.

She tapped in the number for the kitchen. "Hi," she said quietly, just in case her voice carried. Lucas's door was still shut tight. She had changed out of her pajamas into regular clothes—just jeans and t-shirt. She was saving Jupiter's fancy borrowed clothes for work.

"I'd like two orders of your supreme breakfast with waffles and orange juice, please." She waited for them to repeat it back. "Thank you." She set the phone back on the cool marble of the kitchenette counter.

The soft click of a door sounded from the bedrooms.

Lucas stood outside his door, squinting at her. His hair was extreme bed head, practically standing straight up on one side, and he was still in a t-shirt and sleep pants.

"You ordered breakfast." His voice was thick like he was still waking up.

She could imagine he probably hadn't slept much, at least not until the howling stopped. "I'm sorry if I woke you."

He frowned and shook his head, his bare feet padding quietly toward her. When he reached the kitchenette, he scrubbed his face with both hands then braced them on the counter. "I'm sure you didn't get any sleep last night. Not with all the…" He waved a hand vaguely back toward his room.

"I have no idea what you're talking about," she said brightly. "I was watching B-grade horror movies all night. You would not believe how fake those screams can be."

One side of his mouth lifted, and he shook his head again.

"Sit down," she commanded, gesturing to the dinette table and chairs. "I'll make you some coffee."

He frowned. "I can make it—"

She cut him off with a wave, snagged the container from the elaborate coffee-making-contraption on the counter, and started filling it with water. "Sure you could. But I'm fairly certain this Keurig qualifies as heavy machinery, and I think you're probably too sleep deprived to safely operate it. And it's a cooking skill level that might be challenging for me, but I think I can swing it."

He seemed perplexed by her scurrying to grab coffee mugs and K-cups from the bounteous supply in their suite, but then he just shook his head and lumbered over to the table. It wasn't until he let out a small groan when he sat that she saw the slices in his pajama pants and the still-healing scars underneath. *Still healing scars...* those must be incredibly deep, or else they would have healed already. She stumbled in her haste to look away and attend to the coffee machine. She focused on sliding the water container back into place and starting the first cup, then gripped the counter and tried to calm her thudding heart.

He had hurt himself last night.

Her wolf surged under her skin, a protective-ness welling up that wanted to send her back into his arms—to soothe him, kiss him, melt away the pain that drove him into such a frenzy that he would sink his own claws into his body to stop it. Only her grip on the counter kept her in place. She had to wrench her hands off the stone in order to put a second K-cup in the Keurig and start it again for another cup.

Keeping away from him might be harder than

she thought. *Really* hard. But he didn't need her pawing all over him. He needed a friend. And she had to give him what *he* needed, not just what *she* wanted. That's what a good friend did. She hadn't had many of those, and none who understood what it meant to be a shifter, but she could do this for him. She *would* do it.

And she'd keep her hands to herself in the process.

When the second cup was done, she brought both to the table and set one in front of him, taking the seat opposite. The coffee was too hot for her, so she just blew on it and set it down.

She wanted to catch his eye, but he was studiously staring at his mug. When he finally set it down, they both spoke at once.

"Lucas, I—"

"I'm sorry I—"

They both stopped, and he finally met her gaze. His eyes were shot with red and watery.

"You look like hell," she said.

"Good morning to you, too." But he was holding back a smile.

"I'm sorry for yesterday—"

"You've got nothing to be sorry for, Mia." His voice was back to being rough. "None of this is your fault. Or even your concern. I'm the one who should apologize for being such a—"

"Lucas," she said softly. His gaze was caught by hers, and she wasn't letting go until he let her speak. "You lost your *mate*. Don't apologize for being torn up about that."

He seemed like he wanted to say something, but couldn't.

Which worked well because she wasn't done. "I can't imagine how hard that had to be. Hell, I barely know anything about how all this shifter stuff works, much less what it's like to have a mate. But it's not hard to see this isn't the right time for you to have another one. So, I just wanted to say sorry for not understanding that before. But I do now."

He looked away from her, shifting in his chair and pressing a fist to his mouth.

Mia held her breath, afraid maybe she'd overdone it. Or just made him feel worse.

"So…" she said lightly, hoping to bring some bit of levity back to all of this. "I promise not to try to jump your insanely gorgeous body anymore." That drew him back. A smile seemed to be fighting its way onto his face. "Well, you know… unless you *ask* me to. Very nicely. Roses would be good."

He let out a laugh, but the pain under it made her wince.

She let the humor fade out of her voice. "There is one thing I would like from you, though."

The haggard seriousness returned to his face like a landslide. His dark eyes studied her.

"Other than keeping me safe, of course. I don't want to put you and your family in any more danger." She wrapped her hands around her coffee, trying to find just the right words.

He waited.

The small wrinkles at the corners of his eyes had softened, and her heart did a small skip with that observation. Lucas had a lot going on underneath his skin. Some of it seemed deep and primal, like the wolf who howled half the night. Some of it was right at his fingertips, as he showed so readily when he spent a night introducing her to a deep kind of pleasure she hadn't known before. There was so much *to him* that she really wanted to know. Keeping their relationship at the *just friends, no benefits* level was really going to be difficult. Especially if he kept looking at her the way he was now, with an amount of infinite patience. Waiting for his chance to care for her. To figure out the one thing he could do for her. There was an incredible kindness to that... he couldn't know the effect it had on her.

She cleared her throat. "I want to learn more about being a wolf. I feel like I have a whole... *life-time* to catch up on."

He surprised her by reaching across the table and taking one of her hands. He held it gently with just his fingertips. She almost jolted her hand out of his.

His smile was so gentle... "I can't imagine what it would be like growing up as a shifter with no one to guide you. You're a very strong person, Mia."

That rushed heat her face. "I don't know about that."

"I do." He was looking at her that way again, as if he saw something in her face, understood it, appreciated it... only she had no idea what it was. It made her squirm a little in her chair, and she didn't understand that reaction either. She pulled her hand back, even though her wolf snarled a complaint. Touching him just made it more difficult to keep her thoughts trained on helping *him,* rather than helping *herself* to a really big bite of Lucas deliciousness.

Damn, this was not going to be easy.

She wrapped both hands around her mug, using

her coffee as an excuse to reclaim her hands. "How does this pack thing work, anyway?" She stared at the dark, filmy swirls of inky liquid, then looked up. "Do you have to be born into one? Or do they ever, you know, adopt new shifters? Like, maybe ones who don't have a pack of their own?"

He smiled.

The squirm in her seat worked all the way up to her shoulders. It was pretty obvious what she was asking, but it would be really helpful to know her options. Apparently, a lot of her attraction Lucas had to do with her instinctual drive to *belong*, not just the magnetic effect of his insanely masculine presence or the intense sexual promise of his bed. Maybe she could satisfy that first part just by finding a true pack to join.

And then, maybe a mate from there…

"You probably could join my father's pack just by bringing him some coffee one morning and dropping your tail."

Her eyebrows flew up. "Dropping my *tail?*"

His laugh was sudden and light. It was good to hear, although she wasn't entirely sure he wasn't laughing at her.

"Sorry," he said with a mischievous smile. "It means submission."

"Ah, right. Dropping your tail." She pictured the Red wolves submitting to Lucas in the alleyway. "See? I don't even know the lingo here." She took a sip of coffee to buy herself a moment while he grinned at her cluelessness.

Was he serious? Would his father take her into his pack if she asked? Of course, she would have to submit to him… a growl from her wolf told her that might not be as easy as it sounded. Her inner beast had already, in her weird wolfy way, imagined herself submitting to Lucas. Given Mia would have to be in wolf form to submit to anyone… it might be hard to convince her wolf to submit to someone other than him.

Mia set her cup down. "Why would your father take me into his pack?"

Lucas leaned back in his chair, looking more relaxed now. "He's already extended pack protection to you." He gestured with his hand like this was obvious. "And that was when he thought you were human, before he met you. Now…"

Mia shook her head, frowning. She wasn't following. Why did that make a difference?

"He likes you, Mia." Lucas smirked.

"I guess that would be an important part of the Join the Pack application," Mia said lightly. "Liked by the alpha: check!" She frowned again. "Although honestly, I've been nothing but trouble. I'm not sure why he would like that."

Lucas chuckled, but it was a knowing kind. Like he was in on some wolfy secret that she wasn't privy to. "He's an alpha, Mia. We usually like challenges." He winked at her, and her insides did a somersault in response. He really needed to not do things like that, not if he expected her to keep her hands to herself. Before she could respond, he rose up from his seat—gingerly, like his self-inflicted wounds were still paining him—and took his mug with him. "While we're waiting for breakfast to arrive, I'm going to get started on that report again. My father's not going to be happy if I don't have something for him soon."

She rose up, grabbing her mug too. "But he's not your alpha anymore, right?"

Lucas's lips turned down, but his voice was still even. "No, but I do work for him. And this job is more than just a job right now." He gave her a sideways look.

"Right," she said. "But after this job, Lucas…"

He had already started toward the bedrooms to retrieve his work stuff, but he paused mid-stride. "Yes?"

"I want you to teach me more about being a wolf."

He smiled broadly. "That, Ms. Fiore, would be my pleasure."

She flushed, but he didn't seem to notice. Just turned away and strode toward his room with a lighter step than before. She hoped whatever he had in mind wouldn't be some kind of torment for her as she tried to keep her side of the bargain.

But at least he seemed happier again. And that made even her wolf hum with approval.

Chapter Fifteen

L∪CAS RUBBED HIS FACE AND SHOVED THE BREAKFAST dishes away to make room to spread out the Loop-Source market analysis. For the last two hours, he'd been sitting on the floor, his scribbled pages and laptop taking up the entire living room table and half the floor in Mia's hotel suite. The dishes teetered at an unseen edge, buried under the mess, and Mia caught them before they crashed to the floor. Lucas sent her a grateful look... which lingered too long as he watched her sway into the kitchen with them. She was young, but she was all woman with that walk. And her jeans rode her hips the way he wished his hands could. Or possibly his claws, if he was gentle... He grimaced. *That thought was straight from his wolf.*

He closed his eyes and had to physically shake that thought-train from his head. The sooner he was done with this project, the sooner he could leave Mia in the hands of a bodyguard more capable than him… and less likely to be distracted by her every movement.

Besides, Mia made clear she didn't want anything like that from him anymore… and with good reason. He'd been so lost in his wolf last night, he was afraid he'd wake up to find her gone. Frightened off. Instead, she'd ordered breakfast and *apologized*. As if any of this was her fault. And now she was trying to help him work the LoopSource deal. He already knew he was too broken to be a decent alpha for anyone… but the more he looked, the more he saw Mia becoming the female alpha she was destined to be. He didn't want to screw that up by embroiling her any further in this Red pack business.

He tried to focus on the market analysis before him, but the lack of sleep and the distraction of her scent as she swayed back from the kitchenette neatly scrambled his thoughts again. He groaned and scrubbed a hand over his face for the second time in two minutes.

"Do you want me to manufacture another cup

of coffee with the Coffee Machine of Awesome-ness?" she asked.

"If I have any more coffee, I'm going to crawl out of my skin."

She pretended to contemplate his words. "It *would* be tough to do market analysis as a wolf."

"Ha ha." He looked up at her, hands on hips, smirking down at him. "Anyway, I'm not sure how much further analysis is going to help. LoopSource has a good idea, a solid platform, but there's a lot of competition in mobile app creation. There're at least two very strong players in that space and a dozen smaller ones like LoopSource. I'm just not seeing how that plays out well for a company that's still two guys working out of a basement." Lucas didn't know how much she could track with the tech-speak, but it helped him to just say it out loud. There was definitely room for doubt in this deal.

"Seems to me like the key is ease of use." She settled on the couch, close enough that a small wash of her scent reached him. It was a clean-scrubbed smell laced with the faint crispness of soap. He chose this hotel because of its lack of perfumed soaps and cleaning products, along with a killer view, and decent room service. But being here with a woman who appreciated those things as well rumbled a dangerously familiar feeling inside him.

He forced himself to look away from those sparkling blue eyes and focus on the work. "Ease of use is key, but I think that's really just table stakes," he said, gently. He didn't want to discourage her: it was a good point. "Everyone who wants in on this game has to be easy for the end user. I think the functionality of the apps is what's most important. And I'm not sure LoopSource has enough differentiation there."

"You're thinking in terms of business usage." She edged a little closer, propping her elbows on her knees and leaning over her clasped hands. "But this is for your everyday college student or mom or weekend warrior who wants to create an app for their hobby or friends or ten-year reunion. Ease of use is paramount." Her eagerness was infectious.

He twisted to face her from his spot on the floor. "But it has to *do* something, or it's no use at all."

She bit her lip, which made his wolf sit up and take notice, but the human part of him worried again that he had discouraged her. She was his *intern*, for god's sake. Even if he couldn't be her alpha, he could at least try to not completely suck at being her boss.

Before he could come up with something more reassuring, she continued, "Maybe I don't really understand how it all works. But that's just it—I don't have to. The tech guys will figure out how to add cool features. And once it's out there, people like me will say, *Hey, idiots, why don't you add a button here?* And they will."

Lucas's eyes went wide. "They could crowd-source the functionality." His mouth hung open... why hadn't he seen that? It was precisely the kind of idea that SparkTech could bring—together with funding—to make the acquisition a value-add for both parties. "Mia, that's perfect."

She smiled shyly, and it flushed a warm feeling through him. It was no mystery why he had been so distracted this last week. He had a very strong urge to kiss her right then, but instead, he rose up, closed his laptop, and scooped up as many of the papers as he could carry. He wouldn't need the analysis anyway: now he had the core idea he'd been missing all along.

Mia frowned. "What are you doing?" She was looking up at him in a puzzled way that just made her lovely face even sexier. He gave in momentarily and dropped a kiss on her cheek.

"We're going to tell my father your brilliant

idea."

Her pale cheeks flushed pink. He couldn't tell if it was the kiss or the compliment, but getting a reaction like that from her was more dangerous than the kiss itself.

"So you think SparkTech should make an offer?" she asked, eyebrows raised.

"As long as they have a solid base of easy-to-use interfacing, you're absolutely right—the value-add of the functionality will be driven by the market. And there's still a lot of game left to be played there: customized tools not just for retail, but for all kinds of users. Small businesses. Non-profits. Large corporate customers would require more and could be a separate, spun off business, eventually. The point is, it's not what LoopSource has *now*... it's what they're going to have in the future."

"But it's still a risk," she said, frowning. "There's no way to know for sure they'll be able to come through on the tech side."

"And that's just the right time to get in on a deal," he said. "Besides, my father *wants* to do this deal. And so do I. Letting those bastards in the Red pack get their hands on another startup with a bright future that might feed their enterprise is the last thing I want to do."

That made her smile again, and his heart lifted even further. His wolf pawed the ground, wanting a repeat of the kiss. And more. Instead, he took her hands and lifted her from the couch.

"Let's go tell my father now," Lucas said gently. "But as soon as we're done, I'm taking you out to learn a little bit more about being a wolf."

Then he had to turn away and busy his hands with packing up the rest of his things before that broad smile on her face could get him into any more trouble.

THERE WERE FAR TOO MANY WOLVES IN HIS FATHER'S office for Lucas's taste. He'd stumbled in on an impromptu joint pack meeting when he'd brought Mia to SparkTech—and a pack meeting on a Sunday at noon, when they should all be home with their families, was not a good sign.

But his father had readily agreed to hear him out on his LoopSource analysis. Which left Lucas giving his acquisitions pitch in the middle of a room filled with two packs—his father's and his brother Llyr's, both of whom had absorbed several of Lucas's pack members when Tila was killed.

Mia kept close to Lucas's side, but her eyes were wide. She had to know they were all shifters, and this must be more than she'd ever seen in one room together. She returned their stares with nervous attempts at a smile. Lucas could practically see their wolves' ears perking forward. They had to know by now she was an unmated female with no pack, and he clearly wasn't the only male who felt the power of her brilliant blue eyes. Meanwhile, Mia didn't seem to have any idea of the effect she was having on them. He tried to ignore the thrashing his wolf was giving him for allowing all that attention to fall on her, instead focusing on going over the Loop-Source numbers, as well as the reasoning in favor of the acquisition, with his father.

Llyr stood to one side of their father's desk with his beta, Colin. Both were only two years older than Lucas, and Llyr had always been the true alpha son their parents had hoped for. Oldest, tallest, strongest in wolf form, a natural from the start. Even as pups, Llyr always fought harder and demanded submission from both Lucas and Lev. Not that it mattered as children, but it was clear he was destined to have his own pack. He teamed up with Colin as teenagers, splitting from his father's pack even before they went to college. Their father allowed it, no doubt encouraged it. Everyone knew one day Llyr would run the family business. Probably with Colin by his side, unless his beta decided to make an attempt at becoming alpha of his own pack someday. Llyr had already found an alpha female from another pack to mate with, and they were working on building a family of their own, but Colin was still single.

And the way he was sniffing at Mia made Lucas's wolf claw him from the inside out. Or maybe it was his imagination: his wolf's jealousy for something he couldn't have. Both Llyr and Colin wore appropriately grave looks for the discussion at hand. Lucas suspected they had been the leads for the incursion on the Red pack territory ordered by his father.

On the opposite side of his father's desk was his father's long-time beta, Rent. He was as old as his father but less wise. Of the two, Rent had always been the muscle, and his father had been the brains. The elder beta had never taken a mate, and he was the only single wolf in the room who ignored Mia and kept his arms locked and his scowl fixed for Lucas's pitch.

To Rent's right, Lucas's brother Lev stood at attention along with several other young males from his father's pack. They were the next generation that would be called upon for a pack war, should there be one. Lucas hoped his father had at least held Lev back from the previous incursion—and if there were a pack war, Lucas would insist on taking Lev's place in it. Lev was the youngest brother, but old enough to fight—Lucas just couldn't stand the thought of it. Their mother would be an ally in keeping his brother out of any wolf fight, he was sure, but all the better if he could prevent it in the first place. Lev flicked soft-hearted looks of concern over Mia, then elbowed one of his pack mates for the too-hungry look he was giving her. Lev's glances were the only ones she was gathering that didn't infuriate Lucas's jealous inner beast. He knew his younger brother would defend Mia as if she was Lucas's mate.

It was the rest of the unmated wolves who were drooling over her that concerned him.

"So," Lucas said, trying to summarize the lengthy pitch he had just given. "I think making an offer on LoopSource is a smart investment. With our help, they have the potential to become a serious player in the mobile app platform design market."

His father glanced only briefly at the sketched

notes and graphs Lucas had spread out before him, then turned his steady gaze on his middle son. "You're sure, Lucas?"

"As sure as I can be, sir."

Llyr unfolded his arms and stepped forward, encroaching on Mia's space next to Lucas. "Maybe you could be a little more sure than *that*, little brother. If I'm going to be sending my pack to defend our right to make this deal."

All the hairs on the back of Lucas's neck stood on end. His wolf snarled with bared teeth for his alpha older brother. It wasn't so much that Llyr was questioning him. Or that he called Lucas *little brother*. It was the narrow-eyed look he was giving Mia as if he blamed her for the situation with the Reds. Colin, Llyr's beta, hung back a half step, but he had even more eye action for Mia, covering her head to toe with a look that made Lucas curl up a fist. Mia had been silent during the entire pitch, but then Lucas realized she was meeting Colin's visual inspection with one of her own.

Lucas's wolf was ready to rip out Colin's throat.

He forced himself to keep cool. To his hulking older brother, he said, as calmly as he could manage. "Not your call."

His brother met his stare with one that looked ready to start a brawl right here.

Lucas decided he would go for Colin's neck first.

"The call is mine," their father said, breaking into their staring contest. "But I want to be sure as well. Lucas, go over these numbers with me one more time. Everyone else, out."

The bottom dropped out of Lucas's stomach as the pack members around him restlessly jockeyed their way toward the door. "Mia should stay," he said quietly to his father. "She helped with the analysis. The key ideas were hers."

His father's tightly drawn face softened a little, and he threw a smile to Mia. "I'm sure that she did. But I need to talk to you alone, Lucas."

The tension inside him ratcheted up three more notches. Lucas threw a mad glance around the room and caught Lev's eye. His brother broke with his pack mates and hurried over to Mia's side.

"Right this way, new girl!" Lev said brightly, one hand on her elbow, the other gesturing to the door. The sea of wolves parted to let her go through. Mia shot a look back at him, but she didn't argue as Lev led her out of his father's office.

Lucas trusted Lev, implicitly, but his wolf still growled as he watched her go.

Chapter Sixteen

LEV STEERED MIA BY THE ELBOW, GUIDING HER PAST the aimless pack of shifters that had spilled out into the common room outside the elder Mr. Sparks' office. He urged her quickly into her own office. It was darkened, but as soon as he closed the door behind them, Lev scurried to tap some controls by the door. The blinds must be on some kind of automatic control because they parted, slowly spilling the noontime sun into her office and setting it aglow. Lev watched the parting blinds like he'd never seen window treatments in action before in his life.

Mia glanced over her shoulder toward the common room. "Lev? Is there some reason why we're hiding out in my office?" Through the frosted glass, she could see the tall, dark, and sexy figures milling in the open area, waiting to hear the outcome of the conversation that must be raging inside Mr. Sparks' office between the founder and his son. Considering the result would affect them all, she could understand why they were waiting. What she didn't understand was why Lev had hustled her away.

"Oh!" Lev said with a little bit of a jump like he'd just realized he sequestered her away. He shrugged. "The testosterone was getting a little thick in there, don't you think? I figured you'd like a break from all the, you know…"

"All the *what?*" She eyed him as he edged toward her desk and perched on the corner, obviously trying to look casual, but only succeeding in broadcasting massive amounts of awkwardness. Or discomfort.

He dipped his chin. "C'mon, Mia! You're killing me here."

She lifted both hands in the air. "Lev, what in god's name are you talking about?"

He looked at her like he was trying to figure out if she was joking. Then he just shook his head. "Lucas told me you weren't pack-raised, but c'mon new girl. You can't tell me you didn't notice a room full of guys ogling you."

"Ogling?" Her heart took a small skip, and she looked back toward the common room again. "Which one?" She was kind of hoping he meant the tall, green-eyed one who'd been checking her out.

"Which one?" Lev gave her an incredulous look. "More like which one *wasn't*. The answer to that, by the way, is *me*. Because I'm not an asshole, and Lucas is my brother and my alpha——" He stopped, and his jaw worked. "Well, he *used* to be my alpha, and to me, that still counts for something."

Mia's heart melted a little with Lev's devotion. He was still there for Lucas... and, from what Lucas had told her, Lev was there when his brother needed him most as well. It ran a hot flash of guilt through her for the thoughts she'd had in Mr. Sparks' office. She'd never seen so many extremely hot men in one place at one time... and they were *all* shifters. Even the elder Mr. Sparks was handsome and commanding, but the younger wolves... like Lucas, they wore their power in their tall frames and good looks. His brother Llyr was just as handsome as Lucas, only without the soft underside Lucas had demonstrated time and again. Llyr was simply pure *power*. He had an almost overwhelming presence when he was standing still, listening to Lucas make his pitch, but when Llyr spoke... he electrified the room with tension. Lucas had risen immediately to his bait, and that had made her heart pound with fear for him. She couldn't imagine the two hulking brothers in a fight without someone being seriously hurt. Or even killed.

But then the other wolf—Lucas had introduced him as Colin—had raked her with his gaze. It was impudent, and a little terrifying in the context of the high-voltage situation, but her heart rate had quickened with something very different than fear. His green eyes had blazed at her with a possessiveness had flushed her with a trembling heat. That had alarmed her, simply because she would have died of embarrassment if a room full of male wolves had smelled anything like arousal on her. So she'd impudently thrown that look right back at him... but it only seemed to inflame him more. The dead sexy look on his face had been filled with promises...

"Earth to Mia." Lev snapped his fingers in front of her face.

She flushed hot again, caught reliving that intense moment.

His shoulders fell. "Don't tell me all those pheromones were getting to you."

"What?" she asked, focusing on him and trying to rein in her thoughts.

"Look, I'll spell it out, because you're not, you know, pack-raised." He shifted uncomfortably on her desk again, then stood. "Female wolves are kind of rare."

That took her back. Lucas had never mentioned anything like that. "They are?"

"Yes. To begin with, female shifters aren't born at the same rates as males. I don't know why, something to do with shifter hormones and gestation periods and... whatever. I'm not a scientist. And it's not like there's hard data on this, but everyone knows the ratio is pretty whacked. Something like 60-40, males to females. So females are scarce to begin with, and then... well, males shifters aren't the only ones that can't wait to get their hands on them." He took a deep breath and let it out slow. "Did Lucas tell you what happened to his mate?"

Mia winced. Lucas's revelation, and the howling night that came afterward, still haunted her. "Yeah.

It's awful, Lev. I want to... I'd like to help him... heal. If that's possible."

Lev's face softened. "I knew you were good people, new girl. Knew it from the first moment I saw you."

She gave him a shy smile, then frowned again as she thought it through. "I thought what happened to her was just a freak thing. I mean how often are wolves hunted for their..." She couldn't bring herself to say it, just swallowed down the sickness at the back of her throat.

The corners of Lev's mouth turned down. "More often than you might think. Especially the females. They... *you*... carry a lot of powerful magic in your body, Mia, and not just in your heart. Witches hunt wolves, female ones in particular, but even if female wolves weren't hunted, ones like you would still be in high demand."

"What do you mean, *ones like me?*"

He twisted his mouth to the side, thinking. "How can I say this? You're one hot property, new girl. Really hot."

"Lev!"

"I don't mean sexy..." He tipped his head to her. "Although of course you are ridiculously that as well."

Mia shrank inside herself. "Can we talk about something else?"

He shook his head like *she* was the one being ridiculous. "Okay… let me put it this way. There are two types of betas. The kind, loving, and adorable type… like me." He gave her a cheesy grin.

A laugh erupted from her, and she quickly covered her mouth. "Sorry."

"No, it's true." He grinned again, more naturally this time. "I haven't found the right mate yet, but I will. And when I do, she'll be a beta like me. Kind, loving, and very, very hot. Also adorable."

Mia could barely hold in the laugh this time, but she managed.

Lev's humor faded a little. "And then there are betas like Llyr's beta, Colin."

Mia's laugh flew away under the return of her flush.

Lev nodded in a knowing way. "Colin's really an alpha in waiting. All he needs is the right mate, and he could form his own pack. If he could take another alpha's girl, that would be quite the score, but if she was an alpha female in her own right—"

"Wait, what?" she cut him off. "Take an alpha's girl?"

Lev had that awkward look again. "Aren't you and Lucas…? I heard you and he were…"

Mia bit her lip. "It's complicated."

He scowled. "You mean he's an asshole."

"No!" She held her hands out. "I mean… I don't think he wants to be with me. Or I guess with anyone. I hope it's anyone and not just me. Because that would really be… hard…" She was rambling, so she stopped.

He took hold of her hands, which were twisting with each other. "Mia, it's okay. It's not you. It's definitely him. I know he's not… quite ready." His face brightened. "But you have no idea how much better he is with you around. You just gotta stick with him, okay? With you, he might be able to… well, he might come back to us."

By *us*, she knew Lev meant *him*. And Lucas's other pack members. The ones he lost when he lost his mate.

She nodded. "I want that, Lev. I really do."

He smiled broadly, then pulled her into a hug. And it felt so much like *home*, she melted a little more. That was when the door swung open. They broke apart, Lev a little more hastily than her. That brotherly hug just felt so good. But instead of Lucas at the door, it was the tall and sexy wolf who'd painted her with his stare before.

Colin.

He arched an eyebrow, then shot a glare at Lev. "Well, well. I guess being an ex-beta doesn't hold the loyalty it used to."

"Why don't you fuck off?" Lev's voice had dropped an octave, and the words came with a growl.

Colin just looked amused. "Don't worry. I won't tell Lucas you're helping yourself to his girl the moment his back is turned." Then he dipped his head down to bore a look into Lev. Lucas's brother was shorter and leaner, but he didn't shrink under the larger wolf's stare. "Besides, it's time for you to leave."

Lev let out a bitter laugh. "Not happening."

Mia felt frozen through the entire exchange like they were inches away from having the claws come out, and if she said anything, she might just make it worse. Then Colin turned from Lev to her, and his glare evaporated like it was never there. In its place was a smoldering look, the kind he painted her with before. He hadn't said a word to her, but it felt like a kiss and a promise and a hot hand trailing across her body all at once. He was tall and gorgeous and those green eyes…

Her wolf was all bristled out and snarly. *This isn't our alpha.*

Mia knew that, but his stare still made her human knees weak.

Colin took a step closer, extending his hand for her to shake. "It's a pleasure to meet you—"

Lev stepped between them and knocked away Colin's hand. "That's close enough, asshole."

The fury fired back to Colin's face, but he kept his cool. "It's *her* choice, Lev. Not yours. Or Lucas's."

Mia finally found her voice. "Damn straight it's my choice."

Colin's hot gaze snapped back to her, and the corner of his mouth tipped up.

She had a fair guess what choice he was talking about, but in truth, she didn't really have a choice— at least, Lucas wasn't giving her one, not right now. He'd flat out told her *no,* and in spite of what Lev said, she didn't know if his brother would ever be ready for a mate again. And if that was the case, she could do a lot worse than the gorgeous, green-eyed shifter standing before her.

Mia stepped around Lev's body-blockade and held out her hand to Colin. "My name's Mia."

He took her hand, but instead of shaking it, he held it gently but firmly. He turned it wrist up and lightly stroked her palm with his thumb while holding her gaze. It sent lightning bolts racing through her body. His gaze was all for her like Lev had ceased to exist. Lucas's brother had shrunk back, anyway, shoulders caved.

"I know your name, Mia." His voice was commanding, yet smooth, like smoke curling over a steel blade. "It means *Mine*, and that's exactly what I want to make you."

Her entire body heated with those words. The snarling of her wolf reduced to a whimper. He'd barely spoken to her, but he was already claiming her with his words. Something Lucas had consistently refused to do, ever since he knew what she was. Colin, on the other hand, knew exactly what she was and wanted her badly enough to march in and demand it.

It reached inside her and touched a deep need. One even her wolf couldn't muster a complaint against.

"I don't even know you," she managed. It felt weak. Her *knees* felt weak.

He still hadn't let go of her hand. "I can change that." His voice was full of sexual promise, and that just made the rest of her quiver. "Once we're together, Mia, you'll see what I already know: that you belong with me. I'm the wolf you deserve." Without releasing her from his gaze, he tipped his head slightly in Lev's direction. "You don't belong with someone who will always be a beta. You're strong, *Mia mine*. I can see it in your eyes. I can smell it in your lack of fear. My wolf is singing for you— he has from the moment you stepped into that room. A strong wolf like you needs a mate who's just as strong. *Stronger.* You deserve an alpha. And not a broken one."

Mia's heart was pounding so hard, she was afraid he would feel it pulsing through her hand. "I'm the one who decides." Damn, her voice was trembling as much as her knees.

Colin smiled. "The choice is absolutely yours, my queen of wolves." Then he quickly pulled her hand up to his lips, kissed the inside of her wrist, and released her.

A small breath escaped her, but the sound of it was covered by Lev's snarl of disgust. At that same moment, the door opened, and Lucas strode in. Mia gathered her hand back to herself and tucked her arms across her chest. Guilt and powerful surges of attraction warred inside her body, twisting her stomach in knots. She wanted to be with Lucas, and she should try harder to be the kind of friend he needed, too, but there was something magnetic about Colin. Something *primal.* She could too easily picture surrendering to that and never coming up for air again.

Lucas sent glares to both Lev and Colin, and the tension skyrocketed.

"Do you have some news for us?" Mia asked Lucas, her voice still weak. Anything to forestall them from all shifting and going at it right there.

"My father's making an offer to LoopSource as we speak," he said tightly. Then he held out a hand to her. "Come with me. For the next 24 hours, I don't want you anywhere near the office. After that, we can gauge the Red pack's response, and the threat level to you."

Colin's glare for Lucas stepped up a heat level, but Lucas was focused on her, his hand outstretched.

She took it. "Let's go, then."

Lucas towed her from her office and through the common room without another word. His pace was so quick, she nearly had to run to keep up with him. They only paused when they reached the elevators, and even then, he glanced at the door to the stairs, like he was considering jogging down the thirty-two floors.

"Where are we going?" Mia asked to fill the charged silence. "Back to the hotel?"

The sound of her voice seemed to soothe him. His shoulders relaxed, and he turned to face her. "You still want to learn what it means to be a wolf?" There was another question buried in there. Something like, *do you still want to be around me?*

"Yes. Absolutely." She clearly still had much to learn. And she wanted to learn it from *him.*

He smiled, and the tension between them seemed to seep away. "I know just the place."

Chapter Seventeen

THE OLYMPIC NATIONAL PARK... MIA BREATHED IN a giant gulp of air, tasting the earth scents, the multitude of creature smells, the just complete *aliveness* of the place. Her wolf hummed with happiness. Lucas grinned at her from the other side of his car. As soon as he had stopped, she had leaped out of it and run halfway to the trailhead for the hiking path.

The afternoon sun glared overhead, turning the bristly pine trees brilliant green, but the light was dimmed below their branches. The forest was moss-covered and misty and mysterious. The slender dirt path snaked into the underbrush, inviting her inside the wild.

"It's been too long since I've been here," she breathed. They had grabbed sandwiches along the way, gaining some mental and physical distance from the dramatic events at SparkTech. The food had settled her nerves and filled her belly. And now the forest called to her to *run*.

Lucas caught up to her, then beckoned her toward the path with him. "Your wolf needs this connection," he said, a grin still playing on his face as he watched her wide-eyed wonder. "If you attend to your wolf's needs, she'll become stronger, more fully integrated with your human side."

She flashed a look to him. "Is that a good thing?" The echo of his mournful howl the night before still rang in her mind.

He gave a short laugh. "Yes, that's a good thing. You and your wolf are just two parts of you. When each part embraces and respects the other, you're more integrated as a person."

She nodded but wondered if that applied to him as well. He seemed to retreat into his wolf when hurt, and that didn't seem like a good thing. She appreciated his wolf nature, but mostly, she wanted him to be *human* with her. Then again, she wasn't sure what it meant to be *wolf* with him. Her inner beast was too busy yipping with happiness to contribute to that thought.

They had stepped into the attenuated light, the

soft glow of it turning the forest into a fairyland of arching ferns, falling dust motes, and moss-draped branches. A thousand tiny sounds floated in the air, but for the most part, the sighing wind in the branches above them ruled them all. Nature was encroaching on the path, with tendrils winding out to reclaim it and fallen needles carpeting the dirt. As they hiked deeper, she could see a brightness through the trees off to their left. Lucas veered off the path, tromping through the forest and heading for it.

"What's that?" Mia asked.

"A little more breathing room," he said with a smile.

It took a few minutes, but when they reached the edge of the clearing, she could see what he meant: it was a meadow filled with tall grasses past her knee. The flowers were an assault on the nose, and the sun made her shade her eyes until they adjusted, but it was wide and open and beckoning. Lucas stepped out into the thick of it and threw his arms wide, face tipped up to the sun, basking in it. For a moment, she just watched him, fascinated by the unabashed joy on his face.

Then he turned his gaze to her and smirked. "Take your clothes off."

"Excuse me?" she choked.

He stepped through the tall grasses, coming back to her. "You heard me."

"Right here?" She glanced back at the forest they had come through, imagining other hikers on the path.

"No one comes here," he chided. "Correction: no *humans* come here. Trust me, I've spent a lot of time in these woods. This trail doesn't get much use. Plus we're pretty well off the trail."

When she didn't immediately whip off her shirt, unexpectedly shy given they'd already been naked together, he chastised her with a frown. "Do you want to learn about being a wolf or not?"

"I wasn't planning on getting naked to do it." Her hesitation was sounding ridiculous, even to her.

He arched an eyebrow. "Can you shift without getting tangled in your clothes? Or ripping them to shreds?"

"Um… no."

He gestured for her to get on with it.

She sighed and kicked off her shoes. He reached down to whip his shirt off in one quick motion, but he was watching her every move.

She started to unbutton her jeans, but before she slid them down her hips, she said, "Don't look."

"You're kidding, right?" He didn't take his eyes off her.

She inched her pants down and stepped out of them, standing now in just her t-shirt and panties. "I mean it. If we're going to be friends, you can't be ogling my breasts."

"I'm not ogling."

He was definitely ogling. And also unbuttoning his pants. She swallowed and resisted checking him out, but she was pretty sure he was *sans* underwear.

"You're drooling as well," she said.

"Wolves drool. It's what we do." The smirk was firmly planted on his face again.

She grabbed the bottom of her t-shirt. "Don't look. I mean it."

He stopped removing his pants and covered his eyes, one with each hand. "Okay. Not looking."

She pulled the t-shirt off, but by the time she had it over her head, he was watching her again. "Cheater!"

"Guilty." He chuckled and slid his pants down, still watching her.

He was completely naked, while she still had on her bra and panties. He stepped closer, and it was suddenly hard for her to breathe. She thought he might mock her again, but the smile had gentled on his face. She was trying hard not to let her gaze drift down, to see if he was as aroused as she was quickly becoming, but even the sight of his bare chest was making heat gather between her legs. She hoped like heck the bountiful bouquet of the meadow flowers would cover the smell.

He lifted her chin with one finger, bringing her gaze up to his. "No looking." The smirk was back.

"You know, you're really obnoxious when—"

She cut herself off as he reached around and started unhooking her bra. It went slack, and then he slid a finger down each arm, easing the straps off her. She held her breath as he knelt down to remove her panties, using just his fingertips to glide along her skin. Her whole body was trembling with need by the time he stood up again, eyes blazing at her.

"Maybe," she said, breath short, "we can wait on the wolfy part for a bit."

"No waiting." He stepped back, dark eyes still on fire for her. "I want to watch you shift."

She was pretty sure she was blushing from head to toe, but he obviously wasn't going to *touch* her like she achingly wanted him to. There was nothing to do but give him what he asked for.

She closed her eyes and focused on her inner wolf. It took a few seconds because her beast was demanding that she open her eyes again to feast upon Lucas's naked body. Mia forced her wolf's attention back on doing what he wanted.

Your alpha wants you to shift.

When she put it that way, her wolf thrilled with happiness, and the shift happened with wicked speed. It was so fast, it caught her off balance, and she tipped over into the tall grasses surrounding her paws.

When she opened her eyes, she was *wolf.*

Her body had grown more muscular and compact. She clambered up on her four paws, her black fur glistening in the sun. It had been so long since she had shifted, and the shift was so sudden, that her bones and muscles were still settling into place. She stretched out the kinks by bowing low, forepaws straight ahead, digging into the scratchy weeded meadow ground, while her rear and tail were raised high in the air. Then she reversed it, forelegs upright and head raised, hind paws pushed back, tail lowered. A yawn overtook her, but it seemed like everything was finally in place.

I like the show.

She about jumped out of her fur, leaping into the air and landing with teeth bared. A dark brown wolf that had to be Lucas stood facing her, his tongue lolled out, his glittering black eyes trained on her.

She snarled at him, even while admiring the way his fur shone in the sun and the strength of his stance. He was every bit as magnificent as a wolf as he was as a man.

Why thank you.

What in the…? She sat her rump down in the meadow grass, stunned. *You're reading my mind.*

You're kind of broadcasting your thoughts all over the meadow. He dipped his head and walked toward her. *It'll take some time, but you'll learn how to keep them to yourself and only share intentionally.*

This could be embarrassing, she thought.

When he reached her, he rubbed his nose along the side of her face, then gave it a single lick. It welled up such a feeling of comfort that thoughts of shyness flew away. She nudged his muzzle with hers, attempted to lick him, but missed, then ducked her head, feeling foolish again.

He tapped the top of her head with his chin. *If you don't want me to read your thoughts, I'll try to ignore them.* His voice was like a soft whisper in her mind. *But it will make it harder to teach.*

She lifted her head and nuzzled him again. This time she landed a lick on his face. *Teach me what?*

He sat back on his haunches and cocked his head to the side. *How to protect yourself, mainly. If you're ever caught in an alleyway again, I want you to be able to shift and defend. Or at least run.*

She dipped her head again. *Running was probably my only option.*

Then let's see you run, midnight wolf.

Her tail swished the grass, and it embarrassed her that she was *wagging her tail* in response to his pet name. She dragged her head up to look at him. As a wolf, his black eyes were even more beautiful, more mysterious, than in his human form.

Stop admiring my eyes and run.

Run? She glanced around the meadow wondering where she should run *to*, when all of a sudden, he was on her, forepaws knocking her to the ground. Before she knew what had happened, she was pinned. His paws and the weight of his body held her in the weeds, while his bared teeth rasped against the fur on her neck.

No fair! she thought. *I wasn't ready!*

Don't let anyone pin you, midnight. He nipped at her neck, which surged an odd combination of panic and pleasure through her. *You can get hurt in this position.*

As soon as he eased off, she got her legs under

her and *ran*. Bounding across the weeds, she crossed half the meadow in no time. The flowers whipped her muzzle, but it was exhilarating. She thought she had left him far behind, but then something nipped at her tail. She threw a glance back, and he was *right there*. She cut left and increased her speed, galloping across the length of the open space. He was a dozen paces behind now but gaining. Her chest heaved, but she seemed to have more strength, more power, as a wolf than she ever could as a human. She drew on that strength, increased her speed, and dashed toward the forest. He was still a ways behind her when she slipped the boundary of the meadow and plunged into the undergrowth that skirted the trees. Suddenly, all her focus had to be on the forest in front of her. Fallen branches hidden by ferns, rocks large and small, moldering logs she had to jump… it was an insane obstacle course that thrilled her with its challenge. She zigged and zagged until even her wolfy lungs were protesting. Ducking behind a massive lichen-covered boulder, she hid from him, wondering if he would hear her panting in the stillness of the wilderness.

She waited.

Nothing. Not a stirring or a broken twig. A bird twittered high in the branches.

Lucas? she thought. But there was no answer.

She peeked out from behind the rock. The forest was still and barren of wolves. She crept out, her tired legs a little shaky from the run. Her paws made crunching sounds that echoed with each step.

Fear kept her heart racing, even though her body was already recovering from the run. She had lost him. Peering into the dim forest, she realized she had no idea where she was. Or even which direction she had come from. It all looked the same.

She was lost.

A deep and mournful sound worked its way up from her belly and erupted from her snout. Her howl was plaintive and weak. The sound surprised her: both because it happened at all and because she'd never howled before.

A short rustle behind her was the only warning before he pounced.

He knocked her flat, almost instantly pinning her again. A fern dangled over them, poking at her face. She snarled and snapped at him, but he held her fast.

That wasn't fair, either! She struggled against him, but his teeth went to her neck, holding her in a false death grip. She was completely vulnerable to him.

Her heart pounded, thrilled and angry and excited at his nearness.

Dark wolves don't play fair.

What the hell does that mean? The anger surged up to take first place among her warring emotions, and she struggled against him again.

He released her throat, eased back, and sat on his hindquarters next to her. *It means always watch your back.*

She struggled to her feet, then licked at the fur on her shoulders that was mussed from his rough play. *Lev was right about you.*

How's that? He cocked he head to the side.

You are kind of an asshole sometimes.

He bobbed his head and yipped. It was a wolfy kind of laugh.

She was not amused.

Mia snarled and took off again, zipping past him and heading deeper into the forest. Her annoyance sharpened her focus and fueled her speed. She was flying over rocks and under low-drooping branches. After a minute or two of all-out running, she even outran her anger—now she was flying on adrenaline and exhilaration alone.

She was *wolf:* a midnight shadow flitting through the shrouded forest, breathing in the scent of her home. Each paw-fall was a tiny movement that hardly disturbed the forest. She leaped and landed, crouched and leaped again. Her fur bristled to dispel the heat that was growing inside her from the hard, hard run. But still, she kept going. After several minutes, she saw the glow of a clearing and tipped toward it, wondering how she had managed to circle back without noticing. Her legs were finally growing weak with exhaustion, but she pushed on, wanting to score the victory lap before Lucas realized where she was. When she broke out into the sun, she stumbled to a stop, and her weakened legs nearly folded underneath her.

This wasn't the clearing Lucas had brought her to.

This clearing had *wolves.*

A dozen, big hulking brown wolves who instantly turned toward her graceless crash out of the forest. They were fifty feet away, noses and tails in the air, scenting her. She heard the whispers of their thoughts, but there must be a range to the wolfy telepathy or something, because she couldn't make out individual words.

That is until they all coalesced into one. *Female.*

As a pack, they turned and bounded toward her. She scrambled backward, tripping, falling, her legs failing her. By the time she could right herself and turn back toward the forest, they were closing fast. She ran, but she was weak and tired and slow. The first one nipped her tail, but he was hip-checked away, and it was the second one who pinned her. She went down with hardly a fight or a snarl, her muscles too quivery from her run and her mind too terrorized by the onslaught to resist.

He stood over her, holding her down, hot breath puffing across her muzzle.

Well, hello beautiful.

It sent chills through her and bristled out every last hair on her body.

Chapter Eighteen

Lucas hung his head, shaking it. Even in wolf form, he was an idiot. He shouldn't have scared her off like that. She wasn't used to that kind of playing, and he probably just freaked her out. Besides, she wasn't *his* plaything anyway. He should have respected her more than that.

Damn it. What was wrong with him?

He picked up his head and scanned the forest again. He'd followed her scent for a while, but then he'd lost it to some other wolf tracks that had smashed down a good trail of their own through the forest. A pack of some kind had come through recently. It was a few hours old, so he wasn't too concerned, but it fouled her scent well enough that had to hunt around to pick it up again. Meanwhile, she was getting farther away and spending more time thinking he was an asshole.

Not that she was wrong about that.

He swept another circle around the spot where he'd lost her scent. Then another. Then a still wider one. Finally, he detected that fresh-scrubbed-with-soap scent that was hers. He trotted a smaller circle around that until he picked up the next place she had touched down in her sprint. She must have really been pissed—the distance between her scent markers was huge. She had to have been flying through the forest. He growled and took off in that direction, nose keen to follow her trail.

It took about ten minutes before he heard the yips. And the growls.

He threw himself into a flat out run. Up ahead. A clearing. As he neared the forest edge, the growls resolved into the clear sounds of a fight. As he broke out of the trees, he could see it was only two wolves, both brown, snarling and stiff-legged, dashing at each other inside a ring of a dozen others. They were sparring, either for position or mates or whatever other damn thing they had decided to have a throw down over. He dared to hope for a moment that Mia hadn't stumbled upon whatever pack gamesmanship was going on, but then his heart seized when he saw her lying at the edge of the ring. She was on her back, legs tucked up, head turned to the side like she couldn't bear to look at her captor. The shaggy wolf above her only had a single paw to her chest, but Lucas knew that pose: he had already pinned her, and now he was just holding her with the threat of doing it again.

And it was possible she had already submitted to him.

A growl erupted in Lucas's chest, along with white hot anger. His claws dug into the meadow floor, scraping the earth and weeds. If she had already submitted to one of them, he would have almost no chance of getting her to leave with him voluntarily. He had to fight every instinct he had to keep from flying in there and attacking the wolf that held her. Only because Lucas knew he would lose, and then Mia would be lost to their pack.

As he fought through the haze of fury clouding his mind, he realized what the pack's fight was about: *her.* Which meant he *wasn't* too late. They were still fighting over who would claim her. Which meant they probably had held off on having her submit, waiting until they had chosen which one would be her mate.

It might still be possible to get her out.

But how?

Lucas pawed the ground, agitation almost making him shift into human form. They hadn't noticed him yet, and he was out of telepathic range, so he had a moment to come up with a plan. But he was a lone wolf. What could he do against a whole pack already fighting to see who could claim a stray female who had wandered into their meeting? Apparently, that made her fair game. Which made Lucas sick, but he knew there were a lot more packs which gave into their dark sides than there were honorable ones like his father's. And even his brother Llyr's.

He couldn't claim territory, either. The Olympic Park was free range by unspoken decree among the local packs. The city was free for marking, and even the larger wilderness in the other national forests, but this area was too frequently visited by wolves and humans alike for anyone to stake—and keep—it for themselves.

And none of that mattered anyway, because he was *just one wolf.*

His frustration boiled up, and he nearly barked out a taunt to pull their attention, bring the fight. He had to try *something.* But he would lose, and it wasn't just his fur at stake. He needed to be smarter than that. He couldn't take them on his own, and his father's and brother's packs were too far away. By the time he left to get them and returned, one of these dark wolves would have already claimed her.

And then she would never leave.

A bleak despair dragged him down until he realized… this pack didn't know he was alone.

Half a plan formed quickly in his mind. He stood tall, tail erect, and marched toward the pack. It didn't take long for them to notice. The two sparring wolves ceased their grappling, and the entire pack came to attention… focused on him. When he came into thought range, the cacophony of thoughts were thrown at him. He ignored them, searching, one by one, until he found the alpha. He was a slightly darker russet brown wolf, older by the looks of his gray-tufted ears, and one of the larger ones, still in his prime.

What's your business, lone wolf? the alpha asked.

Mia twisted on the ground, just finally noticing him. *Lucas! Oh my god, Lucas.*

He ignored her, hoping she could forgive him for that. *My business is the female. There's something you might want to know about her.* This was the tricky part. Projecting a lying thought to another wolf was no small trick. And Mia was a completely open book.

He hoped she wouldn't think anything that would give him away. He blocked out her thoughts just so he wouldn't react to her pleas and fear. The whites of her eyes showed her panic, so he kept his gaze away from her as well and trained on the alpha.

What do I need to know about her? the alpha asked. *Other than she likes to run around without her pack?* The alpha's thoughts drew a round of yips and bobbed heads. Their cruel laughter made Lucas's stance grow stiffer.

She's been claimed already. He thought the lie with as much conviction as he could. The possibility alone should be enough to give them pause.

So she's your mate? The alpha's thoughts were reserved, as he took Lucas's measure. Lucas was a strong wolf, but he certainly couldn't take on an entire pack. The alpha knew this. Yet, it still might sway them, if they had any decency. *I'm sure there's someone here who would be happy fight you for the right to keep her.*

Or maybe not.

Killing him would break the bond, and she would be released to mate again. And that was the hitch. If he said she was his mate, they would just kill him for it... for *her.* He needed more firepower than just himself.

I'm just a beta, he thought. *She's my alpha's mate, and I was supposed to guard her while we're here, but clearly… I've failed. He'll probably have my throat for it. But I can tell you, if you take his mate, he'll bring the whole pack to find her.*

The alpha snarled at him, baring his teeth. It wasn't just the threat of the pack retribution. If she had already been claimed… and it wasn't him… that meant she was bonded to someone else. And as long as she was bonded, her body would reject the bite, the claiming. If they attempted it, at best, it wouldn't take. At worst… it could kill her, as the magic of two males fought within her body to claim possession.

Lucas didn't know their intentions, but it was unlikely that they just wanted Mia for sex. There were plenty of human females who responded to the were-pheromones of shifters and were happy to please a pack, individually or as a group. But female *wolves* were too rare to waste on mere sexual depredation. These wolves no doubt wanted to bring Mia into the pack and have her whelp for their strongest member, whoever could win the right to claim her. It was ancient and brutal and primal… and effective in making the pack strong.

Her death wouldn't serve them in any way. They wouldn't risk it. Maybe.

There was a rise in the snarling and pawing and general disagreement among the pack as they discussed it in their thoughts. Lucas stepped back and sat down, showing his patience for them to decide. If they sought to keep her and claim her, even though they thought it might risk her life… he wasn't sure what he would do.

Probably die trying to prevent it.

The smarter thing would be to leave, get his father's pack, then come back for her. The feral pack would claim her in the meantime. He would have to break the bond by killing the wolf who took her, something he really would have no trouble with. He just didn't know if he could force himself to walk away, knowing what would happen to her. Knowing that another wolf would *have* her. *Claim* her.

The thought made him want to launch himself at the pack, regardless of the consequences. He stiffened every muscle in his body, holding himself back, waiting for the alpha to make his judgment.

When the grumblings finally settled, the alpha nodded to the wolf holding Mia to the ground. He released her. The relief was like a wash of warm water gushing through Lucas. She scrambled to her paws and ran over to him. He turned away before she reached him, afraid she might lick him or nuzzle him in front of the pack. But Mia was smarter than that: he could see her nose trembling, but she simply came alongside him. They trotted at a reasonable pace to the edge of the clearing, every step filled with tension. At any moment, Lucas expected the pack to change their minds and come after Mia. But none of them made a move, apparently content with their alpha's decision.

As soon as Lucas and Mia were back in the forest, he thought, *Run.*

He didn't have to tell her twice. Her trembling legs pounded the forest floor, and she shot ahead of him. But she was running blindly. He surged forward to take the lead and turn her in the direction that would bring them back to their dropped clothes and his car. They ran hard and fast, and the panic in her thoughts tore at him, but they couldn't stop. And it fueled her shaky legs to move faster, so he supposed that was good. He kept glancing back, but it appeared the pack had truly let them go.

When they reached the meadow where they had first shifted, they came to a stumbling stop where they had shed their clothes. She was shaking so badly, she could hardly stand in one place. All of her fur was standing on end. He rubbed his muzzle all over hers, under her chin and on top of her head, trying to calm her. He ached to reassure her by taking her in his arms, kissing her, holding her.

It's all right, Mia. You're safe now. Safe.

Slowly, her heaving breaths tempered. His need to touch her didn't, though.

Mia, honey, shift for me.

He kept contact as her body responded to his command, lengthening and narrowing under his touch. He shifted with her, slowly, as she figured out how to overcome her primal fear and transform into a vulnerable human again. A moment later she was shivering and naked in his arms. He wrapped his arms around her and squeezed her tight. Then his hands roamed her body, touching her everywhere—over her back, up and down her arms, over her shoulders and into her hair—trying to reassure her, cover her with his presence, calm the tremors that had possessed her. It was working. Her hands moved from their tightly fisted spots at the small of his back: she went from holding onto him like her life depended on it to roaming his back and then to sliding up his arms to reach around the back of his neck. The shaking had stopped, and she was melting into him.

Only he was rock hard for her.

With the high voltage tension of freeing her from the pack, and now with her naked in his arms, clinging to him, needing him, his wolf wanted nothing more than to claim her for his own. The length of her soft body was pressed to his, and his erection strained against it, pressing into the silky skin of her belly.

"Lucas." Her breath was hot, and his cock pulsed as her lips brushed the skin of his chest.

God, he wanted her so badly.

He gathered her hair in his hands, burying his face in it and inhaling her scent. "Mia." It was as much a moan as a word. "I can't resist you like this."

She threaded her fingers up into his hair, urging him to bend down and kiss her.

He nuzzled her instead, telling himself he was just reassuring her, that was all it was, after a moment she wouldn't need it anymore, and he would stop… he didn't have to take her hard against the meadow grass like his body, mind, and soul were aching to do.

"Make me yours," she whispered, and her

words caused a literal ache deep in his belly. It was a primal *need* for her that he couldn't believe he would survive without fulfilling.

"God, Mia, don't torment me like this."

"You can have me. You can take me. Right here. Right now. Lucas, I want you to." Her words were like small prayers whispered against his skin followed by kisses that she dropped up and down his chest, branding his heart with every single one. She lifted up on her toes to reach his neck, dragging the hard tips of her breasts against him and stabbing more deeply into that ache inside him.

"I can't. We shouldn't. It's not fair to you." His protests fell from his lips, but they were useless against the wandering of her hands on his skin, pulling his body tighter against her. God help him, her fingers were trailing hot lines against his skin... he reached down to grab her wrists and stop her hands from burrowing between their bodies and seeking out his cock. If she started with that, they wouldn't stop. And he *couldn't* do that to her again. She deserved someone whole, someone who could truly make her his own. Someone who didn't almost lose her to a pack of dark wolves because he played with her in all the wrong ways. Lucas dragged her wrists up to the safety of his shoulders, but she moaned in protest, and that was like a shot of adrenaline directly to his cock anyway.

Then she pressed her hands flat against his chest and shoved him away.

He was so startled by the instant loss of contact, the afternoon breeze suddenly coming between them, that he didn't realize at first what she was doing. But she held his gaze with a scorching hot look and said, "I want you to be my alpha."

Then she shifted.

It wasn't as fast this time, and he watched in awe as the beautiful curves of her body shifted slowly into her wolf form, and the satiny black curtain of her hair grew and transformed into a glistening coat of fur. She held his gaze until she was completely transformed, then she lowered her eyes, bowed her head, arched her back, and dropped her tail.

Submission.

He felt it like a punch to the gut. She bowed before him, giving herself to him, pledging herself, and the alpha inside him raged so hard against his skin that he couldn't help but transform. He fell to all fours as he shifted, then lunged for her, tackling her sideways into the soft grasses of the meadow. He pinned her. Anger and fear and a nameless emotion that put him on the verge of panic gripped him, and he growled in her ear.

Do not submit to me! he thought.

But I want to be yours. I want—

Shift, Mia! Shift now! He put every ounce of command he had into those thoughts. Surprise seized her face as her body shifted without her intending it. It happened so fast that it snapped the magic bond just as it was forming between them. He could feel it, like his heart breaking. Then he shifted quickly back into human form, still pinning her to the ground with his hands on her wrists and his body covering hers.

She squirmed underneath him, still finishing her shift, but he had managed to stop the submission from taking hold. A breath of relief escaped him, even as his chest heaved against hers. If that had happened… if she had submitted to him… he wouldn't have been able to stop. He knew it. That bond, even if only until the next moon, would have been a constant pull to claim her, even more so than he felt already. There was no way he could have resisted it. In fact, he was certain they wouldn't have left the meadow without him taking her from behind and biting her to complete the claim… and then regretting that act for the rest of his life. Mia was a true alpha herself. She deserved a whole, strong alpha to mate with. Someone who could keep her safe. Someone who wouldn't let her run off in a forest by herself to be captured and enslaved by a rogue pack.

That, if nothing else, proved beyond any doubt that he wasn't worthy of her. Claiming her now, no matter how much she thought she wanted it, was the worst thing he could do.

When she had fully shifted, her body stilled. She stared up into his eyes. His cock still dug into her tender flesh, and her body still molded against him, but now he could see her eyes were glassing over with tears. Her wrists were still trapped by his hands to the meadow floor.

"You don't want me." The pain in her voice gutted him.

"No, no." He released one wrist to bring his fingertips to her lips, to stop any more words like those from coming out. "Mia, I want you so badly, I think I might die if I don't have you." The words were out before he realized what he was saying. They stayed her tears, but he instantly wished he could pull them back in. She would think he meant something he couldn't give.

She slipped her free hand around his neck and stared up into his eyes.

"Prove it," she said, and then moved underneath him. A shooting streak of pleasure reminded him that his cock was still wedged between their bodies. She was purposely grinding against him, bucking her hips against his, all while staring into his eyes and daring him to stop her. He dragged her hand from his neck and held both on the ground above her head.

Her eyes widened slightly. His mouth watered for her. Suddenly it was too much for him. He needed her too much. His body was overriding any sense in his head. And hers was swimming in arousal so intense it was drowning him. He would have to sate both their bodies to have any chance of clearing their minds. Then he could explain to her how it had to be. How she had to find someone else to mate with. And soon, or he wouldn't be able to hold himself back any longer. Even as he thought those words, he couldn't picture actually saying them to her. Not without dying inside.

Instead, he edged forward and leaned down to whisper his lips against hers. "You're going to regret saying that, Miss Fiore."

Then he crashed his lips into hers.

Chapter Nineteen

WHEN LUCAS KISSED HER, IT WAS LIKE A DAM HAD broken inside Mia: relief that he had finally given in to her, a literal gush of wetness between her legs, and an ache as her mouth opened to his devouring tongue. His kiss was so hard, so insistent and deep, that her head sunk into the cushion of the meadow grasses beneath her.

At the same time his kiss tipped her head, arching her back with the force of it, his hand slipped between her legs. She gasped with the sudden contact she had been aching for, but his mouth was commanding hers, filling it and controlling it, so she could barely draw in that surprised breath. His circling fingertips sent shocks of pleasure racing through her core, but then he plunged his fingers inside her, and she had to wrench her head away from his to cry out. She was already drenched with wetness, so his fingers easily slid deep, but the sudden and fierce pumping, working her with his hand, made her back lift off the ground, arching in pleasure. His other hand held her head, pulling it back to expose her neck to the small nips he was making along it. She couldn't catch her breath, her whimpers racing to catch up with the mounting pleasure coiling tight inside her. Then she came, suddenly, like she had hurtled over the top of a hill and soared free. She gripped him, holding on, even as her body bucked and writhed against him, riding his hand as he kept working every last shockwave out of her.

She hadn't even begun to come down when he quickly pulled his fingers free of her body's grip. He reached under her with that hand and lifted her hips slightly away from the grass. She didn't have time to ask or think or move before he thrust his cock inside her. He was so large and filled her so completely, just like that night she spent in his bed, but this time he angled her just right so that his cock buried deeper inside her than it had ever been. She cried out and held onto his shoulders. His growls rumbled through his chest while it slid against hers, his face nuzzling against her cheek, his breath panting against her neck with every thrust. Each pound went deeper and slammed his body harder, hitting her right above her entrance, where the tight nub of her sex screamed pleasure with every touch. Her ankles banged against his back, and the grass burned underneath her with each slam, but she clung to him, urging him on with an incoherent mixture of mumbled words, cries of pleasure, and his name.

His muscular grunts gave way to reverent whispers of her name. He thrust faster, begging her to come, but she was already there: she gasped in a ragged breath as her entire body rocked with it, wave after wave, head to toe, a massive sweep of pleasure that pulled her under and buried her. His long growl and the way he gripped her even harder said he had reached his climax too, but she was still lost in her own orgasm, swimming in a haze that disconnected her from every sound or sensation other than the rocking of his body into hers.

The completeness of it filled her. This was how they were meant to be. Always. His body possessing hers. His fingers digging into her flesh as he milked the last of both their climaxes. Her arms and legs wrapped around him, clinging to him as though he were the entirety of her world.

He was kissing her now, and it was the kisses that brought her back to earth. Tender nibbles of her throat and ears. Soft sweeps across her cheeks and eyelids. And finally, his lips found her mouth, eager for him, but in a hazy, love-soaked way, like they had all the time in the world to touch their lips to one another. Her body was humming with so much pleasure that even when he withdrew and put a small space between them, it was as if he was still deep inside.

She lazily opened her eyes. The bright after-noon sun had moved enough to put them in the shadows. Lucas lay next to her, his head propped on his arm. His fingers trailed a ticklish line across her belly, but she didn't stop him, enjoying even that sweet torment. She took a deep breath, all the oxygen she hadn't been able to pull in while writhing and gasping underneath him, then skimmed her hand along the muscular ridges and valleys of his arm, taking it all the way up to his shoulder, and then his face. She touched his lips with her fingertips and wanted to say something. Anything. But she couldn't think of the words that would express how she felt.

Complete. Whole. Belonging to him.

He was looking at her, but he wouldn't meet her gaze, and instead letting his focus wander over her body as if memorizing it. His lips were pressed together, and his brow had furrowed as if he was thinking some great, ponderous thought—although she couldn't imagine what. Her mind was still awash in the aftermath of their lovemaking. And it *had* been lovemaking, even if it was rough and sudden and an urgent release for bodies too stressed by all the events that had plagued them since they met. She could tell by the tender way he held her now, and the way he gave her body just what it needed before. Even his holding back showed his love for her because she knew it was out of concern for her, no matter how misplaced.

He wasn't a bad wolf or a dark wolf or whatever he seemed to think. It was wolves like the ones who captured her, who fought over who could claim her without a second thought or any regard for her wishes on the matter... *they* were the evil ones in the world, the ones who didn't deserve a mate. Not the kind and gentle wolf she was falling in love with.

She blinked, shocked to stillness with that thought. Her inner wolf had been driving Mia to want Lucas to claim her... she knew that. It was a primal instinct, but like Lucas said, her wolf was part of *her*, not some separate thing that existed independent of her. Her desire to *belong* was based on that primal need… and Mia was all right with that. But the idea that the human part of her was falling in love as well… it made tears well in her eyes. It was the perfect pairing of her human and wolf sides, complete in every way in being with him.

His hand had come to a stop, resting on her belly. He still had that ponderous look, biting his lip as he stared at his hand. The torrent of emotions inside her—love, lust, wonder—finally cooled enough for her brain to engage. She remembered he had still refused to claim her. Had actively prevented it by *forcing* her to shift with the command in his voice, something she didn't even know was possible. That both thrilled and terrified her. He still didn't want to acknowledge they were meant to be together, but maybe now, after their frantic coupling in the grass… maybe he was feeling the same things she was.

She tipped her head back to look up into his face. "I was serious, what I said before."

He frowned and dragged his gaze across her body, up to her eyes. "About what?"

He knew damn well about what. "About having you claim me. I want it, Lucas. I want *you.*"

He slipped his gaze back to her belly, but he removed his hand. Now he wasn't touching her at all, and it made her wolf whine. "No, you don't, Mia. It's just lust. You'll get over it."

A chill swept through her body and stabbed an icy coldness into her heart. "Is it just lust for *you?*" she challenged. She tried not to have tears jump so easily to her eyes, but they were already there.

"It doesn't matter." He rolled away from her and sat up, locking his hands around his propped up knees. He still wouldn't look her in the face. "It's just your wolf wanting *someone* to mate with. It's an instinct. It has nothing to do with me."

She propped herself up on her elbows. "How I feel has *everything* to do with you." The tears were leaking from her eyes now, but he didn't see them. He still wasn't looking at her.

His hands clenched each other like they wanted to strangle something. "It doesn't. You'll feel the same with someone else, I promise. And that's what you need, Mia. You need to find a mate. The sooner, the better. And someone who is not me."

"You don't mean that." Her breathing was coming in short gasps. He was just pushing her away again like he did before. Just trying to resist the pull—

"I *do.*" He met her gaze, jaw clenched. "I'm not going to do this with you anymore, Mia. I'm not going to get us both off just because we can't seem to resist it."

Get them both off... Her mouth dropped open, but he wasn't looking at her face anymore. He was staring at her body like their lovemaking wasn't the sacred thing she thought. Like it was a lustful thing he had tried and failed to resist.

His voice turned hard. Commanding. "It's too hard, Mia. You need to find someone else."

Anger surged up inside her, bubbling up like a noxious volcano that wanted to spew out any remnant of him. He had come inside her body moments ago, and now he was not only pushing her away, he was ordering her to *be with someone else.* Her rage was so inarticulate, she just threw a growl at him and scrambled up from the grass where she lay.

How dare he? How dare he treat her like that? When she'd bared her soul to him. Told him she wanted only him. She hadn't said she loved him, but wasn't he the one who said claiming was more powerful than love? But he didn't want that from her, either.

"Fine!" she shouted when the growl allowed her to find her voice. "Finding a mate who *isn't you* should be no problem." She stomped away, toward their clothes, having no idea what she would do next. Her wolf was crying, working up to a howl. But her inner beast was wounded by his rejection, and she didn't fight Mia's anger, the righteous human side that was rising to their defense.

No one had a right to treat them that way.

Mia found their clothes tossed into the grass and scooped up hers. What was she going to do? Get dressed and have him drive her... where? Back to the hotel? To stay with him?

Screw that.

She glanced back: he was still sitting in the grass, head hung. The hurt and angry part of her wanted him to hurt, too. But she couldn't do that. She couldn't lash out at him again—she just didn't have the heart for it. But she sure as hell wasn't going to hang around and give him more opportunities to tell her how she needed to find someone else to screw.

His jeans lay in the grass next to hers. She bent down, fished the car keys out of his pocket, then stuffed them into the pocket of her jeans. She quickly rolled up her clothes.

And then she shifted.

Mia heard him call out her name somewhere mid-shift. He seemed alarmed, but that wasn't her concern anymore. She grabbed the bundle of clothes in her mouth and took off through the forest, toward the path and the car that brought them here. She ran fast, hoping he wouldn't follow, or if he did, that he was too slow to stop her.

She broke out of the forest and shifted on her way to the car. Quickly grabbing the keys, she opened up the car, threw her stuff in, and hopped into it, naked as the day she was born. His wolf bounded out of the forest just as she slammed and locked the door. He shifted as she started the car. He was calling her name, but she just twisted the wheel and spun the car away from him.

She allowed herself one glance back in the rearview mirror to see him standing naked in the middle of the dirt parking lot, watching her go.

Chapter Twenty

Don't drive angry.

It was a line from that crazy Groundhog Day movie, when the groundhog is at the wheel with Bill Murray, driving like a maniac. Mia felt a little like the groundhog, driving down the mountain buck-naked, leaving behind her wolf lover who didn't want to be her lover anymore. Not in any real way, at least. When she was miles away and approaching civilization, she finally pulled over and put on her clothes. She'd left her shoes behind, but she could get new ones.

Especially if her roommate was home.

It was the middle of a Sunday afternoon, and she had no idea if Jupiter was at their dorm, but if

she were, she'd be the perfect person to talk to…
and the perfect shoulder to cry on. Jeeter wouldn't
hold it against her if the whole *moving out* thing
didn't last, but Mia couldn't come back to stay: the
Red wolves were still out there, and now that Spark-
Tech was acquiring LoopSource, she really did need
to lay low for a while.

Just not with Lucas.

It took her well over an hour to reach the
university and her dorm. Somewhere in the middle,
her phone buzzed in her purse, which she had,
thankfully, left in the car. As soon as she had seen it
was Lucas, she sent it to voicemail. She was still
figuring out her plan, but it certainly wasn't going to
include him. The best thing was probably to go
back home and crash on her mom's couch for a
while. The place was a slum, but that was the whole
reason she was trying to get her degree and a
decent job to begin with. It would refocus her, get
her back on track.

By the time Mia arrived at her dorm and
parked Lucas's ridiculously expensive red and black
Audi in the visitor's lot, she had the plan all worked
out: sob on Jeeter's shoulder for a while, borrow
some clothes so she didn't have to go back to the

hotel, borrow some money so she could take the bus to her mom's, then call Lev. She knew Lucas's brother wanted her and Lucas to be together as much as she did—correction, as much as she *used to* —but he was the only one who would understand why she had left Lucas naked in the national park and his car in visitor parking at McMahon Hall. How they worked out things from there was none of her business.

She sighed as she strolled into the dorm. She'd probably have to get another job, too.

She punched the elevator button and rode it all the way up with her arms crossed in front of her chest. If Jeeter weren't there, Mia would just have to borrow stuff and leave her a note. And call her later. Which made her think… she dug through her purse for her phone and found her room card tucked in the case where she always kept it. Just as she was pulling out the keycard, the face of her phone lit up with an incoming call. It said *No Caller ID*, but that just meant it was her mom. She couldn't afford a cell phone and was always calling from their next-door neighbor, Mr. Bailey, who thought the government was tapping his phone and had Caller ID permanently blocked.

"Hi, Mom." Mia tried to sound like absolutely

nothing in the world was wrong, while simultaneously coming up with some plausible reason why she would be crashing on her mom's couch soon. Her mom knew Mia hated it there.

"Hi, honey! How are you?"

"Great, Mom. Just great." No, that didn't sound sarcastic at all. Mia grimaced and strode out of the elevator as soon as the doors opened.

"You haven't called in a while. I was getting worried."

"Mom, there's nothing to worry about! UDub is totally safe." Mia cringed internally at the lie. She'd said it a million times before when she'd transferred to the university last fall, because her mom had this strange idea that the University of Washington wasn't as safe as her mom's rundown tenement, just because it was far away. Mia scanned her keycard and swung open the door to her room.

A quick glance showed Jupiter wasn't home.

"I don't know," her mother was saying in that classic *worried-Mom* voice that every mother came with pre-installed. "I mean, during the school year, sure, when everyone's there and serious and studying. But during the summer… it just seems like there might be more partying going on. You're not going to parties, are you?"

"No, Mom, no parties," she said with practiced patience. As if dorm parties were a bigger danger than the crackhead gangs in her mother's neighborhood. Who were likely shifters, too. Little did her mom know her own daughter was a shifter. And embroiled in a pack war. Mia sighed into the phone while propping open Jupiter's closet to peer inside. "You know what, though, Mom? I think I could use a break from the big campus life for a while."

"Well, you can always come home," her mom said, gushing relief through Mia. She should have known she wouldn't need an excuse. "I've been saying that from the beginning. There's no reason you can't come home during the summers."

"That sounds great," Mia said, digging some clothes out of the closet. "But just for a few days, okay. Until I... until I miss Jupiter."

"Who's Jupiter?" Her mom always forgot her roommate's name. As if it was forgettable—Mia guessed she was just still in denial that she had actually moved away from home.

"My roommate, Mom. Crazy drama girl, remember? You met her at Thanksgiving."

"Oh, her! I remember now. Very nice girl."

Mia scooped up an armful of clothes and dumped them on the bed to look through them.

"Yeah, she's great. The best roommate anyone——"
Mia cut herself off when she glimpsed something
blue on the floor out of the corner of her eye.

Jeeter's blue feathered purse.

Oh no. Mia glanced quickly around. Jeeter wasn't
hidden under the blankets somewhere, nursing a
hangover. The room was a mess, but Mia had
thought it was just the normal kind of mess... only
the blinds were kinked up like someone had fallen
into them. Some of Jeeter's books were dumped on
the floor. And her half-finished homework was still
sitting on her desk, textbook open, pencil on the
floor.

Jeeter never went anywhere without that damn purse.

"Honey?" her mom said. "Are you still there?"

"I gotta go, Mom," Mia said in a shaky voice.
"I'll be home soon."

She clicked off the phone. And clenched it in
her fist. Maybe Jeeter just left in a hurry. Maybe
some hot Boy of the Week stopped by and swept
her off to his dorm room. Mia stumbled over to
where the purse lay on the carpet and picked it
up. Did her roommate really take this thing *everywhere?* Mia wracked her brain: surely there was a
good explanation for Jeeter just picking up and
leaving.

Mia smacked her forehead: she could just call Jeeter.

Clutching the feather-purse in one hand, Mia spun through the numbers on her phone. She never called Jeeter, they were almost always in the room together. Just as she was getting to the J's, her phone lit up again, kicking her out of the phone book.

No Caller ID.

Mia growled in frustration and clicked the phone back on. "Mom, I swear I'll be home soon."

"I wouldn't be so sure about that." The voice was deep and male and full of way too much amusement.

A chill ran down Mia's back.

"Who is this?"

"The more important question, Mia, is where is your roommate?" The voice was smooth and sinister.

Mia's stomach seized. She forced herself not to be sick. "What have you done with her?" Her voice was trembling.

"Why nothing. Nothing at all. Yet." There was a noise in the background, a scuffling and a muffled, angry yell. Mia's hand with the purse shook as she held her fist to her mouth, trying to stifle her own gasp.

There was a scraping sound like the phone had brushed against something, then Jeeter's voice came through, screeching so loud Mia had to hold it away from her ear.

"Mia! Oh my god, Mia!" Then crying, but the phone had moved away, and Mia could only hear the muffled struggle again.

Tears streamed down her face.

"See?" the voice said. "She's perfectly fine."

"Please don't hurt her." She tried to not let the tears show in her voice.

"It's not her we want, Mia." Smooth, deep-rumbling. It was almost soothing. Except for the words.

"What do you want?" Her voice hitched. She knew. Of course, she knew.

"We want you."

Her heart sank to the bottom of her toes.

"Just come downstairs. We'll have a car waiting for you."

How did they know where she was? How did they even get her number? Then she realized: *they're already here, watching.* And they had Jeeter, so they had Mia's number. But who was she kidding? Red Wolf, beyond being run by an evil pack of shifters, was an *internet* development company. Of course, they had figured out how to find her.

And she'd walked right back into their trap.

When she didn't answer, a hint of impatience crept into the voice of whichever of the Red wolves was on the other end. "Don't make us wait, Mia."

"I'll be right down."

Chapter Twenty-One

Lucas was running as fast as four paws would carry him.

The dirt edge along the paved road winding through the Olympic National Park was clear enough—at least he didn't have to run through the forest, dodging fallen logs and hidden rocks—but carrying his rolled up clothes in his mouth was slowing him down. And he had driven Mia a *long* ways into the forest for their little lessons in being *wolf*. Getting back out again on foot would take far longer. Even in his wolf form, his legs were screaming from the abuse.

Meanwhile, Mia was speeding away in his car, angry. There was no telling where she would go or what she would do.

A sick feeling cramped his stomach. He didn't know if it was the run or the idea that she might do something reckless, but he had to stop. The clothes had to go, so he spit them out, nosed around with his muzzle to get his phone of out his pocket, and dropped it on the dirt to have a look. Still no bars. He didn't know how far he'd have to go before he reached civilization and a cell phone tower, but he didn't have the luxury of hauling clothes along for the ride. He mouthed the phone, trying not to drool on it while he clamped it in his teeth, and started running again.

A half hour later, he was about to pass out. Too hot, even in the shade, panting, he stopped to check his phone again. Two bars this time.

He shifted and flopped naked on the side of the road while dialing Lev's number.

"Hey, brother, what's up?" Lev's cheery voice gushed relief through him.

"Need your help." Lucas had to keep his words short. It was a massive struggle to catch his breath.

"Jesus, what happened to you?" Lev went from zero to DEFCON 5 in just those few words. "Wait… is Mia with you? Is she okay?"

Lucas winced. He was supposed to be guarding her, watching over her while his father's pack made an offer on LoopSource. With the offer in play, Mia would be in even more danger from the Red wolves who wanted to use her as leverage to stop the deal. Instead, Lucas hadn't even kept her out of danger for an hour. And managed to piss her off so badly she took his car and left him behind.

"Mia left me," Lucas managed to get out. He swallowed, panted a few times, then added, "She has my car."

"What in the…?" Lev was confused, but his state of alert dropped a few levels. "All right. What did you do?"

"Pissed her off." His breath was settling down, but the panting was making him dizzy. It didn't help that he was splayed out on the side of the road and not running anymore.

"Obviously." Lev sighed audibly into the phone. "Man, what am I going to do with you? Mia is the freaking best thing to happen to you, and you're *ruining* it."

"Need your help," he repeated. Lucas squeezed his eyes shut, trying to stop the world from spinning.

"Yeah, no kidding. You could have listened to me on Tuesday when I told you—"

"Now," Lev."

Lev's voice took on a little more concern. "Where are you?"

"Olympics."

"Wait… she left you in the Olympic forest?"

"Need clothes, too."

Lucas had to hold the phone away from his ear as Lev howled with laughter on the other end. He let his hand fall to the dirt and lifted his head slightly to peer down the road. Civilization was still miles away. He banged his head back to the ground. He deserved every bit of Lev's mockery, but that wasn't his top concern.

Mia was unprotected. His wolf snarled its reproach, and this time, he was absolutely right. He and Lev both. Lucas had been a complete idiot. He should have turned her over to… *anyone*… other than him for protection. Colin, Llyr's beta, would have taken her in a heartbeat. Any of the wolves in his father's pack would have. Instead, he selfishly wanted her for himself… and now she was gone.

Goddammit. Even if he'd given in to his wolf's demands and claimed her, she would be safer than she was right now, all alone. It was his shitty inability to decide—he couldn't let himself claim her, and he couldn't let her go—that led to all of this. And that was it: as soon as he found her again, he was locking her far, far away from him. He wouldn't even allow himself to be alone with her to explain. He'd send her a text or something later, but he would turn her over immediately to someone who actually had a chance of keeping her safe… because that sure as hell wasn't *him*.

Lev's tinny laughter on the phone in Lucas's hand died away. "Bro? Lucas? Lucas, are you there?" It was just a squeak, but he could make out the words.

Lucas brought the phone back to his ear. "Need your help, Lev." It was the third time he'd said it, and this time his brother sobered immediately.

"Got my keys. On my way. Where are you in the park?"

"That place you pulled me out…" Lucas swallowed again, the dizziness finally fading. "I'm on that road."

"Got it. Be there as soon as I can."

Lev hung up, and Lucas let his phone hand fall again. It would take Lev at least an hour to get there from the city. That would give Lucas time to rest. Or he could get up and run some more and cut a few minutes off the time until he'd be able to go after Mia again.

He glanced at the phone in his hand: or he could call her right now.

He dialed her number. It rang once and went to voice mail.

Dammit. She wasn't going to take his calls.

Lucas shifted, clamped the phone in his mouth, and started running.

"So, what was the fight about?" Lev asked from the driver's seat.

Lucas was still buttoning the shirt his brother had brought, but they were already speeding back toward Seattle. "Doesn't matter." He'd been wracking his brain to think of where Mia might go: the hotel was the only place that was reasonably safe, and all her stuff was there.

"Considering you pissed her off about something, I'm thinking it probably matters. If you want to actually find her, that is."

Lucas glared at him. "That's not funny, Lev."

"No, it's not." Lev returned his glare with sideways looks while watching the road.

Lucas finished with the shirt, then clenched his fist and pressed it against the passenger door next to him. There was no point in telling Lev about their fight—Lucas knew what he was going to say anyway—but it was going to be a long drive if he didn't.

"She wants to be my mate." He kept his gaze out the window at the green blur of pine trees whizzing by.

"Ah, *shit.*" Lev slammed his palm against the steering wheel. "You told her no, didn't you?"

"She's better off with someone else." He glanced at his brother, but his blotched and angry face just drove Lucas to stare back out the window again. "You should know that better than anyone."

"You are such an idiot!" Lev's voice had hiked up.

"Exactly my point." Lucas kept his gaze on the forest. Maybe he would go back there when this was all through. Once Mia was mated with someone else, he wouldn't be good company for anyone for a while.

Lev growled and banged his frustration on the steering wheel several more times.

"Easy on the car, Lev," Lucas said calmly. "We need it in one piece to get Mia back."

Lev blew out a breath. "The hottest unmated female shifter I've seen in *years* drops into your lap, and you tell her no. You take screwing up to a whole 'nother level, you know that?"

"She'll find someone else." Lucas gritted his teeth. He'd rather finish this conversation than drag it out. "Colin would make a good choice."

"*Colin?*" Lev screeched.

"I think they can hear you in Seattle." Lucas refused to look at him, but his knuckles were cracking from how tightly his fists were clenched.

Lev plowed right past his comment. "I can't even believe you would say that," Lev said, disgusted. "You're an even bigger idiot than I thought. Colin's an asshole."

"He'll keep her safe."

Lev was quiet for a moment. Then he said, "You really don't deserve her."

Lucas turned to him, but his brother's eyes were fixed on the road. His knuckles were turning white on the steering wheel.

"That's what I'm saying, Lev."

"No. That is *not* what I mean." Lev threw him a sideways look, then stared at the road again. "She's smart. She's kind. She knows what happened to Tila, and she *still* wants to be with you. You don't deserve someone that good, bro. But it really doesn't matter what you deserve. You get me on this? Alphas don't get what they deserve—they get what they *earn.*"

"I'm not an alpha." Lucas gritted his teeth. Damn Lev for making him say that out loud. Never mind that those words had rumbled through his head every day for a year. His wolf was snapping at him for voicing it, too.

Lev took a deep breath. "Did it ever occur to you that she's your second chance? Your chance to earn back what you lost, what we *all* lost, with Tila? And that this is it? You're not going to get another one."

"Let's just get her back, Lev." Lucas restrained himself from punching the car door. Or his brother. "Let's try the hotel first. If she's not there, we can try the dorm. Later, when she's safe, you can both tell me how stupid I am."

Lev grunted in agreement to that, but at least it shut him up for a while. In fact, they kept an uneasy silence all the way back to the hotel. Except when they got there, she was nowhere to be seen. And her stuff was still there, too.

"Did she have a key to the room?" Lev asked, looking around like he might find her hiding underneath the couch.

"Her purse was in the car," Lucas said. "And

even if she didn't, she could have gotten one at the front desk."

Lev fixed him with a skeptical look. "Have you even tried calling her?"

"She's not taking my calls."

"How many times did you try?"

Lucas didn't answer, just clenched his jaw and picked up her coffee cup from that morning. House-keeping must not have come through, because it still had traces of coffee along the rim where she sipped it.

His brother looked unimpressed with his efforts. "Try again."

"Fine." Lucas rumbled a soft growl while he dug out his phone. "But if she doesn't pick up, we're heading to the dorm."

Lucas dialed. It rang twice then picked up. There was no sound on the other end. Lucas's heart rate kicked up a notch. She was giving him a chance, even if it was a slim one.

"Mia, honey, I'm sorry. All of that came out wrong. Just give me a chance—"

But a male voice cut him off. "You've already had more than one chance, Lucas Sparks."

Lucas gaped. *Who the hell was on Mia's phone?*

"Who is this?" he demanded.

"I'll give you exactly one more chance to save your little human plaything." The voice was gloating and cold. "Retract your LoopSource bid. I'll be nice and give you 24 hours. But I can't guarantee I won't have fun playing with your favorite toy while you make up your mind."

Lucas's body felt like all the blood had been drained from it. He braced himself against the countertop, suddenly dizzy. An image of Tila the way he found her—bloody, broken, a giant fist-sized hole missing in the center—blinded him and suddenly he couldn't see anything but small rivers of blood pooling on the floor.

"Mia." It was a ghost of a whisper, not meant for the male voice on the other end.

But he heard it. "Such a pretty name, I agree. And I can see why you find her attractive. Yes, I can definitely see that."

The way he said it... as if he was already *touching her* with his words... Lucas's wolf roared back to life. *"I will kill you."* It was one long growl of words and anger and frustration as he gripped the phone.

Lev was at his side, hand on his shoulder, but Lucas shoved him away.

The caller on the phone just chuckled in his ear.

Lucas reined in his fury enough to get some intelligible words out. "I want proof she's alive."

A sick, mocking humor clung to the man's voice. "You certainly take your playthings *very* seriously." Then it turned darker. "I've already sent proof to your alpha. That's all you'll get until we close a deal with LoopSource."

Lucas squeezed the phone so tight he thought it might break under his grip.

"You have one day, Lucas."

The wolf on the other end of the line hung up.

Chapter Twenty-Two

I'VE ALREADY SENT PROOF TO YOUR ALPHA.

Mia's heart sank at those words. The Red wolf who said them—the other wolves called him Mace—had already taken her picture, just minutes ago, using her own phone to send it to Lucas's father. And now he was taunting Lucas with his words, an evil smirk on his pretty face while he held her hostage in his Bellevue estate. At least, she thought it was his estate. He acted like he owned the place, but she was still sorting out who was who and what possibilities there might be for escape. For her and for Jupiter.

Only she hadn't seen her roommate yet.

The black car that had been waiting for Mia outside her dorm hadn't been familiar, but she had recognized the wolf inside. Well, one of them, anyway. He was one of the three wolves who attacked her in the alleyway. The driver had called him Beck, and he was the one who had never shifted, his throat being caught in Lucas's wolf-form jaws. Beck would have been handsome, except for the sneers and lecherous looks he kept giving her during the twenty minute ride from her dorm, over Lake Washington, and past a series of foliage-shrouded estates in the boomburb of Bellevue. It was where all the super-rich dot-commers lived once they made their millions and billions. The driver took them down a winding, quarter-mile-long driveway, past a sprawling gray-stone and red-wood estate, to a smaller, regular-sized house—one of several they had passed in the compound. By the time they'd gotten out, they were so deep inside the secluded estate surrounded by forest, she didn't even contemplate screaming for help: no one would hear her.

Inside the house, the other two wolves from the alley had been waiting for her.

"You have one day, Lucas." The one called Mace hung up the phone—*her* phone. It had rung before she could demand to see her roommate, who was nowhere to be seen in the expansive, two-story living area. Her house/prison was as luxurious on the inside as the estate was on the outside, with white leather sofas, dark carved-wood chairs, and a roaring gray-stone fireplace.

Mace looked her over with undressing eyes that made Beck's lecherous looks seem tame. Beck sat uncomfortably close to her on the couch, even though she had edged to the far side. He kept touching her hair with his fingertips and thoroughly creeping her out. The third wolf from the alley leaned against the fireplace stones—he was the one who had leaped from the limo at the SparkTech garage and grabbed her, and he still wore the bruises Lucas gave him for it. Mace was clearly the leader of the three. An ugly smirk sat on his pretty-yet-masculine face, and his cold, dark eyes were already carving her up like she was a delicious steak he planned to feast upon.

"Well, Mia Fiore, apparently Lucas Sparks has quite a thing for you." Whatever Lucas said on the phone seemed to double Mace's pleasure in kidnapping her.

"What did he say?" the bruised wolf by the fireplace asked.

Mace kept his gaze on Mia. "Oh, just that he'd kill me."

"I don't get it," he protested. "She's just a girl."

Mace stepped closer to Mia, inspecting her with that penetrating gaze. "I don't know, Alric. Maybe after screwing his way through the human female population of Seattle, Lucas has finally found one he has a taste for." He gestured for Mia to stand up. "Let's take a look at you, Mia Fiore. Maybe we can figure out what Lucas sees in you."

She was glad to get up and away from Beck, but then she shuddered when he put his hands on her hips and boosted her up from the couch. She stood, teetering, in front of Mace as he raked his gaze over her plain t-shirt and jeans. She'd grabbed Jeeter's sneakers along with her roommate's blue-feathered purse as she'd run out of her dorm and into the waiting stretch sedan of the Red pack. Mia tried to put on a brave face under Mace's scrutiny, but that didn't stop her hands from shaking where they were clenched next to her.

She was in serious *you-might-not-survive-this* trouble.

They were all staring at her, including the driver, who had taken up a station at the two-story entranceway by the front door. He was slightly less hulking than the others and was dressed in a white collared shirt, rather than black silk, but the thing that really set him apart was his constant frown. He seemed as disturbed by the situation as she was—or perhaps he was simply worried she might make a run for it. Either way, he seemed separate from the rest, like maybe he didn't belong with them. Or didn't usually hang out with them. Or something. He was keeping an eye on the front door, but also the rooms upstairs, which was where Mia guessed they were keeping Jeeter.

If only Mia hadn't gotten so mad at Lucas and stormed off like a child having a tantrum. So what if he rejected her? It wasn't like he owed her anything. In fact, *she* owed *him:* her life, a couple times over. At least when she was with him, she was safe. It was when she went running off that she seemed to always find the most trouble possible. And now she had put him and SparkTech in a terrible position. And her roommate in danger as well.

Mace twirled his finger like he wanted her to turn around for his inspection. It was humiliating. She did it anyway. She had gone with them willingly because they had Jupiter. Until her roommate was free, Mia wasn't going to try anything that might get either of them killed.

By the time she had completed her turn, Mace

was licking his bottom lip. "Well, I have to admit Lucas does have good taste."

It struck her as odd that he seemed so familiar with Lucas. But Red Wolf was a competitor, both in the venture capital business and in the *pack business,* as Lucas called it—she guessed it made sense they would know as much as possible about each other.

And now Mace had his enemy's "favorite toy," as he'd called her.

Which made Mia's heart seize up with a fluttery panic: she didn't want to think about the ways Mace might want to "play" with her before releasing her back to Lucas. Assuming she ever got free again. But first, she had to get her roommate out of this mess.

"I want to see Jupiter," Mia demanded, surprising herself with how strong her voice was compared to the shakes running through her.

Mace seemed amused by it, too, throwing a smirk to Beck seated behind her. "Maybe Lucas likes his females feisty." The other two wolves, Beck and Alric, had a chuckle at that.

"I'm only here because you said you wanted me, not her," Mia said angrily. "I want to see her. And then I want you to let her go."

Mace smiled wide at that. "She likes giving

orders, too." He wasn't even talking to her, in spite of his eyes wandering all over her face and body. From the couch, she could hear Beck chuckle darkly.

Mace glanced at the driver by the front door. "Jak. Bring the roommate out."

Mia watched him jog up the stairs and disappear. When she looked back to Mace, he was eyeing her like he was trying to figure out which part to taste first.

"I really should thank your friend, what's her name… Jupiter? If it wasn't for her, it might have taken us a while to figure out how to lure you away. Next time, you might want to be more careful about uploading pictures of yourself to the internet."

The selfie. They must have found out Jeeter was her roommate from there. Or somehow known that they were friends enough that Mia would care… and come for her.

The driver—apparently his name was Jak— came back down the stairs with Jupiter in tow. Her roommate was a mess of wide eyes, running mascara, and trembling lips… but she was alive. Mia held in her sigh of relief and waited for Jak to escort Jeeter into the room, a hand at her elbow, guiding her. As soon as her roommate saw Mia, she broke away and threw her arms around her, holding her so hard that Mia nearly choked.

She hugged her back. Jeeter was crying, sobbing really, and didn't let go. Through her roommate's mass of red hair, Mia threw hateful glares at Mace, who seemed unconcerned by the whole display.

When Jeeter loosened her grip, Mia pulled back and looked her in the face. "Are you okay?"

Her roommate sniffed and nodded quickly, but her mouth was quivering too much for her to speak.

"Did they do anything to you?" Mia asked, with a look for Mace that said, *you better not have.*

Jeeter shook her head in equally small, quivering movements. Mia was about to hug her again when Mace took a quick step towards them, grabbed a handful of Jeeter's long hair, and yanked her out of Mia's grasp.

Jupiter shrieked, then sobbed again, shaking. Mace held her close to his body, head tipped back as if he was about to take a bite out of her throat.

Mia's fists clenched again. "Let her go!" It was almost a growl, and her inner wolf was all bristled out, ready to shift and take a bite out of Mace instead.

He smirked. "You're not the one who gives orders around here, Mia." Then he mashed his lips against Jupiter's, devouring her in a forced kiss that made Mia's whole body jolt. Jeeter squirmed in his hold, but he was too strong for her, holding her fast through the whole thing. It only lasted a second or two, but Mia's wolf nearly leaped out to stop him. She was only able to rein in her beast at the last moment when Mace broke the kiss.

Jeeter sobbed.

The hatred Mia felt for the wolf holding her roommate couldn't have burned any brighter. "You said you would let her go." Her voice was half-wolf and all-growl. She may have to fight her way out of this. If she did, she was going for Mace's throat first.

He just shook his head in amusement and looked over Jeeter's trembling, tear-stained cheeks, like he imagined more than just forced kisses to come. "I said she wasn't the one we wanted. But now that we have her, there's no sense in letting good prey go to waste."

A chill went through Mia. *Dammit.* What was with these Red wolves and their sick games? She wanted to lunge at him and claw out his eyes, but she would have to keep her cool if she wanted to find a way out of this for both of them. Besides, if she shifted, that would just expose her as a wolf. Something Mace and his goons didn't seem to know yet. Apparently, Lucas had a lot of human play-things in the past… she would deal with that later. Right now, letting the Red wolves know she was a shifter was a whole different level of danger: the rogue pack in the forest had immediately wanted to claim her, and she could imagine the Red wolves wanting something even worse… if there was something worse. At the moment she didn't want to picture what that might be.

Mia kept her voice level. "You don't need her. You have me, remember?"

Mace arched an eyebrow but loosened his hold a little on Jeeter.

"I know lots of ways to please a wolf," she said, wondering where she was getting the guts to even *say* that. "I've been with Lucas lots of times. I know just what you want. All you have to do is let my roommate go, and then my mind will be free to focus on you." She glanced at the other wolves, who seemed to have perked to high attention. "All of you. If that's what you want." She tossed him what she hoped was a flirty look, propping her hands on her hips so he wouldn't notice them shaking. Jesus, where was she coming up with this stuff? She only hoped he would bite.

Mace smiled broadly and tipped his head to

Beck, still on the couch. "Come take the girl," he said, obviously meaning Jeeter, not Mia. Her heart pounded as Beck brushed past her, giving her bottom a squeeze as he went, then he clamped a beefy hand around Jeeter's arm. She whimpered but didn't cry out like before.

"Well, you've sparked my curiosity, Mia Fiore," Mace said approvingly. "But I'm afraid I promised Beck he could have your roommate once we were finished with her."

Mia shot a look to Jeeter. Her eyes had gone wide. Beck started slowly dragging her toward the stairs. She tried to resist but got nowhere. He twisted her around and ducked down to hoist her over his shoulder, barely slowing in his progress toward the stairs. And, presumably, the rooms above. Jeeter flailed her arms and legs, then let out a blood-curdling scream that drove an iron stake through Mia's heart.

Oh hell no.

Mia reached down and swiftly tore off her t-shirt. Then she shifted as fast as she could, trying to catch all of them by surprise while not getting snarled in her clothes. She managed to leap out of her pants and shoes, her long, lean wolf legs slipping free, but her bra stretched tight across her chest. As she finished the shift, it snapped and flew off. By then she was nearly upon Beck, who still hadn't seen her.

Jeeter's screaming pitched up another octave as Mia flew at Beck in wolf form. It was enough warning that he turned halfway around by the time she arrived.

She dove for his throat, but he got an arm up to block, so she caught that instead. He roared and shifted. Jeeter tumbled to the floor. Mia held on during the shift, biting harder, then letting go only when she had a good chance of catching his throat. Her jaws snapped closed, but she'd only caught the side of his muzzle. He wrenched his head back and forth, trying to work free, growling like mad and kicking her with all four paws. She almost had him, but he out-weighed her by half, and he soon rolled and pinned her. Mia yelped as Beck's fangs sank into her neck. It stung, and she choked, and then black spots spun in front of her eyes, but he wasn't killing her, or even piercing her skin… just snarling and holding her. And drooling down her neck.

"Enough!" It was Mace's voice.

Mia couldn't move, not with the hold Beck had on her neck, but her wolf body had all four paws braced against him. If he loosened his grip at all, she was out of there. She could hear Jeeter whimpering nearby.

"Do not allow her to submit," Mace said, calmer and closer now. "She's *mine.*"

Beck eased back, still pinning her, but giving her room to twist her head and look at Mace.

He held her gaze as he shifted into wolf form.

Oh no.

Chapter Twenty-Three

LUCAS DROVE LIKE THE HOUNDS OF HELL WERE chasing him.

"Jesus!" Lev said as they took a turn in the Audi that nearly put them up on two wheels. The skyscrapers of downtown Seattle blurred by. When they came out of the turn alive, Lev added, "It's going to be very difficult to rescue Mia from the afterlife."

That cooled the burning rage in Lucas's veins. Just a little.

"Get our father on the phone," he growled, but he slowed the Audi, so they were only about twenty miles over the speed limit as they wound toward SparkTech.

You have one day, Lucas.

The words had frozen him in place for a long moment, still in the grip of that image of Tila's death—the one that had haunted him day and night in the year since her death—but then a fiery rage had billowed up from the depths of his wolfish soul. From that second on, his every thought, every word, every action would be focused on getting Mia back from the wolf who had stolen her from him.

Stolen. Taken… Claimed.

It was a sequence he knew too well, and his wolf growled and snorted and stomped with impatience to *get her back now.* He and his wolf both knew what would happen if he didn't. The sequence was ancient but still the code by which most wolves operated. It didn't help that Lucas knew in sickening detail the habits of this particular wolf, the voice on the phone. SparkTech was an internet development company, but they were really in the business of *information.* And knowing what their competition was capable of—their latest acquisitions, internal political machinations, and personal habits of all kinds—was the kind of information that was invaluable to their business. Although, strictly speaking, the voice could have been any of the Red pack wolves—Lucas had never spoken with any of them, even though he'd beaten the crap out of a couple—he knew exactly which one it had to be.

Mace.

Marcus Crittenden, alpha of the Red pack, had two sons: Mace was the youngest and most cruel. As well as the most ambitious. The two sons were constantly vying for who would be next in line to succeed their father. So far, the oldest was better placed. Which only meant Mace was even more desperate for any advantage in the hierarchy of the pack.

Given any chance at all, Mace would claim Mia.

Lucas knew Mace already had a mate. He also knew the Red pack collected female wolves like they were trophies, mating more than once, and growing a harem to establish their own pack and to show dominance in the larger organization of the Red Wolf company. Having more females also ensured they could welp the strongest possible next genera-tion to carry on their line. It was another ancient practice that some packs still used, although most modern shifters had left it far behind as the brutal remnant of a less civilized time. It wasn't even a *wolf* practice, but rather an ancient *human* one... wolves naturally mated for life, taking a new mate only when separated by death. That was the instinctual draw of the claiming... and why his wolf sang about Mia nearly from the first moment he saw her, even before his human self knew she was a shifter.

It was only *human* males who were backward enough to claim more than one mate.

Lucas swerved the car, taking another turn too fast, and slamming Lev into the side panel. His brother had the phone to his ear, talking to someone. Lucas hoped it was their father.

If they were going to rescue Mia, they needed to move as quickly as possible, and he would need all the resources of all the packs he could draw upon.

Before Mace could figure out what she was and take her for his own.

LUCAS SHOVED OPEN THE FROSTED DOORS TO SparkTech's office space and hurried inside. Lev was just behind him. Their father was expecting them. Apparently, Mace had texted him a picture of Mia, as well as one of another girl they identified as Mia's roommate. His father said the girls both seemed unharmed, and the image of Mia showed her sitting on a white leather couch. There were no identifying features in either of the pictures to locate where they had taken the girls, but Lucas was almost certain they were hidden away in the Red pack compound. Mace was angling for a position within the pack—there was no way he was flying solo on this, and he had to have the approval of his alpha before even setting up to snatch Mia.

Lucas just needed to verify with his father that Mia was likely in the compound, then they could make an assault plan to storm in and pull her out. He expected to get his father's approval before recruiting volunteers from his father's pack as well as Llyr's... what he didn't expect was Colin, Llyr's beta, stopping him in the common area next to the couches and glass tables that populated the area between the offices.

Colin strode right up to him and blocked Lucas's path. "You had *one job*," Colin spat. His anger took Lucas aback, catching him off guard with the beta's on-fire eyes and at-the-ready fists. *"One.* And you had to fuck that up."

Lucas just shook his head and tried to skirt around the human blockade-of-one. He didn't have time for Llyr's beta, whatever his issue was.

Colin grabbed Lucas by the shirt and shoved him hard.

Lucas stumbled back. Why was Llyr's beta choosing this of all moments to come after him? Then he remembered: *Colin, Mia, in her office...* Colin wanted her.

The thought made Lucas physically flinch. His wolf growled low and dangerous.

Colin stabbed a finger in his face. "All you had to do was keep her safe for twenty-four hours. That was *all*. But it just was beyond you, wasn't it?"

Lucas slammed his hands into Colin's shoulders and shoved him back. Llyr's beta was big, so it only set him back a couple of steps. And Lucas wasn't trying to start a fight, not really—he didn't have time for that, either. The clock was ticking for Mia. They could fight over her later, *after* she was safe.

"Get out of my way," Lucas growled. "I'm going after her."

Colin stepped up to him again, blocking his path with fists clenched and teeth bared. "The hell you are. You have no claim on her, and you're nothing but a screw-up. No way am I letting you be part of this operation."

A group of wolves was forming around them. His father's pack. Llyr's pack. The very men Lucas would need to help rescue Mia. There were murmurs.

Lucas kept his voice calm, in control. "It's not up to you—"

Colin gave him a look of disgust. "It's sure as hell not up to *you*. You're not even in this pack." He gestured behind him, arms wide. "Either of them."

Lucas checked the crowd, his entire body coiling, his wolf ready to spring. Lucas's father stood behind the others, watching, but not making any move to interfere. Even Lev was holding back.

Colin nodded, satisfaction spreading across his face. "Go home, Lucas. You're done with this. When I've finished leading the operation to rescue Mia, we'll let you know she's safe."

Lucas had no claim. He had no pack. By any measure, he had no rights in any of this. None of that mattered to him. "I'm going after her." Lucas's wolf growled his agreement.

Colin met his snarl with a cool stare. "No. You're not."

Lucas's wolf wanted Colin's throat. Bad. "You can't just have her—"

"You can't seem to keep her." Colin's dark eyes mocked him.

Lucas was boiling inside: time was slipping by,

second after second grating against him while they stood here arguing. While Mia could be hurt... trapped... claimed by some bastard of a dark wolf.... his claws itched to come out and bring a swift end to Colin's attempt to stop him and take Lucas's rightful place in the rescue as if Mia already belonged to him...

"She belongs with me." Even as the harshly whispered words slipped out of Lucas's mouth, he couldn't quite believe he'd spoken them aloud. His wolf would have howled in triumph, but he was too busy stomping and posturing for Colin.

"She *belongs* with a *true* alpha." Colin narrowed his eyes. "We both know that's not you. She deserves better, and I'm going to make sure she gets it. You've had your chance, with Tila. There's no way I'm going to let Mia end up in a pool of her own blood. She's *mine* now."

The volcano building inside Lucas suddenly burst with a power that made both him and his wolf roar. He swung a blind, raging fist at Colin. The larger man moved surprisingly fast, dodging Lucas's blow and cutting up to plow a fist into Lucas's gut. Lucas huffed from the blow, but that just let him get close and hook an arm around Colin's neck. Lucas pounded his face with a fury that scored four nose-smashing punches before Colin shifted into his wolf and slipped from Lucas's grasp. He was left holding Colin's shirt, which he threw to the ground.

Colin stood on all fours a few paces back, teeth bared and snarling, blood dripping from his mouth. Lucas had drawn first blood, but Colin wasn't backing down. The air was rich with its iron scent and the testosterone of a fresh fight. The rest of the pack had edged away, giving them room.

Silence held rein, all sound suspended like a drop of blood about to fall.

In the next heartbeat, Lucas shifted out of his clothes and leaped into the air. He landed a blow on the way down, knocking Colin's muzzle aside, but it was the beta's neck he wanted. Lucas's jaws snapped closed, but they only caught a scruff of fur, gritty and slipping away. The two wolves tumbled together, knocking against a glass table and tipping it. Colin used his larger mass and momentum to keep them rolling. Lucas had to twist and wrench away. He barely escaped being pinned. He danced to the side, turned, and faced Colin again.

They stood on all fours, nose to nose, only a foot apart. With a snarl, Lucas dashed at him and retreated. Colin sidestepped and snapped back, just missing him on the rebound. They circled, edging sideways while looking for an opening. Colin lunged forward. Lucas slipped to the side, then clamped his jaws, catching Colin's flank. He whipped around and grappled with Lucas. They both went down, rolling and bashing against furniture. The other wolves backed quickly out of the way. Lucas and Colin wrecked the common room, jaws snapping and catching and bloodying each other.

Pain ripped across Lucas's shoulder. He knocked Colin's jaws free with a side-butt of his head. The beta tumbled into a wall, momentarily stunning him and giving Lucas the split second of distraction he needed. He dove in and clamped his jaws hard on Colin's throat. He held fast against the other wolf's desperate pawing and kicking and wrenching attempts to get free. After a dozen long seconds of struggle, it was clear Colin couldn't win his freedom without ripping out his own throat... but still he struggled. Lucas kept his jaws locked and growled, a sound from deep inside that he couldn't have stopped even if he wanted to.

Colin's rasping breaths wheezed out of his gaping mouth, but he didn't stop resisting. Lucas's urge to finish it, to clamp down until he had drained the life from Colin's body, was tempting—overwhelming, in fact, with the taste of blood in his mouth and the adrenaline of the fight pumping through his body. But he didn't want to kill his brother-wolf. There had been too much blood spilled in Lucas's life already.

He just needed Colin to submit.

Slowly, slowly, Colin's paws went slack, falling against the fur on his chest. Even slower, his tail curled up. Finally, after a long stretch of pant-filled seconds, his body went completely limp. Colin tipped his head back, exposing even more of his throat to Lucas.

Submission.

Lucas felt the bond like a jolt of energy surging through his body. It filled him from the inside out, in ways he hadn't even known he was empty. He loosened his grip immediately, then carefully released Colin, so as not to damage him any more than he already had.

Colin stayed in the prone position while Lucas worked himself free from their tangled limbs. They both were dripping blood on their flanks and muzzles, but those wounds would quickly heal. In fact, they would fade much faster than the submission bond that now held Colin still, even without Lucas's fangs clamped around his neck. Colin wouldn't move until Lucas gave him permission to do so.

He stepped back, still panting. *Rise,* he thought.

Colin instantly rolled to his feet. His body shook, but Lucas guessed it was more from hurt pride than any of his injuries. Colin had never been in Lucas's pack—he had always been Llyr's beta— but the fresh hold of the submission bond had him waiting on Lucas's command before he shifted back to human form. For the moment, at least, Lucas was his alpha.

Lucas nodded sharply to Colin, and they shifted together.

They both stood naked in the middle of the wrecked common area. Colin bowed his head slightly: an acknowledgment that the bond held, even in human form. The rest of the men were quiet, but Lucas could see it in their stance... he could smell their relief in the air... it was settled.

No one else would fight him for her.

Mia was *his.*

Lev's smile broke out first, but he didn't say anything. He didn't have to. Lucas could still hear his words from before. *Alphas don't get what they deserve —they get what they earn.*

"Now that that's settled," Lucas said, "let's get my mate back."

The roar that went up was pack-wide—no, *two* packs-wide—and Lucas's heart soared with it. Several of his former pack members were grinning at each other, and even his father had a shadow of a smile on his face. Lucas's clothes had been lost in the smashed furniture of the common room, so he didn't bother—he just strode toward his father's office where they would make their plans. Wolves on all sides crowded in with him, smiling and jostling and eager. He wouldn't have to ask them now. It was unspoken: everyone would help.

Lucas didn't deserve Mia, that much was clear. But he had just earned the right to claim her—if she would still have him. And if he could rescue her from the dark wolves who had stolen her away.

Hold on, Mia. I'm coming for you.

Chapter Twenty-Four

Beck's substantial weight held Mia down, but what really made her panic was watching Mace shift right in front of her. He held her gaze all the way through, his cold, dark eyes turning a glittering blackness with his wolf form, shining like his dark red fur.

When Mia had shifted into her wolf form to save Jeeter, just a moment ago, she knew she was taking a risk. But she couldn't let Beck just haul away her roommate for whatever predations he had in mind. Shifting was a foolish thing for Mia to do —she knew there had been no chance of escape— but now that they knew she was a wolf, they would be much more interested in *her* than in her roommate. The diversion had worked all too well. Mia shuddered to think of what that would mean next.

Mace took two bounds to land next to Mia and Beck. Mace was *alpha*—Mia guessed it before, but now that they were wolf, she could *feel* it. His power radiated from him. Beck eased off, relinquishing his hold to give her over. She tried to roll away during the changeover, but Mace just sunk his teeth into her shoulder and hauled her back.

She yelped, but before she could even try to fight him, he had her pinned again, his teeth buried in the fur of her shoulder and chest. He hadn't pierced her skin—at least, she didn't think so—but it still hurt like hell. She whimpered, and her heart thudded erratically, but she wasn't afraid he would kill her. She was afraid of something much worse. Growling through the pain, she tried to wiggle out of his grasp.

He kept hold of her shoulder with his jaws, then pressed a paw on her muzzle, forcing her head to twist over and shove against the floor. She couldn't see him with her face mashed against the luxurious carpet—all she could see was the driver standing by the door with his arms crossed, watching. Beck and the other wolf, Alric, stood to the side, out of her line of sight. She heard Jupiter sobbing quietly somewhere nearby, but Mia couldn't see her either.

Submit.

The command came like a blanket smothering her. She was lost in it for a moment, but then she fought free.

She growled and thought, *Fuck you.*

Mace's muzzle moved slightly against her neck, and a small huffing sound was coming from his mouth. *Soon enough, Mia Fiore. Very soon. And I'm going to so enjoy it. But first, you must submit.*

His command washed over her again, worse this time. She was drowning in it like thick honey had been poured down her throat. She struggled, then yelped again when he bit harder.

Go ahead, fight me, Mia. Fight hard. Mace's tongue dragged across the fur of her neck, tasting her while still holding her with his jaws. *It will make your submission all the better.*

Panic was a black cloud choking her. She couldn't submit to him—he would claim her right then and there, she knew it. And then she and Jupiter would never get out, never get away... worse, Mia would be magically bound to Mace for the rest of her life. Or the rest of his. Either way, she would be mated. And trapped.

Submit to me. This time he growled with the command.

Her stomach heaved, and if wolves could cry, tears would be running down her face... but her will to fight was slipping away. She was smothered by her alpha's power, his command, his touch, his bite... *no!* He was *not* her alpha. Mia raged on the inside, even though Mace had her pinned, and she was unable to move. If only she hadn't run away from Lucas...

Then his voice came back to her. *Shift, Mia. Shift now!*

Her heart leaped at the idea like it was a life-saver ring thrown in a drowning sea. She closed her eyes and focused every thought on *shifting, shifting, shifting...*

Mace tightened his hold on her neck *No! Submit! Submit now!*

But she could feel herself changing under the grip of his teeth. He growled and shook his head as if he could stop her with his frustration... but then his grip loosened. He was shifting, too, and they were a tangle of human limbs and fur and teeth, all of which quickly sorted out as they completed the transition. The power of Mace's command faded once she was in human form, just as shifting before had broken her submission to Lucas.

She couldn't even attempt to scramble away before Mace's human hands were on her throat. And if being pinned in wolf form by Mace's teeth and paws was bad, having his naked human body lying on top of her, human fingers digging into her flesh and choking her was worse. Much worse. Especially when she realized his erection was pressing into her leg. He was panting against her lips, even as she gasped for air.

"I don't have to be a wolf to kill you, Mia." His voice was soft, but he was laboring to breathe.

She couldn't tell if his heaving breath was anger or excitement... or maybe both. She was too focused on trying to pull in a breath herself. Black spots swam in front of her eyes. She dug her fingers into his hands, trying to pry them from her throat, but he was far too strong. Mia heard Jupiter crying and felt Mace's heated breath on her face, but other than that, everything was starting to dim.

Suddenly the pressure on her throat eased. She gasped in air and coughed, but she still couldn't move—Mace's naked body weighed her down. Her stomach heaved, and she gagged, but nothing came up. Then his hands were in her hair, gripping it and pulling her head back, exposing her throat to him.

"This is how I want you." A soft danger had crept into his voice. He lowered his lips to her neck, as though he might sink his teeth into her, but he only whispered, "Submit to me, Mia. Or I *will* kill you."

Her heart hammered in her chest. She was sure he could feel it, with his bare chest mashed against hers. Or possibly he could see the vein pulsing in her neck—he was that close.

Would he really kill her? He was certainly evil enough. But the other wolves—the rogue pack in the forest, Llyr's beta Colin, all the other drooling wolves in the SparkTech office—they all seem to want her *alive*. Lev had explained how rare unmated females apparently were, and they all seemed to want her for their own purposes, some good, some decidedly not… with the notable exception of Lucas. Even Mace seemed to want her for mating— would he actually kill her if she refused him? It didn't seem like she was any good to him dead.

It was a helluva gamble. But Lucas knew she was here. He may not want her for a mate, but he'd already saved her life twice. She couldn't imagine him not at least *trying* to come for her. But would he reach her in time? She had to stall… find some way to put Mace off… *fight me, Mia. Fight hard.* Mace's thoughts came back to her as he once again ran the tip of his tongue across her neck. *It will make your submission all the better.*

He got some kind of sick thrill out of her resisting. She flashed back to the alleyway, when he and his two beta wolves had first tried to capture her. Back then, he had wanted her to run. *To chase her…* and then do whatever torments he got off on. Maybe that thrill of the chase would be enough to keep her alive a little while longer.

She struggled against the weight of his body and his grip on her hair, twisting around to defiantly face him. "I'd rather die than submit to you." Her lips were trembling, but her voice was strong. It helped that she mostly meant it. Submission to him would quickly be followed by mating… and the idea of having sex with Mace, not just once, but an endless life of being bound to him, at his sexual whim, something that she had no doubt would be dark and painful… death was a reasonable alternative to that.

Mace's eyes flashed, and his hand gripped her

hair tighter, but she could feel his erection pulse against her, and a tiny, cruel smirk took up residence on his face. "I see why Lucas would kill for you. Not just a female shifter but an alpha, too. Which, of course, only means I can't possibly let you go." Then he ran his hands down her side, feeling her naked flesh, while running the tip of his nose up her throat, taking a long whiff. He exhaled across her skin. "I'm going to so enjoy breaking you, Mia Fiore."

Then he pushed up from her, and the sudden lack of weight made her gasp. She felt even more naked, as Mace stood over her, his gaze ravishing her body. She lay there, trembling for a moment, unsure what to do.

Mace turned to Beck standing behind him and said, "Bring me a witch."

Mia's mouth fell open, and her heart lurched.

What had she done?

Jupiter and Mia perched on the edge of the guest bed. Mia couldn't tell which of them was shaking more, but it was Mia's arm around Jeeter's shoulder that was keeping them somewhat together. That and the blue-feathered purse in Jeeter's hands, a reassuring sight for both of them. Mia had gotten it, along with her own purse, back with her clothes —minus the bra that had broken in her hasty shift. The left-over jitters were bad, but at least for the moment, she and Jupiter had escaped the leering looks of Mace and his two betas. The betas had left in search of a witch—that thought made Mia shudder again as she hugged Jeeter harder. Mace had told Jak he had something to take care of and sent him off to guard Mia and Jupiter in the guest bedroom upstairs. That *something* was apparently Mace having loud, wall-banging sex in the bedroom next door if the screaming and moaning were any indications. At least she hoped the shrieks were of pleasure. From her brief encounter with Mace so far, he definitely walked on the sadist side of crazy. Mia was just glad it wasn't *her* on the other side of the wall… at least, for now. When Beck and Alric returned with the witch… Mia swallowed hard, wracking her brain to remember everything Lucas had told her about witches.

Other than they cut the hearts out of female wolves.

Mia remembered the most valuable ones were female wolves who were mated to alphas. Or something like that. Her brain was still swimming in fear hormones and residual, shaky panic. She rubbed Jeeter's arm to reassure herself as much as her roommate. They were still alive. She had somehow managed to buy them some time. And she was sure Lucas would find a way to help them.

Maybe. If he didn't hate her for running away and getting in this mess in the first place.

Jak-the-driver, for his part, seemed supremely annoyed about his guard duty, sending them dark, glowering looks from the doorway. Mia's sympathy was far less than zero, but there was something off about him. He hadn't been lining up to leer or grope or threaten her the way the others had. He hadn't really spoken at all. Now, he stood next to the door with his arms folded, studying them, like they were causing him some kind of trouble.

Maybe he was late for his golf game.

He probably worked for Red Wolf, just like the rest. That made him a creep almost by definition, even if he wasn't as bad as the worst of them. At the moment, he was the only thing standing between her and Jeeter and freedom—except they were so far inside the Red pack's compound that even if somehow she could knock him over the head with a lamp or scratch his eyes out, they still wouldn't make it far without being caught.

Jupiter hiccupped so violently that the whole bed shook. Her sobs had settled a little. Mia held her tighter with her one-armed hug. "Jeeter, it's going to be okay, I promise."

Jak lifted an eyebrow at her words but said nothing.

Her roommate hadn't said a word through the whole ordeal, but somehow Mia speaking directly to her unlocked her mouth. And then she did nothing but stream out a babbling incoherency of words that all ran together.

"Oh my god, Mia, I can't believe it, I can't, they're just… they're *wolves*. And *you're* a wolf. And *he's* probably a wolf." She flicked a hand toward Jak at the door. "What in the ever-living hell… I can't believe it… why… why are they doing this? What's going on!" Jeeter took a breath and held it, tears leaking out of the corners of her eyes again.

"Oh, Jeeter." Mia wrapped both arms around her roommate, glad that she didn't resist or shirk away from her. Of all the ways to find out your roommate is a shifter… "I'm so sorry. I'm going to take care of everything, okay?"

"How?" The one word escaped her on another hiccup.

Well, Mia didn't know how, and even if she did, she couldn't discuss it in front of Jak, the glowering driver. "I'm sorry I didn't tell you before. About being a shifter, I mean."

Mia wouldn't have thought it possible, but Jeeter's eyes grew wider. "You could have told me, Mia! I'm your friend!" Her roommate balled up her fists and pounded them on the bed, one on each side of her, as if *this* was the ultimate betrayal on Mia's part, not ensnarling her friend in a shifter pack war. It seemed slightly ridiculous, given the situation, but if it was possible to overreact to something, she could count on Jupiter to find a way to do it.

"You're right," Mia said, holding back a smile. "I should have told you I have fangs and claws because, you know, that might have been relevant before now."

Jeeter gave her an outraged, *I know, right?* look.

Mia dropped her gaze to the sleek white comforter that covered their bed. "I *am* sorry, Jeeter, for getting you in this mess."

"Hey." Jeeter took Mia's hand, and she was surprised to find her roommate wasn't shaking anymore. "You don't apologize for anything. Holy crap, girl, you were…" Jeeter glanced at Jak, then dropped her voice, so it didn't carry quite so easily over the banging and moaning coming from the other side of the wall. "You were *awesome.*"

Mia snorted a short laugh. "I don't think awesome is the word you're looking for. Maybe stupid. Or stubborn."

Jak didn't even try to hide that he was listening in. In fact, he pushed away from the door, grabbed a chair from the corner by the lamp and the dresser, turned it backward, and sat directly in front of them.

Mia narrowed her eyes. Maybe the driver had decided it was his turn to leer and grope. But he didn't make a move toward them, and the chair was a pretty effective blockade anyway. Still, she gave him a glare, just in case.

The noise next door reached a crescendo, and then suddenly stopped. The silence that followed was almost more creepy… if only because Mace's attention might soon be circling back to her.

Mia was running out of time.

She needed options. And information.

But Jak spoke first. He tilted his head toward the wall-banging wall. "Mace is determined to claim you. It will go easier if you cooperate." But the way he said it was off... he wasn't threatening her or trying to bully her. It was almost as if he wanted to see if she was serious about resisting.

Mia frowned. "It'll go easier on him if he lets us go *now*. Before Lucas shreds his throat."

Jak nodded once and ducked his head. She had the feeling he was hiding a smile, but when he looked up, it was gone. "Even if the Sparks wolf comes for you, he's not going to get in the compound." Again, it was more of a test or a warning than a threat.

Mia scowled. "I think you might be underestimating him."

She couldn't decipher Jak's solemn nod.

"If you resist the witch, it will take longer," he said cryptically.

Mia swallowed. *"What* will take longer?" She shuddered again as she imagined the witch plunging a knife into her chest to carve out her still-beating heart, bloodthirsty-Aztec-style. Maybe that wasn't what Mace had in mind, but Mia couldn't think of anything *worse* he would need a witch for.

This time, Jak seemed genuinely surprised. He leaned back in his chair, eyebrows raised. "The shifting, of course." He looked askance at her as if trying to figure her out anew.

"The shifting," Mia echoed, still warding off visions of blood-dripping hearts. But, of course, that made sense. Mace couldn't force her to shift on his own—he'd already threatened her life, and she'd called that bluff. And Mia knew witches were used to force the shift, but somehow she'd forgotten that in all the trauma.

Jak was examining her closely. "You don't really understand what's going on here, do you?"

Mia pursed her lips tight. She'd probably been talking too much. Jak worked for Mace—just because he wasn't actively assaulting them like the rest didn't mean he was their friend. Far from it.

When she didn't answer, he glanced at Jeeter, then back to her. He slowly nodded. "You've been hiding it," he said.

Mia had a hollow feeling in the pit of her stomach. She had let loose information that was going to somehow hurt them. She kept her mouth shut, and Jeeter's hand slowly found hers and held it. Mia gave it a squeeze.

Jak stood up from the chair and slid it back to the corner. Then he stood before them, arms crossed, a dead serious look on his face. "If you resist the witch, you can delay the shift. If you resist submitting to Mace, you can delay that, too. But once you submit, there's nothing that can stop him from claiming you."

Then he turned and strode back to the door, taking up his station there like he had never left. His words made shivers crawl up her back, but he wasn't telling her anything she didn't already know. Or was he? The part about the witch was both relieving and terrifying. She knew the police used witches to get wolves to shift so they could take DNA samples in both forms. They wouldn't do that if it didn't *work*. Mia might be able to delay the shift, but she wouldn't be able to stop it. Maybe that's what Jak was telling her in his cryptic way.

But why?

Maybe he was telling her to hold out as long as she could. Because once she succumbed to Mace as her alpha, nothing would stop him from claiming her. But she already knew that. Or at least suspected it. Yet... something about Jak's words nagged at her. Before she could think about it too hard, a sharp rap at the door made her and Jeeter both jump.

Jak opened it. In the hall outside the door stood Mace, his face still flushed from his wall-banging activities. Behind him, a tall, drop-dead gorgeous woman smirked and devoured Mia with her eyes.

Mia had never seen her before, but there was no question in her mind: *she was a witch.*

Chapter Twenty-Five

"I'M NOT WAITING UNTIL EVENING," LUCAS growled. "I know where she is. I'm going to get her *now.*"

He slammed his fist down on his father's desk, just because he had nowhere else to put the anger building inside him. His father wanted to *wait*... all while Lucas knew what had to be happening inside the Red Wolf compound: that bastard Mace was putting his hands on Mia, and Lucas wasn't there to bash his face in for it. He had been such an idiot before, mired in his own head and the past and his own damn guilt about Tila. If he had just claimed Mia before, she would at least have some protection. But now... by the time he got her back... it might be too late.

Lucas's father straightened up and examined Lucas's clenched fist. They had been arguing for twenty minutes, circling and circling around the same issue of timing. The rest of the packs—his father's and Llyr's—were crammed into the office with them. The room stank of too many wolves and too much impatience as they spent precious minutes arguing *how* to get Mia out, rather than heading there to actually *do* it.

"I don't want Mia in the Reds' lair any longer than necessary," his father said calmly.

Lucas reined in his fury. His father's cool voice reminded Lucas that he wouldn't get what he needed that way—and he very much needed his father's help. And that of Llyr's pack, too, if he was going to be successful in pulling Mia out, not just going in blazing and getting himself killed in the process.

"I know, I just... you know one of them is going to try to claim her."

"If they know she's a wolf." His father seemed skeptical on that point, but he didn't know Mia the way Lucas did. If she were in trouble, her wolf would come out. Lucas had just finished teaching her to do exactly that. He couldn't imagine it not happening.

"They'll know," Lucas said. "Trust me… they'll know."

His father frowned but didn't argue any further. He just took a breath and leaned forward over his desk, which was strewn with a satellite map of the Red pack's compound that Lev had printed out.

"We all want Mia to join our family here," his father said. "To come home to you and to us. But the Reds aren't going to kill her, Lucas. If they still think she's human, we have a day before their deadline comes around. If they know she's a wolf, we have… less time. But they're also less likely to harm her. So the important thing is not to get there *fast*, but to make sure we can succeed in getting her out. We're only going to get one chance to do this."

Lucas curled up a fist and pressed it into the table. Then he stabbed a finger at one of the outlying houses. "She's here, in Mace's house."

His father cocked an eyebrow. "How do you know that?"

"I know *him*. He's the one orchestrating all of this."

"He *has* been vying to take over his brother's place as favored son for some time." His father nodded. "But why would he keep her there?"

Lucas took a breath. His wolf was still snorting

and howling inside him to *get Mia now*, but his human side had calmed enough to know planning was necessary. At least they were talking specifics now.

"The main house has too many eyes," Lucas said. "Even if this is approved by their alpha, that doesn't mean they want every minor wolf and housekeeper to see what's going down. The outlying houses afford more privacy." His wolf growled at the idea of what Mace would do with that privacy: even if he hadn't claimed Mia, Mace had a reputation for sexual predation, with a special taste for unsuspecting human females. He was the kind of wolf that gave shifters their rep for being brutal criminals and thugs. Lucas squeezed his eyes shut for a moment and forced himself to not think about Mia in Mace's hands. Otherwise, he'd be rushing off in a blind rage at any moment.

His father looked up from the map. "All right. We'll focus on Mace's house first, then have contingencies for scouting the other outlying houses, if she's not there. First, we'll have to breach the outer security. I believe they've electrified the perimeter, but we need to find out what other security systems they have installed. Llyr's pack will take point on that. Lev, I want you and your wolf-brothers to secure some weapons for us. We'll be entering the house as wolves—I don't want to leave any DNA traces, if possible—but we may need weapons on the way in and on the way out. Lucas, you'll stay here and help me work out the strategy."

The men surrounding them were restless, flitting looks to one another and tossing their heads as if they were already in wolf form. They were as eager to get started as Lucas was.

His father straightened and addressed them all. "This isn't a game. I want exactly as much aggression as necessary to bring the girls home, and no more. If nothing else, a massacre at the Red Wolf estate would draw police attention that none of us can afford."

The pack members dipped their head in agreement, but Lucas could smell the spike in testosterone. They were itching to draw some Red pack blood.

"I mean it." His father's voice had grown very quiet. Every wolf perked to listen. "Any wolf who does more than his share will answer to me." That chilled the air a little, but they still seethed, ready to go. "That being said, no one gets captured, and no one gets left behind. Including the girls. We succeed at this, or we fail as a pack. Understood?"

The packs yipped at that, and then broke apart, heading for the door and their respective assignments. Lucas's father held up a hand to stay Llyr and Lev before they trotted out with the rest.

"Meet back here by dusk," he told them. "We'll be ready by then."

Llyr gave him a short nod. Colin, stood next to him, face gaunt and serious. Llyr gestured for Colin to follow him, which he did, fists clenched. Lucas had won the right to claim Mia, but he knew what Colin must be thinking: that Mia may yet turn Lucas down. That Colin could still win her away. And whichever wolf saved Mia would likely win more than just her appreciation. Every instinct of hers would point her toward the stronger wolf as the better mate. And Colin understood instincts as well as Lucas did.

The idea made all the fur on Lucas's inner wolf bristle out, but to his human side, there was only one thing that was important: *getting Mia out.*

Lucas watched Colin leave, then caught Lev's arm before he reached the door. "Back in a minute," Lucas said over his shoulder to his father, then he followed a surprised Lev out the door. He pulled his little brother to the side, out of the crowd of wolves threading through the common room.

Lucas ducked his head, so only Lev could see the expression on his face. "Lev…" he started, then his throat grew thick. He cleared it out. "They might be hurting her."

Lev's look of surprise quickly faded into a stone-cold expression. "They damn well better not."

"But if they have…" Lucas stared up at the ceiling for a moment. He wasn't sure he would survive if he found her hurt. He knew for certain *Mace* wouldn't survive….but Lucas might lose his mind soon thereafter.

"Lucas, Dad's right," Lev said with a lighter, soothing voice. "Mace isn't going to hurt her. Especially if he knows she's a wolf. She's too valuable— not to just any given pack, but to wolves every-where. No wolf in his right mind would hurt a female, especially one as young as Mia. She's got lots of years of mating still ahead of her."

Lucas brought his gaze back down from the heavens. "I'm not entirely sure Mace is in his right mind. But I know for certain he'll claim her. He might have done it already." That thought made his teeth grind, and his wolf's jaws ache with a desire for Mace's throat.

"I know," Lev said quietly. "If that's the case, we'll just have to make sure we kill Mace."

It was enough to pull Lucas out of his seething rage. He gave his brother a small smile. "I was kind of planning on that, actually."

"I recommend we do it just as a precautionary measure."

Lucas snorted a short laugh. "I don't mind going to jail over it, Lev. But I don't even want you on this mission. You stay away from Mace, you hear me?"

"Look at you, all giving orders! One fight with Colin, and you think you're my alpha again? Just you try to stop me, brother." Lev's voice was light, but his face was deadly serious.

Lucas shook his head, but Lev's words swelled something inside him. Lucas had screwed up in the past, but he was a different wolf now. He had to get Mia back first—nothing else came close in priority —but if he could do that, things felt *possible* again. From the moment she came into his life, she'd had that effect: making him feel things that had been long dead. Challenging him to be a better wolf. A better man. Maybe, with her by his side, he could reclaim the other things he'd lost. The other parts of himself. Maybe he could actually be a true alpha again.

First things first.

Lucas put a hand on Lev's shoulder and gave him a small smile. "Just make sure you're in wolf form while you're doing stupid things. I don't want your DNA all over the place if I have to kill Mace."

Lev nodded. "Yeah, okay, boss. But it's going to work out. Mia's strong. Whatever happens, we're going to get her out of there, and you're going to have her back."

Lucas smiled as his younger brother's optimism. He could feel it working its magic on him as well. With his brothers by his side, they could do this.

Lev tipped his head toward his waiting pack-brothers. "I'll see you in an hour?"

"An hour." Lucas watched him go, then took a breath and headed back to his father's office.

They needed to be smart about this. Like his father said, they would only have one chance. And for Lucas, everything hinged on saving the girl who was saving his life.

Chapter Twenty-Six

THE WITCH SWAGGERED INTO THE ROOM WHERE MIA was being held prisoner. She was dressed in a way Mia could only call upscale goth: curve-hugging, slinky purple dress with a flame-like hem flitting around her shapely legs, a plunging neckline that accented her ample cleavage, and a black beaded-chain choker around her neck. The woman's hair hung in tumbling waves to her waist, a sheet of midnight black except for the wide swath of purple-tint. Her stiletto heels made her as tall as the wolves who stayed back by the door.

As the witch approached, Mia stood up from the bed, motioning Jeeter to stay seated—if at all possible, Mia wanted to keep her roommate out of this.

The witch's red-glossed lips curved into a smirk, and her eyes devoured Mia. "So this is your new plaything, Mace?"

"No touching, Hecca," Mace said. "Spells only." He had followed her into the room, closing the door and leaving his betas outside. Jak remained in the room, although Mia thought maybe Mace had forgotten about him, standing to the side, quiet.

Mia's heart was pounding, but she managed to hold her ground against the hungry looks from Hecca the Purple Witch. Then she reached out to lift Mia's chin with a single, long, purple-nailed finger. A shock ran through Mia's body, like the witch's finger was a lightning rod, and it had just conducted a thousand watts through her body, head to toe. Mia jerked violently, more a spasm of her muscles than any actual pain, but it made her gasp, nonetheless. An instant later, Mace knocked the witch's hand away.

"I said no touching," he growled.

The witch gave him an elaborate pout, but her black eyes dance. "But she's such a strong one. Are you sure you won't sell her to me?"

Mace got in the witch's face enough that her smirk faded and a hard, flinty look replaced it. "Don't push me, Hecca. I'm paying you well enough as it is. And I'd hate to have to tell my father that Morgan Art and Media can't be trusted anymore—and not just as partners in acquisitions, but in *all* our activities."

Mia had no idea what he was talking about, but it sounded like Red Wolf was involved in more than just investments. Somehow that didn't surprise her at all.

The witch curled up a lip. "No need to get testy, little wolf." Then she turned to examine Mia more clinically and with less greed. "A simple shifting spell is easily done. Then you can have your playmate, and I'll be on my way. I have an important social media branding meeting in an hour anyway."

Mace's voice was cool again. "I appreciate you coming on such short notice."

Mia braced herself as the witch looked her over. Jak was still standing quietly in the corner, watching. He said Mia could draw out the shift by resisting, so that's exactly what she planned. But she flinched when the witch reached toward her face again. Mace growled a warning, but Hecca only pinched a single strand of Mia's long hair between her fingers and plucked it out.

Mia's heart hammered. A smile grew on the witch's face. She rolled Mia's single hair between her palms, balling the long black strand into a tiny tangle, then she held up her palm in front of Mia's face with the ball resting in the center. The witch's eyes glittered as she focused it, and her red lips moved, but no sound came out. Then she smirked... and a half second later, the hair burst into flame. It was quickly consumed, and the witch gently blew the drift of smoke into Mia's face. It made her eyes water, and it smelled of burnt hair, but also of mint and lilac and a musky under scent that was pure...*wolf*.

Pain wrenched Mia's gut.

She doubled over with it, choking and coughing out the smoke of the witch's spell.

"Mia!" Jeeter's voice behind her was quickly followed by her roommate's hands on her shoulders, propping her up. Something sharp dug into Mia's thighs, where she was bracing herself. When she looked down, she could see her claws had come out, her hands already half wolf.

No, no, no. Mia shrugged off Jeeter's help—she didn't want her roommate getting too close, in case this went badly—then she closed her eyes and fought against the shift. It was like wrestling a vaporous snake that was seeping into her mouth, her nose, her every pore... the spell was a toxin let loose upon her body, sending tendrils of change throughout her system. The tiny shifts, the parts of her that were forced to be wolf, crashed against the parts that were still human. It wrenched a moan of agony out of her. Even her wolf was crying, confused and in pain, tucking her paws up and shaking her head to ward off the force of the spell.

It's okay, we can do this, we can do this... she was speaking straight to her wolf. She whimpered but calmed with Mia's words. *You're already part of me.* That seemed to relax her wolf even more, and the pain subsided, leaving an echo in the form of twinges and cramps that made it tough to stand up straight.

But Mia forced herself to.

Then she looked the witch straight in her black-sparkle eyes. "Is that all you've got?" Mia asked, wondering what the hell she was doing. But her words wiped the look of surprise off the witch's face and replaced it with one of pure evil. It shuddered fear through Mia's still-aching body.

The witch turned her glare on Mace. "I didn't think this was going to take all afternoon." Irritation made her voice squeaky like a small child's.

"Sorry to break up your day," Mace said, not sounding sorry at all. He was raking a gaze over in

Mia's straight-backed stance like it made his mouth water. "I told you she was strong." He licked his bottom lip like he already tasted her in his imagination.

The witch huffed her disgust, then dashed a hand toward Mia. She reflexively leaned back, but the witch caught one of her hairs and plucked it out again. Only this time, Hecca the Purple Witch came away with several long black strands. She quickly balled them up and repeated whatever silent spell she cast to set them on fire.

The cloud of smoke was thicker, grayer, and smelled like roasted wolf on a spit. Mia tried not to breathe it in, but it didn't matter. The pain hit her like a brick to the face, and she couldn't help sucking in gasps of air along with it. Her wolf screamed, and Mia wasn't sure if the sound had come out of her own mouth or not. She dropped to her knees, her arms clutched around her stomach... but then she saw that her knees weren't knees at all, but wolfy legs. She could see her muzzle lengthen her face, and this time, the whining reached her ears. It was definitely her wolf, not her human voice.

Human, human, human... the mantra sang in her head and throughout her body. It pushed against the wolfish parts, but that only ramped up the pain more. Mia moaned, and the sound seemed to ripple throughout her body.

"Stop it!" Jeeter's hands were on her again, so Mia knew she was close by, but her voice seemed so far away… "You're hurting her! Leave her alone!"

Mia wanted to tell her not to bother, but she couldn't form human words. *Human words… I need to speak… I have things to say…* the aching desire to tell the witch off helped Mia push through the pain. Slowly, her muzzle shortened into a nose. Her forearms lengthened and held her stomach once more. After a long moment, once she thought she was almost human again, she braced herself against her roommate and struggled to stand.

"You know," Mia said, breathless from the struggle. "I'm really starting to hate witches."

Mace's grin was so wolfish she thought *he* might shift at any moment. Even Jak, behind them, had unfolded his arms and was watching her with an open mouth.

The witch was aghast. "She shouldn't be able to…" She left it hanging there but then scowled at Mia.

Mace glanced at the witch, a sudden frown on

his face. "I'm only paying you if you get the job done, Hecca. Don't tell me you can't——"

She cut him off with a flick of her purple painted nails. "Of course I *can.*" The witch eyed Mia. "But I may need to... *touch* her. *If* you don't mind."

He arched a brow at the witch and pressed his lips together. He seemed to mull his choices, gave Mia another hungry look, and then said, "Do it. But anything other than shifting, and I'll have your throat for it, witch."

Hecca the Witch snorted at his threat as if that didn't concern her much at all. She turned her dark eyes on Mia and slowly eased within reach. Mia couldn't help the shakes that were rumbling through her body.

She swallowed.

The witch reached a single finger toward her.

Mia turned her head away, even though she knew it wouldn't matter.

"Please don't hurt her——" Jeeter's plea was cut off by Mia's scream.

The witch's finger on her cheek burned like a crackling fire had ignited on that spot and was now consuming her. It spread from that point like light-ning across her face, down her neck, across her back and out to the tips of her fingers. When Mia stopped screaming and gasped in a breath, she realized her face was mashed against the floor.

No, not her face. Her muzzle.

Her tongue lolled out. The bitter, scratchy taste of the carpet brushed against it. Her whole body quivered from head to toe. The shift had been sudden and complete and had burned her to the ground. She barely had the strength to whimper, but that sound came out regardless. She felt Jeeter's hands on her, petting her, soothing her. Mia tried to lift her head, but everything ached. She let it lie back on the floor. Her wolf eyes could barely see what was happening in the rest of the room, so she closed them. But she could hear the voices.

"You didn't harm her, did you?"

"She's fine, Mace."

"Then go."

"Not even a *thank you, Ma'am?*"

"Get out."

The door opening and closing.

Mia struggled to open her eyes. She blinked, and the room came into focus. Mace loomed over her. Jak still stood by the door, impassive. What had he said? That she could delay it, but she couldn't stop it: the shifting. *The submission.* That was coming next, but she didn't think she had any strength to withstand it. She felt about as strong as a wet paper towel: one particularly strong tug, and she would rip apart.

"Get up." It was Mace's voice, but she was unsure who he was talking to. Jeeter's hands left her body, and Mia missed their touch, but even so, she felt a little of her strength returning. That wolfy ability to recover from just about anything—anything short of a carved-out heart—was making itself known. But still, she was weak. So weak. Even more, it felt like her spirit was breaking. This was what Mace wanted: to break her. She didn't want to give him the pleasure, but if he ordered her to submit to him... she didn't know if she could fight it.

She whined and looked to Jak again. But he was as still as a statue next to the door. If she couldn't fight the submission, Mace would claim her. Probably right now. Would he order Jak away or would he stay and watch? What about Jeeter? It was humiliating to even think about.

Something deep inside her welled up and protested. She wasn't supposed to be mated to Mace. *Lucas* was the one she belonged with. And

Lucas was coming for her if she could just hold on…

"Get her off the floor." Mace's voice again.

A scrape of hard-soled shoes, and Jak's hands were on her, lifting her gently. He held her upright as her legs wobbled under her. He didn't say anything, but his touch was careful like he knew exactly how fragile she was at that moment.

Mace stepped in front of her, looking down. She peered up at him, giving him all the hatred she could in her glare… but he was all smiles.

"Well fought, Mia," he said. "You're even stronger than I guessed. You'll make a fine addition to my harem."

Mia's stomach heaved. *Harem?* Seriously? This guy was a piece of work. Lucas wouldn't even claim her when she *wanted* him to, simply because he thought he couldn't protect her the way she deserved. He was everything Mace was not—good and kind and decent.

Jak's hands left her, and she teetered but managed to stay upright.

To her horror, though, Mace shifted until he was in wolf form before her.

Submit.

The command almost knocked her over. It swept like a wave through her already jittery system.

No, she thought. *You can't have me.* She had no idea if that thought would keep her from submitting, but it was how she truly felt, regardless.

Mia, Mia, Mace thought. He stepped forward and rubbed his muzzle all over hers. She turned her head away in disgust, but he just licked the side of her face. *You're perfect. Strong. Resistant. A fighter to the last. Such a challenge. Exactly the kind of mate I want in my bed. And you'll welp the strongest of wolves for my pack. Don't you see? You were meant to belong to me, Mia.*

I do not belong to you! she thought.

Oh, but you will, he thought. *Submit.*

Her head bowed with the strength of the command. *No,* she thought, but her resistance was fading.

Submit to your alpha.

You're not my alpha, she thought, but she leaned back, forepaws stretched before her. It was like her body was weighed down by a tremendously heavy blanket, and she couldn't help but assume the position of submission.

Submit to me, Mia, and you will forever belong to me.

No, she thought, but the last vestige of her resistance fell away like a mist. *I belong to Lucas.* Then her tail tucked between her legs, and her submission was complete. She could feel the bond seizing her, a magical thing that stretched between her and her alpha: *Mace.*

He stepped back to glare his dark wolf eyes into hers. *What?*

I belong to Lucas and nothing you say or do can change that. Somewhere from within her, she held onto that core belief, even in submission. She would do whatever Mace told her. She couldn't resist her alpha. His will was her command. But she could still speak the truth to him. And that was the truth: she belonged to Lucas, and no matter what Mace did to her, that would always be true.

Mace growled, then he shifted quickly into human form. The submission bond dimmed a little, but she was still in her wolf form, and it still gripped her like a physical force. She wouldn't move or shift or do anything until he allowed it.

She waited.

He growled, stomping around the room and shoving on his clothes. She couldn't understand why he was upset, but she waited patiently for his command to release her.

Mace stalked up to Jak, whose arms were folded as he stood by the door.

"Has Lucas claimed her?" Mace shouted in his face.

"What?" Jak asked, then shot a look at Mia. She could barely see them with her eyes downcast, awaiting Mace's commands.

"The Sparks wolf! Has he taken a new mate? Why haven't I heard of this before?"

Jak's eyes narrowed, still examining Mia. "I don't know." He paused, then looked to Mace. "But if she's his, you can't claim her."

"The hell I can't!" Mace spun away from him and stalked over to her. "Rise!" he commanded her.

Her muscles screamed their protest, but her alpha's command was absolute. She rose up from her submission pose and shifted all in one motion. Only when she stood naked and shaking in front of him did she notice the clothes she shed in the rapid shift the witch's spell had commanded. They lay at her feet.

Before she could decide whether she should pick them up and get dressed, Mace had grabbed hold of her around the waist and yanked her close to him. Her bare skin slid against his chest and the silky fabric of his still-open shirt, but it evoked nothing but horror. This was it. He wasn't even going to wait for the others to leave. Shudders ran across her back, and every hair on her body stood on end.

With his other hand, Mace grabbed her hair and bent her head back. He growled into her neck like he was itching to bite her. "Has another wolf claimed you?"

Her mind was whirring. What had Lucas said about the claiming? Her head was dizzy with trying to think: the bond was for life. It could only be broken by the death of the male. She remembered a male could have more than one mate, but Lucas had never explained what stopped the reverse from happening. Could a female be bound to more than one male? He didn't really say... just that she would be bound. For life. Did that mean... would a second claiming kill her?

Mace shook her. "Answer me!"

She didn't know the right answer—would it stop him, if he thought Lucas had actually claimed her already? Or would it anger him, spur him on? Behind Mace, Jak had edged up to them. He gave her a small nod. She wasn't entirely certain, but she took a guess. He was trying to help her delay him again.

"Yes," Mia eeked out, her teeth clamped against

the pain of Mace's hold on her hair. "Lucas is my mate."

Mace growled and gripped her hair even tighter. "I don't care who has claimed you, I *will* make you mine. Maybe Lucas needs to find a convenient way to die."

Mia's eyes went wide. *No! She couldn't let that—*

"Your father would not be happy to see a dead female wolf in his lair." Jak's voice was soft, but it froze Mace. Anger rippled across his face, but his hold on Mia relaxed.

A dead wolf? Mia swallowed. So it would kill her. Or at least, it would if she was actually mated.

Mace released her and shoved her back on the bed. He stared at her with a hateful loathing that made her skin crawl. Jeeter had scooped up her clothes from the floor and vainly tried to cover Mia with them. Mia couldn't look away from her alpha —the bond's power was intense, even now in human form. She held her t-shirt over her chest, even as his stare kept her captive.

"She's lying." Mace's voice was cold. And dangerous. Mia had the sense she would pay for lying to him if he found out.

"Perhaps," Jak said evenly. "But if she's not…"

Mace growled, but looked away from her to

glare at Jak, thus releasing her from his stare. Mia's hands were shaking so badly, Jeeter had to help her get her t-shirt on over her head.

"There's a simple test," Jak said, his tone cool. "Better safe than sorry."

"Bring it. Tell me the moment you know." Mace spun away and angrily strode from the room.

Jak waited until the door closed behind him, then turned to Mia. "I didn't know you were already mated."

Mia tried to keep a neutral face. "I forgot to bring it up earlier. Things were a little... tense."

He arched an eyebrow but nodded. "It will take a little time to get the test and the results. No more than a few hours, though."

Mia nodded. As he turned to leave the room, she couldn't help wondering why he was helping her. Or even if he really *was* helping her. But she couldn't worry about that now.

As soon as the door closed behind Jak, her roommate started saying, "Oh my god, Mia," over and over. Finally, she broke that pattern with a shaky breath. "I was so scared for you."

Then she stopped rambling and helped Mia get dressed. The two of them curled up on the bed, holding each other in silence. Exhaustion swept over Mia. She couldn't believe she felt sleepy with everything that had happened—the terror of Mace's grasp, the horror of submitting to him, the scoring marks all of it left across her soul—but she was tired. Deathly tired.

Mia burrowed her head into the pillow and let herself drift into sleep.

SOMETIME LATER, JAK BROUGHT IN A SHORT WOMAN who drew some blood from Mia and then left. She barely roused from her sleep for it, lapsing back again as soon as they were gone. By the time Mia awoke again, night had fallen. It was utterly dark in their room except for the sliver of moonlight falling between the curtains. Jeeter slept next to her. Soft snores told Mia her roommate was just as wiped out from the ordeal as she was, even without the witch spell and forced submission.

The echo of that bond still shivered through her. Even in human form, she could feel its hold on her, like a heavy blanket holding her down. The perimeters of it were the limits of what she could do. She could feel it binding her to this place: her alpha's home. Now it was her home, too. It was where she belonged, and where she would always belong. That belonging would be even more complete when her alpha came to claim her, which would happen as soon as he knew the truth about her not being mated to anyone else.

She had always had a sense that something was missing in her life, but she never had quite known what it was. No father. No pack. Not even a mother who knew anything about what Mia truly was. Before she discovered this world of wolves, she didn't even have words for that essential thing was missing, but now she knew: her wolf wanted to belong. To a pack. To a mate. It called to the core of her being to not be alone in the world. Her wolf knew she shouldn't have to fight through life, every step of the way, all by herself.

And now she wouldn't. Even if Mace wasn't the alpha she might have wished for, he was the alpha she had. And her wolf sense told her the magic of the submission bond was just a glimmer of what the claiming would be like: when her alpha took her, the sense of belonging would be utter and complete. He would care for her, and his home would forever be hers. Part of her mind fought valiantly against the idea that this house of Mace's was her *home*, but the submission bond was so strong that it didn't matter. Something deep in her bones cemented her to this place. With Mace.

And soon he would claim her.

Her mind fought against that thought, too. Before submitting to Mace, she really *had* belonged with Lucas. If only he had been ready for a mate. Being with him would have been so much better: Lucas would have cared for *her*. She would have been more than a worthy conquest. More than just a vehicle for welping more, stronger wolves. Lucas would have cared for her human side as much as her wolf.

But he had lied to her when he said it would feel the same with someone else. Even with her submission bond to Mace muddling her brain, she knew that wasn't true. It *wasn't* the same with Mace… it would never be that all-consuming, burning heat she had with Lucas… but none of that really mattered.

This was the life she would have now.

She would have to make the best of it.

She tried to picture Mace claiming her, taking her into his bed, as a good thing. But her body rebelled and shook so hard, she nearly woke up Jeeter. Mia took a deep breath and tried again to prepare her mind for what was coming. Jak said it would be a few hours at most. She needed to be ready when the time actually arrived. It would be better that way. Or maybe *better* wasn't the right word.

Tolerable, perhaps.

As she wrestled with that idea, the door to her room slowly creaked open. Mia twisted her head to see Jak slip in and close the door behind him. He didn't turn the lights on, probably because he didn't want to startle them. Mia tried to ease up to sitting without waking Jeeter.

"Did you get the test results back?" she asked quietly, stretching the sore spots from her arms and neck. She knew the test would show she was unmated. That Mace could claim her without killing her. She was a little surprised he would care, but apparently his father would. Or someone. Enough that it stopped Mace.

But now that he knew the truth, he would be free to do what he wanted with her. Forever.

"I'm not here about the test results." Jak eased onto the bed next to her. He still hadn't turned on the light. "I've come to help you escape."

Chapter Twenty-Seven

"WHAT DO YOU MEAN, YOU'RE RESCUING ME?" MIA stared at Jak, the Red pack wolf who had been helping her all along with delaying Mace's attempt to claim her. But she had already submitted to her alpha. As soon as he found out she wasn't already mated to another wolf, he would come for her. "What about the test results?"

"I've delayed the results as long as I can," Jak said, "but they'll probably finish the analysis within the hour. You have to leave before then."

"Leave?" Mia frowned and looked down at the bed she was sitting on. Her roommate, Jupiter, was sleeping next to her. Night had fallen while she and Jeeter had been sleeping, and Jak hadn't turned on the light when he came in. There was just the moonlight blanketing everything with its silver sheen. She looked back up at Jak. "I can't leave. Mace will be here any minute."

The dark-haired, dark-eyed shifter gave her a soft look. "It's the submission bond, Mia. It's confusing you. You *want* to escape."

Escape? She couldn't simply walk out of Mace's house. Not just because she knew the doors were locked, but because this was where she belonged. Mia shook her head, literally trying to fling those thoughts, those *feelings*, out of her head. She *did* want to escape. If that was possible. Even as she thought it, she doubted it.

"Wake your roommate," Jak insisted. "Ask her if she wants to leave."

Jupiter stirred next to her, their voices disturbing her sleep. Jeeter would want to leave, of course. She wasn't a wolf. Mace wasn't her alpha. Some of the clouds cleared from Mia's mind. If Jak could get Jeeter out, she had to help him.

"Jeeter," she said in a hoarse whisper while she shook her roommate's shoulder. "Jeeter, wake up."

Her roommate slowly opened her eyes and squinted at her. "Mia?"

"Jak's going to help you escape." The more she thought about it, the more urgent the idea became. Mia scrambled up from the bed and urged Jupiter to do the same. She was slower moving, still waking up, but she managed it.

"I'm helping you *both* escape." There was disappointment in Jak's voice, a sadness that made Mia frown. Oh, right—he wanted them *both* to leave. And that seemed like a legit thing to do, although as soon as she thought that, her mind got fuzzy again. Like a haze had settled on her brain and blurred everything at the edges. Her wolf didn't want to leave, that much she was certain about. But what about her human side? Did *she* want to escape?

Mia pictured being claimed by Mace. It made her human body shudder.

She nodded to herself then looked up into Jak's concerned face. "I want to escape, too."

Relief made his shoulders drop. "Good. Let's go."

Mia held Jupiter's hand and followed Jak to the door. He peeked out into the hall, then motioned for them to follow. The hallway and stairwells were dark, but there was light coming from underneath the bedroom door next to hers: *Mace's bedroom.* Mia hesitated by the door, straining to hear, afraid their footfalls might make the floor creak. Muffled sounds came from behind the door, not quite voices. Jak urged them toward the stairwell, and she reluctantly followed. As they descended, he put a finger over his lips to keep them quiet. At the bottom, she saw Mace's beta, Alric, passed out on the white leather couch. Beer bottles littered the nearby table. Mia's wolf bristled: Mace's beta was supposed to be guarding her, but he'd apparently drunk himself into a stupor instead.

She frowned. That thought didn't fit with the fact that she was sneaking out with Jupiter and Jak. *Escaping.* The word rolled around in her mind, but it still felt strange: *why would she leave her alpha?*

Jak had taken her by the elbow, steering her toward the front door. Jupiter was already outside in the moon-drenched front yard, which looked like it could be any suburban home in Seattle: lush carpet of grass, decorative bushes, and a few broad-leafed trees lining the driveway. The other houses cast yellow spotlights to compete with the moon's silver frosting over the landscape, including the black drive that wound through the Red pack compound.

Mia stood in the open doorway, her stomach

twisted in knots. This was Mace's domain. His territory was marked: she could *feel* the presence of him hanging over her. Jak and Jeeter were urging her forward, but her feet were welded in place. *Why was she leaving?*

Jak looked desperate, glancing behind him, in the house, all around. He clearly didn't want to be seen leaving with her. "Mia! We have to go *now.*"

Her stomach heaved at the words. She shook her head and took a step back.

Jak reached in, grabbed her arm, and hauled her across the threshold. Just as she was about to yell out her protest, his hand clamped over her mouth, then he dragged her farther from the door, kicking and flailing. She would have screamed, but she couldn't suck in a breath. When he finally let her go, about ten feet from the door, she tumbled over her own feet and landed on the lawn. Once she was able to pull in a breath, she was about to let loose a yell for help... then stopped.

The grass was wet under her hands. The cool air, perfumed by the nearby forest, bathed her face. The fog in her mind cleared out. *Freedom.*

The submission bond was still there—she could feel it deep inside her, a tiny tug back toward the house, toward Mace—but it no longer clouded her thoughts. Jak had gotten her out, but it had required him literally dragging her from Mace's territory. The residual anxiety of leaving turned to disgust. She scrambled to her feet and gave Jak a sharp nod. He was watching her carefully, and Jupiter's eyes were wide as if Mia had just lost her mind.

"Let's go," Mia said as loud as she dared, glancing around to see if anyone else would hear.

Jak smirked and tipped his head toward the nearby forest. "Follow me."

Mia took Jupiter's hand, and the three of them ran for the wall of trees surrounding the estate. Once they had sunk into the cover of darkness, they had to slow down, so as not to trip over the gnarled undergrowth. The moon pierced the canopy overhead, but only in spots, like weak streetlamps that dotted a path through the darkness. They stumbled along in silence for a short while.

"No flashlights?" Mia asked Jak quietly.

He was still smiling. "Too easy for them to find you."

Jupiter had let go of her hand to keep balance, but now she was ahead of Mia in picking her way through the forest.

Jeeter glanced back. "What in the actual hell

was all that back there?" she asked. "Are you okay, Mia?" She looked forward again just in time to duck under a low-lying branch.

A flush of embarrassment ran through Mia. She knew it was the submission bond, but she didn't know how to explain it to her roommate.

Jak jumped in. "She's bound to her alpha," he said to Jeeter. "Leaving his territory causes a lot of anxiety if it's contrary to his wishes. Mia knew Mace didn't want her to leave. Her wolf knew it even more. Even the strongest of wolves would have had a hard time breaking the wishes of their alpha."

Mia nodded. "It's a compulsion to obey. Not impossible to break... but almost." They were Lucas's words, but she understood them so much better now.

"Good grief," Jeeter said, aghast. "What is with all this mating and claiming and submission crap? I don't get it. Like at all."

It had to seem strange. Mia couldn't entirely disagree. And Mace really twisted all of it to be just... *wrong.* "It's complicated."

"Yeah." Jeeter frowned at her. "You say that a lot." She was miffed, but that sent a strange zing of happiness through Mia. She would rather have

Jeeter pissed at her than crying and screaming and sobbing, like she had been for the past half day they'd been held at the Red pack estate.

Jak held a branch back for Mia to pass. "I didn't think you were going to make it there for a minute. But the witch wasn't kidding when she said you were strong."

She passed him, frowning. "Why exactly are you helping us?"

He gave a sigh. "Not everyone in the Crittenden pack believes in treating females the way Mace does."

"How many *not everyones?*" Jupiter asked. "Because as far as I can tell, all wolves are complete assholes."

Jak gave a light-hearted laugh, and Mia frowned. It had to look that way to her roommate.

A half-beat later, Jeeter seemed to realize what she had said. "Wait… I mean, not *you guys*. I didn't mean that, Mia. I just… it's been so crazy and…"

"Jeeter," Mia cut her off. "It's okay. They *are* assholes."

Jak was chuckling.

Mia grimaced. "But there are a whole lot of wolves that are, well, amazing and awesome and…" She stopped because even those words felt inadequate to describe how she felt. "Wolves like Lucas." Tears jumped to her eyes, making it even harder to stumble through the dark. She might actually get to see him again. And if she did, she was going to spend the next several months apologizing constantly about running off like a child. And begging forgiveness for everything. And hoping he might at least still want to be friends, like she had tried and failed at so miserably. Or maybe just hug him…

"Wait, you mean *Lucas* is a wolf, too?" Jeeter's screeching voice pulled Mia out of her crazy thought-train and back into the present: they still had to finish their escape. "Dammit, is everyone a wolf? Because this is starting to really freak me out. I mean, I knew there were shifters out there, but jeez—"

"Yes, Lucas is a wolf." Mia sighed. She still had to catch Jeeter up on *so much*. "He's one of the good ones. And there's apparently at least one good wolf in the Red pack, too." She tossed a *thank you* look to Jak as he led them through the forest.

His grin caught a stray moonbeam and flashed white. "We're not all bad."

"So… what *are* you?" Mia asked. At his arched

eyebrow, she elaborated, "You're not in Mace's pack, are you?"

"No. I'm his older brother's beta." He grimaced.

Mia frowned. "So you're disobeying your alpha by helping us?" That seemed wrong, not to mention extremely difficult to pull off. Mia had just experienced firsthand how hard it was to go against her alpha's wishes.

"No." Jak seemed very clear about that but took a moment to explain further. "My alpha sent me to keep an eye on Mace during this whole... operation. There's a lot of infighting. And that was before we knew you were a shifter. Securing a female like you as a mate would be a big boost for Mace within the larger structure of Red Wolf. My alpha has no interest in seeing that happen."

"So this is all about a quarrel between the brothers?" Mia was mildly disgusted. Not that Mace didn't do much worse things, but that seemed so... petty.

"I suppose that's one way to look at it." He came to a stop, so Mia and Jeeter stopped with him. "But I'm helping you, Mia, because I couldn't..." He seemed to struggle for words, then glanced back in the direction of Mace's house. When he looked at her again, his jaw was set, and even with the soft glow of moonlight around him, Mia could see the strength of his determination. "I couldn't stand by and let another female fall under Mace's control."

She frowned, not exactly sure what that was all about, but she recognized the tone and the sentiment: he was what Lev called an alpha-in-waiting. And the kind-hearted, protective type, like Lucas.

"Thank you," was all she managed to get out.

He dipped his head, but then he reached back to pull something out of his pocket. It was a phone —*her* phone—and a wad of bills.

"You're going to need these." He handed them to her.

"Wait, wait, wait," Jeeter said, working her way through the undergrowth back to them. "What are you talking about? You can't just leave us here in the forest."

"You're going to be fine," he said. "I've programmed Mia's phone GPS with a location just beyond the perimeter. I've left a moped for you there. Worst comes to worst, you can take the moped all the way back to Seattle. But there's also money for a cab, which would be better. Harder to track."

"You're not coming because you don't want to be seen helping us," Mia guessed.

He smiled. "The perimeter has cameras. The section where the moped is stationed should be less visible, but still. I really would rather not have Mace discover who let his prized alpha female loose—for a number of reasons, but not least because he would have my throat for it. Besides, you need to get outside the perimeter fence, and it's electrified."

"Okay…" Jeeter said. "Exactly how are we supposed to do that? I can't just, like, shift and jump over it, you know. We're not *all* wolves."

Jak grinned wider. "Neither could I. It's about eight feet tall." He sobered quickly. "Follow the GPS. When you get to the fence, wait for my signal. I'll relieve the security guy who monitors the fence from the command center in the main house. He'll be happy to go. He likes to take smoke breaks, and our alpha won't allow smoking in the house."

"Well, I'm glad you wolves are progressive about that at least." Jupiter crossed her arms and cocked her hip to the side.

Jak shook his head but ignored her. "As soon as I have the fence turned off, I'll send you a text. You've got five minutes to get over, then I'll have to turn it back on. Just make sure you get across in time."

Mia nodded. "As soon as you text us, we'll be out of here."

"Good." He pressed his lips together, like he wanted to say something more, then thought better of it and turned to head back the way they came.

"Hey, Jak," Mia called. She waited for him to stop. "Thanks for yanking me out of the house."

He smiled wide at that, then ducked his head, like he was shy about what he'd done, which was just crazy. He had saved her life and probably her sanity as well. Not to mention Jeeter's. Mia watched as he strode back through the forest toward the compound. Then she turned on her phone and quickly navigated to the GPS he had set up for her. The soft glow lit the way through the forest for them. Mia knew that was dangerous, so she took her bearing, then covered the face of the phone with her hand.

"C'mon, let's go," she said to Jupiter.

They tromped through the darkened forest. It seemed like it went on forever, and there was no way she could have made it without frequent checks of the GPS, but it didn't actually take long for them to reach the perimeter. Maybe five minutes.

The fence was tall and hummed, but it looked possible to climb. Beyond it, through another dozen yards of thick undergrowth and trees, the moonlight reflected off a road.

And a moped.

"That Jak guy totally just saved us, didn't he?" Jeeter asked.

"Yeah. He did."

"I still don't really understand why."

Mia frowned. "You know... I think some wolves are just like that. The good ones at least. Did I ever tell you how I met Lucas?" Of course, she hadn't— she *couldn't*. Until a few hours ago, she didn't have any friends she could tell anything like that. Not human ones, anyway.

"Did he save you from another pack of blood-thirsty wolves bent on claiming you for their wolfy princess harem?" Jeeter asked suspiciously. "Because I'm starting to think this is like an everyday occurrence for you, girl."

Mia had to laugh at that. Partly because it was nearly true. And partly because only Jeeter could come out of all this with her sense of humor intact. "Almost. He saved me from Mace and his goons in an alley outside *The Deviation.*"

"*The Deviation?*" Jeeter shook her head. "Good

thing you quit that job. The place was full of losers."

Mia grinned.

"So… what do we do now?" her roommate asked.

Mia peeked at the messages on her phone. Nothing yet. "Now… we wait."

Chapter Twenty-Eight

LUCAS HUNCHED DOWN BEHIND A FALLEN LOG. The forest stretched in front of him to the humming perimeter fence of the Red pack's compound. He and his father's pack held back while Llyr and his pack tackled the fence. They all wore a set of infrared LEDs strapped to their foreheads, looking like ridiculous miners wearing headlamps only without the lamps. Lev assured them the infrared signal would disrupt the surveillance cameras if they happened to sweep by this stretch of the perimeter at the wrong moment. Instead of seeing their stealthy black-clad bodies, the cameras would record a bright-white spot where each pack member's face should be. It would essentially prevent a recording of their identity while breaking and entering.

Get in, get out, no evidence, no casualties. Those were his father's orders, and between Lev's technology, the stun gun weapons, and the grounding device for the electric-fence that Llyr and Colin were setting up, they had a fair chance at it.

The kicker would be the alarm system. It would be triggered as soon as the fence was blown. So they also had to get in *fast*—which meant shifting, running like hell, and hitting Mace hard where he lived before the rest of the Red pack could be rallied to his defense. From what they could tell from the satellite imagery, the standalone houses were mostly single-family. The majority of the non-mated pack members would be in the main house, which their assault force wouldn't be hitting at all, if possible. Hopefully having an overwhelming force of wolves descend upon Mace's house would be sufficient to get the girls out without casualties. And without leaving DNA evidence.

Just to be safe, they would be splitting into two teams: the first with shifters going in fast but weaponless, because carrying a stun gun in your mouth wasn't the smartest plan; and the second team in human form, coming up from behind with stun guns. While the first team took Mace's house, the second would search the others, shifting if they found the girls and had to penetrate one of the houses. They would only engage in human form if weapons were needed. Mainly, the second team would serve as cover for the extraction, once the first team had pulled out the girls.

The first team would be Lucas and his father's pack, including Lev, his father's beta, Rent, and four of the younger wolves. The second team was Llyr, Colin, and a half dozen wolves from his pack. In wolf form, they would communicate telepathically; otherwise, they would rely on the shortwave headsets Lev had obtained for them.

Llyr signaled from the fence that they were ready.

"Hold for my mark," Lucas's father said through the headsets, bringing everyone on his team to attention. Scaling the fence would be tough with paws, so they would climb first and shift second, dropping their clothes and gear by the fence. They'd pick their clothes up on the way out, assuming they weren't hauling ass and didn't have time to get dressed.

"Now!" His father's voice came through the headset. The hum of the fence crackled and then sparked out with a flash. A few electric bolts arced to the ground near Llyr's team. They jumped back just as Lucas, Lev, and the others on their team surged forward. By prearrangement, Rent went first, testing that the live wire was dead, then they all took the fence right behind him, wasting no time in scrambling over. Llyr's team was right on their heels. As soon as Lucas and the first team members dropped to the other side, they shed their clothes, leaving the headlamp for last in case of cameras, finally shifting out of that and leaving it in a pile with the rest of their gear.

Then they ran like crazy through the forest.

Spots of moonlight penetrated the branches above, but the Red's private forest preserve was deep enough that they couldn't see the lights from the compound. The pack's collective sense of direction kept them on a straight line to the estate buried inside. Lucas heard Llyr's team following them, crashing through the underbrush with their human bodies and boots, but they were much slower. With any luck, the first team would have things wrapped up and well in hand by the time Llyr's team arrived. The first team quickly reached the edge of the forest, and the lights of the main house shone brightly in the night.

Hold up, Lucas's father thought, and as a single pack, they came to a stop and kept from breaching into the moonlight frosted lawn. *Hug the edge until we reach the target.*

The instructions weren't necessary—they had pre-planned their route, and this path would take them around the main house and closest to Mace's before breaking cover—but his father's signal helped to keep them tightly coordinated as a group. As Lucas surged along with them, a part of him drank in the pack unity like a man ten days in the desert. The thrill of moving as one, of having one thought, one purpose, and in this case, such a righteous one… it brought a feeling of completeness he hadn't experienced since Tila died. A sensation of brotherhood and honor he thought he would never have again. He surged to the front of the pack, the exhilaration and adrenaline bringing his strength and speed to the fore.

Hold up, Lucas's father repeated, and they came to a noisy stop at the edge of the underbrush. They were within sight of Mace's house now, and every single one of them was on high alert: looking, sniffing, listening for any sign of movement. There were eight of them altogether: even if Mace had a couple of his betas on guard with him in the house, the team should be able to overwhelm them quickly enough. The trick would be getting inside the house without knocking on the front door. For that, Lev carried in his mouth a small pack with an electronic lock scrambler as well as some old-fashioned picks. He'd have to shift briefly to human to use them, but he had gloves, and it would allow them to take the place by surprise. They could throw a brick through a window, but that wasn't going to gain them entry without someone getting hurt.

Lucas pawed the dirt, waiting for his father's command. If it was up to him, or if Lev took too long, Lucas would just shift and kick the door in. Right as he was about to question why they were waiting, a group of four men broke from the main house and ran toward Mace's.

Pack of four, Lucas thought.

I see them, his father replied.

The team pawed the ground restlessly as they waited for his command.

We'll take them from behind as they enter Mace's house. Gain entry that way, his father thought.

Lucas liked that plan… a lot. Lev spit out the toolkit, and the entire team tensed, ready for the signal. Lucas gauged the distance… the Red pack team was nearly to the lawn of Mace's house…

Now! his father commanded.

They surged as one, breaking from the cover of the forest and loping with pounding speed toward the house. Because of the angle, they could no longer see the four Red wolves as they approached the front door of Mace's house, but that was good: it meant the Reds wouldn't see them either, not until Lucas's team was right on top of them.

In a rush of fur and adrenaline, they rounded the corner of the house and bounded across the lawn. They had perfect timing: the four Red wolves had the door open but were still filing in. Without a single growl among them for warning, the team attacked from behind. Lucas surged ahead, so he reached them first, but he was just the tip of an avalanche of fur and teeth mowing down the pack members in the doorway. Two of the Reds reflexively shifted—Lev and one of the younger wolves wrestled with them, rolling in a ball of claws and clothes across the entranceway. Lucas's father and Rent took the two in human form, knocking them down and getting jaws to throat in no time. The Reds still fought back, but Lucas knew they were caught. He plowed forward into the living area, looking for Mia. He and Lev were tasked with extracting the girls, but Lev was occupied, so Lucas would secure them first, then figure out the situation for retreat.

There were no girls in the living area, but the place had plenty of beer bottles. A growl rumbled in his chest with the thought of Mia being held not only by that bastard Mace, but a drunken pack of his wolves as well. Lucas sniffed and ran—through the kitchen, hallway, rear bedroom, and bath—but they were empty. It had only been a few seconds since they'd entered, but that commotion couldn't have been missed by anyone else inside the house. Lucas stopped and listened... sure enough, shouts of alarm came from upstairs.

He ran back to the front, where the four Red wolves were now subdued, just as he expected, then bounded up the stairs, three at a time. He heard someone following behind him, one of his father's pack, but Lucas had speed and a head start and reached the second floor first. It was a hallway with several bedroom doors. Most were closed, but the closest one was open, spilling light into the hall. Lucas rushed the room, hoping to catch whoever was inside by surprise. The pack brother who had followed him up the stairs was right behind him.

Lucas pulled up short when he saw the gun.

But it was too late.

Mace fired.

The sound jerked through Lucas's body, jolting him and making him crouch. But after a half second, he realized he wasn't shot. In the other half of that second, he took in the scene: Mace standing with the gun; a female huddled behind him; two of Mace's betas, weapons drawn. Lucas's legs unlocked, and he scrambled backward. He was seriously outmatched. More importantly: the female wasn't Mia or her roommate.

"Stay where you are, or I'll shoot you, too." Mace's growled words only registered when Lucas backed into something warm and furry in his retreat. He whipped his head back: a wolf lay on the floor, and two more were standing just outside the door. The one on the floor whimpered and whined and tried to drag himself back. He left a smear of blood across the pure white carpet... all the air went out of Lucas.

It was Lev.

THE MOPED BEYOND THE ELECTRIFIED FENCE SHONE in the moonlight, like a beacon calling to Mia. So close... yet so far...

"What is taking so long?" Jupiter asked. It was only the fourth time in about a minute.

"Maybe the guard already took his smoke break." Mia tried to sound calm, but her nerves were ramping up, too. "I'm sure Jak's working on it."

Jupiter picked her way through the undergrowth to stand next to Mia again. Her roommate had been pacing between the fence and the trees, peering into the forest as if she could force Jak to shut down the fence with the power of her glare.

Mia's phone lit up, sending an eerie glow out in a circle around her. It caught Jupiter's eye, too. Mia quickly scanned the text: it was from Jak, but it didn't make any sense.

"What does it say?" Jupiter demanded.

Mia frowned. "He's asking if we did something to the fence."

They both looked at the fence. It was still humming and looked the same.

"Is it still live?" Jupiter asked. They'd already figured out that Mia could hear the fence's electric hum, while her roommate couldn't. Mia's inner wolf enhanced her hearing somewhat, but nowhere near as much as her smell. The hum must be just inside the range she could detect but normal humans couldn't.

"Yeah, it's still live," Mia said. "Don't touch it." She bent over the phone and rapidly texted back, *fence still live.*

They both waited for his response.

Part of fence breached. Find it. Get out.

Mia showed it to Jupiter, then quickly scanned up and down the length of the fence. She was sure it went for a good mile or more. The estate was *huge*, and the fence had to run the whole perimeter. How would they find the section that was out?

"What the heck does he mean by *breached?*" Jupiter asked.

Mia was wondering the same thing. "Maybe Lucas has come for me."

Jupiter raised an eyebrow.

"Trust me," Mia said. "It's totally something he would do."

Jupiter nodded, but then she frowned at the fence. "So... do we just scout along until we find the part that's broken?"

A *bang* cracked through the air, like a car backfiring or a transformer blowing. It jolted through Mia, and they both turned toward the estate where the sound had come from.

That sounded like a gunshot. Fear gripped her heart, but it wasn't for herself. Or even Jupiter. Mia was sure Lucas had come for her. If he was already inside…

"What was that?" Jupiter's voice had pitched up.

"We have to go." Mia grabbed her roommate's hand and dragged her along the perimeter. She had no idea which way to go, how close the breach was, or if they could reach it in time, but they had to move. *Fast.*

Except the dark and the underbrush were slowing them down. Mia uncovered her phone, using it as a flashlight to shine ahead of them, and they were able to make better time. She strained to hear the fence over the shuffling and stomping of their feet through the underbrush. Every fifty feet or so, she stopped to listen, to check to see if the hum was still there, and then they started running again.

They were getting farther and farther from the moped, but that didn't matter—they could always double back along the fence, or if nothing else, she had the phone's GPS. She and Jupiter were both getting winded with the run, and her roommate fell once, but she got right back up and kept going. The next time they stopped, they had to hold their breath for a moment so she could hear the fence over their panting.

It was still humming… and there was something else in the woods as well.

Mia whipped her head around, peering into the forest toward the estate, her nostrils automatically flaring to try to catch the scent of whatever was making that noise: *something* was moving through the underbrush. And it was coming closer.

Mia grabbed her roommate's arm and yanked. *"Run!"* she said in a harsh whisper. They picked up speed, making way too much noise, but Mia figured they had probably already seen her phone bobbing through the forest.

They kept running. The forest seemed to creep in on them, dark fingers reaching out from the underbrush to grab at their legs and feet. Jupiter was keeping up, but Mia could tell she was flagging, either from the run or the terror. They stopped for a moment to listen again. The fence was buzzing, but Mia almost couldn't hear it over the crashing through the forest toward them. She still couldn't see them through the dark, but there was definitely more than one. And they were moving *fast*.

Then up ahead, Mia spied something attached to the fence… *on the outside.*

"Come on!" Mia ran ahead, as fast as her human legs could carry her. When she reached the part of the fence with the elaborate cables and insulated lines on the outside, it was easy to tell this was where the fence had been breached: it no longer hummed, and there were men's clothes scattered all along the forest floor.

Jupiter caught up to her. "What in the world?" she asked, breathless.

"This is where Lucas came in." Mia gestured to the clothes. "And he brought friends."

The crashing through the forest sounded closer. Mia and Jupiter both turned to see dark shapes bounding straight for them.

"Go, go, go!" Mia shoved Jupiter toward the fence. But she could tell it was already too late—even if they made it over, the wolves were too fast. They would catch them. If it was only Mia, she might have a chance of outrunning them, but Jupiter…

Mia grabbed Jupiter's hand and shoved her phone into it. "Take this and go! I'll hold them off."

"What?" Jupiter screeched, then her eyes went wide watching the black shapes close in on them. "Mia, that's crazy! I'm not leaving without you."

"They want *me*, not you. This is stupid shifter

business. And they're not going to hurt me. But *you*... dammit, just *go!*"

Her roommate didn't move for a horribly long second, then she shoved Mia's phone in her pocket and scaled the fence like a monkey. Mia turned her back to the fence and faced the oncoming wolves. She couldn't shift—one of them might be Mace. She had a hard enough time leaving his house in human form, much less fighting him in wolf form. But she would surrender quickly. Or fight and scream. Or possibly shift. Whatever was necessary to distract them from her fleeing roommate.

Four of them exploded from the forest, teeth bared and snarling, red and brown coats glistening in the moonlight that rimmed the cleared space around the fence. They pulled up short, keeping a ten-foot distance from her. They seemed to not expect to find her there, especially not crouched in a defensive pose, as if she was going to fight them with her bare human hands. They took a long moment, probably talking amongst themselves. Mia resisted a very strong urge to look behind her, to see if Jupiter had gotten away undetected. But as long as the wolves weren't scaling the fence, she wouldn't give them any ideas.

They seemed to decide something, and

suddenly, they shifted. Four hulking, muscular, naked men stood before her. None of them were Mace or his betas, but one... Jak stood as strong-jawed and merciless as the rest. The dark look in all their eyes ran a shiver through her, but Jak most of all.

"Come with us." All the softness was gone from Jak's voice.

Chapter Twenty-Nine

MACE WAS STILL POINTING A GUN AT HIM, BUT Lucas didn't care. He shifted back to human form and went to Lev, stepping over the blood trail he had left on Mace's bedroom carpet.

"Lev," he said softly. His brother would be getting up if the injury were minor, but Lucas could see the dark, gaping hole in his chest. The blood was flowing freely down his brown fur and creating a small puddle on the floor.

Lucas put pressure on the wound. "Hang in there." His throat was closing up, making his voice so soft, he didn't know if Lev could hear him. But his brother's wolf eyes moved to focus on him, so maybe. Lev wasn't whining, but the look of pain in his eyes nearly killed Lucas on the spot.

He clenched his teeth, and the room seemed unsteady for a moment. But he shoved aside his horror at seeing a blood-soaked hole in his brother's chest and focused on finding a way out of this. Two of his brother's pack-mates were outside the doorway to Mace's bedroom, holding back after Mace shot Lev. Downstairs, Lucas's father and Rent were probably still subduing Mace's pack members, but here in the bedroom, they were seriously outgunned. Mace was armed, and so were his two betas. And there was Mace's mate in the room as well.

Lucas couldn't risk any more bullets flying around.

"He needs a healer," Lucas called over his shoulder. Crouching naked on Mace's floor over his bleeding-out brother didn't exactly put him in a position to make demands. But that wasn't going to stop him, either. "Let me take him out of here." Maybe he could carry Lev off the property. Mace didn't need a dead wolf on the estate. Lucas still hadn't found Mia, and that wrenched a hot poker through his chest, but at least she wasn't with Mace, either. Hopefully, Llyr's team would find her in one of the other houses. Or come for Lucas and Lev's team once they didn't extract on time.

"Take him?" Mace asked with derision.

When Lucas turned to face him, Mace was waving the gun around, gesturing his disbelief.

"You come into my home and assault me, and you want me to just let you walk out and get a healer? You should have thought of that before you set your pack on me, Lucas Sparks."

Damn, this was a mess.

"Oh wait... that's right... you lost your pack, didn't you?" He sneered. "So, now you're getting pack members killed who aren't even yours."

Lucas winced.

Mace gestured to his two betas with the guns. They edged toward Lucas.

"Pick up your father's wolf," Mace said to Lucas, "and get his bleeding carcass out of my bedroom. You can take him downstairs until we wrap this up. And tell the wolves in the hall to surrender, so I'm not forced to shoot them, too. Not that it would bother me to bury a bunch of wolves in the woods. No one would even need to know you were here."

Lucas's mind was reeling as to how to find a way out of this. But for the moment, Mace held all the cards. Lucas lifted his brother's body into his arms and carried him out into the hall. Lev whimpered, and the blood surged out of his wound now that Lucas wasn't putting pressure on it anymore. He felt the warmth of his brother's blood on his chest, dripping down. He moved quickly, signaling Lev's pack mates to join him. They growled but trotted behind him down the stairs.

When Lucas reached the bottom of the stairs, his father came to full attention, ears forward, tail up. He quickly shifted into human form. Mace's betas were right behind Lucas, so he didn't have to explain. He simply hurried over to the white leather couch in the middle of the living room and laid Lev out. His brother moaned and closed his eyes. His chest was moving rapidly, panting, and a dark anger rose up inside Lucas. His brother couldn't shift in this state so they couldn't take him to a regular hospital. That left a healer who could properly stitch up a wolf before Lev lost too much blood. Shifters could survive extraordinary wounds, but only if they had a chance to recover. And didn't lose too much of the blood that carried the magic of shifting within it.

If Lev died before Lucas could get him to a healer, he would rip out Mace's throat. He didn't care if Mace shot him in the process, as long as Lucas could sink his teeth in first.

Mace followed his betas into the living room, all three brandishing their guns and growling orders. They corralled all eight of Lucas's team into the center of the room. The two Red wolves that had shifted under their attack were back to human, putting on their clothes, while the other two guarded the now-closed front door. Lucas had no idea what Mace's intention was, but at least he had the good sense to leave his mate in the relative safety of the upstairs bedroom.

One of Lev's pack mates shifted human and bent over Lev, applying pressure and talking to him softly. Lucas's father was in human form as well and looked like he was having the same thoughts about ripping out Mace's throat. Rent had remained wolf, along with the three other young pack members. Lucas had no doubt they were mentally discussing their strategy for escape, with Rent leading that discussion, and Lucas's father shifting human to negotiate with Mace.

Only Mace didn't seem interested in talking. At least not to them.

He turned to one of his betas. "We've got this in hand. Give your gun to one of the others and take care of that business we discussed."

Lucas's stomach roiled. He was certain Mace

was referring to the girls somehow. Whatever he had planned there, Lucas hoped Llyr would reach Mia first.

Mace turned to him. "Now, Lucas Sparks." He had a cruel smirk on his face. "Give me a good reason why I shouldn't kill you right now."

MIA'S HEART HAD ALREADY SUNK TO THE BOTTOM OF her stomach when Jak and the other Red wolves surrounded her and marched her through the forest toward the estate. But when the five of them broke from the trees and started crossing the lawn toward Mace's house, her heart sinking all the way to her toes. Each step closer buried it deeper into the earth.

They were taking her back. As soon as she crossed that threshold, she knew the submission bond would smother her again. Jak knew it, too—but he refused to look at her, just kept his gaze straight ahead. She thought she saw his jaw flinch, but she couldn't be sure.

He obviously wouldn't be saving her this time.

As they approached the front door of Mace's house, she couldn't help dragging her feet. Two of the Red wolves simply took one arm each and ushered her toward the door. All four were naked, but that only exposed the extent of their rippling muscles. There was no point in trying to resist. And she wasn't slowing because she hoped to escape; it was simply a reflex, a revulsion to the idea of being once again under Mace's roof.

They flung open the door. As she crossed the threshold, the bond hit her like a punch to the gut. It was good they were holding her up, because her knees buckled, and she had to fight to find her footing. When she did and looked up… she nearly tripped again over what she saw.

Lucas standing naked in the living room, blood covering his chest.

"*No.*" It was half sob, but she couldn't help herself.

His mouth fell open when he saw her, then he closed his eyes briefly. He looked like she was the last thing he wanted to see, and she could completely understand why: *Mace now had them both.*

The submission bond kept her from struggling against the hold the Red wolves had on her, but it didn't stop her from quickly taking in the scene, hoping against hope that it wasn't as bad as she feared.

Instead, it was *worse*.

Mace, Beck, and Alric all held guns on the naked men and wolves in the center of the living room. The elder Mr. Sparks stood next to his son. Four wolves huddled nearby. Another man bent over a wolf on the couch.

"Ah, Mia!" Mace said, his grin wide. "So glad you could join our little party." Then he lowered his voice. "Come closer."

It was a command. From her alpha. She didn't need the urging of the wolves on either side of her to stumble toward him. But as she got closer, horror froze her steps: the wolf on the couch was bleeding, and there was blood everywhere. On him. On the hands of the man trying to keep him from bleeding to death. Smeared all over the white leather of the couch.

And on Lucas's chest. Her heart seized up. The wolf... *was it Lev?*

Mia couldn't hold in her sob. Tears brimmed her eyes, and she sought out Lucas's face. The agony there nearly ripped her in two.

"I said come here." Mace's voice was soft but dangerous, and that only made the compulsion stronger. Her feet dragged her forward. Lucas's gaze followed and darkened as she went. He had to know she'd submitted to Mace. Every wolf in the room had to have figured it out by now.

Mace's gaze flitted back and forth between her and Lucas. When she arrived at Mace's side, he slipped an arm possessively around her waist and drew her close. She was afraid he might force her to kiss him, so she turned her face to the side. But that only made her see Lucas's rage-filled face staring at both of them.

"Oh yes, Lucas Sparks," Mace said with a sick amount of glee in his voice. "I have your mate, don't I? Too bad you won't live to see me claim her."

Mace raised his gun to point at Lucas's head.

"*No!*" Mia screamed. Her hand reflexively grabbed Mace's arm, but he was far too strong for her to wrestle him away. She managed to summon words instead. "I lied, Mace! I lied."

That pulled Mace's attention back to her. He held her close enough that he could kiss her, but instead, he just peered intently into her eyes. "You shouldn't lie to your alpha."

"Lucas isn't my mate," she said in a rush. "I lied about that. I... I..." She flailed for a plausible reason for lying because she couldn't bring herself to say the truth while in Mace's arms, under submission to him: that she loved Lucas, that her heart would always belong to him, and that she had only *wished* he had wanted her for a mate. "I lied because I was afraid. Afraid to become your mate. I've never done that before. But I'm… I'm not afraid anymore." It sounded ridiculous in her ears —she had never been more afraid in her life. Afraid Mace would shoot Lucas. Afraid of Lev dying on Mace's couch. And not least, afraid of actually, finally having to become Mace's mate for real.

But her words, her *lie,* seemed to have an effect on Mace. "You're not afraid, are you?" He licked his lips and squeezed her waist.

Mia heard Lucas growl, but she couldn't look away from her alpha when he stared into her eyes like that.

"I expected you to be a challenge, Mia," Mace said, a small smile coming out. "And you do not disappoint."

Mia's heart was breaking and pounding out of her chest at the same time, but she couldn't look away. "I will do whatever you want. But spare the Sparks wolves. Please. Do it for me. They… helped bring me to you." She felt like she might throw up, but she prayed Mace would believe her. And the truth was: it wasn't a lie. She had already submitted to him. She would end up doing what he wished. She might as well save Lucas and Lev and the others in the process. Lucas never wanted her for a mate anyway... but she could repay him for all the times he saved her life by doing this one final thing to save his.

Mace's gaze was still holding her captive. His hand snaked up from her waist and bunched the hair falling down her back. He was feeling it slip through his fingers.

"Such a noble wolf you are." His eyes shone with what seemed like genuine admiration. But she knew it was only because she had been so hard to get, such a challenge, that he wanted her at all. He would make her his mate for what she would do for him: status, prestige, the satisfaction of the conquer. Lucas would have loved her for who she was. But that would never happen now. Especially when she had just given herself to Mace in front of him.

Her heart broke into a million tiny pieces.

Mace finally broke his stare to look to one of his betas. "Hold them here, Beck. When I'm done, we'll wake my father and show him the neatly wrapped Sparks present I have for him."

He shifted his hold on Mia and returned his attention to her. With her firmly clamped to his side, he walked her toward the stairs. She heard Lucas growl behind them, but she couldn't even look back, because Mace had captured her gaze again.

"Don't look so horrified, Mia," he said softly, a small curl in his lips. "It won't be so bad being the second mate of the next leader of the Red pack. In fact, I think you'll very much enjoy it."

"Promise me you'll let them go." Her heart was hammering in her ears with every step closer, but she couldn't even drag her feet this time. The submission bond wouldn't let her disobey, and the desire rolling of Mace told her how very much he wanted her.

"Afterward," he said. "If you do just as I say... I'll consider it."

It was a lie. She knew it. He would torment them or worse. At least she was buying them time to maybe escape. She could have tried to convince him further, but her brain was muddled by the bond and the terror as they approached the stairs. Mace released her gaze just before they started to ascend, and for one brief moment, she caught Jak's gaze.

The pain in them tugged at her, begged her to resist. But he should know better than anyone she couldn't, not now. When they were halfway up the stairs, Mace's hands started running up her back and working into her hair.

She couldn't stop either his hands or the shudders that went along with every touch.

LUCAS ALMOST WISHED MACE HAD SHOT HIM instead of making him watch as he commanded Mia upstairs with him. He would claim her while Lucas sat prisoner downstairs, knowing full well what was happening. Lucas was certain the only true reason he was still alive was that Mace thought he would suffer more this way.

And he was right.

His heart was breaking, not only because Mace was claiming the girl he loved, but because of her incredible bravery in attempting to spare all their lives. He knew she was strong, but to selflessly try to save them... when by all rights, they should be saving *her*...

Mace and Mia hadn't even reached the stairs when the growl started deep inside him. It was primal and powerful and overwhelming. An echo of it rumbled in the chests of his father, Rent, and the wolves gathered with him. He didn't have to read their minds to know: all of them, to a one, were unwilling to stand by and watch this happen.

Lucas was ready to die to stop it. A flicked look to his father told him he was as well.

As Mia and Mace disappeared around the corner, ascending the stairs, Lucas quickly evaluated the room. Two armed Red wolves and eight unarmed ones, for a total of ten. On the Sparks side, they had only six, not counting Lev and his pack-mate working to keep him alive. They were outmatched; some of them might die. But not *all* of them. If a few of them rushed the armed Red wolves, only a couple would likely catch bullets. The rest could fight past the other wolves and stop Mace and Mia.

Just as Lucas gave a small nod to his father, something slammed into the front door, jerking everyone's attention that way.

Once, twice, and then it flew open.

Llyr's team.

Eight armed men stormed in the door. Lucas didn't hesitate—he sprang for the armed beta closest to him, lunging for the man's gun hand. It went off before Lucas could grab it. Pain ripped through Lucas's shoulder. The man's hand jerked back from the recoil, but Lucas caught hold of it.

He shoved the gun up in the air while pounding his fist into the beta's gut over and over.

Lucas heard a second shot, but it wasn't from their gun. Then a third shot and a grunt. But he couldn't look. The beta hit back, catching Lucas in the face. He reeled, but kept a grip on the beta's gun hand, then came raging back with a punch to the Red wolf's face. He went down and stayed down. Lucas wrenched the gun from his hand on the way.

The rest of the room was in chaos: a melee of fur and skin.

His father was on the floor, bleeding, clutching his leg. Two of his pack had taken out the second beta with the gun, but apparently not before his father had been shot. The rest were still up and fighting.

His father waved away his concerned look and growled, "Get her."

Lucas sidestepped a pair of wrestling wolves and two more Red wolves who were curled up, twitching while Llyr's stun gun electric wires delivered a voltage punch. Llyr himself was down on the floor with another wolf, but Colin crouch near him, by the door. Colin jammed his stun gun into the neck of a Red pack wolf and sent him shivering to the floor.

"Where is she?" Colin yelled over the mayhem.

Lucas jabbed his thumb at the stairs—Colin was closer and would reach her sooner, but Lucas would be damned if he wasn't right behind him. He fought past another pair of wrestling wolves. Then one of his father's pack members grabbed hold of the gun from Mace's beta and pointed it at the crowd, trying to find a clean shot in the fight. Lucas put a hand on his arm to stop him from firing and possibly hitting one of their own. He was young, probably had never been in a pack fight before.

"Guard your alpha," Lucas commanded him.

He nodded, kept the gun up, but backed to a defensive position next to Lucas's father. Lucas shoved aside a Red wolf surging for him then swung his own gun in his attacker's direction. He jerked back, stumbling into a glass table, but Lucas wasn't interested in him.

He turned and threaded through the fight, heading for the stairs.

Colin had already gone after Mia. Lucas's wolf clawed at him, jealous and wanting out, but Lucas had a gun—and every intention of using it on Mace. Besides, the human side of him didn't care who got there first as long as *someone* stopped Mace. Lucas kept his wolf contained as he took the stairs two at a time.

He found Colin kicking the door but having no luck. Lucas joined him, and just as the door gave way, he heard another shot go off. This time something punched him hard and sent him sailing back against the hallway wall.

Colin stared wide-eyed at him, but before Lucas could tell him to *go get her*, the pain hit like a truck landing on his chest. He couldn't breathe. Colin flattened himself against the wall opposite then peeked through the doorway, pointing his stun gun into the bedroom. Lucas fought for air, trying desperately to breathe past the pain and *move*.

Then he heard Mia scream.

Every part of him was electrified by that sound. He braced himself against the wall and struggled up from the floor. Colin did another peek check and fired his electric weapon. Cables flew into the room, and he rushed after them. The sound of another shot jolted Lucas as he lumbered forward, one hand holding the wound in his side, the other holding the gun. He made it into the room, weakly raising the gun ahead of him.

Mia was on the bed, up on her knees, t-shirt

missing and arms wrapped around herself, but she seemed unharmed. She stared down at Colin beating the crap out of Mace on the floor. Electric wires hung limp around Mace's body, and his gun had fallen to the carpet.

Colin was turning his face into hamburger.

Lucas wanted Mace dead as much as anyone, but they were both in human form. With DNA everywhere for God's sake. They couldn't murder him.

"Colin, stop," Lucas wheezed, scooping up Mace's gun. He was pretty well unconscious, but they might yet need it on the way out.

Colin's chest was heaving, but he shook out his bloodied fists and rose up from Mace's inert form. Lucas prayed he wasn't actually dead. He handed the gun to Colin.

Then he turned to Mia. She was pale and shaking with mile-wide eyes, but she scrambled off the bed and stumbled to him. Her arms went around him and squeezed, and he nearly went down with the pain. The room spun for a moment, but he managed to hold her with one arm, keeping the gun well away from her.

"Please tell me he didn't hurt you." Lucas wheezed through the words.

"I'm okay." Her voice was shaky but surprisingly strong.

He couldn't believe how good those words sounded to him.

"We have to get her out, Lucas." Colin's face had lost the fury from before, when he was pounding Mace, but it was replaced with a hunger Lucas understood: he wanted Mia. He had been the first to reach her, yet she'd gone to Lucas.

Only Lucas could barely keep himself standing.

With great reluctance and no small amount of pain, he worked his way out of Mia's grasp. He gave a pointed look to the gun in Colin's hand. "You need to take her with you."

Mia frowned, but Lucas handed her over to Colin. He took her hand. Just in time, too, as a wave of dizziness washed over Lucas. He was losing too much blood. He knew that. He blinked to clear his vision and swallowed the thick feeling in his throat.

Colin glanced at the wound in Lucas's side. "I'll send someone up to help you."

"Just go." Lucas wheezed again. "I'll be right behind you."

Mia seemed unwilling to move, fixating on the bloody hole in Lucas's side. Colin had to urge her to go with him, pulling on their clasped hands. Lucas would have said something, but he was barely managing to stay upright, and he was afraid the pain might show in his voice.

Finally, Colin bent down to her and said quietly, "Mia, they'll keep fighting downstairs until they know you're all right. We need to stop the fight before anyone else is injured."

That convinced her. She bit her lip and let Colin lead her from the room.

As soon as she was gone, Lucas sagged to his knees. The room swam around him, the bed tipping up at a crazy angle. He dragged himself over to it and pulled down the sheet. He bunched it up and pressed it to the bloody mess that was his side. It might stem the bleeding for a little while, just long enough until... suddenly his eyelids were too heavy to keep open. Like a witch had snuck into Mace's bedroom and blown a sleeping spell on him. It commanded him to close his eyes, and he couldn't do anything but obey.

Chapter Thirty

To Mia, it looked like the scene out of a war movie. Maybe an x-rated one, with all the naked men. Or perhaps this was how war really was, back in the days when tribes fought each other like packs of wolves: for territory, for conquest, for females.

Once the Red pack wolves saw Mia walking down the steps, they realized their alpha had been subdued, and they had quickly given up. A few of the Sparks wolves threw unnecessary punches in the heat of the end of the fight, and Mia had to restrain herself from asking them not to hit Jak. She wasn't sure, but she guessed a few bruises from a Sparks wolf was much less punishment than he would receive at the hands of the Red pack if they had any inkling Jak was the one who almost set her free.

So she didn't say a word as they beat and bound up Jak along with the rest of them.

Once the Red wolves were contained, the entire Sparks group made a run back for the forest. Lev had to be carried, of course, and so did Lucas's father. That took four of the Sparks wolves right there. And then Lucas... her heart squeezed as she watched Lucas's naked body being hauled through the forest with Llyr on one side and another wolf on the other. She wasn't even sure Lucas was conscious half the time, as his bare feet dragged through the ferns and banged against the rocks. He had passed out by the time someone had gone back up for him. They'd tied a sheet around his waist, but it was already soaked in his blood. The white part glowed in the moonlight patches as they dragged him past, but the red looked as dark as ink. She wasn't sure if it was actually slowing the bleeding, or just covering up the hole Mace's shot had torn through him.

Mace. With him passed out, it was easier for her to leave the house. And with the house left behind in the Red pack grounds, she was able to think more clearly—and loathe him more fully. He hadn't gotten far in claiming her, but she could still feel his hands roaming her, undressing her, running his fingers and lips over her skin… she couldn't repay Lucas and Colin for coming to rescue her, but the price that Lucas was paying… that they were all paying…

"Are you sure he's going to be okay?" Mia asked Colin. He was staying by her side, guarding her. She would have preferred he helped carry Lucas or tend to one of the other injured—she was the least hurt among all of them—but once Lucas had handed her over to Colin, he hadn't let go.

"He's lost a lot of blood," Colin said grimly. "So has Lev. We'll need to find a healer for them as soon as we're away."

"A healer?"

He smiled down at her like he thought her ignorance was charming. Her face just heated up, and she hoped her hands weren't sweating along with them.

"A healer is a doctor with a specialization in shifters." Even if his smile made her feel embarrassed, his voice was gentle enough. He wasn't making fun of her.

"I didn't know they were teaching that in medical school these days."

He grinned. "They don't. Healers are usually shifters themselves. They have the normal training, plus some special training through their pack. Or another they've been apprenticed out to."

"Apprenticed." An intern, like her. She peered into the murky depths of the forest and the bloodied shifters who had all risked their lives to come for her. A simple intern. An unmated female. Someone who wasn't even part of their pack, but somehow got twisted up in their business. "There's so much I don't know about shifters. Or packs. Or really any of it."

She glanced at him, her face heating up again.

He squeezed her hand a little, just a gentle thing. Sweet and encouraging. "I could teach you anything you want to know." His voice was lower now, just for her, not the entourage around them. She didn't think it was her imagination that there was more to his words than he was saying.

He'd flat out told her before that he wanted her for a mate. And she didn't exactly mind holding his hand as they completed their escape—he was one of the few clothed men marching them all out to safety, and it certainly would have been a lot more awkward if she'd been ushered by one of the naked ones.

But it was more than that.

They lapsed into silence, but the air around

them was heavy with the looks he was giving her. Hungry looks, but in a respectful way. Like he wanted her but didn't want her to feel pressured in any way about it. He *had* saved her from Mace, something she would never find enough words to thank him for. And with her hand in his and those smoldering looks... she had to admit there was more than a little chemistry between them.

She forced herself to peer ahead into the darkness. She had told Mace she belonged to Lucas. Even Lucas had heard the lie. What did he make of that? Probably figured it was just her wishful thinking... or a canny attempt to escape being claimed by Mace. Then she had given herself to Mace right in front of Lucas. He hadn't wanted her for a mate before. She couldn't imagine any of those things would make him want her *more*.

He had saved her life, many times over. She had tried to return the favor. But that wasn't love, necessarily. She wasn't quite sure what it was... at least for him.

Mia watched Lucas's head loll from one side to the other. Mostly it hung down to his chest as they hoisted him through the underbrush.

"Are you sure he's going to be okay?" Mia asked Colin again, without looking at him.

She heard him sigh, but she couldn't tear her eyes away from the growing red stain on Lucas's sheet.

"I promise you, we'll do everything we can."

Mia nodded, eyes still on Lucas, when she realized they were nearing the fence. And just beyond it, her roommate, Jupiter, was jumping up and down and waving frantically to her. Mia wrenched her hand free of Colin and ran past the troop of wolves. As she got closer, she realized that four hulking guys stood just behind her roommate, peering into the forest at the coming crowd.

"Jeeter!" Mia cried, fingers lacing through the deactivated fence. "What are you doing here?"

"I brought you some help!" Jupiter said.

Mia glanced behind her. She hadn't given it a second thought, but all the Sparks wolves were in human form to help with carrying the injured... with the exception of Lev, who couldn't safely shift. She looked nervously back to the people Jeeter had brought—what could they possibly make of a bunch of naked men carrying a wolf out of the forest?

Jeeter must have read her mind. Or the look of horror on her face. "Oh, don't worry, Mia," she said. "They all know you're shifters."

"They what?" Mia hissed.

Colin had trotted up behind her. "Are these people you know, Mia?"

She desperately cast a look around at them... and recognized Cade, the theatre guy that Jupiter had tried to set her up with. "Um... yeah," she said.

Cade gave her a small smile.

"Remember those guys I told you about?" Jupiter asked. "The ones who were *really big?* And could help out if you needed it?"

"Yeah," Mia said, vaguely recalling Jeeter's frantic concerns about Lucas being some kind of control freak that was forcing her to move out of their dorm. Which, of course, he wasn't, but that was before Jeeter knew she was a shifter.

"Well..." Jeeter said, sheepishly.

Mia cut a look at her. *Sheepish* just wasn't Jeeter's thing. "What?"

"Turns out they're kinda shifters, too."

Mia's eyebrows flew up, and she jerked back from the fence. Colin's arm was instantly around her, then he moved so his body was between hers and the fence. She had to fight him to even be able to see her roommate.

"Jeeter, what the hell are you talking about?" Mia asked harshly. "Did you bring another pack here?" God, she told her roommate to *run away*, not bring more trouble.

"No, no, no!" Jeeter said. "I told them what happened, and they wanted to help."

Mia peered at Cade, desperately trying to remember what she knew about him. Last time she had seen him, he was making a pass at her outside her dorm. He had crystalline blue eyes, a commanding presence, and moved with restrained power. Now she wondered why she hadn't seen it before.

"What pack are you?" she asked Cade.

"I'm not a wolf, Mia," he said calmly.

"But I thought Jeeter said..." She didn't understand.

Colin let out a low sound that wasn't quite a growl. "He's a cat."

Cade narrowed his eyes. "Tiger. If you must know."

No way. "Seriously? Wait... Jeeter, did you *know* this, all this time?"

"No!" Jeeter shoved a fist into Cade's shoulder. It barely jostled him. "Jerk!"

Cade smirked but didn't answer.

Jupiter put her hand on her hips and cocked them to one side. "But when I called up a guy who *I thought* was my best friend…" Another pinched glare for Cade. "…and told him my roommate was secretly a shifter and needed rescuing from a pack of wolves… well, it turned out Cade had a few friends of his own."

Mia took in the other three guys standing quietly behind Cade. They were all tall and blue-eyed like him, muscular under those tight t-shirts, and looked like they could tear right through the chain link fence if they wanted to.

"I swear," Jupiter said, "I think I'm the only human left. It's starting to seriously freak me out."

"We don't need you here, cat," Colin said, coolly. "This is pack business."

"Yeah?" Cade took in the scene. "Looks like business is going well."

The troops were starting to arrive, injured ones coming first. They were bloody and broken and limping. They didn't really need four shifters—four tigers, she reminded herself with a shake of her head—to rescue them anymore. But maybe they could help them get over the fence.

Colin growled softly. "Nothing a good healer can't fix."

"Then you're in luck," Cade said. "Parker is pre-med." He gestured to one of his fellow tigers, a dark-haired guy with intense blue eyes that seemed to reflect the moonlight.

"I have my kit in the car," Parker said.

Colin glared. "What would cat know about stitching up a wolf?"

"As much as any pre-med veterinary student who grew up in a collective might."

A collective? Mia looked at Colin, but he wasn't surprised. In fact, he seemed to have a new appreciation for the enigmatic Parker.

"We have three with serious injuries," Colin said. "The rest will heal soon enough not to be of concern."

Parker dipped his head in acknowledgment then spun to run back through the short stretch of forest out to the road. There were several vehicles parked there... including a moped. Mia felt relief trickle through her body. Somehow, someway... Jeeter had brought them a healer. The thing Lucas needed most of all.

"If you've got wounded, you won't want to hoist them over the fence," Cade said calmly. "If you could step back, ladies, we can take care of that for you."

Mia's eyebrows lifted, and she flicked a look to Jeeter, but she just shrugged. All of them backed away from the fence. Cade and his two shifter friends slipped their shirts over their heads and shifted so fast that Mia could barely see them in transition.

"Holy crap!" Jeeter cried, apparently deciding she needed a lot more space between her and her friends, who were suddenly enormous, two hundred pound tigers. She backed up until she was a good twenty feet from the fence.

Cade and his friends took positions at different spots and reared up to place their forepaws on the fence. Their claws made her wolf claws look like tiny playthings—these were six inch long daggers. They sliced through the chain link fence like it was spaghetti. They peeled back the raw edges, creating a gap big enough to easily carry through the injured members of their party—and all the people she loved. *Lucas. Lev. The elder Mr. Sparks.* How quickly she had come to think of them as *hers.* Even if they weren't her mate, or her brother, or her father… they were her *friends.* And they risked their lives for her.

She only hoped there might be a place for her in one of their packs.

Tears sprung to her eyes as she stepped back and watched them get carried through the fence and into the forest. They were heading for the cars... and the healer Cade had brought with him. Another friend who she had more in common with than she knew.

The rest of the wolves gathered up the dropped clothes and gear, slipping them on or simply carrying them through the tiger-made hole in the fence. Cade and his friends had shifted back and were getting dressed as well. Mia tried to keep her gaze discretely on the ground while she passed through the hole to Jupiter.

She hugged her roommate hard. "Jeeter." She didn't know what to say after that.

"Let's go home," her roommate said.

For the moment, those words swelled Mia's heart. Once everyone was healed, she could worry about exactly where that home was.

Chapter Thirty-One

IT WAS A SOLEMN CARAVAN, ONE MIA HOPED NEVER to be in again.

Three cars carried sixteen members of the Sparks pack, most bloodied but already healing. Mia and Jupiter rode in the van with the three injured wolves—Lucas, his brother Lev, and their father. Their wounds were so severe, they needed a healer. Not a doctor, but someone who could stitch up wolves whose injury was so deep it would drain their magic life-giving blood before they could heal. Lucas and his father were in human form, with Lucas unconscious on the floor and his father propped up to sitting nearby. Lev was still in wolf form, lying next to them. He wouldn't be able to shift human until the healer had stitched him up.

In a separate car behind them, Jupiter's friend Cade and his buddies comprised the tail end of the parade through the nighttime streets of Bellevue. Cade had come to help simply because Mia was being held captive. He and his friends were all hulking young men who were apparently shifters as well, only their animal forms were tigers. That they had come in the dead of night to help a girl they barely knew told Mia they were the kind of shifter Lucas was... even if their animal was different. She recognized the type by now, and she was in awe of how selfless these shifters were. Mace proved all too well during her captivity in his house that not all shifters were that way. As awful as that had been, her heart swelled all the more to be back with people who were *her kind*—not just in form but in spirit as well.

Except her three favorite shifters in the world lay bleeding in front of her.

Parker, the tiger shifter who was also a pre-med student and a healer, rode in the van with them. He insisted they only drive a short distance away from the Red Wolf estate before stopping to let him do his work. Colin was driving the van, and he quickly found an empty parking lot in front of a convenience store, dark except for a few lampposts and the ever-present moonlight. The trauma of the night wore on Mia. The rocking motion of the van pulled at her eyelids, wanting them to close, but there was no way she could rest. Not until she knew Lucas would be all right.

The van eased to a stop, and Parker went to work immediately. Someone had found pants for Lucas and slipped them on, leaving the bullet wound in his side bare for the healer. Mia thought he had been shot in the shoulder as well, but she couldn't be sure with all the blood smeared everywhere. Lev was just as bad off, but his dark fur masked most of the damage. The senior Mr. Sparks was the only one conscious, his leg wound a lot less severe, but still bleeding profusely. No one had spoken during the ride.

Parker opened his kit and pulled out several needles and thread and handfuls of bandages—the butterfly kind that basically glued your skin together. As he dug into Lucas's wound, the air was suddenly too warm and thick for Mia. She just couldn't watch.

"Are you okay?" Jupiter asked.

But Mia just covered her mouth, afraid she might finally lose the contents of her stomach, and headed for the door at the back of the van. She burst out into the cool night air. Her roommate was right behind her, but she waved Jeeter back and closed the van door as gently as she could. Mia rested there, needing a moment to herself while she pulled in deep lungfuls of air. The iron scent of blood was less overwhelming outside, but still too painfully present. Mia shuffled around to lean against the side of the van and close her eyes. She heard the driver's door open, and she sensed Colin's presence hovering protectively over her.

"Are you all right?" he asked.

She opened her eyes. "I'm not the one bleeding all over your van."

He tipped up a one-sided smile. "There's not a wolf here who isn't glad he's bleeding instead of you."

She knew he was right, and it filled her with a strange mixture of guilt and pleasure: as if she was glad to be so loved at the same time as wishing it didn't cost those who loved her so dearly. She wasn't even sure *love* was the right word. Protective, maybe. Or possessive. Chivalrous even, if this were the Middle Ages, and her wolves were knights in shining armor, not sexy venture capitalists.

Her wolves.

She really was beginning to think of them that

way. They belonged to her, and she to them. As if they truly were her home, her people. She just didn't know exactly what that meant in terms of things like mates and packs.

She looked up into Colin's attentive face. "I really can't thank you enough… thank everyone really… for coming for me. I don't think I have the right words for that kind of thank you."

He smiled softly. "Then it's a good thing words aren't necessary."

She couldn't help returning his smile, but it was hesitant. "What happens now?"

He leaned his shoulder against the van and peered down at her. "In what regard?"

"I mean, didn't we just make the Red Wolf pack angrier? Won't they just come after us—after me—again?" She bit her lip, too easily imagining an endless pack war all because of her.

"I seriously doubt it." Colin's gaze wandered over her face like he was really looking at her for the first time. He didn't seem put off by what he saw there. The opposite, actually. "Mace will assume you will mate soon after escaping. He knows that will protect you, and we wouldn't intentionally leave you unprotected like that again." He dipped his chin. "I personally never want to see you left unprotected in any way."

Mia felt her face heat up, and she suddenly realized how close they were huddled against the van. She eased back from their nearness, and he lifted an eyebrow but didn't say anything.

"Just to be safe," Colin said in their momentary awkward silence, "you should continue to stay at the hotel. Probably your roommate as well. At least for a little while." He pressed his hand against the van and pushed away from it until he was standing free. "We're bruised and bloodied, but we handed Mace a rather humiliating defeat. We breached their compound and retrieved what they had stolen. Now, the most dangerous time will be the next 24 hours."

"Because they might strike back."

"Precisely," he said. "Mace is fairly unstable, so perhaps in the heat of the moment, the rage at the embarrassment, he might do something foolish. But after he's had a day to cool off, I think it's highly unlikely he'll make any attempt at retaliation. I think this was Mace's idea, and now that he's been disgraced, I can't see their alpha authorizing any more immediate attacks on the Sparks pack. Especially if LoopSource accepts our offer."

"Because then Red Wolf won't be competing with SparkTech for the deal anymore."

Colin gave her an appreciative smile. "Yes. Although there will always be future deals. But for now, they won't have much incentive to provoke another conflict between the packs."

She peered up into his soft brown eyes. "Is it always like this? Bloody and fighting and drama? Because I'm not sure I'm cut out for this life."

He smiled wide and seemed to be holding in a laugh. "No. Usually, it's quite boring." He held her gaze. It wasn't a commanding stare, like Mace's, where she couldn't look away, but it was compelling nonetheless. "You've brought quite a bit of excitement to our pack here recently. Something I hope you keep doing for some time." He touched the tip of his finger to her nose.

That small touch was both cute and little too familiar. Mia eased back again, and Colin withdrew his hands, folding them across his chest as if promising not to touch her again.

People had started to spill out of the other cars, taking a stretch break or patching up their own residual wounds. Some were still getting dressed. They were all waiting to see how the surgery went in the van. Cade and his tigers hung back, separate from the others, but he caught her eye across the parking lot, and with a lift of his chin, started across the pavement toward her.

Colin seemed to tense up, dropping his hands to his sides, and training his stare on Cade as he approached. Mia didn't know if it was a *Wolves Hate Cats* thing or just two different shifters that didn't know each other... or simply that Colin was jealous their little moment alone was about to be interrupted. She was too tired to worry about any of it. Besides, Cade had brought them the healer who was now saving wolf lives, even though he didn't have to—that was worth of a whole lot of gratitude in her book.

"Hey, Mia," Cade said casually, hands tucked into the pockets of his jeans as he approached. "How's the sewing up going?"

"Good. I think. I couldn't..." She waved her hand at the van. "I'm not good with lots of blood and needles."

"Yeah." Cade eyed Colin's rigid stance, cocked an eyebrow, then seemed to decide to let it pass.

"Cade," Mia said, frowning and doubting if she had words for this one either. "Thanks so much for coming out to help tonight."

He waved her off. "Hey, it's not often I have a

chance to get out the claws and do some serious fence damage."

She smiled. Colin didn't. Mia rolled her eyes. Okay, this overprotective thing had its limits. And was silly when there were three people whose lives were hanging in the balance.

"I don't know anything about these healers," Mia said, directing her clueless admission to both Cade and Colin. "How does it work? I mean, will everyone be fine in a few weeks or what?"

"Weeks?" Cade snorted, and it was a lighthearted college-boy sound, not so serious as the dark looks Colin was still giving the tiger shifter. Mia was grateful for the lightening of the tension, along with everything else Cade brought. "Assuming Parker can actually stop the bleeding and piece together what needs piecing, they'll be off to another pack rumble tomorrow." His tone was a little too sarcastic—she couldn't be sure if he really meant it.

"Tomorrow?" This time, she directed her question to Colin.

"Leave it to a cat to be flip about whether wolves live or die." Colin's glare turned up another notch.

"Hey, that's totally uncalled for." Cade's protest

was a little too dramatic. "That's my buddy in there, helping your shaggy, er…" He glanced at Mia and sobered. "But yeah. If Parker can stitch 'em, they'll be fine in the morning."

"I don't understand," said Mia. "I mean, I know shifters heal fast, but these guys are hurt really bad."

Colin placed a hand on her shoulder, then quickly withdrew it, like he hadn't really meant to touch her. "What the cat is trying to say is that shifter healing needs two vital things. Enough blood—"

"He means *magic*," Cade said, cutting him off.

Colin growled. "Enough *blood*, which for shifters, contains properties you might call magic—"

"It's magic," Cade cut him off again.

"Oh for God's sake!" Mia had to repress a laugh. She pointed a finger at Cade in mock fury. "Shut it."

Cade grinned. "Yes, Ma'am." Somehow he seemed too pleased with that scolding.

"As I was saying," Colin continued, overly irritated for the minor offense. "Shifters need two things: blood and the possibility of healing."

Mia frowned. "What do you mean, *possibility?*"

"If you were dying of something that has no cure, say a missing head..." He threw a glare at Cade, who returned it with a look of disgust. "... then no shifter could stitch you back together. But if the parts that are damaged are ones that can normally heal themselves—a broken bone, ripped muscles, even a damaged kidney—then the healer stitches the damaged parts together or sets the bone, and the shifter will heal just as rapidly as normal. If parts are missing altogether—"

"Like a missing heart." Mia swallowed. She could see how that would be a problem.

Colin frowned. "Like a missing heart... then the shifter would die. We can't regenerate parts that are simply gone."

"So it depends on whether Lucas was... if he's missing..." Her throat was suddenly closing up.

"Mia, he's going to be fine." Colin's frown grew deeper. "I don't think the bullet took out anything that can't be stitched."

Cade was watching the two of them, quiet, one eyebrow lifted.

"Is it the same for you?" Mia asked. "Tigers, I mean."

Cade crossed his arms. "Yeah, pretty much. All shifters, if I'm not mistaken. Of course, tigers are less likely to get into this kind of trouble in the first place." He tipped his head to Mia. "Unless we're helping a friend, of course."

"Why is that?" she asked.

"Because cats are loners by nature," Colin said with disgust, and Mia could understand why. *Belonging* was so integral to being *wolf.* The pack, the mating, the submission… it was a huge part of what being a shifter was all about. For her, at least. But then she was a wolf.

Cade gave him another look of disgust. "Like running around with a mob mentality is something to be proud of."

"At least we know the meaning of loyalty," Colin said.

Cade unlocked his folded arms and threw his hands out. "Okay, whatever. As much fun as it is hanging out with your doggie friends, Mia, I think my guys are ready to shove off. As soon as Parker's done, we're going to split."

He was starting to edge away, so Mia scurried forward to give him a hug. She must have caught him by surprise because his arms didn't immediately go around her to hug her back. But when she heard Colin growl behind her, then Cade's hands found a home, splaying all across her back and squeezing her to him. He was totally trying to aggravate Colin.

She shoved Cade away, laughing. "You are so doing that on purpose."

He smirked. "Every chance I get."

She couldn't help but laugh again, but she backed away.

Cade waved goodbye. "Call me if you need me, Mia." He gave a mock salute to Colin that no doubt was intended to provoke him further.

Colin just rumbled low in his chest. "Be glad you're not a cat, Mia. They're not loyal, they sleep with everything and anything, and it's a lonely life, every cat for himself."

She gave him a skeptical look. "Cade came and helped us tonight," she pointed out.

Colin narrowed his eyes, still staring after the tiger shifter. "I'm sure there was something in it for him."

Mia just shook her head.

The back door of the van swung open, and Parker jumped out, landing silently on his tennis shoes. He looked like he'd just stepped out of a horror movie—or an ER ward—covered up to his elbows and all down his front in blood.

Wolf blood. That magical substance Colin said

Lucas needed to survive… only it looked like a whole lot of it had emptied out onto Parker's clothes.

Mia stepped up cautiously. Parker was stripping down. Jupiter had followed him out of the van with a handful of towelettes for him to clean up with.

"How does it look?" Mia asked.

He glanced at her but kept scrubbing the blood from his hands. "They'll be fine. I had to go pretty deep on Lucas, but he started healing even before I had backed all the way out. Lev didn't have as much tissue damage, but he bled out pretty bad. I wasn't sure if maybe it was too much loss, but by the time I had Mr. Sparks stitched, Lev had started to heal as well, at least on the surface. That's usually a good indication that tissue knitting is happening at the deeper levels as well. They'll have more than a few scars to show for it, and I suggest they sleep in and take it easy for a couple days, but they should all recover fully."

Mia let out the breath she had been holding during his entire explanation. "Thank you."

Parker smiled. It was the first time Mia had seen anything other than a dire-serious look on his face. "No problem. Nice to practice my skills for a change. Pre-med doesn't allow us any real opportunities for that, and I haven't had much occasion to stitch up my feline friends lately."

Then he lapsed into quietness again, like that was more talking than he normally did in an entire day. He gave Jupiter a nod, handed her the soiled towels, and strode off in just his underwear toward the car with Cade and his other friends. He had come, helped, and left without so much as a *Hi, nice to meet you.* It was odd, but when it mattered, these tiger shifters were there to help with just a phone call. Cade had promised as much in his parting words. In spite of what Colin said about them, Mia couldn't help being impressed.

Colin edged up to her. "Come on, Mia. Let's get you home."

She still wasn't sure where that was, but for tonight, her bed would apparently be in a down-town Seattle hotel. They climbed back in the van, and Mia watched Lucas and Lev sleep all the way back to the city.

Chapter Thirty-Two

THE CARAVAN STOPPED AT LUCAS'S APARTMENT, BUT only long enough for the healed-up wolves to carry the injured ones inside. Mia wanted to stay, or talk to Lucas, or *something*, but Parker had given sedatives to all three of the wolves he stitched—Lucas, Lev, and their father. Besides, it was late. Llyr was nominally in charge, with his father out of commission, and he ordered everyone to sleep in and not come to work the next morning until noon.

Mia could hardly believe that it was only Monday. Well, Monday at 2 am, but still.

She and Jupiter and Colin drove back to the hotel where Mia had been staying with Lucas. Jupiter kept falling asleep on Mia's shoulder on the way, and Mia was able to stay awake only because she had the nagging sense that she should have stayed at Lucas's apartment. What if he woke up in the night in pain? He should have someone there to help him, besides his injured brother and father. Of course, Llyr had assigned two wolves to guard them, but that wasn't what she meant. She wanted to be there to *care* for him. Although she didn't really have any right to do that.

Eventually, she found herself stumbling into the luxury hotel with her roommate and Colin. He took Lucas's room, and the two girls stayed in Mia's room. They were all dead on their feet, so it didn't much matter where she laid down. She was asleep the instant she was horizontal.

The next morning woke her up with the smell of eggs and bacon.

She peeked out of her room to verify that Colin had ordered them breakfast, but she was too self-conscious to come out in her rumpled PJs and bed head. Jupiter gushed about the view and the giant luxury bathroom, but all Mia could think was that she would much rather have *Lucas* in the next room. Even if he was surly and had been up half the night howling. She tried to ignore those thoughts as she showered away the last memories of her time as Mace's prisoner—it was already fading from her mind, like a horrible nightmare she wanted to shake off. And even if her heart was still worried about Lucas, Colin had also been there to save her. And was looking out for her still. Her wolf yipped in agreement. The least she could do was put on a presentable face and be gracious while he watched over her. And who knew—maybe there could be something between them. Lucas wasn't ready for a mate, but *she* was. Or at least a pack to belong to. Like Colin said, finding a mate would give her an extra level of protection, in case Mace decided to come after her again. But it was far more than that... life was too short and precarious to not seize the chance to belong to something. Especially something as wondrous as all of Sparks wolf packs seemed to be.

She wanted to find her place there.

For once, Jupiter had to borrow clothes from Mia, given they hadn't had time to stop by the dorm and pick up any extras. Fortunately, Mia still had the black slacks and brilliant blue silk shirt Jupiter had loaned her before. Mia had never had a chance to wear them before they both were kidnapped, rescued, and squirreled away in a luxury hotel.

"Are you sure you don't want to wear these?"

Mia asked, indicating the professional outfit she was wearing courtesy of Jupiter's closet.

"You're going to work today, right?" Jupiter was flopped on the oversized bed they shared, hanging her head off the edge and looking at Mia upside down. "You gotta look hot for all those sexy shifter men you work with. Damn, girl, I need to get a job like that."

Mia grinned. "Well, there are some downsides."

"Like what?" Jupiter flipped over and propped her head in her hands. "Having to watch hot man flesh all day? Or having them all court you like some oil magnate princess?"

Mia's grin faded to a scowl. She turned away to check her clothes in the mirror, hoping Jeeter wouldn't see her face heat up. "I don't know what you're talking about."

"Oh, come on! The way Cade and Colin were ready to throw down over you last night?" Jupiter clambered off the bed and came to stand behind Mia, looking over her shoulder in the mirror. "I mean, it makes sense... you're young and gorgeous..."

"Jeeter!"

"Don't interrupt." Jupiter pulled Mia's long black hair back over her shoulder. "You're beautiful, and you know it. Or you should, anyway. By the way, this blouse is perfect for you. See how it sets off your eyes? I'm a serious clothing genius."

Mia sighed. "What I need is a relationship genius. Because I'm swimming without a life preserver in this mess, Jeeter."

Her roommate's gushing faded a little. "Yeah, well, I'm no expert in shifter romance. I mean, who knew there were even enough of you people to have such a thing? Seriously, my mind is still freakin' on that. I'm starting to think my Psychology professor is secretly a baboon—"

"Jeeter, I mean it."

"So do I! Have you seen that guy's face?" Jupiter pulled an exaggerated expression in the mirror that only a drama major would even contemplate making.

Mia shoved her out of mirror range. "You are so strange."

Jeeter gave her a skeptical look. "Says the girl who howls at night."

Blood rushed to Mia's face. "I do not."

"You so did!" Jeeter backed up until her knees bumped the bed, then she flopped down on it again, flinging her arms wide. "Oh, Lucas! Take me now!"

Mia rushed forward, her face on fire. She slapped Mia's knee slightly then climbed onto the bed with her. "Oh god. Tell me I didn't say that."

Jeeter sat up on her elbows. "Not loud enough for Wolfy McCutie next door to hear if that's what you're worried about."

Mia's shoulders dropped, in relief but also desperation. "Oh, Jeeter. What am I going to do?"

Her roommate sat up farther and folded her legs. "I'm not sure I completely understand the question." Her face was finally serious, although that could simply be an act, too.

"I think I might be in love with Lucas."

Jupiter nodded. "That's not actually a question, you know."

Mia sighed. How could she explain when she wasn't even sure what all the moving parts of shifter mating were herself? Although she had a pretty good idea now, even better after all the trauma with the Red wolves. "Shifters mate for life. Well... the wolf ones, anyway. Lucas lost his mate, and he's still pretty devastated about it."

Jeeter frowned, and the seriousness was for real this time. "Oh man. That's awful."

"Right? I mean, I don't know how anyone gets over that." Mia smoothed out some wrinkles in the super fluffy comforter. "I mean, I know he's attracted to me, but he's made it pretty clear he's not ready for a mate."

Jeeter nodded. "But that Colin guy is totally into you."

Mia gave her a pained smile. "And he's super nice."

"Not to mention outrageously hot." Jeeter's nod was a little more enthusiastic.

"And he helped save me, and he wants to protect me, and he's *totally* looking for a mate, and—"

"Mia." Her roommate's touch on her knee stopped Mia's rambling. "Do you love him?"

"Well, no, not yet… I mean, I just met him! But maybe I could. Someday." Mia heard the weakness in her own voice. And she knew in her heart that her answer would be very different if Jeeter had asked if she loved Lucas. But that option wasn't really on the table.

"Well, there's no rush, is there?" Jeeter asked. "Jesus, Mia, you're only twenty-one. Why don't you date him for a while and see?"

Mia bit her lip. "That makes sense. I know it does. And if I was only human, I would totally do that. Hell, a week ago, I wouldn't even consider—"

Mating. It was this amazing and profound experience, and she hadn't even known about it a week ago. But now that her inner wolf had awoken, the idea of *mating* spoke to her in a way she couldn't ignore.

"Consider *what?*" Jeeter had that *what have you gotten into* look again like she did when she thought Mia was moving in with Lucas.

Mia took a deep breath and tried to put the tangle of feeling rumbling around inside her chest, inside her *wolf,* into words. "Wolves mate for life. And my inner wolf is ready for that. *Wants it,* badly. It's the human part of me that's not quite sure. I think with the right man, the right *wolf,* I would be. But I just don't know. This is all so new to me." An ache in her chest made her wish she could just talk to Lucas about it… even just as a friend. He would tell her the truth about how it all worked. He would help her sort it out. And he would make sure she made the right choice.

Jupiter frowned and didn't say anything for a moment. She pursed her lips and looked over Mia's professional outfit. Finally, her face softened. "I'm kind of out of my depth here, girl. But it seems like whether you're human or wolf shouldn't really matter for this sort of thing."

Mia frowned. "What do you mean?"

Jupiter shrugged. "Seems like, when it comes to love, you've just got to follow your heart."

Mia nodded, but her roommate's words only unsettled her more. How could she follow her heart, when it kept leading her down a dead end?

"Look," Jeeter said as she squeezed Mia's knee, "my personal rule—and this had never steered me wrong, so I highly recommend you heed it—is *Never Make Massively Difficult Decisions On An Empty Stomach.*" She tilted her head to their hotel bedroom door. "Let's go eat some of that awesome hotel food, Wolfish McHottie has ordered up for us."

Mia gave a small laugh. "His name is Colin. Please, please, don't call him McHottie to his face."

Jeeter swept off the bed, unfolding her legs and striding toward the door. "SweetMercy McHotness?"

"No." Mia scrambled after her, straightening her skirt on the way.

"Wolfman McStudmuffin." Jeeter's hand was on the door.

"Jeeter, I'm begging you."

"Ah, you're no fun at all." She flung open the door and flounced into the main part of their hotel suite, where Colin waited. He looked up from the breakfast table expectantly, his gaze searching for Mia.

She took a deep breath and tried to keep her steps light as she followed after her roommate.

COLIN'S GAZE SELDOM LEFT MIA DURING BREAKFAST. He kept up with Jupiter's wild forays in conversation, but mostly he seemed to be waiting for something... she wasn't quite sure what, but his eyes never wandered away from her for long.

Mia and Colin left Jupiter at the hotel with an admonition not to go back to the dorm. Mia didn't think it would be a problem: Jeeter was camped out with leftover room-service, Wi-Fi, and a rental laptop from the hotel. She barely waved as Mia left.

Colin kept up the frequent glances in Mia's direction all along the drive in to SparkTech. He had mentioned something about her clothes being nice, and she supposed her buttoned-up blouse could have been buttoned-up farther, but she had a feeling that wasn't what the stares were about. At least, not entirely. He wanted to talk to her, and for some reason, he was waiting. For what, she didn't know. But the staring was so obvious Mia was afraid they might crash his gorgeous sports car right into one of the glass skyscrapers of downtown Seattle.

Somehow they managed to arrive at the Russell building in one piece.

The SparkTech offices on the 32nd floor were still fairly empty. Mia immediately checked, but Lucas, Lev, and their father still hadn't come in. But Lena, the receptionist, was there, and it was after twelve o'clock noon, so while Colin went off to his office to work, Mia ventured to ask Lena straight out if her three favorite wolves had made it through the night.

"Honey, they're fine," Lena said. She was impeccably dressed, as always, and had a kind, knowing smile for Mia. "Mr. Sparks called in this morning to let me know the boys were recovering very quickly."

The boys. She meant Lucas and Lev.

"Are they staying home today, then?" Mia asked.

"If I know them, they will be in here as soon as they can manage it." She smiled again, but Mia had the sense that she really didn't know any more than she was saying.

Mia nodded her thanks and wandered back to her office. The sun outside was brilliant on the bay, sparkling in a magical way that turned the sea into a jeweled blue-green blanket. It reminded her of that time in the hotel with Lucas, when he was desperately trying to analyze the LoopSource deal so he could find a way to keep her safe. It had been only a few days ago, but it felt like a lifetime had happened in between. Even then, he had been devoted to protecting her... all while refusing to consider her as a potential mate.

And now? Now she was safe, especially if the LoopSource deal went through. Then there would be no need for him to protect her anymore. They could still work together—his office was only a few doors down from hers—but there were no pack wars or dark wolves or crazy witches forcing her into danger. And in need of his protection.

Somehow that didn't stop her from feeling like she *needed* him.

A small tap at her door drew her attention away from the window and the longing inside her.

"Hey." Colin stuck his head in, hand on the doorknob. "I have good news."

"Really? I could use some good news." She smiled, her heart lifting a bit. Maybe he was bringing more news about the injured wolves.

He stepped inside, leaving the door slightly

open in his wake, and came around her giant wooden desk to stand by the window with her. He hesitated, like he wanted to touch her, but was holding himself back.

"Yes?" She gave him a questioning smile, not knowing whether she should encourage him or not.

He peered down into her eyes for a moment, holding her gaze with those blazing green eyes of his. "LoopSource has accepted our offer."

A small breath escaped Mia. "Really?"

He smiled. "Yes, really."

"Oh, that's... that's great news." A shadow crossed over her heart. This was it... things would go back to normal now. She could return to the dorm and live her life without worrying about dark wolves. Lucas wouldn't need to protect her any longer.

Her wolf whined a little at the pain creeping into her chest.

Colin placed a hand against the window and leaned closer. "Mia, I know it's been hard. I can't even imagine how frightening all of this must have been for you." He shook his head. "From the moment I saw you, I could tell you were strong, but I had no idea... my packmates told me what happened at Mace's house."

Mia's face ran hot. The intensity of his green eyes, the sun beating through the window, the memory of Mace forcing her to walk up those stairs… the temperature all around her was rising to flaming hot. "I'd rather just forget all that if you don't mind."

Colin's face softened. "Of course. None of that should have happened in the first place. If it was up to me…" He paused, looking out the window and seeming to hold something back. When his gaze returned, it was on fire for her again. The way it had been when they first met in her office before she was kidnapped, when he strode in and told her in no uncertain terms that he wanted to claim her.

"Mia, I will never let something like that happen to you again." He edged closer and gently touched her cheek with his fingertips, trailing them down until he barely grazed her bottom lip.

She was frozen, captivated by his touch and the intensity in his eyes.

"I want you," he whispered. "Every minute I'm near you, my wolf is singing your name. You're beautiful and strong and everything I could ever want in a mate. You're a Queen among wolves, Mia, and I want to make you mine."

She let out the breath that was trapped inside

her. "I'm barely a wolf. I'm only just now figuring these things out."

His eyes lit up. "Let me show you." He closed the distance between them until his face was only inches from hers—close enough to kiss as they huddled against the window and the shining view of Seattle. "You have no idea how much I want to bring out the full alpha female that you are. When I make you mine, I'll show you a world you've never seen."

Her wolf whimpered under the hot sexual promise in his tone. She recognized the alpha in his voice, in his stance, in his commanding touch even as his fingers barely skimmed her hair. Mia's inner wolf wouldn't fight her on this: Colin saved her from the worst fate she could imagine. Her instincts were begging her to submit to this alpha who so clearly wanted to claim her. But what about her human side?

His nearness made it difficult for her human parts to breathe. "This is all so new to me."

"I know." He touched her again, and this time, it was more intimate and slow. He was enjoying the softness of her skin as he glided his fingertips over it. "And, to be honest, that's part of what excites me. You have no idea what you can become. What we can become together. I want to show it all to you, Mia."

He leaned closer. If she didn't move, he would kiss her. But she couldn't decide: was this what she wanted? Colin's touch and hot promises were undeniably building heat inside her, making her wolf whimper with need, and making her human body flush with arousal. He was gorgeous, commanding, and wanted her *badly*... but was that enough?

"I just... this all seems so sudden." Her words were breathless. His hot touch was stealing the oxygen straight out of her lungs.

"I know it has to seem strange to you." His slow fingertip touches were sliding down to her neck. "I know it's incredibly fast." He bent forward and was whispering close to her face now. "But if you become mine, Mia, I will love you and protect you all the days of my life."

He finally closed the last whisper of space between them, and his lips touched hers. It wasn't a forceful, passionate kiss... more like the ghost of a future kiss. A light sweep that promised more to come. Only... it felt wrong. Like a shoe that was one size too large, loose and ill-fitting. He said he would love and protect her... but not that he was *in love* with her. Maybe that would come later. Maybe that was what he meant, but it just came out wrong. But as those thoughts tumbled through her head, she realized none of that mattered: she wasn't *in love* with him.

And she should be.

Colin's hand moved to the back of her head, and he leaned in to kiss her again. Only this time, Mia could tell it would be no light feather-brush of lips.

She leaned away and slipped her hand up to his face, holding him back with her fingertips.

He frowned like he wasn't quite sure why she was stopping him.

Mia gazed up into those sexy, green eyes, hooded with desire. Jeeter was right: he *was* incredibly hot. And she was going to tell him *no* anyway. She hoped she wasn't going to regret this for the rest of her life.

"Colin, I'm sorry." It came out in a rush. "I'm in love with Lucas."

He didn't move away, just he briefly closed his eyes, then lowered his gaze to the thousand-foot drop out the window next to them. The pain on his face stabbed guilt through her chest.

"Are you sure?" he asked without looking at her.

She could say that she *wasn't* sure. That maybe

she could grow to love Colin instead. Or that it didn't really matter if she loved Lucas, because he would never want her for a mate anyway.

But none of that mattered, either.

Mia slipped her arms around Colin's neck, reaching up to hug him tight. He was surprised: she could tell by the way he hesitated before putting his arms around her.

"I'm sure," she whispered in his ear, then gave him a small kiss on the cheek before pulling completely back. "But thank you. For saving my life. For wanting me for a mate. And for letting me decide."

His lips pressed into a tight line, and the way his eyes pinched at the edges made her heart hurt. She didn't want to reject him or ruin all his plans. But he was a good man, and he deserved to know the truth.

And the truth was she loved the broken alpha who might never love her back. Strangely, that didn't matter either. She could wait until he was ready. Or just be his friend.

Somehow, even a dead end with Lucas was better than not having him at all.

Colin just nodded, then leaned forward and dropped a sweet kiss on her forehead. That made her blush more than anything that had gone before.

Then he smiled. "If you change your mind, Mia Fiore, you know where to find me."

Then the only decent shifter who had ever wanted her for a mate turned and walked away.

Chapter Thirty-Three

THE ELEVATOR RIDE UP TO THE 32ND FLOOR WAS
more comfortable than the car ride to SparkTech,
but Lucas still found himself moving his weight
from one foot to the other and arching his back to
stretch a little. His brother, Lev, was doing the same
subtle stretch-and-twist motion, while their father
seemed to have healed completely.

Not bad for an old man.

It wasn't that Lucas was still in pain so much as
the deep hole in his gut was still knitting itself back
together, and the stitches the healer had left inside
hadn't dissolved yet. So they pulled and twinged
and generally made an annoying habit of
reminding him he wasn't quite healed yet.

His father lifted his chin in Lucas's direction. "You didn't have to come in, son."

"Of course he did." Lev stretched an arm overhead, more obviously working out the kinks. "But I call dibs on talking to Mia first." He threw a smirk to Lucas.

"She was there when you were shot, Lev." Lucas shook his head but had to work to suppress his grin. "She already knows all about your heroics."

"I think she needs a complete recounting to get the full effect." Lev glanced at the numbers counting up to the 32nd floor.

"A complete recounting?" Lucas asked. "Jesus, I *am* going home."

"What?" his father said with a full smile. "And miss your own opportunity to brag?"

"Oh, is *that* how it's going to be?" Lucas shook his head in mock disgust, but the truth was he had missed this light-hearted banter. The mission, and its aftermath, had wiped away everything that had gone before and restored this sense of belonging to the family again. He wouldn't trade it for anything, even with all the harassment that came with it.

Especially with the harassment.

Lucas hooked a thumb at his father's healed leg. "I noticed you only managed to get shot in the leg, old man. Next time, maybe you could commit a little more to the mission."

His father chuckled. "I'm thinking the wolves *not* catching bullets were probably the smart ones."

"Hey, I never claimed to be smart!" Lev said cheerily. "Llyr's the badass genius of the family. I got the good looks and charm. Poor Lucas had to settle for surliness and general bad hygiene."

"Ok, that is just…" Right as the elevator doors opened, Lucas grabbed his little brother by his black silk shirt and folded him over into a headlock. "… uncalled for."

Lev made a few sad attempts at punching his way out of Lucas's hold while he dragged Lev from the elevator.

"Oh, come on, man, I just ironed this!" Lev's muffled voice from under Lucas's armpit made him chuckle so hard he was sure he pulled one of his stitches. Lucas let him go and gave him a good-natured shove toward the frosted-glass doors.

"Ironing? *Ironing, Lev?* You've got soft, man. It's a sad thing to see."

Lev was walking backward toward the door, flinging his finger out at Lucas. "Hey, just because *you* have no style, doesn't mean all the Sparks brothers like to live primal."

"That was low, bro," Lucas said with a shake of his head and a barely concealed smirk. "Really low."

"You wrinkled my shirt," Lev said as if that justified any level of retribution he might choose.

Lena was beaming at them as they cruised by and pushed through the doors. As much as he was bursting with this joy of brotherhood he hadn't felt in so long, Lucas couldn't help immediately sweeping his gaze across the offices and the common area, looking for Mia. There were a couple members of his father's pack sharing coffee and lingering in the common area, but most of the offices were still closed up... except Mia's door, which was slightly open. He gave Lev a sideways look, and they both raced toward her door, each grabbing the other and trying to hold him back. They checked their head-long rush as they reached the door and saw inside...

Mia and Colin. Kissing.

Lucas came to a dead stop, staring, then he wrenched his gaze away and stared at the floor.

"No fucking way," Lev said under his breath.

Lucas shook his head, searching the carpet. He was too late. He should have known Colin would make his move while he was out of the picture. A roaring, growling thunder was growing inside Lucas. His wolf wanted to charge in and beat the crap out of Colin for presuming to even try. The only thing that stopped him: *Mia was kissing him.*

He had already lost.

"I'm gonna kill him," Lev growled.

Lucas shot a hand out to grab him by the shoulder. Lev's face was livid, a reflection of all the anger and jealousy boiling under Lucas's skin. But he didn't understand: it wasn't Colin who had done anything wrong. It was Lucas. He failed her so many times in so many ways… pushed her away… and now, he was simply too late.

"I'll take care of this, Lev." Those words sent a pain ripping through his gut that had nothing to do with gunshot wounds or stitches. Lucas looked back inside Mia's office: she had her arms around him, hugging Colin like he was a life preserver. His hands were on her back. Lucas gritted his teeth and forced himself to watch… until she kissed him on the cheek, and then he had to look away. He pulled a shock-faced Lev to the side, away from the door and out of Mia's line-of-sight.

"This is so wrong, bro." Lev was shaking his head. "So wrong."

Their father had held back, face pinched.

Waiting to see Lucas's reaction, he imagined.

"I'll take care of it," Lucas said to his father. "Lev, just… give me some space, okay?"

Lev gave him an exasperated look like he couldn't believe everything had unraveled so fast. And Lucas couldn't bear to see that expression on his face. Not again. Not after everything. That alone would have broken his heart if it wasn't already in shreds.

Colin emerged from Mia's office, barely sparing a glance for them as he strode toward his office. Lucas had to hold Lev back again.

"Just let me have a little talk with him," Lev said through gritted teeth. "Beta to beta."

"Hey." Lucas grabbed Lev's face in his two hands and pulled him back to look at him. "You *are* my beta. You will *always* be my beta, no matter what. Do you understand me, Lev?"

Lev's wild look calmed slightly. "Always have been. Always will be, Lucas."

"I know." Emotion swelled Lucas's throat, but he pushed past it. "As your alpha, I'm telling you: *leave it alone.* I will handle it."

Lev's heaving breath calmed a little more. He pulled out of Lucas's grasp, but then he nodded his agreement.

"I'm going…" The words were getting more difficult. "I'm going to talk to Mia first. Then the asshole."

Lev smirked.

"Then I might need a really strong drink. And possibly more stitches. Think you could fix me up?"

Lev's smirk died, and he was back to looking murderous.

"Wait for me, Lev." Lucas said it as a command, even though he knew he didn't need to. His brother would be waiting to pick up the pieces, just like he had always been.

Lucas left him standing in the hall and stepped toward Mia's office. The door was still slightly open. He pushed it wide as he stepped inside, then quietly closed it behind him. She hadn't noticed him as she stared at the Seattle skyline, the sparkling bay, and the Olympic National Park beyond. Her dark hair fell in a lovely cascade down her back. He didn't have to see her eyes to know her blue silk shirt was a dead match for them. Her slim black skirt hugged her curves and made his heart ache.

"Mia." His voice was soft, partly because he didn't want to startle her, partly because his throat was closing up.

She still jumped, but not too badly. "Lucas!" But

she wasn't chastising him for scaring her, like that time in her office when he first kissed her. Or in his apartment after they'd had sex for the first time, and before the second. No, this time, she seemed full of heart-breaking joy at seeing him and ran toward him from her spot by the window. She was moving so fast, he had to catch her around the waist to keep her from crashing into him. Her arms went around his neck… and just like that, she was in his arms again. He automatically held her close and bent his head to bury his face in her soft cloud of hair. A giant hole formed inside him: this was what he had blown. This was what he wouldn't ever have again.

"Oh my god, Lucas, are you all right? Tell me you're all right!" She was clinging to him, and her grip on him, her worried words… it was like the sweetest home he had ever known. He didn't want her to let go. Ever. But he was sure the hug was just Mia being… Mia. Her worry was about an injury that was nearly healed… not the hole that was carving deeper into him by the second. He didn't think this new wound would ever go away.

Lucas didn't want to let go, but she was pulling away. And she wasn't his to keep.

She didn't go far. When she put her soft hands on his cheeks and searched his face with those beautiful blue eyes, it nearly undid him. He almost had to turn and go. But he came into her office because he had something to tell her. And he wasn't leaving until he did.

"Please say something," Mia said, hands still on his face. "Tell me you're going to live."

He gave her a pained smile. "I'm going to live." He was saying it to himself as much as her, but part of him doubted it was true. A very large part.

She dropped her hands and took a step back, creating a space between them. He ached to bring her back. A small frown came to rest on her forehead. He wanted to touch it and make it disappear. But he didn't have a right to that, either.

She bit her lip. "I should... I mean, I wanted to thank you—"

"You don't need to thank me." God, he wanted to kiss her so badly.

She frowned. "That's what Colin said, too."

He winced. *Colin's name on her lips.* Lucas wasn't sure he could do this. He sucked in some air and breathed through the pain in his chest. "Mia."

She peered up at him, lovely and waiting. He had to say it. Then he would leave. Forget Colin— he wouldn't waste any time there. He would just get out and get thoroughly drunk with Lev.

"I had something I needed to tell you," he started, then was suddenly unsure how to make the words come out right. He took another breath and reminded himself of all the courage she had shown. And all he had put her through.

Her frown grew a little deeper. "You don't have to tell me any—"

"But I do," he cut her off. Then he couldn't help it, he had to touch her. A strand of her hair was mussed from their hug. He reached out and tucked it behind her ear. Her big eyes just watched him as she waited. Patient. He'd made her wait too long. Probably the biggest mistake he would ever make.

"I was in such a dark place for so long," he said quietly, dipping his head a little to peer into her gorgeous eyes. "I was dead. Dead to my family, dead to my pack... even dead to myself. And then this... *girl* came into my life, and suddenly I was doing things, feeling things, that I hadn't since... since I lost Tila."

Her eyes went a little wider, but that only made them softer, more beautiful.

He shook his head a little and gave a small laugh. "Mind you, I didn't *want* to feel those things. I pushed you away, because... well, I just couldn't face it. But you made me feel alive, Mia. You made me *want* something. Protecting you was the only decent thing I've done in a long time. From the moment you came into my life, you challenged me to be better. A better man. A better wolf. A true alpha, not some broken excuse for…" He paused, his throat thick.

She seemed distressed by what he was saying. "Lucas, you're a good man."

"I'm a better man with *you.*" He choked on those words and the simple truth in them. A truth he'd figured out just a little too late.

She reached for him, then stopped. She seemed on the verge of saying something, so he pushed on, trying to get the last out before the fact that he was too late overwhelmed him.

"Before I go," he said, "I just wanted to thank you for… all of it. Every single minute."

She pulled back, and tears glassed the corners of her eyes. He could barely stand the sight of it.

"Before you *go?*" Her voice hiked up. "Where are you going?"

He hadn't really thought about that. But it didn't matter. "I can't really stay around while you…"

"While I *what?*" Her alarm had stepped up

another notch, and her hands were wringing one another. Her distress almost forced him to touch her again, soothe her, but he held back.

"Mia, I understand. And I know it's my fault. I waited too long. I'm an idiot."

She flung her clenched hands to the side. "Dammit, Lucas, what are you talking about!"

He gritted his teeth. She was going to force him to say it. "Mia, I *know*. I saw you with Colin. I'm sorry, I just can't stick around and watch that."

"What?" She grabbed his shoulders in frustration like she was going to shake him. "Lucas, I told him *no.*"

"You… wait, what?" A rush of exhilaration in his brain left him uncertain like the world had moved under his feet.

"He asked me to be his mate. I told him no."

"You're not going to mate with him?" His mouth gaped open. Did he hear her right? Was his mind spinning tricks, making him misunderstand?

"Lucas." She was smiling. At the same time tiny tears, leaked from the corners of her eyes and leaked down her cheeks. "I already told you: I want to be with *you.*"

All the rush in his brain washed down and forced the air out of his lungs in one long huff. He wasn't too late. Colin had tried… and *failed*. Because she wanted *him*.

"Mia." He barely got the word out before his hands were on her. He slid them around her back and crushed her to his chest. His lips found hers and devoured them. His hands slid up the silkiness of her shirt and wound into her hair until he was holding her head with both hands, angling it so he could plunge deeper into her mouth and claim her with his kiss. His tongue warred with hers, then he pulled back to taste her lips again, a flurry of hungry kisses that he simply couldn't hold back.

His wolf roared inside him, a triumph so complete in that one kiss that he couldn't imagine anything better… short of actually claiming her.

Claiming her.

He pulled back, breathing hard. Her eyes were half-lidded, and her lips were swollen with his kiss. He'd never seen anything so damn sexy in his life.

He still held her head in his hands, breathing hard. "Mia." He waited for her to open her eyes. "I want you. Now and forever. I want to make you mine."

Her smile was tremulous like she wasn't sure he was really saying it.

He wanted to make her sure. He wanted her to

know *exactly* how much he wanted her. He slid one hand down her back, feeling every curve along the way, then he grabbed her by the bottom and pulled her hard against him. She pulled in a short gasp, but he was just getting started. He held her tight against him as he walked her backward and pinned her to the translucent office door. His one hand was still in her hair, holding her head, but now with his body pressed flush against hers, his other hand was free to work its way up her side, making clear that this was what he wanted: *all of her.* Every inch, every curve, every thought and feeling, all of it, belonging to him and only him.

Mine, his wolf growled.

Lucas's hand reached her throat, and he stroked his fingers up her silky soft skin to her face. He lingered there a moment, relishing the ability to touch her like this, then trailed his fingers slowly back down to her chest. He shoved aside the flimsy cloth of her blouse to reveal her bare shoulder. Her breast lay just below his hand, pressed between their bodies, and bulging up in a way that made his mouth water. He painted a line across her creamy skin with his finger. This was where he would bite her. This is where he would mark her and forever make her his.

She let out a small moan.

He dragged his gaze back up to her eyes. "I want you to understand exactly what I'm going to do to you." His voice was husky with need, and his cock was swollen and hard against the deep softness of her body. Even through their clothes, he could feel her heat. He brushed his lips against hers but didn't kiss her. He whispered against them instead. "If you say yes, I'm going to take you, now and every day for the rest of your life. I'm going to claim your body with my love and with my bite, and you will forever be mine, Mia. You'll be forever bound to me, and I will forever protect and care for you. If you say yes to me now, Mia, I won't stop until we're mated." He was breathing hard against her, his chest heaving with hers. He wouldn't be *able* to stop. He knew this. Nor did he have any desire to.

"Yes." Her lips barely moved with the word. It was as soft as a feather-light kiss and like a trumpet blaring to every instinct inside him. His wolf growled for him to take her *now*, right up against the translucent door where he was sure everyone in the common room could see exactly what they were doing. He would be lucky if they made it to somewhere with any kind of privacy.

His wolf's growl worked up into his throat as he kissed her again and again. Then he worked his way down her throat, bending to reach the delicate bones of her shoulder and chest. He trailed his tongue across her skin, tasting her, relishing the thought of the claiming to come and what it would mean. How it would make him whole. How it would make her *his*.

"Oh god, Mia," he breathed against her skin. "I need you right now."

Her hands were in his hair, kneading through and encouraging him to go lower. One hand still in her hair, he clenched it tight and held her up against the wall as his other hand slid under her bra, freeing her breast for his mouth to enjoy. He cupped it in his hand while his tongue roamed the hard bud of her nipple. He nipped at it with his teeth, and her moan went straight to his cock. Which was seriously in need of contact with her. His canines were already coming out, and his mouth was watering, but he would hold back that part. The claiming was too special—*she* was too special—to take her hard against the door as his body was aching to do.

He straightened and smoothed her clothes back into place. "We need to go."

Chapter Thirty-Four

LUCAS SMILED AS MIA'S FACE FLUSHED A BEAUTIFUL pink.

"Where are we going?" she asked.

"My apartment," he said, releasing her hair and grabbing her hand instead. He pulled her from where he had pinned her against her office door and gave her a tiny space in which to straighten her clothes. "I don't think the boss will mind if we take the rest of the day off."

She blushed even more furiously, her eyes going wide. "You're not going to tell him…!"

He held back his chuckle for her sake. "If we make a run for it, maybe he won't notice." He knew that was a lie—if he dragged Mia from her office while he sported a raging hard-on, every wolf in

SparkTech would know exactly what he intended to do with her. The only question they would have was what took him so long.

Mia smoothed down her hair as if that would give them away, not the pink in her cheeks. "Maybe you should go first. I'll meet you downstairs."

He pulled her against him with their joined hands. "No way in hell am I letting you out of my sight, Mia Fiore." He grinned as her cheeks pinked up even more. "Now be a good girl and come with me."

He didn't wait for her assent, just spun her around and towed her toward the door. Besides, it would be easier for her if they went quickly: she'd be less likely to notice the stares. He strode quickly through the mostly empty common room with Mia right behind him. The stares followed them, but he made no attempt to hide. They pushed through the entrance doors, only to find Lena and Lev whispering over her desk in the reception area. Lev's eyebrows almost flew off his face, they were hiked so high. Lucas gave him a nod but didn't slow on their way to the front doors and the elevator beyond. Mia ducked her head, and he wasn't sure if she even made eye contact with Lev, but they were out the door before anyone could say anything.

Lucas punched the elevator button and pulled Mia into his arms.

She buried her face in his chest while they waited. "Oh my god, they totally know, don't they?"

He chuckled. The feel of her hands gripping his shirt and hiding her face against him was only feeding his hard-on. "Oh yeah."

She groaned her embarrassment, but he didn't want her to feel that way. Not about this. Not about being with him. He slid a hand up to her face and lifted her chin. "I want them to know. I want every wolf at SparkTech to know you belong to me."

That seemed to relax her a little because she melted against him and peered at him with those big blue eyes. He bent to kiss her. She tasted like sweetness and musk, and the perfume of her arousal was heating up again, making his wolf growl his need for her. He was just getting serious about exploring her mouth when the elevator dinged. Fortunately, it was empty. He pulled her inside, hit the button for the parking garage, and even before the doors were closed, he had her up against the smooth stainless of the wall, his body welded to hers, his mouth claiming her again.

His hands slid down her sides, over the curve of her hips and down to the back of her knee. He slipped his hand under her skirt and hiked it up. She hooked her leg over his hip and strained against him, grinding against his rock-hard cock. He gripped her soft bottom, pulling her tight to him. Her moan sent a shiver of want through his body. He palmed her breast with his other hand, relishing the weight of it and anticipating the moment when there would be no clothes between them. She arched her back as he nipped at her neck.

"God, Mia," he whispered into her sweet-tasting skin. "This is how I should have had you from the beginning. So much wasted time…"

"Lucas." She was already whispering his name and digging her hands into his back. It sent his wolf into a small frenzy. He shifted his body until his cock pressed between her legs, grinding her into the elevator wall until he made the contact she was craving. Even with clothes between them, it must have hit the right spot because she arched even more and let loose one of those delicious moans.

"I want to make up for all that lost time," he panted against her neck. "All of it."

She slid her hands up to his head, gripping his hair and pulling his face up from feasting on her throat. The look in her eyes—filled with love and lust and understanding far beyond anything he deserved —went straight to his core. He *needed* this beautiful woman more than he needed air to breathe.

"Lucas," she said, her breath short. "I've never wanted anything the way I want you. The way I want *this.*" And he knew she meant all of it: him, their bodies entwined, the forever bond that would come soon… and not soon enough for him.

His lips found hers and gently brushed against them. Their bodies were gripped tight, but their lips were free to say the things that needed saying. The things he should have been saying all along.

"I could give you everything I have, my whole heart and soul, Mia, and it wouldn't be enough." His words were close and whispered and just for her. "It would never be enough to repay what you've already given me." He slid his hand up from exploring her body to cupping the back of her head. He kissed her thoroughly and with everything he had.

When they paused for air, she whispered, "You don't owe me anything. *You* saved *me.*"

He smiled and kissed her again. "That's where you're wrong, sweet Mia of mine," he whispered. "But that's all right. You just keep thinking that. I'm going to spend the rest of my life trying to find new ways to pay you back."

Just as he dove in for another deep kiss, the elevator lurched to a stop. He reluctantly released her, and she hastened to smooth out her clothes, but there was no one in the parking garage when the doors opened.

Hands clasped, they dashed down the line of cars, her heels clacking against the cement, his shoes pounding his impatience to get her to his apartment. He was caught up in her secret grins and flushed cheeks and was only absently scanning for his car when they came upon the SparkTech van they had used the night before in the rescue. He pulled up short—he had forgotten he had driven it into work with his father and brother. Fortunately, he still had the keys in his pocket.

He clicked it unlocked, then opened the front cab passenger door for her. The cab seat was one long bench, and it was high off the ground. Mia's heels and tight skirt made it difficult for her to negotiate a way into the truck. She tried stepping up a few different ways, but finally just climbed up on her hands and knees, leaving him with a dangerously nice view of her rear end as she summited the bench seat.

It was far too tempting, and he was done resisting anything when it came to Mia Fiore. She belonged to him now, and he would have her whenever and wherever and however he desired. He climbed into the van cab after her, his only question being whether or not making Mia come in the parking garage would pink up her cheeks with embarrassment in that delightful way again. He skimmed his hand over her delicious rear and closed the door behind him.

She squeaked with surprise. "What are you doing?" She had a hard time turning in that tight skirt and was momentarily at the mercy of his hands cupping her bottom.

He sat on the seat, grabbed hold of her hips, and pulled her down to sit on his lap, facing forward. He moaned as her bottom hit his cock. To make matters worse, she squirmed on him, twisting around to see what he was doing.

"Lucas, what in the——"

Her words cut off as he slid both his hands up her skirt. He groaned again as she squirmed some more, turning in time to see his hands slip under her panties and find her sex.

"Oh!" she said in surprise, but it quickly changed to a gasp as he sunk his fingers into her already-dripping core. He pumped fast, no desire to take anything slow. Her gasps quickly turned to moans. With one hand pumping inside her, and the other working the sensitive, slick bud of her sex, the kinds of protests she was making weren't protests at all.

"Lucas... Oh god..." Her head tipped back against him. His hands kept working her, slowly increasing his pace. The way she was moving against him, grinding her hot bottom against his cock, writhing and moaning in his arms, it was everything he could do to keep his own climax from coming way too soon. Her head rested against his shoulder, her heaving breaths coming harder and faster. He tipped his head in to nuzzle and nip at her earlobe and cheeks and neck as she writhed in his lap.

"Mia, baby, come for me," he whispered. His hands pumped faster and circled harder, making her back arch more. Then he felt her body squeezing down on his fingers. He held her tight as she bucked and came and moaned his name. It was insanely beautiful and erotic to hold her this way, to feel her coming undone in his arms. He could hardly breathe.

As soon as it seemed that she was starting to

come down, he withdrew his hands from inside her, lifted her bottom, and slipped her panties down her legs. She was still gasping, still reeling from her orgasm, but he had already decided there was no way he could wait until they got back to his apartment. He needed to be inside her *now*.

He carefully used his hard leather shoes to nudge her off her dangling heels and slide her underwear past her feet. Then he boosted her off his lap, setting her momentarily next to him on the bench. He worked furiously to get his pants undone, while she braced herself against the dash and seemed dazed.

He grinned. "Are you light-headed, my love?"

"God, Lucas," she said, blinking and staring out the windshield. "You need to warn me when you're going to do that."

He lifted his hips to slide his pants and underwear to his knees, freeing his aching cock to bob in the increasingly steamy air of the van cab. That finally caught Mia's attention. Her eyes went wide.

He reached for her waist. "What would be the fun of that?" He hauled her back into his lap again, only this time, face-to-face. Her hands went to his shoulders, trying to catch her balance while she straddled him.

"What are you doing?" she asked, wide-eyed.

"Do they teach you *nothing* in college these days?" he asked with a playful smile.

She twisted to look over her shoulder out the windshield. "But what if someone one comes?"

He smirked. "I plan on having at least *two* some-ones coming." With his hands on her hips, he held her up slightly from his lap as he slid down on the seat, working his way into position. His cock grazed her still-dripping sex, and she twisted back to peer down at him, mouth agape. Her hands gripped his shoulders.

"I can't believe we're——"

He cut off her protests with a finger across her lips. Then he slid his hand up into her hair, holding her there, and gripping her hip with his other hand. He positioned his cock just at her entrance, then peered up into her eyes.

"Ride me, Mia," he whispered, as he urged her to ease down onto him.

Her eyes went a little wider, but she shifted slightly forward, just enough so that she could take him inside her. He couldn't help the groan that came out as her hot tightness surrounded him. But he didn't want to just have her ride him—so when she had sunk halfway down his cock, he arched up into her, thrusting hard the rest of the way in.

She gasped in surprise, but he held her tight in place. *God, she feels so good.*

He peered up into her half-lidded eyes, and he knew she felt it, too. This joining together of their bodies—it was what they were meant to do. It was where he belonged, inside her, part of her. They were made for each other, made for *this*—a holy and beautiful thing that was the perfect joining of more than just their bodies.

He eased back to the seat, his cock still half buried in her. "Now," he said, his voice husky with need for her. "You need to hold onto me and hold perfectly still. Do you understand, Mia of mine?"

Her lips were parted and panting. She nodded, as much as she could with his hand gripping her hair and holding her firmly in place. He felt her grip on his shoulders harden and her body tense around him. He slid his hand from her hips to the heated wetness between her legs.

She whimpered as he found her swollen nub, still sensitive from when she came before.

He smiled, then tensed and thrust up into her again. She gasped, and he could feel the tremors running through her body. He thrust again and again, each time stroking her harder with his thumb. She gasped with each thrust, and after a moment, she lifted up and matched his thrusts with downward ones of her own. His moan reverberated throughout the van, a soul-shaking climax building inside him so fast it felt like a freight train bearing down on him.

His head fell back against the cab seat, and he pounded up into her, holding tight as she rode him, and he took her, all at the same time, perfectly matched, perfectly building... until she cried out his name, and he came undone. The pleasure of the release was almost too much, like a wave pulling him under. He was drowning in it, in her, in the fact that he had finally found a way to have her and keep her. His pace slowed, but he kept pumping as long as he could, drawing it out for her. Then the pleasure sunk him, draining the last of his energy. He pulled her down to his chest, still joined together, but now calming. He hugged her, molding her body to his. She shivered with pleasure, small aftershocks shaking her while he cradled her in his arms. Her head tucked into the crook of his neck, and he nuzzled her, finally finding her lips to kiss her softly, again and again.

"I think," she said, breathless. "You need to warn me when you're going to do that, too."

His chuckle was low and deep and shook both of their bodies. They relaxed even further into each other, connected and calming. He relished the softness of every part of her, including her long, silky hair on his fingertips.

"Consider yourself warned, Mia Fiore." He softly kissed her temple and across her eyelids. "I'm just getting started with you."

She shivered. He held her close for a minute, then two.

Finally, as their bodies began to cool, he said, "Time for me to take you home."

Chapter Thirty-Five

ALL THE WAY TO LUCAS'S APARTMENT, MIA FLOATED in the afterglow of the most amazing sex she had ever had in her life. Of course, all of the amazing sex she had experienced in her life had been with Lucas, but this was... beyond. Her body was still heated, still thrumming with pleasure, when they eventually parked the van in Lucas's apartment garage. They held hands on the way to the elevator, and if the gray-uniformed doorman could tell they had just had raging hot sex twenty minutes before, he didn't show it.

They hadn't said much on the ride over, but it had been a comfortable, snuggling kind of silence. She was still in shock somewhat—not because of the hot sex, but because of the words he had said, before, during, and after. He wasn't going to push her away this time. He truly was hers now. But as they rode the elevator to the 15th floor, a creeping nervousness snuck into her humming body and chilled it.

They were going to his apartment, so he could claim her.

She wanted it—she knew that was true—but that didn't stop butterflies from coming to life in her stomach and dancing around like they'd been electrified. Part of her was excited—mainly her wolf, who was running yippy circles in her mind while basking in the afterglow of hot sex with her alpha. And the human part between her legs was still hot, damp, and ready for more of the commanding sex Lucas had been dishing out in the van. *Holy hotness.* The way he told her what he wanted her to do and just how to go about it… that whole thing had scratched a very, very deep itch inside her. One she wanted to be scratched again and again.

All those parts of her couldn't wait for what would happen in Lucas's apartment. But as he opened the door and let her go in first, it was the front part of her brain that was revving up the butterflies in her stomach. Would the bite hurt? Would the magic that would bind them together be… strange? A pall hung over her from her submission to Mace. She was far from him now, but that bond wouldn't be wiped away until the new moon. More importantly, she could still feel the horror of it in her mind: Mace had controlled her in a way that, even now, gave her the utter creeps to think about. And she hadn't tried to think about it —in fact, she'd pushed it from her mind as much as possible. But as Lucas dropped his keys on the kitchen counter and took her hand, leading her straight to the bedroom, that feeling came rushing back, chilling her.

Lucas turned, all sexy smiles, and drew her into his arms.

But he must have sensed something because a frown quickly took over his face. "What's wrong, Mia?"

She stared at his chest, frowning. "Just nervous, I guess."

Lucas released her and took her hand, leading her to the bed. He sat on it and drew her down onto his lap, sitting sideways. He touched her hair, smoothing it back from her face.

"I would never hurt you," he said very softly. "Can you trust me when I tell you the claiming isn't going to hurt, not really?"

She couldn't look him in the eyes, even though he was trying to catch her gaze. "I'm not really worried about that." And she wasn't—now that she thought about it, the pain of the bite was the least of her concerns. It was the *magic* that worried her.

"What is it, then?" Lucas asked. "Tell me."

It wasn't a command, but his insistent tone made her drag her gaze up to meet his. There was such love in his eyes that it melted away a lot of her concerns right there. This gentle man, this kind, self-sacrificing alpha, would never let anything hurt her. She knew that, down deep in her bones and in her wolf-heart.

"When I was at Mace's..." But then the words got stuck in her throat.

His frown was dark and dangerous, but she knew it wasn't for her. It was Mace that made him glower like he wanted to kill something.

"Did he hurt you?"

She could tell the words pained him just to say.

"No." She shook her head for emphasis. Then she swallowed. "But I submitted to him, Lucas."

His shoulders relaxed. "I know. It's all right, Mia, you didn't have a choice."

She frowned. "I didn't want to."

"I know."

"And I fought him." Her stomach clenched at the memory.

"I would have been surprised at anything else." He gave her a soft smile.

"It's just that it felt…" Horrible. Awful. Like it was her own fault. Like he was messing with her mind. Like a terrible, wet, heavy blanket on her soul.

He touched her cheek, bringing her gaze back to his soft brown eyes. "It will be different with us, Mia."

A weight lifted from her chest, and she sucked in a breath. "Are you sure?"

"I promise you." He cupped her cheeks in his hands and kissed the tip of her nose. "But we can wait if you want. If you're not ready." Pain crinkled the edges of his eyes. It would hurt him to have her delay this, she could tell.

And hurting Lucas was the last thing she ever wanted to do. As simple as that, her worries fled, like cockroaches before a light. If this would make Lucas happy, would banish the pain from his eyes, then that was all she had ever wanted anyway. And she trusted him with her life… she could trust him with her heart and soul as well.

She rose up from his lap. His eyebrows lifted as she took his hands and hauled him up, too.

She reached up to touch his cheek. "Lucas Sparks, I want you to be my alpha."

The look on his face was something that would sear into her mind forever: love, need, hunger, and a kind of softness like she was giving him a precious gift that he didn't deserve but that meant the world to him.

And if that were even close to true, she didn't want to wait one moment more.

She stepped back and held his gaze while she slowly unbuttoned her silk top. He watched as she dropped the blouse to the floor, then reached back to remove her bra and toss that aside. His eyes darkened, and she could see the lust rise up in them. As she reached back to unzip her skirt, he started removing his clothes as well, first his black silk shirt, then his shoes and pants. In moments, they both stood naked. She could see his chest heaving, but he didn't move otherwise, just devoured her body with his eyes.

Then she shifted, and before she was done, he was in wolf form as well.

He stood proud before her, tail erect, head high, ears forward. She met his gaze but waited for him to command her to submit. She could have done it without the command, but for some reason, it felt important to have it happen that way.

Submit to me, Mia, my love, he thought.

Those words, ringing through her mind, lifted her heart in a rush, like a rising hot air balloon taking soundless flight. Her body relaxed, stretching forward with her forepaws and lifting her rear end into the air. She bowed her head, and lastly, tucked her tail down. She felt the bond immediately, like a warm blanket surrounding her—only instead of weighing her down, it comforted her and lifted her up. It was as though Lucas's strong arms were constantly holding her, keeping her from falling, buttressing her against anything in the world that might ever seek to tear her down. It was a magic borne of love, and it wiped away all her fears. All the memories of Mace and his ugliness faded into the shadows. She didn't want to move from that position of submission, that invisible embrace, for fear of shattering that feeling of being so completely loved.

Rise, my love. Lucas thoughts nudged her up from her tucked position, and her heart swelled to see him looking at her with such love in his dark wolf eyes.

She leaped to him, landing by his side to nuzzle him and lick his face and bump the top of her head into his. He nuzzled her back, and little huff of breath puffed on her face. She was sure he was laughing at her silliness, but her heart was so filled with joy, she couldn't even begin to feel embarrassed for it.

He touched the tip of his nose to hers, nudging her slightly back. *Shift for me, Mia.*

It was a command, but it felt like a kiss.

She shifted with such blinding speed that she found herself tumbling to the polished wooden floor of Lucas's bedroom. He had shifted with her and managed to catch her before she hit, holding her gently.

"Oh, Mia," he said, breathless. He pulled them both upright. His hand found her cheek, his burning gaze holding hers. "Tell me you're ready, my love, because I'm not sure if I can stand one more minute without having you."

Her naked body flushed with his words. "I'm yours, Lucas. Always."

MIA'S WORDS WERE AN ELIXIR FOR LUCAS.

He had already been floating on the submission bond—like when Colin had submitted to him, only a hundred times better. A flood of energy filled him from the inside out, enervating his entire body, empowering him in a way that burned him down to the core and then rebuilt him again, stronger, more capable, the true alpha that Mia needed him to be. She would always be his now, and he would fulfill every promise he had ever made to her: to protect her, to love her, to satisfy her every need.

And now that she was ready for him to claim her, his physical need to have her body pressed against his, to be inside of her, obliterated every other thought in his mind. She stood naked before him, that pink flush all over her now, from the rosy tint on her breasts to the heat in her cheeks. His cock was at attention, aching for her.

"Climb on the bed, Mia," he said.

Her eyes flashed, then she did as he asked. Her rosy skin stood out beautifully against his white comforter, but as she crawled up to the mountain of pillows pushed up against the iron headboard bars, she looked back over her shoulder, uncertain. He would definitely be taking her from behind for the claiming, but first, he wanted to pleasure her, make sure she was absolutely ready for it. He crawled across the bed, and when he reached her, he ran his hand across the smooth skin of her back.

"On your back," he said, his breath already coming short. "At first."

He lifted her hands from the comforter, then pressed them over head, leaning her back onto the pillows behind her.

"Grab onto the bars and keep your hands there."

As she reached over her head to grab on, her lips parted. Her breasts moved with her heaving chest, and the spike in her arousal was like a heady cocktail of pheromones straight to his groin. He grabbed one of the pillows and lifted her bottom to place it under her, leaving her stretched out on a nest of pillows, perfect for maximum pleasure for her and the ability to sink deep inside for him.

He started with her breasts, heavy in his hands, lavishing his attention in small kisses and nips on one and then the other. She arched under him, and one of her hands drifted down to wind into his hair.

He stopped. "Hands on the bars, Mia."

She sucked in a breath and immediately returned to grasping hold of them.

He smirked as he returned to nibbling her breasts. It wasn't that he didn't want her hands on him—very much the opposite—but her pleasure would build faster this way, her climax would come harder. And then… she would really be ready for him.

A hand between her legs found her sopping wet. She jerked with need as he touched her, so he gave her what she wanted, at least for the moment, plunging his fingers in and making her moan.

"Lucas, please…" There was so much need in her voice, he couldn't hold back any longer.

He shifted to position himself between her legs and thrust inside. She cried out, holding tight to the bars like he told her. He angled the pillow beneath her hips so he could sink even farther. His wolf was growling for him to take her hard, so he did. Hovering over her, his thrusts went deep and strong, wrenching small whimpers from her and grunts of pleasure from him with each one. He hooked his arm behind one of her knees dragging it forward and grabbing hold of the bars of the headboard to gain more leverage. Her moans escalated to shrieks, and she seemed desperately close to release, but not quite there. The tension was coiling deep in his belly as well, but he needed her to get there first. He stepped up the pace even further, and that tipped her over the edge. She gasped, and her body convulsed under him, her climax almost bringing him to the edge as well. But he held back, working her body with his thrusts even as he slowed.

Before she could come down too far, he said, "Now I want you from behind."

HER BODY PULSED FROM THE PLEASURE LUCAS HAD just wrung from her. She hadn't thought she could come again, not after twice already in the van, but he had taken her so hard and fast that it had pushed her right over the edge. And now that she was breathless and dizzy, he finally wanted to claim her.

He slipped out of her, leaving her craving him still.

"On your hands and knees," he said. "Hold the bars with one hand."

They were commands, and her wolf thrilled to them. Every muscle in her body felt loose and quivery, but she managed to comply, grasping the cold iron bar in one hand, with the other sinking deep into a pillow. Lucas shoved aside the other pillows below her, and with hands on her hips, thrust into her from behind.

It was without warning, but the new position

crashed a flush of pleasure through her core, making her quiver even more. Lucas groaned and started a steady pounding that quickly matched the frenzy that had brought her to climax so fast the first time. She felt his claws come out, gripping her hips, holding her for each slamming thrust. The small pinpricks of pain raced straight between her legs, heightening her pleasure with an aching fierceness. She felt the claws retract and his hand smooth its way up her back. His thrusts were shorter now, deeper, fully inside her and filling her in a way she had only imagined was possible. He was bending over her back, still taking her but threading his fingers into her hair until he reached her head. He grasped a fistful of it and pulled. The slight burn on her scalp again charged her with pleasure as he exposed her neck to him. She could just see him behind her, his face coming closer as he bent to kiss her shoulder.

Out of the corner of her eye, she saw the canines, long and sharp and white, extending from his mouth and reaching for her. She shivered with anticipation, but when he reached her, he only ran his tongue across the top of her shoulder.

"Mine," he said, and it was half growl.

Yes, she thought, but she was too consumed to

say anything and too held tightly to move. He was inside her, holding her, possessing her. Just when she thought he might delay it further, twin pains pierced her shoulder, and she let out a guttural moan. The pain quickly ramped up the tension low in her belly and pushed her over the edge. A cascade of pleasure pulsed through her body from head to toe. Once his teeth sunk into her, he clamped his full mouth onto her shoulder. He kept riding her while grasping her with his bite and tasting her with his tongue. Suddenly, his body tensed, and his groan worked out around his mouth's hold on her. His climax seemed to last and last, but then finally, his whole body shuddered, and he slowed. His canines withdrew from her, and he released her from his mouth. His breathing was heavy and hard, but his grip on her hair and hip eased. He gave a long wet kiss to her shoulder, then he pulled back completely, leaving her body and falling onto the bed beside her. Before she could think or move, he pulled her down with him, spooning her from behind.

"Mia, my love, my love." He was brushing aside her hair, seeking out the tiny wounds he had given her. She was certain they were already healed, or on their way with wolfy fast-healing, but it felt like there was a clean fire burning where he had bitten her. As she lay next to him, it quickly spread, down her arm, across her chest, to her belly and below. Her entire body heated with it, but it didn't hurt—in fact, she had never felt more alive. She felt his heart beating through his chest, pressed to her back.

"Mia, my love, say something."

Her lips were numb, burning with the same fire that had spread throughout her body, but her alpha wanted something from her, and every fiber of her being wanted to give it to him. She twisted in his arms until she could face him and take his cheeks in her hands.

"I am yours," was all she could think to say. Every cell in her body felt connected to his. This alive feeling, was it the magic? Was it the claiming bond? It had to be. Her body was singing for him.

He was smiling at her with love in his eyes. "And I am yours, Mia Fiore."

She could feel it: he would forever be a part of her now. It settled her soul in a way so profound, she was in awe of it. It was as though the pain of the claiming had birthed something new in her. Something permanent. It wasn't a thought or a wish, but a physical thing that bonded them together.

She would always *belong* to him, and him to her.

"I didn't think it would feel so... *new.*" She blinked a couple of times, still adjusting to the feel of it.

He grinned. "Should I have warned you about that, too?"

"I think you did."

His smile calmed into something more intense. "I don't think anyone can ever be prepared for something like the claiming." He touched the tip of his nose to hers. "Or for falling in love."

She peered into his eyes. "Did you fall in love? Is it someone I know?"

His chuckle was so deep it shook the bed next to her. "I certainly hope so."

She grinned. "Is it Jupiter?"

"No."

She pretended to think about it, then arched an eyebrow at him. "Is it a Red pack girl-wolf? That would be very scandalous."

"No." He was working hard to hold back a grin.

She wrinkled up her nose. "It's not Lena, is it? Because she's like your dad's age."

He coughed. "She's my dad's sister."

"So that's a no?"

"No more guessing." He leaned in and gave her a delicious kiss, followed by small nibbles that warmed her heart, and remarkably, other parts of her body as well. She wouldn't have thought it was even possible, but Lucas Sparks seemed determined to wring every ounce of pleasure from her that he could. Something she could hardly argue with.

"Wait!" she said, both hands on his chest, holding him off from nibbling her some more. "I have one more guess."

"How about I simply prove my love for you instead?" His alpha eyes were blazing for her.

She decided that was an offer she would never refuse.

Mia and Lucas have found their Happy Ending, but the Red pack is still causing trouble… and breaking hearts.

Saving Arianna (Dot Com Wolves 2)

Subscribe to Alisa's newsletter

for new releases and giveaways

http://smarturl.it/AWsubscribeBARDS

About the Author

Alisa Woods lives in the Midwest with her husband and family, but her heart will always belong to the beaches and mountains where she grew up. She writes sexy paranormal romances about complicated men and the strong women who love them. Her books explore the struggles we all have, where we resist—and succumb to—our most tempting vices as well as our greatest desires. No matter the challenge, Alisa firmly believes that hearts can mend and love will triumph over all.

www.AlisaWoodsAuthor.com

Made in the
USA
Columbia, SC